Rainbow in the Morning

Rainbow in the Morning

by

Mary-Frazier Paul

**This book is dedicated to my nephew, Allan Paul, who has always been there for me.
Love,**

Aunt Mary-Frazier

Fiction Publishing, Inc
5626 Travelers Way
Ft. Pierce, Florida 34982

The characters and events in this book are fictitious. Any similarity to real persons, living or dead is coincidental and not intended by the author.

ISBN 13: 978-0-9819727-3-2
Printed in the United States of America

Rainbow in the Morning

Chapter One

On an unusually warm November morning in 1886, Megan Riley stood with her Uncle Jim, watching a sailing vessel move slowly in the harbor of the Port of New York. When the schooner neared the dock, Meg could make out its name.

"Uncle, it's the Annie Marie!"

"So it is, Meg. We'll soon be on our way."

Meg watched as the three-masted schooner prepared to dock. She felt a thrill of anticipation because this was the ship that would take her to Jupiter, Florida, her former home where her father was the Jupiter lighthouse bookkeeper. He had been a physician, but had contracted malaria, and his consequent poor health forced him to give up his practice. Two years after her mother died of smallpox, Dr. Riley had sent his daughter to live with her Aunt Julie and Uncle Jim, who was a lawyer in New York City. Now after nine years Meg was finally on her way home.

1

"Uncle Jim, we're so lucky to have booked passage on the Annie Marie. They don't usually carry passengers, but fortunately, with your influence on Captain Wade Guthrie, you were able to talk him into taking us along. I'm so glad even though it's a cargo ship. The passenger ship wouldn't be leaving for another month. I can't wait to see father. He'll be surprised to discover that I am a responsible woman now," Megan said.

Jim Styron looked at his beautiful red-haired niece. She was tall and slender, like her mother, his beloved older sister. Her long, thick hair and porcelain complexion accented her jade-green eyes.

"Your father will be amazed at the change from a gangly twelve-year-old to a pretty young woman."

"And a mature school marm, don't forget," Meg added. Megan had graduated from a Normal School, receiving her teaching certificate. "I want to teach the Seminole children around Jupiter."

"We'll see what the situation is when we arrive. That may or may not be feasible. We'd better find Captain Guthrie and see about getting our luggage aboard."

Meg followed behind him. By now the crew had secured the lines. Jim spoke to one of the crewmen. "Can you direct me to Captain Guthrie? We will be passengers on the Annie Marie and need to stow our luggage."

"I'll take you to him, Sir. Follow me."

"Thank you. Meg, you stay here with the trunk and suitcases. I'll find Wade and be back shortly."

"Okay, I'll wait right here," answered Megan, reluctantly.

Jim turned and followed the young man up a short gangplank. Meg sniffed the tangy air, filled with the strong odor of salt mullet and shad roe, evidently the vessel's cargo. Everything was interesting and exciting. She watched another ship offload barrels of pitch and whale oil. Tiny sea creatures that looked like centipedes swarmed over the pilings and barnacles and oysters were attached to every pole. More ships entered the harbor and Meg could see that their hailing ports were far and wide. The quays became busier by the minute. To Meg's delight, a steam packet entered the harbor, its paddle wheels churning up a white, frothy wake. The sights and smells were so fascinating that Meg could have stayed all day. She was tempted to stroll to a nearby chandlery store and look at all the candles and supplies for ships. But she resisted since she had told her uncle she would remain where she was. She sat on the trunk wondering how long it would take them to reach Jupiter Inlet. Both her father and the Styrons wanted her to find a job in New York, but Meg stood her ground, eager to return to Florida. She wasn't afraid of the semi-wilderness and indeed, thought of it as a challenge. Though she dearly loved her guardians and had enjoyed the opportunities that a city had to offer, she always knew in her heart that when she became twenty-one, she would return to her roots.

"Megan, come meet Captain Guthrie."

Meg stood up and observed a truly amazing man approaching with her uncle. He had burgundy-red hair and equally red mutton chops. In the setting sun, he seemed to have a flaming nimbus 'round his head. His six-foot five frame was sinewy and gaunt. He might well have posed as a mizzen-mast spar so unfleshed was his body. When he came closer, Meg saw that his old, weather-beaten face was as lined and cracked as a ship lying in six months dry dock. The deep-water, sea-blue eyes were curiously innocent, as though he expected the very best in human nature and usually found it. Meg discovered herself warming towards the man though they had not exchanged a single word.

"Meg, this is my long-time friend, Captain Wade Guthrie and Wade, this is my determined niece, Megan Riley."

Captain Guthrie smiled and said he was honored to meet her. Meg held out her hand, which was engulfed in his gnarled, big one.

"I have heard so many stories about your exploits from my uncle," said Meg.

"Jim's a mite prone to exaggeration."

3

"I don't believe that for a minute. You have the reputation of being one of the best skippers to sail the seven seas. I'll feel perfectly safe on our trip to Jupiter Inlet."

Jim turned to Meg. "We may not be sailing tomorrow."

"What do you mean?" asked Meg, disappointment written all over her face.

"Wade says that some ships coming into the harbor have reported a storm brewing off Bermuda."

"Oh, Uncle, I want to go now. Can't we sail around it, go farther out to sea?" Meg asked, turning to Captain Guthrie.

"I don't know exactly where it is. It might have reversed direction."

"What do you think, Wade? Should we chance it?"

"The trip should take about nine days. Less time if the weather is right. If you still want to go, we'll sail at first light tomorrow morning, Jim."

"Good. It's settled then," said Meg.

"Why don't you and Miss Riley go to your cabins and make yourself comfortable. I'll have the boys stow your trunk and luggage in there. You can freshen up for dinner and spend the night on the ship. That way you won't have to get up so early. If you stay in a hotel, you'd have to get up at 4:00 a.m. in order to arrive here for the rising tide."

"That's fine with me. I don't fancy getting up with the roosters," said Jim.

"Let's head to the cabins then. Dinner's at six so you'll have about an hour to relax."

Meg wasn't enthusiastic about going to her cabin. She was too excited and wanted to watch all the interesting sights around her, but she didn't wish to start an argument with her uncle the very first thing. Meg had a mind of her own and she found it difficult to simply obey as any young lady was expected to do. So she thanked the Captain for his consideration and followed docilely along as her uncle and Captain Guthrie reminisced. At a later time she planned to explore every inch of the Annie Marie

4

and to talk to any seaman who would talk to her. After all, she didn't have red hair for nothing. She suspected that the redheaded captain was used to having his way too, in spite of his trusting eyes.

They reached the cabins and Meg was left to "rest" while her uncle and the captain went to his quarters to continue their talk and have a drink or two. In a semi-rebellious mood, Meg flounced on the bunk and pulled out her diary. She faithfully recorded any interesting events each day. Up until now her diary was as dull as Letitia Brown's coming-out party, but now she was going to fill it with fascinating details of her new adventures.

Chapter Two

At dinner that night Meg was seated between the captain and the steward, Priam Jones, a slightly rotund man with stringy hair whose spectacles perched on his nose like two saucers. Her uncle sat to the right of Mr. Jones. On the other side of the captain was the boson, Anson Davis, who looked as if he might have been a retired bantamweight fighter. His nose was crooked and was rosy from the sun or rum. Meg couldn't decide which. To his left sat Davy Guthrie, a young, likeable, fresh-faced lad who was the first mate and grandson of Captain Guthrie. Twelve more crewmen completed the mess.

Meg spoke to Mr. Jones. "This seems like a big boat. How long is she?" Meg was secretly proud that she knew boats were always referred to in the female gender.

"Well ma'am, the Annie Marie's 65 feet long, of some 800 tons and when she's that big, we call her a ship."

"Oh," was all the slightly deflated Meg could muster.

Having paid his due to polite conversation, the steward turned his attention back to his dinner, hunching over his plate so he could more easily shovel the food into his mouth.

Seeing her conversation with Mr. Jones had reached a stalemate, Meg listened to the comments around her.

"Yes, Oi runaway to sea at ten years old and have lived a life of adventure, but it's been a hard-workin' time too, from swabbin' decks, to cookin', to spottin' whales from the Crow's

Nest," Anson said to her uncle. "Oi was gone home from Beaufort long before you was born, Jim."

Her uncle nodded appreciatively.

"Wade and Oi have sailed together for many a year, ever since he got his own ship and hired me as boson.

"So you knew each other as boys?" Meg asked.

"That we did."

Jim smiled and turned to the shy young man across from him. "How long have you been your granddaddy's first mate, Davy?"

"Two years, Sir, ever since I turned sixteen."

Meg glanced at Davy in surprise. He seemed so young, she wouldn't have thought he was more than fifteen now.

Almost as if he knew what she was thinking, Davy blurted out, "I've learned a lot from my granddad. He trusts me to carry out my duties."

"I'm sure you're a very good first mate, said Meg.

"I have to put up with those doubting looks all the time. Grandma says it's because I have rosy cheeks and innocent blue eyes."

They all chuckled at his naïve remarks, making him blush all the more.

"Never you mind, Davy. Looks belie your ability," said his grandfather. "Well, we have to cast off early lads, so let's batten down for the night."

They all rose from the table and the cook and cabin boy began removing dishes. Though it was only eight o'clock, Meg did feel a little tired. She started to protest that it was too early to retire, but thought the better of it. Her uncle walked her to her cabin door.

"Good night, Uncle Jim. Sleep well!"

"Good night, Meg. Don't stay up late. I know how your mind conjures up impossible fantasies!"

"I won't." Meg turned in, undressed quickly, and soon slept the deep, peaceful sleep of the innocent.

8

At sunup, the ship suddenly was alive with activity. Within twenty minutes, the sailors had trimmed the yards and cast off the lines. The Annie Marie glided smoothly south for the Port of Savannah, Georgia, her first port of call. Meg jumped out of bed and dispensed with her morning ablutions. She found a thunder mug under her bunk and a pitcher of water and basin on a table by the bunk. She began dressing as quickly as she could, eager to see the ship's launching.

Finally dressed after struggling with her corsets, Meg noticed that the ship was rolling and pitching much more than it had when she first awakened. She left her cabin and listened for sounds of movement at her uncle's door, but heard nothing. She decided to go up on deck alone to enjoy her self without a chaperone, for once. She strolled along the deck, absorbing the mystic beauty of early morning as they headed for the open rolling sea. Within thirty minutes they had cleared the harbor and she could no longer see the wispy outlines of the shore. A rainbow curved across the horizon. The lively vessel skimmed like a Petrel over the water. Meg thought the full-rigged schooner was a magnificent sight with her fluttering, cream puff sails challenging the wind and her sleek hull glistening with the constant swish of waves splashing against her sides. She stood on the poop deck, holding down her hat, and watched the sea birds- gulls, terns, cormorants, and skimmers follow their wake, hoping the cook would throw the remains of breakfast overboard. The birds were not disappointed and began to swoop and dive with shrill, raucous cries. She leaned over the rail and watched the flying fish, lovely as Japanese kites soaring up, gliding, and then landing gracefully on iridescent, filigree wings. Her uncle joined her at the rail.

"So you're finally up, lazy bones," said Meg, almost sliding down the deck with the sudden listing of the ship.

"Yes, my little phoebe bird. I heard you warbling in your cabin so early this morning and I knew you wanted to venture out a bit on your own." He spoke as he buttoned the last button on his under-waistcoat.

Meg smiled as she admired her uncle's sartorial splendor. Even on a ship with brawny seamen as an audience, Jim Styron dressed like Diamond Jim Brady, as though he had just stepped on stage for a Broadway revue.

Grasping his arm for support against the increasingly unsteady movement of the ship, they made their way to the dining room. Passing by the galley, they could see that the cook was having some difficulty as the pots and pans were sliding back and forth on the stove. Looking over her shoulder, Meg noticed that the sun had vanished almost as quickly as it had appeared.

"We'll go ahead and have breakfast," said Jim. "Wade told me to sleep as late as we wished and to eat whenever we wanted to since the crew would have breakfasted at five o'clock."

"Okay, but I don't feel very hungry."

They sat down and tried to anchor their plates and cups that moved like fingers on a seaman's Ouija board being jerked around by some unseen force.

"Uncle Jim, look out the porthole at those waves!" Megan stared nervously as the once calm seas thrashed angrily against the small windows, as if trying to gain entrance.

"That's starting to be a ferocious sea."

"It was so calm when we left port. The skies were blue. The sun was shining and now there's a scattering of rain, but I can still glimpse the fading colors of the rainbow. Do you think we're in any danger?" asked Meg.

Jim looked with some apprehension at the boiling sea. "Well, Wade and Anson have sailed through some rough weather. So I guess if this develops into something more than a light blow, they can handle it." He spoke trying to reassure his niece, though he felt distinctly uneasy about the increasing turbulence.

The cook asked them what they'd like for breakfast.

"Just tea and toast for me," said Meg.

"That will do for me, too. At this point I don't think my stomach is up to bacon and eggs," said Jim.

10

"Coming right up, Sir," said the cook, completely unaffected by the tilting, listing ship.

"You most certainly have sea legs," said Meg, marveling as he placed the teacup before her without spilling a drop, along with a plate of crisp, buttered toast.

"Here's lemon, cream and sugar. Anything else, Sir?"

Meg noticed that the crew almost always addressed her uncle unless she asked them a direct question. 'Was that because women were considered bad luck on a ship?' she wondered.

"That's all we need. Thank you," replied her uncle.

They finished breakfast, eating just a bite or two of the toast, but drinking the tea. As they rose Jim said, "I have a few notes to finish writing in my room. You go on, if you like. I don't think you can get into any trouble." He smiled as he spoke to his strong-minded niece.

"All right. I do want to finish my promenade around the ship." Meg moved as best she could, for more often than not, the Annie Marie's bow rose and then fell suddenly like a bucking bronco in Buffalo Bill's Wild West show. As she approached the Captain's quarters, she heard him talking to Mr. Davis, the boson. They did not notice her standing further along the railing.

"The wind's picking up. I don't like the feel of it. And that rainbow boded no good," Captain Guthrie spoke in an undertone.

"No, Oi'm in agreement. "Rainbow in the morning, sailor take warning.' The Sea's like that old siren a'calling Oddy--. What was that Greek sailor's name?"

"You mean Odysseus?"

"Aye, that's the one. Oi believe we're in for a good blow afore this voyage is over." Anson looked at his friend expectantly. "What do you think we ought to do? Head her back in?"

The captain squinted anxiously at the sky; the vessel, as if compelled to obey her master's omen, began to pitch and roll. "It's too late for that now. We'll have to try to ride it out and hope the Annie Marie is as good a ship as I think she is."

11

As the ship began to roll, Meg lost her balance and fell against a tarp. Both men heard her cry and hanging onto the rail, made their way towards her. They reached her after almost being tossed overboard themselves.

"Miss Riley, you'll have to go below and stay there unless we tell you to come topside," the captain shouted above the rising wind. Meg wasn't in any mood to disagree. She nodded her head.

"Mr. Davis, help her to her cabin and then join me in the wheelhouse."

"Aye, Sir." The two made an unsteady journey to her cabin and Meg staggered gratefully inside. The boson fought his way back to the captain. In an instant the sky had become sunless and gray and the ocean changed from a mirror glass to a washboard.

"Wade, this is startin' to be a rip-roarin' sou'easter! Reminds me a bit of the gale in '58!"

"Yes, but this one will be worse. We'll be lucky if we have a spar standing, much less a sail, when this blows over. Somehow, this gale is different- odd. I don't know how to explain the feeling. I don't like the sound of the wind."

They stood together, two old cronies, secure in their friendship and sure of the vessel. Outwardly, they were an odd physical contrast, but within they were kindred souls who had lived through fifty or more storms together and who had known each other's families. Davy staggered in, thrown almost across the room by a capricious puff of wind.

"I had the men secure everything they could on deck. They're mustered outside, waiting your orders."

"Good, Davy. What is our position, Mr. Davis?" the captain asked.

"As near as Oi can calculate, about now we must be 300 miles east of Sandy Hook, New Jersey."

The captain stepped out onto the deck, grasping the stair rail to keep from being blown into the seething ocean. Outside the wind intensified to full hurricane force. Captain Guthrie watched

12

the breakers crashing over the stern, each comber rising higher than the last, and gave orders to the crew.

"Drop the mainsail and furl the sails. We'll have to scud under bare poles."

There was nothing more they could do except hope they wouldn't be sent to a watery perdition. "You remember that old hymn, 'Peace Be Still'?" Wade asked his friend.

"Oi sure do and Oi hope the Master of the winds and waves is with us now," Anson said fervently.

"I hope so, too. Otherwise, we are going to be bunking in Davy Jones' Locker. This is the worst weather I have ever experienced in all my years of sailing."

"Oi'll not gainsay you there."

They ran before the gale. For four days they were blown .by the wind and lashed by the waves. Every time the sea broke over the stern, the concussion was so great it stove in the bulkheads and shattered glass in the portholes far from where it struck. Meg sustained a small cut on her forehead from the flying glass. Her uncle had tied her to the bunk to keep her from being thrown about the cabin, but she still felt like a ball being bounced back and forth. To make matters worse, she was seasick. At this moment, she wished the ship would sink and her with it.

The captain could not believe the amazing force of the sea. It actually lifted the deck fore and aft of the pilothouse. The boson returned from his cursory survey of the storm damage.

"Wade, the storm has made an opening about one inch wide the whole length of the vessel and the water's pouring into her sponsons[1] every time she ships a sea. She's rolling like a fallen timber in the water," said Anson as he entered the cabin shaking water from his head.

---

[1] A projection from the sides of a ship to help keep balance

The captain glanced through the portholes. The breakers were running masthead high and with the combined force of the wind, everything was swept by the boards.

Davy slid across the deck to his grandfather. "We've done everything we can, Sir. I ordered the men to tie themselves to the masts." He hung on precariously to a door lintel as he spoke. Wade looked proudly at his grandson. Davy was both brave and responsible. What more could a parent ask for?

"That was the right thing to do. All we can do is ride her out. It's in God's hands now."

The ship's bell was an ominous accompaniment to the Captain's words. It tolled with the shock of each wave, as though sounding the funeral knell of all on board. Wade listened and a queer dread formed around his heart. All along since the start of this voyage, he'd had a premonition, a deep feeling of uneasiness. As he looked at the furious storm, he noticed that every sea stove in a new place. The billows rose as high as the top mainsail mast and as they curled and broke, they struck with a force so great the captain couldn't understand how the Annie Marie withstood it. He stared into the yawning gulf below, just waiting for the ship to be swallowed up. The whole sea was white with foam and the wind blew up the water in such quantities that the atmosphere was thick with it. Anson and Wade both felt they were breathing in foam instead of air. Then the rainsqualls came, howling as though they were hag-ridden. To Wade, it seemed that sea, wind, and rain all conspired to destroy them. With every thunderous crash of the sea, the ship creaked and groaned and all the while, the bell rang with a foreboding sound.

"Davy, get Tom Midgett in here. It'll take two men to manage the helm now since the rudder is damaged. It's only responding about half the time."

Davy ran back out into the maelstrom and came back with a bedraggled Tom.

"Help Joey there, Tom. That helm's like a runaway carriage without a horse. It'll take two of you to hold it."

14

"Aye, Sir," said Tom as he held onto the helm with all his strength. Wade and Anson stood braced as a constant stream of water swept the decks filling the scupper holes. At eight bells, the captain sounded the pumps and found three feet of water in the hold. "Anson, help me set the force pumps to work. We'll also have to heave the overdeck load." They began tossing everything overboard that wasn't attached. "You men," said the captain, "help us heave this stuff!" The crew responded while trying to keep themselves from following the stowage into the sea.

Wade made his way towards the bow to see what else could be done. He discovered that even the forepeak scuttle had begun to ship water. He felt as if he were at Manassas again dodging bullets as lanterns, bolts of canvas, coils of rope, and the medicine chest all became lethal as they were hurled from port to starboard and bow to stern. "Forget the stowage," he shouted to the men nearest him, "and lash yourselves to the masts again. You'll be blown overboard!"

They rode out the night and by first light of the next morning, the mouth of the Chesapeake was left far behind. They passed over Wimble Shoals off Chicamacomico and crossed the bar. At about seven bells into the second watch, the after davit carried away on the jolly boat and the captain thought he could save her.

"Belay that line 'round the fife rail, boys, and hold the jolly boat tight!" They passed a line around the boat and bent it to the mizzen-mast halyard and were trying to hoist her when a twenty-foot wave boarded and breached them from stem to stern.

"Watch out!" yelled Davy. "The boat's coming over the taff-rail!" He looked in horror as the boat caught the captain between it and the wheel box. He and the crew sprang to release the captain as he was pinned beneath the boat.

"Hurry up! Get it off him!" Davy cried, trying to free his grandfather. As they attempted to reach the captain, the mizzenmast top broke out and crashed down on deck. If this had not happened, nearly all hands would have been swept overboard.

All Davy could think of was his grandfather, even though most of the crew were injured and tangled in the rigging. The wrecking crew finally managed to cut away the gear even with the wind tearing at them and the rain blinding them. Each time they cut through the shrouds, the ship stood on its bow and they were thrown forward. If they had not been tied together and to the mast, they would have slid helplessly into the sea. They finally freed the captain and got him down below.

The captain was muttering as they laid him down on the bunk. "Anson, seek refuge under the first lee. The Annie Marie can't take too many more blows." He sank back, as if he had used his last ounce of strength to speak.

"Tim, go topside and relay the captain's orders," Davy said to the crewman. Tim left. Davy, Priam and Anson gathered around the captain. Davy couldn't stop the tears. "Granddad, don't leave me!"

"Davy boy, you're a man now and you'll have to take care of your grandmother." Wade paused for breath. "You've been exactly the kind of son your father could have wished for and as for me, I have been blessed in having you by my side all these years. I wouldn't have had you one whit different. Tell Annie I thought of her and I'm sorry we won't sit on the porch like we'd planned and look out across Taylor's Creek anymore." He stopped speaking and tried to sit up. Davy clasped his beloved, callused hand.

"Lie back down, Granddad. Save your strength."

"No, Anson, raise me up. I can't see." The old boson lifted his friend in his arms, but the captain's hand fell back lifeless and they knew he was gone. He had lived only two hours. Davy put his arm around his grandfather, hugging him for a final time.

Sorrowfully, the others went topside. "Men, what a sorry plight we're in. Over half the crew is injured and we still need two men to manage the helm," said Anson. "Tom, you and Joey try to keep the sea on our starboard quarter, if possible. We're going to have to try to run out the storm."

16

Somehow, they managed to do that and after first light on the fifth day, the wind hauled further to the northwest and fell out somewhat. At two bells of the second watch, they sighted land.

"Oi haven't been able to get a fix, but by dead reckoning, Oi think we're approaching the outer cape of Hatteras," Anson told the crew.

Then, as if they hadn't endured the worst that nature could offer, a spindrift now surrounded the ship. However, they knew they had seen the loom of land, and they were able to make out the breakers on the starboard bow.

"Men, beat off some and give these shoals a wide berth. Keep her steady as she goes," said Davy, who had come topside after paying his final respects to his grandfather.

The wind and current were carrying them down along shore and the sea began to be calmer, though the fury of the storm had not lessened. By this occurrence, Mr. Davis was inclined to believe they had doubled the cape and were coming under its lee.

"Oi think we're going to make it, boys," he said.

At mid-day, both the tide and wind had abated, and they knew they had to give the captain a burial at sea. By this time, Meg and her uncle had come topside. Meg couldn't believe the gallant captain was dead, nor could his friend, Jim.

"How can this be? He was so full of life, so knowledgeable, so vibrant," said Meg.

"It's hard to accept, Meg, but every seaman knows that life is fleeting. Wade knew it, but this was the life he chose and I know he would not have changed it even if he had known the result," said Jim.

They both looked at the sad face of the captain's grandson, knowing that his sorrow was far greater then theirs.

"Have the sail maker sew up the captain in brand new canvas and put ample weight at his feet," said Davy. "Mr. Davis, will you give the eulogy? You were his best friend and knew him well."

"Aye, Sir."

17

When the sail maker had finished his sad chore, the Captain's shroud-covered body was brought on deck. They dropped anchor and all hands assembled, along with Meg and Jim. Mr. Davis stood near the deckhouse, abaft the mainmast. His short, stumpy body leaned against an upended carpenter's bench for support. The old seaman's clothes were tattered and his grizzly beard and hair were wet with sea and rain. He looked at the crew for some minutes, gazing from face to face and finally his weathered gray eyes found the sad young face of the captain's grandson.

"Captain Wade Guthrie was my life-long friend. Oi've never know'd a better man or a better pilot. We scouted Taylor's Creek and Cart Island Slough as shirt-tailed boys, and we sailed to many a foreign port as men. And Captain Guthrie, well, he could guide his ship just like a pilot whale through the channel with shoals a'looming on both sides. He was some captain. Yes, he was! In the years Oi know'd him, he never run her aground."

The old boson looked out to sea, a single tear coursing his cheek over crevasses created by a thousand sunlights. He seemed to see something far out on the horizon- a half century of memories shimmering in sea-dappled sunbeams. His big, calloused hands, browned and aging, grasped the thwart and he shook his head.

"And now he's casting out to sea in a jerry-rigged foresail for the last time. There's no seaman living that don't see death. It's always a'looming on the horizon. Oi've seen it beckoning from fifteen fathoms deep- dark and shadowy, like a hundert sharks, waiting, waiting. But you know, it's a funny thing. Captain Guthrie weren't afraid to die. He said to me once, 'Oi've lived righteous all my life. Oi've tried to follow the Lord's way and He's been my co-pilot. He guided me through many a shoal and stormy sea and Oi believe he'll guide me even in death past the wrecks and whirlpools to the Promised Land.'"

The aged boson watched the crew with unwavering stare, and then his eyes softened and he looked at the bedraggled men with a radiant smile.

"Oi can tell all hands assembled he was a man who weathered every storm and now he's ready to meet his maker and seek refuge under the lee. Raise the plank, boys, and let him find a grave in the deep."

The inboard plank was lifted and they watched the weighted canvas slip quietly into the sea with hardly a splash. Only the shrill cries of the scavenger seagulls could be heard as the Annie Marie moved into jeweled waters, her wake a silver path leading from the watery gravesite. They all saw the ripples as they swirled over the captain's final resting place. A blue heron swooped low as if to say "Goodbye".

"That was the most beautiful and moving eulogy I have ever heard," said Meg, with tears in her eyes.

"It was," said her uncle, his own eyes wet with tears. "Alfred Lord Tennyson said it well too."

"Twilight and evening star and one clear call for me. And let there be no moaning at the bar when I put out to sea."

Chapter Three

The crew went back to their posts and Davy took command of the Annie Marie. They had been blown about thirty miles south of Cape Hatteras, on the north edge of the Gulf Stream. They continued their course carried by the current, if not by sail, and on Thanksgiving Day of 1886, they lumbered into the bight of Cape Lookout. They dropped anchor there, attempting to repair the ship. Meg thought sadly of her naïve comments about eating wild turkey and Indian maize on Thanksgiving Day. How wrong she had been! Some crewmembers took Meg and her uncle ashore in the one remaining jolly boat. They explored the island while the ship was being patched together to make it seaworthy enough at least to get them into Beaufort.

When they returned, the jolly boat was there and Joe rowed them back to the Annie Marie under bright, sunny skies.

After several days, Mr. Lewis and Davy deemed the ship seaworthy enough to reach Beaufort. The boson stood gazing out to sea, lost in memories, as they moved up Core Sound, past Harkers Island and Diamond City on Shackleford Banks.

The Annie Marie moved slowly up the sound towards Beaufort Inlet and Davy headed her towards the bell buoy marking the entrance of the Beaufort bar. The buoy swayed and swirled in the rushing tide while the bell clanged mournfully as the waves pushed it back and forth. The Annie Marie listed as she rode the waves, propelled only by the jib.

"Hope that south wind holds 'til we get into the harbor," Davy said to Anson. "Otherwise, we'll drift right on back out to sea!"

"It'll hold. We didn't survive that storm for nothin'. The breeze is freshenin' roit now." As he spoke, the ship rolled forward towards the harbor, pushed by wind and wave. Meg looked eagerly towards Beaufort as they gradually approached Taylor's Creek. She could see the houses that lined the narrow, sparkling, white shell street. Boardwalks were built out over the water and the lower end of the shell street terminated in a boardwalk three quarters of a mile long. The full tide rose beneath it, swirling among the pilings. The homes were connected with it and each had its own little boardwalk, some of these running on out toward the channel.

"Uncle, each house has its own boat landing".

"They do and each has a bath house attached, too."

"How interesting. What a quaint town. You must have had a good time growing up here. I wish I could have been here."

"It was fun. You know, every boy knew how to swim. My father threw me off the Inlet Inn dock and said 'Swim or drown'. "That was a Beaufort slogan. Of course, I well knew my father would dive in after me if I had started to go under.

"Look at that house. It's the tallest house in town. I guess that's because it is on a hill," said Meg, leaning out over the railing.

"That's the Hammock House. It is said to have been Blackbeard's home. The story goes that he caught his wife with her paramour, killed them both, and buried her beneath the live oak tree. Folks claim that her ghost can be seen roaming the halls and the bloodstains remain on the steps. No amount of scrubbing can remove them."

"I don't believe it! I'd just like to see those spots. I'll bet they're not even there!"

"Megan, the present owners are tired of strangers knocking on the door, day and night, asking to see the bloodstains. We won't be part of the nuisance."

"Fiddle! I never do anything exciting!"

"I should think that storm you came through would be enough excitement for a lifetime!"

"That's different. There were no pirates or ghosts on board."

"The Hammock House is not the only house in Beaufort with ghostly inhabitants," said Jim.

"You mean there's another one? Tell me about it. Where is it?"

"You see that house on down the shell street about one hundred yards with the white picket fence around it and the upstairs porch?"

"Yes, I see it. Is that haunted too?"

"Most definitely. Mr. Sabiston was captain on a sailing vessel and often made trips to foreign ports. His wife would pace back and forth on the upstairs porch, or widow's walk, looking out at the Inlet, hoping to catch a glimpse of a sail as it crossed the bar. One night she heard her husband's voice calling her. Overcome with joy, she ran outside and down the front walk, expecting to greet her husband. To her surprise and disappointment, he wasn't there. She scanned the dock but saw no sign of his boat. She watched all night but never saw her husband. Three weeks later a sailing vessel entered the harbor. It was Capt. Beveridge's boat. When he docked, the captain came to see Mrs. Sabiston.

'Dear lady, I'm so sorry to bring you bad tidings of your husband. John's ship went down off the coast of Bermuda during a storm and all hands perished.'

Mrs. Sabiston sank to the couch in shock. 'When did this happen?'

'Three weeks ago,' Capt. Beveridge replied.

'At eight o'clock in the evening, three weeks ago, I heard John call my name. I ran outside but he was not there.' The poor, distraught woman began to cry.

'But that's impossible.'

'No, it isn't. John tried to come home to me. He did!'

"Capt. Beveridge left shortly thereafter, unable to console Mrs. Sabiston. She died a few weeks later still convinced her husband had called her. Her two daughters live in the house now and they claim they hear footsteps coming up the walk on a windy night and they vow they have seen their mother on the upstairs porch."

Meg listened avidly to the tale of heartbreak and ghosts, eager to walk along the shell street for a closer look at the house.

While Jim spoke, the Annie Marie glided slowly up Taylor's Creek with barely a puff of wind catching her flapping sail.

Meg sniffed deeply of the salty air. "Ugh!" she said. "What is that awful, horrible stink?"

Jim laughed. "People in Beaufort say that smells like money!"

"Money?"

"You see that ship just passing us so low in the water you can't see the copper paint water lines? That's a Menhaden fish boat. She's loaded with shad or Menhaden and that's what you smell."

"I don't see how they stand it," said Meg, wrinkling her nose.

"You get used to it after a while. The fish factory is east of Cart Island."

Davy walked up beside them. "We're going around Gallants Channel to the Town Creek boat ways in West Beaufort and haul the Annie Marie up on the railways for repairs, but we'll drop you off at the Davis House landing. I'll have a couple of the crew take your bags up for you."

"Thanks, Davy. I guess then you'll go directly home to your grandmother?" Jim looked at him sympathetically.

"Mr. Davis is going with me," Davy said, his sad young face showing how distressed he was. They had reached the pier in front of the Davis House.

"Tom, after you've secured the line, you and Samese take Miss Riley's and Mr. Styron's luggage up to their rooms," said Davy.

"Aye Sir."

Meg walked gingerly down the gangplank with her uncle close behind.

"Be careful, Miss Meg. We don't want you swimming in Taylor's Creek! That's a strong current rippling under the dock and you'd be at Guthrie's Shoal before you knew it!"

Meg had a death grip on Davy's hand. "Don't worry. If I go, you're going with me!" She jumped nimbly onto the dock, in spite of her long skirt, and Jim followed close behind, easily moving down the swinging gangplank. They walked to the end of the wharf and headed for a long white, two-story, balconied structure. Several people were sitting on rockers scattered along the veranda, enjoying the southerly breeze and talking among themselves.

"What a view they have of the inlet and shoals," said Meg.

"That's part of the appeal. They can see the harbor filled with ships, old Topsail Inlet, Shackleford Banks, and on a very clear day, Cape Lookout lighthouse," said Jim.

"Do you think we'll have a room on the second floor with a door leading onto the porch?"

"I wouldn't be a bit surprised. Mrs. Jones and I are old friends and she shows special hospitality to friends!"

Chapter Four

A tall stranger, standing unobserved on the next dock, watched with interest as Meg and Jim crossed Front Street to the Davis House. His lean frame was casually propped against the railing and he puffed on an expensive cheroot. Andre Lafitte, grandson of the notorious pirate Jean Lafitte, smiled as he noticed the sun glint on Meg's hair making a rosy cloud around her fair face. Lafitte had other business to attend to, but he always found time to appreciate a pretty face. He watched as they approached the boarding house and made a mental note to dine at Miss Amy and Anna's table tonight, where he was sure they would have dinner.

After watching Meg until she was out of sight, Andre walked over to Rumley's Feed Store for an assignation with Dory, his cohort in crime. The two had been on the run with a Pinkerton man hot on the trail, eventually landing in Beaufort on their way to Florida where Andre thought they could find sanctuary among the Seminoles, and rob them while they were at it. Meanwhile, Meg and Jim had unpacked and freshened up. They then decided to take a stroll around Beaufort.

"Uncle Jim, what fun it must have been growing up here. I wish I could have been thrown off the Inlet Inn dock and have gone fishing every day!"

"You would have drowned for sure in all those petticoats!"

"No, I wouldn't have. I enjoyed growing up running barefoot in Florida, playing with the Indian children, and paddling their canoes, but Mother and Father were both so busy taking care of their Indian friends' medical needs that we didn't have much time to do things together."

They had walked to the end of the boardwalk and were looking towards Piver's Island.

"The Naptha launch will be coming here from Shepherd's Point shortly. We'll watch the passengers disembark."

They stopped and sat down on a bench across from the Duncan house.

"What a beautiful house," said Meg as she admired the gable roof and broad porches. A white picket fence surrounded the house, and wind-swept cedars, battered by nor'easters, were bent and twisted into leafy, bizarre topiary. A tremendous wind-flattened live oak's fronds swept the earth like feathery arms that had thrashed to the ground during a hurricane. Hardy pittosporum made a lustrous dark green border around the house while the orange-red fruit of the ligustrum added bright patches of color in the yard. The red berries of the holly tree gave a hint of Christmas. Meg was momentarily distracted from her absorption in the house by the sight of a boat rounding Piver's Island. Its paddles were churning the water, leaving a white frothy wake.

Meg said, "Oh, look! Here comes the launch and there are quite a few people on it."

Fluttering parasols held by ladies protecting their delicate complexions from the morning sun looked like a cloud of brightly colored butterflies hovering in the stern of the boat. The pilot maneuvered the launch into its mooring across from the Davis House without a single jar against the bumper guards.

"I think I see an acquaintance of mine from New York. That's unbelievable that we should meet in Beaufort, of all places."

"Who is it, Uncle Jim?"

"It is Raymond Seymore."

"I managed to get a reduced sentence for his nephew."

As the passengers began to disembark, Jim and Meg walked quickly down the street to greet them. An extremely portly man with a moon face and full beard stepped off, helped by two men, one on each side. He was joined by a tall, skinny woman who was dressed in a high-waisted, mustard-green muslin frock with a protruding bustle on which a seagull might have perched.

"Raymond, what a surprise to meet you in this part of the world! And Henrietta, what a pleasure."

Mrs. Seymore inclined her head in a brief acknowledgement and presented a lank, gloved hand. "The heat is quite enervating, I find," she spoke in a faint voice as if at any moment she might swoon. "I simply could not survive the day without Lydia Pinkham's nostrum. It is such a restorative for my weak condition."

"Er, yes the heat certainly can be devastating, but I am sure you will find our delightful zephyrs will restore your health." Turning to Mr. Seymore he asked, "What brings you to Beaufort, of all places?"

"A wedding. My wife's niece was married in New Bern. We decided to extend our vacation and visit Beaufort. What brings you here?" asked Raymond as the two men shook hands.

I am escorting my niece who insists on returning to Florida. Unfortunately, we were caught in a hurricane on the way and had to come into Beaufort to repair the ship."

"May I present my niece?" he turned to Henrietta. "Mrs. Seymore, may I present my niece Megan Riley."

"How do you do?" said Meg.

"Oh, I do feel quite bilious. It is the heat, you know." Mrs. Seymore had taken out her lorgnette, and holding it to her eyes stared suspiciously at Meg's fiery hair.

"Megan, this is Mr. Raymond Seymore. My niece, Megan Riley."

"How do you do, young lady? And a pretty one, I might add."

"Very well, thank you. I know you will both enjoy visiting Beaufort. I've just started to explore it myself."

29

Mrs. Seymore sniffed in disgust. "Mr. Seymore insisted that we visit this God-forsaken countryside in spite of my vigorous protests. He knows how delicate I am. Why, I heard that there are Indians still inhabiting the woods!"

Jim said, "My dear Mrs. Seymore, you need have no fear of wild Indians here. Now if you visited Florida, the Seminole Indians roam freely there."

"Indeed! I shall certainly make it a point never to travel to that barbaric land. Come Raymond, I must rest. The tedious journey from New York and the train ride from New Bern and that ridiculous rocking boat quite exhausted me." She fanned herself vigorously as if bathing in ninety-six degree heat though the temperature was only fifty-five degrees.

"Are you staying at the Davis House?" Jim asked.

"Yes, we are. I have been told it is quite pleasant," said Mr. Seymore.

"Humph, if you ask me, we should have stayed at the Ocean View Hotel or the Inlet Inn, but Mr. Seymour always wants to get a room at the cheapest place."

"Now, Henrietta, that is not true," said Raymond, his face reddening.

Jim intervened before they could continue. "I assure you, Mrs. Seymore that you will find your accommodations quite comfortable and attractive. Besides that, you are right next door to the best eating place in town and I insist that you be my guests for dinner this evening."

Mrs. Seymore, somewhat mollified by the offer of a free dinner replied, "I suppose it might be satisfactory then. My delicate condition requires it." Having had the last word, she turned to her husband. "Mr. Seymore, shall we go?"

"Of course, my dear. Thank you, Jim, for the invitation. What time shall we dine?"

"How does seven o'clock sound? That should give you time to rest before dinner."

"Fine, Jim. Until seven."

The couple departed, followed by two seamen staggering under the weight of a Saratoga trunk. They still had to return for two other sizeable suitcases. Mrs. Seymore glanced back over her shoulder, and then whispered to her husband, "I am appalled that Miss Riley is not wearing a bustle. It is outrageous!" she mouthed behind her fan. "The impropriety of young women these days is not to be believed!"

Meg could barely suppress a giggle. "Her delicate condition must require that she recuperate for two months. She certainly brought enough clothes for an extended stay!"

"Now Meg," said Jim.

"Wonder what she'll think of the tin bath tub out back of the house at five cents a bath? Poor Mr. Seymore! I don't believe he'll fit in it!" Meg burst into laughter then.

"Let us continue our exploration and leave the Seymores to their own devices. Hurry up! They might hear you laughing!" Jim took her elbow and urged her along. Meg sobered up and they strolled along the boardwalk, watching the beehive activity in the harbor.

They strolled along companionably as Jim helped Meg over puddles. "You know Bogue Sound watermelon have the best flavor of any grown in the U.S., according to old John Todd. He could be prejudiced though, since he grows them. People come down to the docks early in the morning to buy local produce, or to purchase fish and oysters off the boats. Of course, there is Ramsey's grocery store further down for those who don't get here early enough."

Meg found the sights and smells just as exciting as those in New York's harbor.

"Meg, look across the sound to the west. Can you see the jetties surrounding Fort Macon?"

"Where?" asked Meg, squinting to see. Jim pointed to a spot to the left of Piver's Island.

"You can just make them out. Can you see them yet?"

"Yes, now I do."

"When General Robert E. Lee was a young lieutenant, he designed those jetties surrounding the fort. We even had a female Confederate spy, right here in Beaufort."

"You did? You never told me about that before. Was she a relative of mine?"

"No, she was not and I know you are disappointed about that. Her name was Emeline Pigott. She carried confidential information, sewn in her petticoats, to the Confederate forces outside the line. She would have continued her activities, undetected, right until the end if someone had not reported her. She was arrested as a spy and confined. We never knew who the informer was. If we had, he would have been strung up from the Crow's Nest by his, or her, thumbs. Emeline was quite a person." By now they had reached Turner Street and were walking towards Ann Street.

"I wish I could have known her. What a life she led."

"I thought Annie Oakley was your inspiration!"

"She is! Can you imagine? From thirty paces she can shoot a playing card in half, held on its edge! She can hit an Indian Head penny thrown into the air. Not even Buffalo Bill can do that. And her husband lets her cut a cigarette from his lips. William Tell was a piker compared to Annie Oakley."

"So what do you want to be when you grow up? If you ever do. A trick shot markswoman, a spy who clandestinely acquires information, or a savior of the Seminole Nation?" asked Jim.

"All right, joke if you will, but you may be surprised at what I do."

"Meg, Meg, whatever will your father do with you?"

"He will find me a great help!"

"No doubt. If his hair is not already gray, it will be. Just look at mine," said Jim as he touched his jet-black hair.

"Yes, it's as gray as a Pennsylvania coal mine!"

"Dear Meg, it is just that you are so idealistic and so naïve. I worry that people will take advantage of you. You may be twenty-one years old, but you have led such a sheltered life. And yet you are a rebel. What a paradox you are! Your Aunt Julie looks at you almost as if you were a changeling left by the wee folk. She dearly loves you, but fears for you because you do not fit the mold of a young lady anno Domini 1886. She cannot understand why you do not heed Mrs. John Sherwood's rules of social behavior. How many times have you read Manners and Social Usages?"

"At least five times! I've also curled up with Sensible Etiquette of the Best Society on a rainy night. I know never to leave a spoon in the cup, or never to visit an artist's studio alone, though I don't know where I'd ever meet an artist. But Uncle, I don't want to spend my life fanning vigorously to avoid the vapors, or waste time behind a tea cart pouring tea for the local ladies' society." Meg tossed her hair rebelliously like a young filly. "You understand me, don't you, Uncle Jim?"

"I do, but dearest niece, you make this poor, old heart beat anxiously. As difficult as it is, you must try to conform. Unfortunately, there has always been a double standard for men and women, doubly reinforced by Queen Victoria's code of conduct. Besides revolting against the strictures society imposes, you are a dreamer. You cannot look at life through rose-colored glasses. Life has too much black and gray in it." He gazed at his niece whom he loved as if she were his own child. "Okay, lecture's over. Let's go to the apothecary shop. Dr. Brown's office is next to it and I would like to say hello to him if he is still practicing."

Both Jim and Meg stepped back as a wagon rattled by them. 'Dr. Corkey's Horse Ambulance' was painted on the side of it. Another wagon from Collins Coal Company was going the other way and passed by with barely inches to spare. Jim waved at the drivers.

"Afternoon, Ruffus."

Meg was somewhat dejected by her uncle's lecture for she dearly loved him. She walked with her head down, barely noticing the activity going on around her.

"Cheer up, Megan. You can still enjoy life and be circumspect at the same time."

"I know, I know, but it's hard to do!"

By now they were passing the Custom House, which also had a telegraph office and post office inside, and stagecoach stop on the corner of Turner and Ann Streets. A tethered horse was drinking cool, fresh water out of a moss-covered trough that had been hollowed from a log. Across the street was a chandler shop.

"Do you want to go in and look around? Maybe you will find something to interest you."

"No, let's go to the apothecary shop." They crossed the street and entered Dr. Brown's Family Medicine Company. Dr. Brown owned the apothecary shop and had his office in the same building. The interior was cool and shadowy and had a slightly medicinal smell. The shelves were filled with dozens of bottles and jars containing medicines for every disease known to mankind. Many of these nostrums were quite popular, particularly the tonics which contained 21 percent alcohol which kept it and the consumer from freezing in the winter.

Jim was amused by the labels. "Ah, here is a good one-"Radway's Ready Relief'. Many a soldier returning from the war eased his pain with a shot of this!"

Meg read some more labels. " 'Hostetter's Celebrated Stomach Bitters.' You remember old Mr. Donleavy? He used to drink a pint of that a day for indigestion. Here's 'Ayer's Sarsaparilla' for chronic fatigue. Mrs. Seymour needs to get a supply of that! You think I should buy her a bottle?"

"Now Meg, leave the poor woman alone. She would be shocked at the alcoholic content!"

"Ha, I'll bet!" said Meg. "We could take a bottle of Barkers Liniment 'Joy to the World, Relief Has Come' to Mr. Seymour for his aching muscles after he got out of the bathtub."

Jim tried to be serious, but Meg's laughter was infectious and he fell into the spirit. "Here's some Egyptian Regulator teas which will bring 'graceful plumpness' to flat-chested girls. Henrietta could use some of that, too!"

"And Mr. Seymore could benefit from a flagon of this Rengo medicine guaranteed to 'turn fat into muscle; for flabby men'." By now both Meg and Jim were laughing.

The apothecary approached them with a frown on his face. "May I help you with something, Sir?" He looked severely at Jim as if to say that he at least should behave in a seemly manner.

"Please forgive us. It was just an amusing story. We'll be quiet," said Jim apologetically. He noticed that several other customers were looking at them disapprovingly.

They tried to compose themselves and walked past elixirs for those who felt they lacked sex appeal, Kickapoo Indian Salve, and at least two dozen bottles of Carter's Little Liver Pills for nervousness and dyspepsia. They reached the end of the counter where two ladies were thumbing through patent medicine almanacs. Each had a bottle of Lydia Pinkham's Vegetable Compound in her hand. The apothecary had returned to his post behind the counter.

"I came in to speak with Dr. Brown. Is he in?" asked Jim.

"I am not his secretary," answered the apothecary.

"Of course, I realize you are in charge here. I am an old friend of the doctor and just thought you might know if he had left. I noticed that there were no lights on in his office."

"He has gone for the day."

"Oh, too bad. I will buy an almanac. How much?"

The pharmacist brightened somewhat at the prospect of a sale. "That will be ten cents."

Jim handed him the money. "Here you are. No bag necessary. Thank you very much. Let's go, Meg. We will barely have time to change for dinner." He picked up his book and they left the store.

"I do not think he appreciated our humor," said Jim.

"No. Maybe three or four of Carter's Little Liver Pills would help. He certainly looked dyspeptic!"

"He did indeed! Let's walk back on Ann Street and then turn up Moore Street. That way you can see a little more of Beaufort."

The streets were busy with horse-drawn wagons. One carried furniture; another refrigerated wagon was delivering meat to the Episcopal Parish house for a picnic on the grounds.

"We don't have time to go there now but the blacksmith shop is at the end of the street. They shod horses, make nails, scythes, harness fastenings, pots and pans, plowshares. You name it, they do it. Sometimes the blacksmith even makes swords and knives."

"Who needs a sword nowdays? The days of sword play and pirating are over."

They continued their walk and Meg admired the lovely houses along the way, each enclosed by a white picket fence. "They are pretty, but why do all the houses have fences?"

"To keep the chickens, pigs, or cattle from grazing or trampling on their carefully cultivated plants. The chickens get under the house and they make a mess in the yard. The pigs nose out bulbs and squeal half the night."

"You never see this in New York."

"That is true. Beaufort is still a small fishing and farming town with one policeman whose biggest job is trying to get a cat out of a tree, though he did have to chase a pig out of Mrs. Robinson's petunias."

"That explains it then. But what happens when you have a real crime, or doesn't that happen here?"

"I am kidding. We do have an occasional theft or drunk on the rampage, and Telford takes care of it. If more serious crimes occur, he just deputizes some of the local citizenry."

As they continued along Ann Street, the elms on both sides of the street made a thin canopy overhead and autumn's fallen leaves of crimson, gold and vivid orange blanketed the path under their feet. Meg shivered

There it is a chill in the air. It is starting to get colder."

"Yes, it is. I knew this Indian summer would not last long."

"Look," said Meg. "There's a billboard saying 'Corcoran's Circus' coming to town on December tenth. What fun that will be! Can we go? I enjoy those dime shows. I hope they have a bearded lady and a sword swallower!"

"If we are not snowed in by then," Jim said, huddling inside his jacket.

The wind began to blow harder from the North and stung their faces. They picked up their pace, eager to return now.

"A fire in the fireplace will feel good tonight," said Meg as she pulled on her mittens. A mist that had been forming in the northwest suddenly changed to rain.

"Oh no!" yelped Meg as the first chilly drops hit her. "Now I wish I had my parasol!"

"Let's run for it!" Meg gathered up her skirts and dashed for shelter, with Jim running beside her. By the time they reached the Davis House, both were soaked. They stood dripping in the foyer and Jim pulled out his pocket watch.

"It's after six now. I shall tap on your door at quarter of seven and we will go over to Miss Amy's boarding house. We want to be sure to arrive before the Seymores do."

"All right. I'll hurry though it's not easy to do with all these fastenings and layers of clothes," Meg said as she climbed the stairs. "This is the time I really need Abigail to help me dress!"

"I wish we could have brought her with us but she was adamant about not leaving New York. She said she was not going to be murdered by roving Indians," Jim said.

"It's okay, I'll make do. See you shortly!"

Chapter Five

Andre finally found Dory in the stables near the boatyard where the Annie Marie was lying like a beached whale on the railways. Dory was talking to the stable hand.

"Wot do ye get for that piece of 'orse flesh?" Dory asked.

"She's a fine mare. Mr. Willis is asking two hundred and he'll throw in a saddle, too."

"Two hundred! In California I could buy meself two 'orses for that price!"

"Well, you're not out West now. He'll not come down on it. I can tell you that!" the stable hand said.

"Bloody bugger."

"Come on, Dory," said Andre, foreseeing a squabble. "We've got business to discuss."

With Dory still muttering to himself, they walked outside.

"You were supposed to be at Rumley's Feed store. I've been looking all over for you," said Andre.

"Oi got tired waiting and Oi wanted to see some 'orses."

"Bother the horses! Mate, you're going to have to batten down that temper of yours. We don't want to get run out of town here. Remember Galveston? Two nights in the pokey and a shotgun escort out of the burg, with that Pinkerton bloke not far behind. He's like a baying dog, slathering at my heels."

"All roit. Wot's the plan? 'Ow long 'ave we got to stay in this 'ere pesthole? Not a single pub in town to wet me whistle!"

"There is bound to be a tavern somewhere on the outskirts of this town. Scout around and find it. Then go into the bar and look for a lightskirt. Make sure she's pretty. Don't talk directly to her but find out where she lives. Do you understand?"

"Oi understand. Oi need some jack to buy me ale."

Andre handed him money. "Now be quick about it. I need a woman now."

Dory scuttled down the street like a molting crab, his face as cracked and peeling as a blue crab shell. He knew too well what would happen to him if he failed. He saw two fishermen sitting on the end of the dock opening oysters. He sidled up to them.

"Mates, would you know where to find a pint of bitters?"

Surprised, the men looked up at Dory's scarred face.

"Well," said one, "there's a place about a half mile past the fish factory that sells any kind of spirits you want."

"Wot direction is it in?" asked Dory.

"You just walk straight down Front Street. When you start smelling them rotten fish, you're on the right trail. Go past the factory 'bout a half mile and you'll see a building back in the woods. There is a picture of a near-naked woman on the front." The fisherman turned away and began opening oysters again.

Dory muttered to himself as he walked back down the dock, "Bloody buggers."

Walking and swearing to himself he finally reached the tavern. Two hours later he returned to town with news for 'Marcel'. He went to the Ocean View Hotel and banged on Andre's door. The door flew open and Dory rushed in.

"Oi've found just wot ye wanted, Marcel. Not too young, but pretty. She said she could use some money."

"I told you not to talk to her!"

"Weren't nobody else to talk to."

"Where can I meet her?"

Dorey said. "She lives back in the woods behind the tavern. It's the only 'ouse there. She'll be there right now. 'er name's Maxine."

"Good work, Dory. I knew I could depend on you. Now go to your room and stay there." Andre shoved the loathsome creature out the door. He considered taking Dory with him. That would give the broad a jolt being raped by both of them. But then he decided he would get more enjoyment being alone with her. He made sure his derringer was in his pocket, along with his money bag and two other items.

A half an hour later, he knocked on the door of a ramshackle house. A woman opened the door.

"Are you Maxine?" asked Andre.

"I am that very one. Come on in, Dearie."

He entered the gloomy room. A bed with a filthy cover was against one wall. Near by was a bucket of water. The only other furniture was a small table with an oil lamp and a chair. The room smelled like unwashed bodies. In the dim light Andre could see that she was an older woman, but she did have a pretty face.

"Ready for some fun? Come over and sit on the bed and Maxine will make you feel real good."

"Maxine," said Andre, "I'm going to make you feel –uh real good."

"Ooh, a Frenchie. I like that."

Suddenly Andre reached into his pocket, grabbed Maxine's arms and tied her to the bed post.

She started to protest when he ripped off her clothes.

"Hey, wait a minute. Take it easy. That's my best dress."

The smiling invitation on her face changed. Her eyes bulged with terror as the whip descended. She screamed and screamed in pain as the whip lashed her tender skin, and Andre's eyes gleamed with an unholy light. He raised the whip again and again. The woman howled, cried, and begged him to stop. She screamed until she could scream no more, but just moaned in agony.

As the whip struck, Andre remembered, even heard his mother's screams as his drunken father beat his slut of a mother, night after night.

Finally after fifteen minutes, Andre put down the whip. He took off his clothes, pulled her legs apart, and pushed savagely inside her. He found sudden relief and a moment of ecstasy, the same rush of feeling that he had experienced when he plunged the dagger into his father's throat.

His face was slick with sweat from his exertions. He got up and looked down at her tear-streaked face in disgust.

"Well, Maxine, You've earned your keep tonight."

He walked over to the water bucket and washed her blood from his body. Then he put on his clothes.

Maxine cringed as he came towards her. He untied her hands and then put ten gold coins on the bed. He leaned close to her face. "If you say anything about this to anyone, I will come back and slit your throat. Understand, Cherie?"

The terrified woman could only nod her head.

"Bon. Sweet dreams. I may be back in a few days. I know you'll be waiting for me." His smile was cherubic as he walked out the door, whistling.

Now he needed to find Dory again before the idiot made trouble. When Andre reached town, he discovered him walking towards the Annie Marie.

"What do you think you're doing? I told you to stay put. Now listen. I think I can persuade that young captain of the Annie Marie to take us on as passengers. I heard some of the crew talking. When their ship is seaworthy, they're heading for Jupiter Inlet in the south of Florida. That's where we want to try our luck. The Indians should be easy pickings. Even more so than the Chinese we conned in San Francisco. I still have thirty thousand dollars left to set up a 'respectable' business. We'll see how the land lies when we arrive. We can always travel further south, if it doesn't appear profitable."

"Oi'm agreed. The sooner, the better," Dory said.

"We'll have dinner at the boarding house, but you will need to change clothes. I don't think those manure-covered boots would add to the dinner table ambiance."

"Stuff your ambiance, wotever the 'ell that is!"

"Just watch yourself and don't foul up my plans," warned Andre with a distinctly ominous look.

Dory said nothing more. He knew only too well not to cross Lafitte. He had seen more than one man who had crossed him turned into shark food. They walked to their rooms at the Ocean View Hotel with a brisk chilly wind at their backs, and Dory wondering for the hundredth time how a man who looked like the angel Gabrielle could actually be the devil, Old Scratch, himself.

"We'll have rain before night," Dory predicted. "My bloody knee is aching!"

"Good barometer, your knee. Comes in handy. Black Boris must have known what he was doing when he gaffed you with that grappling hook!" Andre took great pleasure in baiting Dory when no one else was around.

"One day you're goin' too far, Matey," said Dory with a murderous gleam in his eye.

"Ah, Dory, can't you take a joke? After all, poor Boris paid the price. The last time I saw him he was staring out of sightless eyes!"

Andre whistled a bar room song, his good humor restored. "This rain you are predicting will probably turn into sleet. But I don't mind if I'm in front of a blazing fire with a glass of port in one hand and a good Havana cigar in the other," said Andre, and he thought to himself, 'a pretty red-haired wench sitting next to me.' "Remember Dory, we may be here for several weeks, so don't cause trouble at dinner tonight, or any other night. Above all, keep your hand out of the till wherever we go!" With that last warning, they went their separate ways. When Andre reached his room, he bathed, shaved, dressed carefully for his encounter with the delectable redhead. He wondered how she would look tied to the bed.

The dining room was rapidly filling when Megan and Jim arrived. One long table laden with savory-smelling dishes was set up in the center of the room. Two waitresses were bringing in more bowls and platters of steaming hot vegetables, meat and soup. Numerous chairs had been placed around the table and several small tables and chairs were lined against the walls. Gas lights cast a soft glow about the room. Jim looked around for the Seymores.

"Good, they aren't here yet."

"I've never seen so much food in my life!" exclaimed Meg, watching the bowls being handed around to the diners.

"It is referred to as family-style. You can take as many helpings as you want. I've seen my friend, Billy, eat six pieces of fried mullet alone, not to mention all the other dishes. Here are the Seymores."

Jim walked over to greet them. "I hope you rested well."

"Quite well, thank you. Those feather beds were so comfortable I almost missed dinner!" responded Mr. Seymore.

"And Henrietta, did you rest comfortably too?"

"Hardly, since my delicate skin is so sensitive. I am distantly related to the Royal family of England, so I am like the Princess and the Pea. I could feel the slightest bump through five mattresses, I am quite sure."

"Did you feel a bump?" asked Meg, fascinated at the thought.

"Only a small one," said Mrs. Seymore, who had snored loudly enough for her neighbors across the hall to hear.

Jim said apologetically, "I am afraid we will have to sit at the long table. All the small tables have been taken."

"If we must," said Mrs. Seymore with a sniff. "I do hope we will not have to sit beside any unsavory characters."

"I see some vacant chairs by some friends of mine." He waved to Anson Davis and Priam Jones who were sitting by

44

Leland Carter and his wife, Stephanie. Carter was a Beaufort lawyer and old school friend of Jim's.

"Leland, how's business? Any more lawsuits against Miss Alligood and her nine cats?" Jim asked.

Leland laughed. "There's always been a feud between her and Clem Potter. He's got four fat, spoiled dogs including one toy terrier that insists on being carried everywhere. Sweetie Pie has probably forgotten how to walk! She almost had a canine version of the vapors when Muffin, Miss Alligood's sixteen pound cat, glared at her from the fence."

Meg was enjoying the story. She had a smile on her face as she glanced at her fellow diners. Priam, as usual, was almost head first into his plate, while Anson entertained Mr. Seymore with seaman's folklore. Mrs. Seymore gazed loftily at the riff raff, then turned her attention to the aromatic dishes placed before her. Meg looked up to see a tall, brawny man standing in the doorway. He didn't appear to be local. He was dressed in a brown, woolen jacket and sharply creased trousers, worn with a wide leather belt. A bright red handkerchief, tied loosely around his neck, stood out against his crisp, white, linen shirt. His brown leather boots almost sparkled they were so highly polished, and he wore a ten-gallon hat that he quickly removed. He brushed a tanned hand across his long gleaming, flaxen-colored hair, which was pulled back with a ribbon. When Meg looked directly at his face, she thought he was the most handsome man she had ever seen.

'I'm staring at him like some gawky, spindly-legged, pert young chit,' Meg scolded herself. Tearing her eyes from his face, Meg glanced beneath her lowered lashes around the room. Every female was staring at this Adonis with the exception of Mrs. Seymore who was eying the smorgasbord laid out before her with much the same expression that Meg imagined was on her own face. 'This is ridiculous,' she thought. 'I'm looking at the man like he's a sugar- coated confection! Uncle would consider this most unladylike.' She sneaked a glance at Jim half expecting he could read her thoughts. To Meg's surprise, he too was staring at the stranger who was now approaching the table, and Jim's expression was grim and unfriendly.

"Good evening," said the stranger, his deep voice resonating around the table. "May I join you? This seems to be the only place available."

Meg thought his accent was charming, a touch of French perhaps. He had not looked at her yet and addressed his comments to Jim. She glanced at her uncle. Had she imagined the look of distaste earlier? For now, his countenance was devoid of expression.

"Certainly," he said, "please be seated. I am Jim Styron and this is my niece, Megan Riley."

The two men shook hands. "How do you do?" responded the stranger, formally to Jim. "My name is Andre Lafitte." He turned to Megan. His probing blue eyes almost mesmerized her. "Very nice to meet you, Miss Riley," he spoke in a low voice that seemed meant only for her ears, and bowed slightly.

"Nice to meet you, too," responded Meg in a muted tone quite unlike her usual, lyrical voice.

Andre smiled at her then turned away and seated himself between Anson and Leland.

" I am Leland Carter and this is Stephanie, my wife," said Leland extending his hand. They shook hands and Stephanie nodded and said," Hello."

"What brings you to Beaufort?" asked Leland, obviously more curious than polite.

Andre served himself some fried hard crabs. "Haven't had these since I left Borneo. What a delightful surprise!"

All conversation had ceased at the table, forks raised in the air. Many strangers, both from passenger and commercial vessels, made stop-offs at the small port of Beaufort, but this was a visitor who commanded attention.

"I have traveled extensively- the Near East, the Far East, Europe, Africa. Ah, delicious," Andre murmured in appreciation as he bit into the succulent crab. He helped himself to fried oysters and cornbread.

"Europe? Do I detect a French accent? Are you from France?" Leland was persistent, noting the clever avoidance to direct questions. He had not been a lawyer for twenty years for nothing.

"How astute of you, my dear fellow. I am indeed originally from France, though I haven't lived there in recent years." He turned to the waitress who was passing around clam fritters. "Please give my compliments to the chef," said Andre as he transferred two fritters to his plate.

Maryanne almost dropped the platter. "Uh, I sure will, though Miss Molly Gillikin ain't no chef. She's been cooking for Miss Anna long's I can remember." Maryanne wanted to smooth back her hair because she knew it must look untidy from the stove's heat, but she had both hands on the platter and couldn't.

"Thank you," he said, giving her a dazzling smile.

"Yer welcome," she croaked, and fled for the kitchen.

Several diners left the dining room and no one appeared to notice the swarthy fellow with a jagged scar from his right eye to his mouth slip into a chair at a side table. Andre saw him however, and was thankful that Dory was sitting by himself. He hoped no one would sit with him. Dory's volatile temper could erupt at the slightest provocation and Andre, at all costs, wanted to avoid that.

Jim had been quietly watching Andre, not missing any of the by-play. He, too, had observed the scurvy-looking sailor enter the dining room. He felt that Andre recognized the second stranger, but did not want it known. All of Jim's nerve endings tingled with alarm for he instinctively mistrusted the man calling himself Andre Lafitte, and Jim's instincts were seldom wrong. He had spent too many years in the courtroom not to recognize a con artist. But even more than that, Jim sensed a core of evil beneath the glamorous, charming façade. He was apprehensive, not for himself, but for his beloved Meg. She, in her innocence, would be no match for this man. The man's magnetism was apparent. Even

Anson was charmed and was telling him of foreign ports he had visited. Priam was staring transfixed, offering bits of conversation, food forgotten and Mr. Seymore was trying to interject politics into the conversation.

"You have an unusual name. Are you a relative of the late Jean Lafitte?" Jim asked across the table. There was a pause as if time had been momentarily suspended. No one spoke.

Andre hesitated, taking Jim's measure. He recognized an opponent and realized he must tread carefully with this man who would not be so easily bamboozled. "I am his grandson, though I never met him. I only know of his exploits through what little my own father told me. He did not know him either. I can, and have offered condolences for his deeds, though he did help your American General Jackson." Andre had chosen his words carefully, as though he were metaphorically picking his way through a field of broken glass.

"Certainly, one cannot choose one's relatives, nor be accountable for their actions," interposed Mr. Seymore., as he passed a plate of vegetables to Priam.

"No, of course not," said Jim, though he knew for a certainty that the seed of treachery and murder had been passed down from Jean Lafitte to his grandson.

Dallas Smith, a local fisherman, spoke from the end of the table. "Anson, Oi was shore sorry to hear about Wade." This remark momentarily distracted the others from the startling revelation about Andre Lafitte.

"Thank you, Dallas. It still don't seem possible."

"That storm must have been 'bout as bad as the one that foundered the Crissie Wright," said Dallas. He took a sip of tea, preparing to tell his story of the shipwreck.

"Prob'ly worse. We was just lucky it weren't a blizzard. Near ever foot of sail was blown off the Annie Marie. The main mast crashed to the deck and we scudded under bare poles for four days," said Anson.

"Did another ship go through a hurricane like we did?" asked Meg.

"For shore, Miss Roiley, but it were a terrible tragedy." Dallas said.

"Oi was visitin' my Uncle Charlie at Wades Shore over on Shackleford Banks. One minute the weather were as shiney as a new silver dollar, but it was some cold. We had a foir a'roaring in the foirplace, but my fingers was as cold as mullets in a salt barrel. I seen a big, black cloud puffin' up in the northeast. 'We're in for a bad 'un,' Oi told my Uncle Charlie. It was so cold them marsh tackies [2] was roit up to the door tryin' to git warm. "Bout that toime, Oi looked out the winder and seen a sail five miles off shore, just east of the Cape. 'Uncle Charlie,' Oi sez, 'That's a ship standing in towards the beach!' 'Let's go, boy,' sez he. So we grabbed oir oil skins and a armful of foirwood and run outside and down to the shore. The wind was a'howlin' and snow so thick Oi could barely make out the ship. Foive or six others from Diamond City come up a'luggin' wood. We seen the crew had dropped the hook, but it was a'draggin'. They was about two hundred yords from the beach and we knew they was headin' for the reef. Then she come ashore stern first, roit on top of the reef, and rolled on her side with the sea a'breachin' her starboard, larboard, fore and aft." He paused for another drink.

"We couldn't do nothin' to help. We couldn't launch a dory in them fifteen-foot waves. So we built a foir to let 'em know we was thar if they could make it in to shore. By then, they had clum up to the mizzen mast shroud and tied theirselves to the ratlines. But the weather got worser and worser. It must of dropped to ten degrees. We watched through the noit and it got colder' than froze up flounder. We could see 'em as the sun come up through a black cloud. They was slowly freezin' to death and

---

[2] Banker ponies

49

we couldn't do nothin' but pray.   When the waves come down enough to launch the whale boats, Oi jumped in with Captain Seef Willis and his whalin' crew.   Uncle Charlie went with Captain John Lewis and his crew.   When we reached the Crissie Wright, there weren't no movement on board.   The crew was froze solid in the shrouds and there were no sign of Captain Collins.   We figured he had froze and fallen overboard."

"How horrible!" said Meg.   "Did everyone die?"

"Not all, ma'am.   We seen a lump in the jibsul and found four men wrapped together in the sail.   The top three was froze to death, but the man on the bottom was still breathin'.   We brung 'em all ashore and slowly thawed out the livin' man.   Later they was all took to Beaufort, and Robert Johnson, that was his name, was took to the Naval Hospital at Charleston, South Carolina.   The other men was buried in the burying ground near Purvis Chapel."

"When did this happen?" asked Mr. Seymore, filling his plate yet again.

"Almost one year ago on January eleventh.   Oi'll never forgit that oice cold day," said Dallas.

Anson said, "Me and Wade was fishin' off Nova Scotia when it happened.   Oi remember jist how cold it was.   We come into Beaufort a month later and heard the awful news.   Ain't nothin' nobody can do 'bout the wither, except hope it spares you one more toime."   Anson shook his his head as he took another bite of cornbread.

Andre hardly listened to the tale.   He eyed Meg, covertly, planning his campaign to seduce her.

Dallas realized that his friend, Anson, was sad, so he thought to cheer him up.   "Anybody heard 'bout the paper canoe?" he asked, glancing around the table.

"Yes, I have," answered Jim.   "I read about it in the New York Herald some years ago.   Then several years later, the voyager himself wrote about his trip and I read that.   It was called The Voyage of the Paper Canoe and it was a fascinating account.   He actually rowed all the way from Canada to Florida and back."

"He came right by Beaufort." It was about twelve years ago. I didn't actually see him, but I heard people talking about it." said Leland as he passed the plate of fried oysters to Stephanie.

"How could you possibly travel all those miles in a paper boat? It would get waterlogged and sink," scoffed Meg, relieved to have something to think about other than a Greek god's disturbing blue eyes. She sneaked a look in the god's direction and was completely nonplussed to discover that he was gone. 'Here I've been deliberately refusing to look at him and he wasn't even there!' she pushed her plate away, no longer hungry.

Andre had taken the opportunity to leave while the diners were engrossed in the seaman's story of the Crissie Wright. He had signaled to Dory who followed him out.

Jim had watched Lafitte unobtrusively slip away. 'Now I wonder why he left without a "by-your-leave",' he thought.

"But it is possible," said Mr. Seymore. "In fact, the Cornell College Navy had a victorious season using paper shells."

"They are quite sturdy evidently, from what I have read about it," said Jim. "The paper can be pressed into any desirable shape. After that, it is waterproofed with pure rubber gum"

"How much did his boat weigh?" asked Meg.

"His canoe only weighed fifty-eight pounds. He could actually portage it across small sections of land. It also had greater strength as well as stiffness, durability and speed. Even more so than a wooden boat of the same size. You see, after the water-proofing has dried and hardened, it can be polished. The paper doesn't shrink or swell, doesn't have any cracks, so it will not leak. The canoe will float and it is lighter than wood. Not only that, the molded paper retains its shape perfectly and it will not warp as does wood."

Mrs. Seymore said huffily between bites of fried trout, "Such poppycock! I suppose you will be telling us next that they will make paper steamboats. No sensible man would risk his life upon the turbulent waters in a paper canoe. It is all part of the monstrous lies put out by that Joseph Pulitzer. He would do

51

anything to sell a newspaper. You could not pay me enough money to read The New York World!" She looked self-righteously around the room as if daring anyone to disagree with her. Jim wasn't afraid to rise to the occasion.

"Henrietta, don't you know his favorite expression? 'Accuracy is to a newspaper what virtue is to a woman.' The New York World has produced the best stories and most accurately written ones including the tale of how Jean Lafitte, along with Andrew Jackson, defeated the British in the battle of New Orleans."

"That may be so, but he and that Horace Greeley of the New York Tribune are sensation seekers, pure and simple. Any promotional stunt to gain readers."

"What about the New York Herald sending Henry Stanley to Africa to find the long-missing Dr. Livingston?" asked Jim.

"Publicity. That's all it was. Dr. Livingston was perfectly happy until he was found, although how he could have been among those savages I will never know. This paper canoe business is just more of these same promotional stunts."

"You are right about one thing. It certainly boosted the sale of newspapers. But the story of the paper canoe was not a promotional stunt."

"That's true, Henrietta. I read about that fellow in the newspaper myself, and in his book, too," said Mr. Seymore.

Stephanie noticed that Meg looked a little forlorn and her maternal instincts were aroused.

"Meg dear, my husband, Leland, and Jim have always been intrigued by ships and hurricanes. What you went through must have been traumatic. Nothing would terrify me more than being on a ship during a hurricane."

Meg turned at the sound of a sympathetic voice. "Oh, it was so frightening. I thought I'd never make it to Florida. But the good thing about it was that it brought me to Beaufort. I'm getting to meet all of Uncle Jim's friends, and to see where he grew up." And she thought to herself, 'I never would have met Andre.'

"Good. We're so happy to meet you, too. Through the years, Jim has written, glowingly, about you. I feel as if I already know you. Meg, you're not eating. Try the trout. You know it's fresh because the tail is turned up."

"Really? Well, maybe just a bite."

Stephanie smiled at Meg and they both turned to listen to Dallas's narrative.

"My granny still lives o'er to Hattres and she seen that paper boat herself," chimed in Dallas. "When he come a'rowin' by, everbody on the oiland was waitin', 'cause the telegraph sent a message from Norfolk sayin' he was a'comin'. Folks thought he was crazy as a loon, but real noice and polite. When he come ashore, my granny lifted the bow up hoi, then lowered it. She told him she reckoned she wouldn't take no chance o' dyin' crossing a creek in 'er. And Joe Rose didn't want to hurt the pore travellin' feller's feelin's none, but he jist had to say his thoughts. He told Granny, 'That feller's goin' to make a shiney coffin for himself out of that yer gincrack of an eggshell. It's all a man's loif is worth to git in 'er'. Then little Leroy Mason troid his best to punch a hole in 'er, but she held fast."

The diners paused in their eating and listened in rapt attention to this tale of the paper canoe

Jim said, "You know what really amazed me about the story was the danger he encountered around Hatteras from sharks and porpoises."

Anson had been listening intently. He wasn't really hungry, still thinking of his friend, Wade. He had eaten only a small piece of cornbread. "Them Hattres fishermen has to have a good supply of oars. The sharks think them oars is fish movin' through the water and they'll snap them blades like they was kindlin'wood."

"Yeh, that's roit," said Dallas. "Joe warned that feller about it. He said them white paddles a shinin' in the water would attract them sharks just like a silver spoon bait. The feller said he appreciated the warnin', but he vowed he had more trouble with porpoises 'cause they always wanted to play."

"I read about that," said Jim. "The porpoises appeared and disappeared leaping from the waves all around him, diving under the boat and reappearing on the opposite side. They would lash the current with their tails and snort and blow all the while, according to the canoe traveler. It seemed that that the faster he rowed, the more they multiplied, ploughing the sea in erratic directions so that he could hardly row a straight course. Now you realize these were big fish, from five to seven feet long, and weighing from two hundred to four hundred pounds each."

"I heard that a dolphin will push a drowning person in to shore," said Meg.

"It moit be, but he weren't about to jump o'erboard to test the theory. Them porpoises don't mean no harm like a shark does, but they're shore playful, and a four hundert pound playmate aint one oi'd be like to choose." said Anson..

Jim continued, "Evidently, they had summoned all their neighbors to join the games and they chased him, rowing as hard as he could, into three feet of water. At this point, they turned on their tails and left for deep water." Jim signaled Maryanne to bring them more tea.

"Absolutely amazing," marveled Leland. "I definitely would not have wanted to be in that canoe, surrounded by por-poises, no matter how friendly they were, not to mention being bumped and snapped at by sharks. I wonder how he provided for food and water? There can't have been too much room in the boat."

"Evidently," said Jim, "It was heavily laden with con-densed goods, rubber blankets and an alcohol stove. He also had a canvas deck cover that was fastened by buttons along each gunnel of the canoe. That way, if a wash caused by tugboats on the lakes, or large schooners, or if stormy seas occurred, his cargo was protected. He even carried a flannel suit carefully rolled in a water-proof cloth."

Though listening to the conversation, Meg was wondering why Andre left without speaking to her.

"That's what I call 'rugged individualism'," said Leland, pushing back his plate. "But surely the canoe was not completely impervious to tears or rips if he found himself dragging over oyster beds or hidden projections like cypress knobs or stumps."

"The man was prepared for every contingency. He kept a double paddle in reserve against accidents to oars and oarlocks, and he carried an iron and shellac. Then when he reached sanctuary in some kind-hearted fisherman's home, he heated the iron on top of the stove, and applied shellac with the heated iron to the cuts made by oyster shells. This made the craft just as good as new. After supper and a good night's sleep, he continued his voyage.

"Then he probably did not use many of his supplies, did he?" asked Meg.

"He did, actually. Many nights he camped on swampy islands. He would pull his shallop³ well onto the beach, with no danger of a rising tide catching it. Then he'd search for a large clam shell and get fresh water by digging with the shell two or three feet into the sand."

"Hmph! It's a modern miracle he didn't catch malaria, chills, or the ague sleeping on that wet ground like an Indian," muttered Mrs. Seymore as she polished off a sweet potato slathered in butter.

"I agree with that, my dear! He must have been in superb physical condition to have resisted infection in those fetid unhealthy swamplands," said Mr. Seymore.

"With all that rowing, he had to have been," agreed Stephanie.

"I cannot help but envy him," said Jim. "What a challenge he had, swashy seas, howling winds, storm-tossed trees, mischievous fish, unique people! What more can you ask?"

---

³ A small wooden boat propelled by oars or sail

"A warm feather bed with a heated brick at my feet and a solid roof over my head," said Mrs. Seymore, pushing her fork around her plate to catch an elusive morsel of crab.

Anson and Dallas shook their heads at the infinite folly of man.

Priam, like Mrs. Seymore, had sampled every dish on the table including six kinds of vegetables, fig preserves, fried chicken, home-made pickles, spiced oysters and all the other bountiful seafood harvested from Cart Island Slough and beyond. Meg marveled at their infinite capacity.

Maryanne was clearing the table. "Now ye save yerselves room for Miss Gillikin's specialty!"

"What is that?" asked Mrs. Seymore, her eyes aglow in anticipation.

"Angel food cake with blueberry fool!"

"I most certainly 'have room' for that," said Mrs. Seymore, slipping into the vernacular. She was in an expansive mood, heightened by the ingestion of succulent food.

"I do, too," agreed Priam, as he took another bite of cole slaw.

Jim, Meg, Leland and Stephanie all refused dessert. Jim, who had been about to leave, settled back into his chair.

"I will have another cup of that tea," said Meg. "It's quite a refreshing drink. What kind of tea is it?"

"That's yaupon tea, ma'am."

"What is yaupon?" asked Meg.

"It's a tree someun' like a holly that grows hereabouts. We droi the leaves and twigs and then boil 'em."

"It's an old, Indian drink, Meg. The settlers learned about it from them."

When Maryanne left to get the dessert, Meg whispered to her uncle, "Everything else was wonderful, but I almost choked on that coffee! What kind was it?"

Jim chuckled. "Meg, you are going to have to learn to be a pioneer woman when you reach Florida. Although Miss Amy and

Miss Anna do not skimp on the food, sometimes they show a streak of frugality. They save coffee grounds for repeated use."

"You mean----?"

"Exactly. They put the coffee grounds in the pot, toss egg shells on top of them, fill up the pot with water and boil the coffee."

"Yuk! Why do they put in egg shells?" asked Meg.

"To keep the grounds at the bottom. Now you wouldn't want a mouthful of two-week old grounds, would you?".

Meg just looked at him. "I noticed that Mr. Davis and Mr. Jones were the only two drinking coffee."

"They are accustomed to it. Months at sea will get one used to anything, I suppose. By the way, did you know that a diamondback terrapin will eat five bushels of shrimp in an hour at feeding time?"

Meg appeared startled by the abrupt change of subject, and then burst into laughter. She knew Jim was comparing Priam and Henrietta to the terrapin.

Leland tried to discreetly look at his pocket watch. They had been in the dining room three hours and all the other diners had long ago come and gone. Poor Maryanne looked disheveled and tired, but too timid to say anything. Jim decided to stop Priam and Henrietta before they had seconds and thirds of dessert.

"While the traveler was at Hatteras, a small storm passed over and the turbulent seas disinterred many coffins that began floating away. The lids flew open and rows of toads were sitting inside the coffins!"

"Eek!" yelped Mrs. Seymore, her fork suspended in mid-air. "How ghastly! Raymond, I think it is time we left. I have lost my appetite."

"Yes, dear. I do, too. Maryanne looks quite exhausted, poor girl."

"Who is that? Come, Raymond," she ordered, as she spooned the last blueberries into her mouth.

Mr. Seymore managed to move his more than ample bulk back from the table, pushed up and then pulled out his wife's chair.

Everyone got up at the same time. The meals had been paid for at the door, twenty-five cents per person. Jim walked over to Maryanne and put three dollars in her hand.

"Maryanne, you are the very best waitress I have ever seen and that includes waitresses in the nicest restaurants in New York City!"

"Mr. Styron, you give me too much money. Oi was jist doin' moi job," stuttered Maryanne, looking at the money as if it were about to burn her hands.

"Please take it. You deserve it. Good night. Let's go, Meg, it is getting late."

"Noit! Thanks!" said Maryanne, cramming the money in her skirt pocket. Meg and Jim bid goodnight to everyone and all left, with Mrs. Seymore indignantly grumbling about coffins and horrid toads and Priam gazing longingly over his shoulder at the last piece of Angel food cake.

Chapter Six

Meg awakened the next morning to the sound of a northwest wind whispering under the eaves of the house. She snuggled under the warm quilts listening to the popping and cracking noises of the rafters and standing timbers. The gusty, soughing wind pushed against the old wood frame house as if trying to gain entrance. Some time in the pre-dawn hours, the rain had turned to sleet and it clicked against the windows with icy fingernails. She watched the smoldering embers on the hearth, giving off a faint rosy glow as they crumbled into ash. Her uncle had started a roaring fire in her fireplace the night before and Meg felt so warm and comfortable she dreaded to leave her cozy nest. Her lids closed sleepily and she dozed another half hour. With a start, she jerked awake.

"Get up, you sluggard," she chided herself. By now, the sleet had stopped and the sky was rapidly clearing. The sun had already climbed above the horizon and Meg called herself several other uncomplimentary names before she finally found the courage to put one foot on the chilly floor.

"Oh, that's cold!" she yelped. Then with a valiant effort she threw back the covers and walked over to the window. A cottontail rabbit jumped across the lawn, leaving a trail of tiny prints. A sparkling frost coated the leaves. The Spanish Dagger's limbs, heavy laden with purple fruit, made a colorful splash in the yard and a holly tree's bright red berries foretold of Christmas. She could hear the loud, sharp and clear honks of wild Canada geese flying overhead seeking haven in the lakes and marshes where they could find food and water.

"What a beautiful morning," she thought. Padding to the armoire, she found a wrapper of green cashmere, put it on and tied the satin ribbon sash tightly about her waist. She tucked her feet into satin slippers, picked up her brush and sat in a cushioned window seat. The now unbroken azure sky reminded her of Andre's eyes. 'Why am I mooning about him? The man obviously didn't think much of me or he would have at least said goodbye.' Meg was curious. Where did he come from? Why was he in Beaufort, of all places? Where was he going? She brushed her hair and the red-gold ringlets tumbled about her face and down her back. Little did she know he had been and was still thinking about her! Thinking how she would look tied to the bed.

Andre had been on the alert when two men sat down at the table with Dory and had decided to leave when he heard voices raised at their table. He was also annoyed that this interfered with his subtle plan of seduction of the beautiful red-haired Meg.

Meg idly wondered what she would do today. Her uncle had suggested that she might enjoy visiting Miss Amy's kitchen and learn something by talking with the old cook. He suggested that Meg really had no idea now privileged a life she had led. They had a telephone in their house on Fifth Avenue and there were not that many in all the United States. The kitchen was a modern wonder, but Meg had never actually worked in it since they had many servants to do the work. Meg sighed. "Tempest fugit. What to wear?" she pondered. She decided on her green and blue wool dress. "That, along with nine dozen petticoats," she fumed. She wished she lived in a country where they did not wear petticoats or hoops at all. Mrs. Seymore would collapse at the thought. Meg giggled as she pictured the look of outrage on Henrietta's face at such a scandalous idea. With a final look in the mirror, she went downstairs. Jim had told her to do as she liked since he and Anson would be visiting Wade's wife and grandson. He had said he'd be tied up most of the day visiting and taking care of business. 'Evidently it is "de rigueur" for young ladies to walk unchaperoned along the streets of Beaufort," thought Meg, thankfully. It would have been considered improper in New York.

She tripped lightly down the porch steps. When she stepped outside, there was a sting in the air and she breathed in the crisp, cool breeze. Walking briskly, she made her way to the rear of Miss Amy's house. It was quite early and she did not want to disturb the sisters if they were still sleeping. As she approached the kitchen, her nose was tickled with the delicious aroma of freshly-baked bread. "I can't possibly be hungry after last night!" she thought. She tapped on the door.

"Come on in," called out a wavery voice. She entered the room and saw a wizened , old lady sitting at the kitchen table. She looked like Meg imagined a cheerful sprite would look, her brown eyes dancing with mischief. Her red-bandanaed head barely peeped over the table's edge. As Meg approached, she noticed that the little mother was seated on several pillows.

"Good mornin' to ye," said the fairy-like creature.

"Good morning to you. I am Megan Riley. You must be Molly Gillikin."

"I be her,' said the wee creature as she stood up and walked to the stove. Meg thought she could not be more than four feet eight inches tall. Molly began removing home-cured ham from a cast iron spider. She placed the slices on a plate, then took two crusty, brown, clabber biscuits from the oven and placed them on the plate.

Meg looked at the food hungrily, amazed that she could even think about eating after last night. Molly added a generous amount of fig preserves to the plate and placed a bowl of freshly churned butter beside it. She then went to the sink and began pumping water from a pump that was inside the sink, into a pot. She placed the pot on the stove to heat the water, and then added dried leaves and twigs.

"Now then, you jist sit here at the table and have yourself breakfast. Yer yaupon tea'll be ready quick as a ram kin shake his tail. I figures you don't want no coffee," she added, her brown eyes twinkling.

"Oh, this looks wonderful. And you're right, I don't want coffee. The meal last night was unbelievably good. I don't think I've ever tasted anything better."

"Wait 'til you tries them clabber biscuits with my home-made fig preserves!" said Molly, her nut-brown face wreathed in a smile.

"I can't wait," said Meg as she sat down and bit into the hot, buttery biscuit. "Umm, delicious! How long have you been cooking for Miss Amy?"

"I been with her fifteen years. Before that, I was a house servant to the Pelletiers since before the war."

"Well, Miss Amy is certainly lucky to have you!"

Maryanne came in carrying a load of clothes that almost hid her face.

"What? Not wash time already? I ain't even started my pine bark muddle yit!"

"Monday morning wash and with all them visitors, we got a pile as hoigh as Hummuck Hill,' sighed Maryanne.

"Good morning, Maryanne!" Meg greeted the girl with a warm smile. "You must be tired after last night."

"Oi was so toired, Oi fell roit to sleep. So now Oi'm rested."

"Maryanne, you sort out dem clothes whilst I heats some water." Meg watched as the tiny old lady bustled about the kitchen.

"You do the cooking and washing both?" asked Meg, amazed at her energy.

"Me and Maryanne does de cookin', washin' and cleanin'." Molly spoke as she filled four pots of water and placed them on the stove. "Now den, let's see 'bout de soap." She walked over to a three-legged pot that rested in a corner of the kitchen. The kettle was filled with homemade soap made from animal fat and skins and some lye.

"How's de weather? I ain't been outside dis morning," Molly asked Maryanne. "I wants to wash outside, if I kin."

"It's warmed up some. Oi don't believe them clothes'll freeze up."

"Do you sleep here in the kitchen?" asked Meg in surprise.

"No ma'am. Me and Maryanne lives here. We has rooms upstairs."

"Oh, I see."

"Maryanne, while dis water am boilin', you go 'round de house and fill all de lamps with oil. Den trim de wicks and wash de globes and chimleys. I wants 'em sparkling and clean so's I kin see my face in 'em. I'll jist take a dip o' my snuff while she's at it," said Molly, winking at Meg.

Molly walked over to a sideboard and picked up her snuff and snuff paddle. There was a corncob pipe next to them. "Most the time I likes a piece of sweet gum in my jaw, but this mornin' I feels like tobaccy." She put a generous supply of snuff in her mouth that puffed out her cheek like an apple. Then she pulled out a washboard and a wooden paddle from beneath the sink and carried them to the door.

"Maryanne's a good'un. She do her work and don't complain none. That lazy Sally Mae afore her weren't good fo' nothin'! Chile, eat more of that ham! You needs some meat on yer bones. Heh, heh, heh! Men don't like no skinny girls!" Molly chuckled and hummed a tune like a cheerful cricket as she busied herself around the kitchen.

"It's absolutely delicious! I ate two biscuits also! But I simply cannot eat another bite!" said Meg. By this time, Maryanne had returned.

"Dis water's 'bout hot enough. Let's git them clothes done so's I kin git working on my muddle. It'll take three or fo' wash pots full if them people eats like they done last night." They all went outside and Maryanne got two washtubs from the porch and carried them out into the yard.

"Let me help you with those clothes," offered Meg, for the tiny woman was completely hidden by the mounds of dirty clothes she carried in her arms. It looked as though the clothes were marching by themselves.

"Don't need no help, thankee," said Molly as she dropped her burden to the ground by the washtub. Maryanne had gotten the pots of boiling water and poured them into the washtub. Then she added a plentiful supply of soap. She dumped the clothes into the scrub bucket and began stirring them with the paddle. She pulled a soapy, steaming dress onto the scrub board and began vigorously scrubbing the clothes against the washboard. After overseeing the work, Molly turned to Meg and said, "Let's go out to de storage house. I needs some sweet taters and mebe a few pears."

Meg followed along to the back of the yard where there was an old storage house. The house had a juniper rail fence around it. The building was long and narrow with an oval, shoulder-high sharp roof. It had a low door, just large enough for a person to crawl inside. At the moment, the door was swinging in the northeast wind.

"Now who is the culpit who done left de door open?" asked Molly. "I bet it was dat Tommy. He sneaks in dere to git hisself a pear. Lestways he chopped some logs fo' de fireplace. He better put dem on de porch, though." Meg saw a plentiful supply of small logs in the woodpile near the chopping block.

"We keeps a year's supply of taters in dis shed." The frame part was made of wood and covered with about two feet of light brown pine straw and soil about fifteen inches thick was placed on the straw to form the outside of the potato house. "My nephew, Joshua, built dis house for Miss Amy and Miss Anna. He grows sweet taters, corn, pumpkins and collards on his farm. Miss Amy buys 'em from him. An' we has a great big pear tree right here in de yard."

Molly walked inside the barn to get her potatoes and pears. Meg bent down and looked inside. Fresh dry, smooth straw formed a dense thicket that nearly covered the floor where potatoes

64

had been cautiously poured and stored for the winter. Bartlett pears, carefully selected and picked to prevent bruising, were laid along the floor with the sweet potatoes and several large pumpkins sat side by side on the barn floor, just waiting to be made into fresh pumpkin pies. Meg saw three small barrels resting against the wall.

"What's in those barrels?" she asked.

"Dem be salt spots and mullets. We kin have fish all de winter when dem fishes goes to de bottom. Can't kitch 'em den."

"And what's in that big barrel near the door?" Meg asked.

"Dat's my yaupon. I cuts de leaves and twigs, den I heats some stones 'til dey is red hot. I puts a layer of de stones in de barrel, den a layer of de twigs 'en leaves. I keeps on making de layers 'til it reaches de top. Den I puts de cover on real tight. After it cools, I hangs de yaupon on dis line right by de barrel 'til it's dried. I makes some money sellin' it, but mostly I makes it fo' Miss Amy.,"

"So you actually make your own yaupon for tea?" asked Meg, amazed by Molly's constant hard work.

"Sho' does and I cans and preserves dem pears, but it be nice to eat a fresh pear during de winter time too. I don't smoke no hams myself, though. I gits 'em from my nephew. He raises hogs and chickens, too. When it gits too cold, I lights de lantern to keep dem taters and pears from freezing. Den I covers 'em with more straw."

"Somebody must be sleeping in here," said Meg. "I hear him snoring!" She looked all around but found no recumbent form.

"Heh, heh, heh! Dat's the barn owl you hears asnorin'!"

"Barn owls snore?"

"Dey sho does! Maryanne, come in here and pick me a pumpkin," ordered Molly, her own hands full of sweet potatoes and pears.

"I can do it," offered Meg. "Which one?"

"Dat smallest one'll do. I kin git three pies out of it."
Maryanne was halfway to the door. "Git on back to dat washin'.
We'uns got de pumpkin." Meg smiled to herself. Maryanne
would make three of Molly, but a domineering attitude bested
height any time. By now, she had half the clothes in the rinse
bucket and was starting to ring them out by hand. Once the clothes
were hung out to dry, they would be stiff as a board.

"Hurry up, girl! Dem clothes has got to dry 'fore it rains,"
Meg held the door and they went back into the kitchen.
"Monday's wash day and Tuesday's iron day. I doesn't want no
'ruption to my skedul," said Molly as she put down her potatoes
and pears. "I thinks I'll just fix me some fry bread 'fore I gits
goin' with my cookin'."

Meg sat down at the table and watched as the little old
woman mixed flour, lard and clabber milk into a dough. She broke
off portions of the dough and rolled it into strips. Then she put
grease in the frying pan and dropped in the dough strips. She fed
the wood stove with kindling and fried the bread dough on top of
the stove.

"Ain't nothin' better'n fry bread. Did you poke a hole in
your biscuit and pour in molasses?" Molly asked Meg.

"No, your fig preserves were so good I just kept eating that
instead!" Meg coughed several times.

Molly placed the leftover biscuits on the warming shelves
on top of the stove. "You catching a cold?"

"I do have a sore throat. I probably am catching cold after
being out in the chilly rain and wind yesterday."

"I has jist the thing for it," said Molly as she pulled a bottle
from the shelf. She poured some black liquid into a glass. "Here,
you drink all dis. It'll cure yer sore throat 'fore dinner tonight."

Meg took the glass gingerly. She sniffed its pungent odor.
"What is it?"

"Niver mind. It's cured near everybody in Beaufort one
time or 'nother." Meg held her nose and drank. She choked and

sputtered.. "That's awful! It's a case of cure or kill! Am I still breathing?"

"Worst it taste, the better it be! Turpentine and sugar. All my chillin's got a dose ever time they done sneezed!"

"Turpentine! I will be dead before morning!"

"Ain't nobody died from it yit."

By this time Maryanne had finished her washing and walked in. "Miss Molly is better'n that 'pothecary man. Oi bet she's cured more people then the doctor!"

Meg looked skeptical. "Do you get your medicine from the apothecary shop?"

Molly snorted in disgust. "He ain't no better'n a medicine man in a travellin' show. My medicine is guaranteed to cure and don't nobody git drunk on it neither."

"Oh, and what else do you have in your magic cupboard?" asked Meg.

"I got a jar of leaves and bark from a toothache tree. You jist makes a paste from 'em and puts it around that misery tooth."

"And that relieves the pain, does it?"

"Sho do. But my all 'round cure is my asafetida bag." Molly handed a net bag filled with some sort of herbs to Meg. "Jist hang that 'round yer neck and ye'll fight off de rheumatics, ague and swamp fever."

"No, thank you!" Meg thought it smelled worse than the fish factory fumes. It would probably ward off Dracula!

Meg was intrigued by Molly. 'She could be a character in a vaudeville show,' she thought. 'But she is not a fictional character. She's real and as Uncle Jim says, I can learn some things from her that may help me when I go to Florida.'

"Do you mind if I watch what you do?" she asked.

"Sakes, no. I enjoys pretty young peoples, if they minds their business. That coffee and fry bread sho was good. Now I needs to start cookin' for dinner tonight. Praise de Lord, I don't have to do no noontime meal. Maryanne, git on upstairs and dust all de furniture and shake out de beds unlessen they still be a body in 'em."

Maryanne flew upstairs, tying on a new apron as she ran.

"What is that pine bark muddle you were talking about?" Meg asked.

"I don't rightly know where it come by that name, 'ceptin' you throw everything into it, sorta in a muddle and you cooks it over a fire made from loblolly pine bark."

As she was talking, Molly was chopping at least three pounds of onions and frying as much salt pork. She diced six cups of potatoes. Next she removed the cracklings from the drippings and then fried the onions in the drippings. She was like a tiny whirlwind circling the kitchen. Meg was amazed at her energy and efficiency for she must be at least ninety years old. She put fifteen or more pieces of fish on to boil. Then she cut up five pounds of tomatoes and put those onto cook. "I cooks de fish jist enuff to take out de bones. Now we is goin' to carry all dis vittles outside and put 'em in my iron wash pots."

Molly filled the caldrons with water and got a fire made of pine bark going under each kettle. By this time, the fish and tomatoes were partially cooked. After picking out the bones, she dumped fish, tomatoes, onions, cracklings, crumbled crackers and six-dozen eggs into the mixture. "I'll jist let dis cook a minute, then add de butter 'en salt 'en pepper. Now it can stew awhile," she said with satisfaction. "I is now ready for my nap. Dat Maryanne kin cook de collards with dis piece of backbone boiled down with some salt. Later on we'll bake some sweet taters."

"Oh, she does some of the cooking, too?"

"Eny old body kin cook collards and sweet taters," said Molly, dismissively. "She can throw in some blueberry dumplings. They turns green in that collard juice. I wouldn't trust her none with a pumpkin pie. Once I 'lowed her to make a huckleberry pie. It were as sour as a persimmon a'fore the frost hits it. The payin' folks said they wasn't comin' back to eat no more. I had to 'splain to de folks it weren't my cookin'. And I promised I'd niver let Maryanne cook no pies no more."

"Poor Maryanne!"

"Well, eberbody kin do somethin'. I kin cook 'en Maryanne can clean. We is happy doin' what we does. If you 'scuse me, I is goin' to my room 'en curl up under them quilts and sleep 'til suppertime." She trotted out of the kitchen and up the stairs.

"Goodbye," Meg said, but she was talking to empty air. She wandered into the parlor, deciding to leave by the front door this time. Indian clay pipes and arrowheads decorated the mantel above the fireplace. The fire screen was held in place by two metal mallard ducks, one on each side of the screen. She noticed an old family Bible on the pie table. She carefully leafed through the brown worn and faded pages, noting a record of the family genealogy going back four generations. A spinet piano was tucked into the corner, its legs and case draped with a lace cloth. Meg was amused. The effect of Queen Victoria was felt even in this out-of-the-way place. She had decreed that the display of piano legs was vulgar. Thus, piano legs throughout the United Kingdom and in its worldwide environs were covered. A quilting frame faced a spindle-back chair, waiting for its mistress's nimble fingers to continue their work. The frame had multi-colored squares of cloth sewn together which were stretched across the frame. Meg wondered whose artistic hand had created the lovely pattern. For a moment, she felt very inadequate, afraid even. She had never had a needle in hand, so much as boiled water or dusted the magnificent mahogany furniture in her uncle's home. She was quite talented at sketching and painting and better than average at performing on the piano. Admirers thought her contralto singing voice most appealing. And, of course, she had her teaching certificate. In short, her abilities were impractical except for the teaching, but would she even find enough Indian children to teach? Suddenly, she was assailed with doubts. Were her father, uncle and aunt right all along? Should she have stayed in New York, protected and cosseted, the rest of her life? She didn't have to work. She knew her uncle wanted her safely married with the obligation of his loving protection transferred to an equally loving husband.

'Am I capable of existing and thriving on my own?' Meg pondered. 'You've come so far. You can't go back. That would be admitting failure before you've even tried. Can I prove to my father I can do this?' Meg threw back her shoulders, visibly forcing herself out of the doldrums. 'I am capable, and I will thrive. Jupiter Inlet, here I come!' She walked over to a walnut étagère and gazed at the treasured knickknacks displayed. With a guilty look behind her, Meg opened a blue enameled hair box. A long, black curled strand of hair nestled on a velvet cushion. Was this once the treasured memento of an ardent lover? Meg knew she was romanticizing. She doubted the spinster sisters entertained such thoughts. She wondered if Andre would treasure a lock of her hair. Beside the blue box was a cloisonné snuffbox. There were numerous small oval miniatures of proud family members, all with proper but grim expressions.

She idly looked at the few books placed at random on a bookshelf. Horatio Alger's <u>Ragged Dick</u>, the first of many rags-to-riches novels, was conspicuously displayed. Next to it was <u>Little Lord Fauntleroy</u> by Frances Hodgson Burnett and <u>The Secret Garden</u>, both variations on the theme. Mark Twain's <u>The Prince and The Pauper</u> was dog-eared, obviously read over and over by a dreamer.

"There is a romantic in the house," said Meg as she picked up Charlotte Bronte's <u>Jane Eyre</u> and her tragic sister's <u>Wuthering Heights</u>. "Wonder who emphatized with Jane's passion for Rochester?" There was an Episcopal <u>Book of Prayer</u>, along with several books of etiquette. Ah, she knew those only too well. <u>Godey's Lady's Book</u> and <u>The Farmer's Almanac</u>, both offering current information, were well thumbed. Two copies of America's best-selling schoolbook, <u>McGuffey's Reader</u>, rounded out the eclectic literary offering.

The pleasant chiming of a grandfather clock in the hallway reminded Meg of the time. 'Wonder if Uncle Jim is back yet?'

Chapter Seven

Meg ran outside and down the steps as Jim was approaching the Davis House. "Uncle Jim!" she called. "Good Morning! Isn't it a glorious day? I saw geese flying overhead in a perfect V formation. How can they do that?"

"Instinct, dear. They are born knowing how. Incidentally, I sent a letter to your father today. I saw a friend of mine in town this morning. Kemp Morris is captain of a steamboat and he is headed for the Bahamas tomorrow. Jupiter Inlet is on his way, so he said he would be glad to stop there and deliver the letter to Sean. It will be much quicker than waiting for the mail boat which is not due until next week."

"Good. Father must be worried by now, wondering why we haven't arrived. I really enjoyed visiting with Miss Molly. What a personality! What a worker, and at her age!" They continued walking down the street, not willing to go inside on such a perfect day.

"She is amazing. Oh, by the way, Leland and Stephanie have invited us for punch and appetizers at their home this evening. Dr. and Mrs. Brown will be there, the Seymores, the Episcopal minister Thomas Alligood, who is an old friend of mine, and the new young Baptist minister, Ralph Day, and their wives, of course."

"I'm sorry about the circumstances that brought us to Beaufort, but I am enjoying meeting your friends and seeing where you grew up. Why did you sell your house?"

"When both my parents died and left the house to me and your mother, we knew that neither of us would be returning here. I had a prosperous law practice in New York, and Theresa was dedicated to helping your father in his clinic in Florida. So we decided the best thing to do would be to sell it. Leland and Stephanie have graciously asked us to stay at their house while we are here, but Christmas is not far away and I know their children and grandchildren will be coming to visit for the holidays. It would be too crowded. So I told him I appreciated it, but we were fine at the Davis House."

"Do you think we'll still be here through Christmas?' asked Meg.

"Yes, I talked to Davy and he says the repairs to the ship will take even longer than expected, at least until mid-January. I know your father will be disappointed. He has been looking forward to seeing you for so long."

"I'm not so sure about that."

"Why would you say that? He loves you dearly," said Jim in a shocked voice.

"I always felt that I was an inconvenience to my parents. They were so completely involved with each other that there was no room in their lives for a third person. You have been more of a father to me than my own father ever was." Meg looked so downcast that Jim was at a loss, particularly since he had never suspected that Meg's relationship with her parents was unhappy.

"Surely, Meg, you must be mistaken. I know they were dedicated to their work, but certainly not to the exclusion of their only child."

"It's true, Uncle Jim. Some people have a love that is all-consuming, that requires no one else, which allows no one else within that unbroken circle. Oh, I never suffered from physical want or was scolded or punished. I was almost like an unwanted stranger, who was granted their hospitality, but not their love." Meg looked up at her uncle with tears in her eyes and saw the distress and compassion in his. Impulsively, she put her arms

74

around him. "Dearest Uncle Jim, I only wish I could have lived with you and Aunt Julie all my life. You loved me far more than my own parents did. When my mother died, I think my father's heart was broken and part of him died, too. He worked even harder in the clinic, day and night, but he couldn't forget her, or remember me."

"I never even suspected this. If it were true, what a terrible loss for them never to have known their dear, sweet, wonderful daughter." Jim's voice cracked with emotion as he spoke. How could they have excluded this warm loving child? He simply could not believe it.

"Uncle Jim, I did suffer from their rejection as a child, but when I went to live with you and Aunt Julie, my whole world changed. I soon knew that you loved and cherished me and my life was different. I wouldn't trade precious gold for that. You made me realize that I was worthwhile, that I was someone who could be loved. You turned my whole life around, but now I want to prove that I am somebody to my father and that I am capable to myself. I'm not leaving you forever. You'll visit often, won't you?"

"Yes, we will. We'll miss you so much, you'll have to keep us away!"

"Never! Do you understand why I want to go back? It's as though something were unfinished."

"I do understand now. I thought you were simply rebelling, trying your wings like a fledgling. Perhaps this journey will bring you a sense of peace."

They had been slowly walking along the waterfront and Jim pointed out a lovely old home, its high steps leading to a wide veranda.

"That's Leland and Stephanie's house. They have furnished it beautifully. I know you will appreciate Stephanie's delicate touch."

"I look forward to seeing it tonight."

Jim pulled out his pocket watch, looking at it in surprise. "It is way past lunchtime. Let's go to the Inlet Inn. They have sandwiches and delicious clam chowder."

"If we keep this up, I am going to weight one hundred and fifty pounds Miss Molly says I am too skinny to attract the male population. Evidently, I need to look like a tub of lard to be alluring, and I'm well on the way!"

"Megan, every male eye follows in your direction when you waltz by! Besides, you eat so sparingly, you will never be in the running in a fat ladies contest. But just in case you are seriously worried, let's run the rest of the way."

"All right, but hold my parasol!"

Meg grabbed her skirts and ran along the shell street with Jim in the lead. Quite a few astonished strollers watched as they sped by. They reached the Inlet Inn laughing and out of breath. Jim was happy to see that Meg was no longer depressed. Andre was standing at the top of the steps, enjoying the sight of Meg flying along, her cheeks flushed and her hair tumbling about her shoulders.

"Good afternoon. I see you're in fine fettle. Nothing like brisk run to keep healthy," said Andre as he offered Meg his hand to help her up the last step.

Meg was glad her face was already flushed from the exercise; otherwise he would have seen her blush. "Oh, thank you. It was invigorating!" she said as she clamped his hand. "Uncle Jim and I are going to have lunch here."

"Good afternoon to you, Sir," he spoke politely to Jim. "You will enjoy it. The clam chowder was excellent."

Jim's pleasant mood dissipated. "I'm sure we will. Come Megan, let's go in before they stop serving."

Andre released Meg's hand and stepped aside to allow them passage. "I look forward to seeing you this evening. Mrs. Carter was kind enough to send me an invitation to their party. I sent my acceptance back to her this afternoon." He smiled pleasantly, tipped his hat to Meg and walked down the steps. Meg thought she heard him whistling as he walked away.

Meg and Jim went inside and Meg noticed Jim's frown. "What is it, Uncle? Why are you scowling like an old bear with a sore paw?"

"I'm not scowling, am I? It is just that I was surprised that Stephanie invited him. I wonder if Leland knows."

"What an odd thing to say. Why shouldn't she invite him and why would Leland not want to invite him?"

"For one thing, he is a complete stranger. For another, he's a little too smooth for my taste. We don't really know anything about him. He could be an axe murderer, for all I know."

Meg turned to look at her uncle in astonishment. "Axe murderer! Uncle, really! I can't believe you said that. Why would you think such a thing? He's quite charming and pleasant, and he's so...."

"Good-looking?"

"Well, yes. What's wrong with that?"

"Nothing, of course. But what lies beneath that handsome veneer?"

"He appears to me to be a perfect gentleman. What has he said or done that makes you think otherwise?"

"It's hard to explain, Meg. Experience, intuition tells me he is not what he seems." Jim didn't want to be too negative because he knew Meg would staunchly defend him. "Maybe I'm just being a fussy, over-protective father figure. Let's forget about it and enjoy lunch."

When he said this, Meg relaxed and they went inside. The clam chowder exceeded its reputation and Meg ate every bite though she resisted the cracklin' cornbread. They left the dining room and decided to walk up Pollock Street.

"I'm so sleepy, I think I'll take a nap before the party tonight."

"Good idea. I still have some matters to take care of, or I'd do the same thing. Let's stop by the Post Office. I left this address with my New York office because I knew Wade planned to stop by Beaufort for a day or two to see his wife, and I thought any urgent mail could reach me here."

They entered the building and stood waiting for the mail, but there was nothing for him.

"Well, at least nothing momentous has happened or Elise would have forwarded the mail. I was expecting some word about the McCrimmons case."

They walked outside and Jim pointed out another building. "That's the Carteret Academy, also known as the Beaufort Female Academy. This is a school for girls from the Outer Banks. Maybe you might like to teach here. I'm sure they would hire you. Teachers are not easy to come by, especially qualified ones. Sometimes they have to use girls with just a high school education."

"I would be interested if I hadn't already planned to teach in Florida." She looked curiously at the school, wondering what it would feel like to be mistress of the classroom. She'd soon find out if all went as she had planned.

"The bill for tuition, including room and board, is seventy dollars. That is quite a bit of money for those fishermen, but somehow they manage to do it. Oftentimes the churches contribute supplies- books, paper, pens, ink."

"I'm sure I'll have to supply materials to the Indian children too," said Meg, already planning what she would need. "You've given me enough money to outfit an army!"

Meg was remembering her father's clinic. Patients gave what they could, but it was mostly chickens and pigs they raised or vegetables they grew.

"I remember one old Indian squaw gave him six strings of beads, her most prized possession, when he saved her grand-daughter's life," said Meg. She was also thinking about her childhood Seminole friends.

"You know, I haven't thought about Micco in years. That's strange because he once saved my life."

"Who is Micco?" asked Jim.

"He was an Indian boy who helped my parents in the clinic. I was just a little girl at the time, maybe five years old. Micco was older, about ten, I think. I was out in the canoe with three or four other older children and I fell overboard. We weren't that far out on the river, but far enough for me to have drowned if Micco hadn't happened along. He dove into the water and quickly swam to me and grabbed me, then brought me to shore. I was more frightened than hurt because he rescued me before I swallowed much water. I have never seen anyone so angry, but not with me. He turned on Gray Wolf and told him that I was never to be taken in the boat again until I could swim. 'From now on, that is your job. You will teach her!' he ordered, like some chieftain rebuking his subject. And Gray Wolf did. A year later, I could swim as well as the other children. It's funny how I remember that now. I haven't thought about Micco in years. I wonder how he is? He was always so clever. His father, Tall Chief, died when Micco was about thirteen and my father had him help out at the clinic. He ran errands, delivered medicine, cleaned and did any odd jobs required. By the time I left to come to New York, Father actually depended on him. He even assisted with patients."

"Perhaps you will see him when you return to Jupiter Inlet."

"Oh, I hope so. Micco Ravenwing, are you just as autocratic today as you were then? I wonder?"

"He sounds like an interesting fellow. I look forward to meeting the person who saved my Meg. I hope he hasn't left the tribe to seek his fortune elsewhere."

"I do, too. Now, I really want to see him again!"

They had crossed Ann Street and were walking past the Carteret Academy, up Turner Street.

"There's the firehouse and fire engine," Jim pointed out. "Every time I see that engine I am reminded of Ben Clawson's old horse. Ben's horse, Jumper, pulled the fire engine. He had done it ever since he was two years old. Ben never tied up Jumper at the house because the horse was trained to stay in his own yard. He was also trained to go straight to the firehouse when the alarm bell sounded. It was funny to see that horse galloping down the road with the siren blasting. He's go right up to the fire engine, and stomping the ground eagerly, wait to be hitched.   Jumper responded to many a fire bell for over twenty years, but then he started to go blind. Ben couldn't let him pull the engine any more and it was so sad to see that poor, half-blind horse, still trying to gallop down the street. He just could not understand why his master wouldn't let him do his job anymore."

"Poor, dear horse. I'll bet they never had another one as smart as that," said Meg.

"No, they didn't. Jumper was a special horse. He was every bit as smart as William Cody's trained horse in the Wild West show. That performing horse went into his act when a gun was fired. At the tour's end, Buffalo Bill gave his friend, Sitting Bull, this rare, prized horse when Sitting Bull went back to his own people. He had been part of the show and became good friends with Bill."

"Let's get back to our rooms. You can nap until the party tonight. I won't say 'Get your beauty sleep', because you don't need that. We really won't have to worry about dinner because I feel sure Stephanie's canapés will be as filling as a full-course meal." By now, they had reached the boarding house.

"I'll wake you up at five-thirty. That will give you a couple of hours of sleep. We are to be at the Carter's home at six-thirty." He gave Meg a peck on the cheek and left.

Meg walked to her room, thinking about Micco. She really wanted to see him. What would he look like now? He had been a handsome, if skinny boy with flashing brown eyes, quick to take offense at wrongs, and quick to laugh at Meg's childish babble. She had completely forgotten her friend in the bustle and excitement of New York City. She hoped he had not forgotten her. Then her thoughts flitted to Andre. She was excited at the thought of seeing him tonight. What should she wear to impress him?

Since it was a party, she could really dress up. She decided on a frock of apricot-colored, silk-lawn fichu with undersleeves and a daintily stitched muslin apron covering her quilted petticoat. This would display her figure to the best advantage. 'If this doesn't attract him what would?' she thought with a smug smile.

Meg stretched out on the bed and soon her eyes closed. When Jim knocked on the door two hours later, she was so groggy she didn't know where she was at the moment and thought she was back in her bed in New York.

"Meg, wake up. I know how long it takes for you to get dressed. We don't want to be late," called out Jim. "Are you awake?"

"Yes, I am now. I'll be ready!"

"All right. See you in a little while."

Fortunately, Meg had one of the few rooms that contained a bathtub. She knew she probably had her uncle to thank for that. She ran downstairs and found the maid in the parlor dusting the furniture.

"Could you please heat water for my bath?" she asked.

The maid looked surprised. "Yer goin' to take a bath and its only Monday? You better be kerful or you'll rub off yer skin fer sure."

Meg smiled. "I often take a bath several times a week. Saturday night is no special night to me. If it is especially hot and sticky, I might even take one every day!"

"Sakes, alive! Yer gonna peel jist like an onion, but Oi'll heat the water fer yer," said the young maid, shaking her head. "Oi'll bring it up to ya when it's a'boilin'."

"Thank you." Meg turned and ran upstairs, eager to lay out her clothes.

She took her dress from the armoire and laid it carefully on the bed.

"Ooh, ain't that a purty dress!", the maid exclaimed as she came into the room, staggering under the weight of two steaming kettles, one in each hand. She put them down next to the tub, then caught her breath and poured the water from each into the tub. Meg added bath salts and a sweet fragrance filled the room.

"Did you want anything else, ma'am? There's fresh towels and wash cloths on the towel rail."

"No, thank you. Everything is fine. What is your name?"

"My name's Sally Louise," answered the maid.

"Sally Louise. That's a pretty name. My name is Meg. Please take this for all your help," said Meg, handing her fifty cents.

The maid's eyes were as big as saucers. "Thank you, Miss Meg," she said, pocketing the money. "Jist call me if you need anything."

"Oh, wait a minute. I forgot to speak to Mrs. Seymore. Sally Louise, would you mind coming back in about twenty minutes? I can not lace up my corset by myself."

"Yes, Oi'll come back."

Meg tested the water, and then poured in cold water from a pitcher on the washstand. She quickly disrobed and stepped into the inviting steamy water.

"Ah! That feels heavenly!" She chuckled as she soaped her body. "I better be careful because I don't want to peel like an onion!" She soaked for twenty blissful minutes and glancing at the lady's boudoir clock on a side table, she stepped out, wrapping herself in a big, fluffy towel. After hurriedly drying herself, she stepped into her drawers and put on a chemise. Just then, Sally Louise tapped on the door.

"Come in!" By then, she had put her corset on over the chemise. Turning her back, she muttered, "Now, let's tighten this torture device!" Her helper tugged and pulled until Meg was gasping for breath.

"There now, yer all tied up!"

"Thank you, I guess!"

Meg finished dressing and she dabbed 'Verte et Blanc', an expensive French perfume, from her glass bottle. Her uncle had ordered it from Paris for her twenty-first birthday and it was her favorite fragrance.

She finally pulled her dress over her head and slipped into her evening shoes. She brushed out her curls.

"Do I dare add just a touch of rouge to my lips? Why not?" she asked the girl in the mirror. "Go ahead," it answered. "This is 1886, not 1850. Queen Victoria notwithstanding."

Meg had just finished placing her velvet hat with pale orange ostrich plumes on her head when Jim knocked on the door.

"Are you ready? It's six-twenty."

"I'm ready," Meg said as she opened the door, "bustle and all!"

Jim looked at her admiringly. "You'll be a daffodil among weeds!" Meg laughed and took his arm.

"And your sartorial splendor will make the other men think they have on work clothes."

They walked quickly to the Carter home for the sun was sinking and the northeast wind nipped their cheeks. When they climbed the steps and into the porch, ringing the doorbell, the hall clock was just striking the half-hour.

"Enter, friends! Welcome," said Leland and Stephanie. As they passed through the door, Meg was delighted by two alabaster cloisonné jardinières on either side of the portal that were filled with pine fronds, pine cones and sprays of holly leaves and bright red berries.

"How lovely! It gets me in a holiday mood."

"You must help me decorate for Christmas," said Stephanie. "I'm starting tomorrow on decorations for the tree. I've made my fruitcakes already. They're drenched with wine and slices of red apples. They are my children's favorite!"

"No wonder," said Leland. "My wife makes the best fruit cake in Beaufort."

"I think Martha Alligood would disagree with you there!"

"I'd love to help you decorate. What time?" asked Meg .

"Oh, come around ten o'clock." They were still congregated in the foyer and Meg admired a gilt wood mirror with a pierced basket and floral carved crest above a grapevine carved frame.

"That mirror is magnificent!" she exclaimed.

"It is a Louis XVI. Leland purchased it at an estate sale in Philadelphia last year." They continued to the drawing room where a fire was crackling in the huge fireplace.

"That feels good," said Meg as she pulled off her hat and coat and warmed her fingers.

"Come sit close to the fire," Stephanie said as she took Meg's hat and coat. "You look lovely, dear. That color becomes you."

"Thank you. I am a little chilly. It has become cold again. I was getting a sore throat, but Miss Molly administered one of her home remedies. I thought death was eminent when I swallowed it, but it must have worked."

Stephanie laughed, "She has wrought some miraculous cures."

"It looked like a snow sky earlier today," said Jim, rubbing his hands before the blaze. "I wouldn't be surprised to see snow before morning."

"Will you have Episcopal punch or Baptist punch or mulled cider?" Leland asked.

"What is Episcopal punch and Baptist punch?' asked Meg.

"Punch with spirits added is Episcopal punch. Unadulterated punch is Baptist punch!" said Stephanie with a smile.

"I'll have the mulled cider and Meg will have the Baptist punch," said Jim quickly.

"Uncle Jim, on Christmas Eve, do you think I'll be the only one drinking eggnog without the nog?" After all, I am twenty-one now!"

"We'll see."

Stephanie went for the drinks while Leland answered the doorbell.

"Come in. Nippy, isn't it?"

He led the nine people who all arrived at the same time into the drawing room. "Dr. and Mrs. Brown, this is Meg Riley, Jim's niece."

Meg exchanged greetings with the distinguished-looking couple. Dr. Brown had a handlebar mustache and stood quite erect as if he had been in the military. Mrs. Brown was stylishly dressed and both appeared to be in their sixties.

Jim shook hands with Dr. Brown. "It is good to see you, Albert and Jennifer. You haven't aged one day, my dear. What is your secret?"

She smiled and waved her fan at him. "You must be kin to an Irishman and every one of them has kissed the Blarney Stone!"

"Thomas, how are you?" said Jim, shaking hands and patting his friend the minister, on the back. "Martha, you are as lovely as ever. May I present my niece, Megan Riley."

"Charmed, my dear. I am Thomas Alligood, a longtime friend of your uncle, and this is my wife, Martha."

Meg shook hands with both. 'What pleasant people,' she thought. They were about the same age as her uncle, and while the Reverend Alligood wore his clerical collar and black suit, his plump little wife was dressed in blue velvet trimmed in silver. Reverend Alligood continued with the introductions.

"This is Ralph Day and his wife, Lois Jean. You'll probably be seeing them in church Sunday, I believe. Reverend Day is our new Baptist minister and his charming wife is the music director." Both were young, almost as young as Meg and both were quite cheerful and friendly. Reverend Day had a ruddy complexion, reddish-blond hair and twinkling light blue eyes. Meg thought that he probably injected some humor into his sermons. He was rather short and quite husky, more like a boxer than a minister. Lois Jean was slender and as tall as her husband. Her pale blond hair was pulled back unfashionably into a chignon, as befitted a minister's wife. Evidently, this young woman did not adhere to society's rage for ringlets, but her hazel eyes were as merry as her husband's, dispelling a look of severity. They all exchanged greetings. The Seymores were introduced and joined in the conversation. The last person to enter the room was Andre. He stood waiting to be introduced.

Stephanie said, "This is Andre Lafitte. He is a stranger in town, but let's change that."

The men shook hands and Andre bowed slightly to each lady. Mrs. Brown had a speculative look in her eye, and both Mrs. Alligood and Mrs. Day were staring unabashedly at this handsome man. Mrs. Seymore was examining the punch bowl and trying to see in the dining room. Jim exchanged civilities, as did Leland, but with no smile on his face. Meg was trying not to stare, but it was difficult. He matched her uncle in sartorial splendor. His blue waistcoat, threaded with gold, heightened the blue of his eyes and his hair gleamed like spun gold under the candelabra. 'Even his complexion is perfect,' thought Meg. He smiled at her and his eyes seemed to say, 'You are the only one I really want to talk to.'

Stephanie asked what they wanted and then served the drinks in clear glasses with cranberry flashing from a silver, rose punch bowl with a ruby glass liner. She dipped the punch with a sterling silver ladle. Meg had never seen such a lovely set, even in her aunt's house. Andre turned on the charm. He soon had Dr. Brown discussing his latest cases. The good doctor was amazed at Andre's knowledge, especially about gunshot wounds and knife wounds. "Young man, you will have to visit my office next week if you're still here," he said jovially, patting Andre on the shoulder.

"I'd be happy to, Sir. It would be an honor."

Andre discovered that Mrs. Brown was an avid gardener. He discussed the magnificent flowers of Hawaii and Tahiti. "The hibiscus in California seems lusterless in comparison. Do you grow them here?"

"Yes, though they die back in the winter. How I'd love to travel to those exotic places," she said.

He discussed religions of the world with Rev. Alligood and his wife, mentioning the strange customs of the Moslems. Both the Alligoods and the Days found him to be knowledgeable and unprejudiced. He expressed an interest in music and hoped Mrs. Day would play and sing for them. Mrs. Day felt that he really did want her to perform and she would certainly oblige him. Andre tried to include Mrs. Seymore in the discussions, but met failure for once in his life. She was impervious to charm or good looks. But Mr. Seymore hung on his every work. Jim was talking to Leland and both men glanced, unobtrusively, at Andre from time to time. Meg was left to chat with Mrs. Seymore, which was downhill all the way.

After about thirty minutes, Stephanie rang the dinner bell.

"Please come into the dining room. Serve yourselves and sit where ever you like."

Mrs. Seymore was the first in line. Somehow, Andre was suddenly standing beside Meg.

"May I escort you?" he asked, offering her his arm. Meg, at five feet seven inches tall, had to look up at him. 'He must be at least six feet three,' she thought.

"Thank you." She took his arm and everyone in the room except Jim, Leland and Mrs. Seymore thought what a strikingly handsome couple they made.

To their left was a marble top buffet server. A tremendous silver soup tureen was filled with a thick, aromatic vegetable soup. The maid was just bringing in a tray of warm blueberry popovers, fresh from the oven. Platters of dainty open-faced sandwiches topped with egg salad, a ham and chutney spread, raisin and nut, thinly sliced turkey, and cucumber and chives, filled the sideboard. The maid had returned, bringing hot crab canapés, tiny sausage biscuits, melted cheese in a thin crusty roll topped with onion, and fried oyster rolls. There was also a bowl of spiced oysters. At the end of the buffet, thin slices of cherry jelly cake were placed attractively in a silver cake basket that was embossed with beads and scrolls with a leafy border.

"Shall we have the soup first?" Andre asked Meg.

"Yes. Oh, my. Another night with food enough to feed the entire nation of starving Chinese."

He ladled two cups of soup and carried them to the lace-covered mahogany table that seated twelve. There were individual bowls of toasted pine nuts beside each table setting. After placing the cups of soup on the table, he pulled out a chair for Meg. Bending low, he whispered in her ear, "May I say you are ravishingly beautiful. You are exquisite!" He straightened and said aloud, "I'll get us those delicious-looking popovers."

Meg blushed. She knew men admired her, but the men of her acquaintance would never have been so bold. She supposed, compared to Andre, they were callow boys.

Andre had moved beside Meg so quickly that Jim found several people in line before him. He was almost gritting his teeth in frustration. By the time he went through the buffet, the chairs on both sides of Meg and Andre were taken. He sat down across from them.

Meg was admiring the centerpiece. It was a pale blue glass epergne that sparkled from the surrounding candlelight. The central vase was filled with branches of holly and berries and was flanked by a matching pair of smaller vases filled with greenery. A pair of spiral stem branches were suspending baskets that were filled with painted nuts of gold and silver and fruit- red raspberries, purple grapes, raisins and greengage plums. The opalescent borders had turquoise glass rims.

Meg turned to Mrs. Seymore, who was on her right. "The centerpiece is breathtaking, don't you think?"

"Ostentatious," she said with a sniff, barely glancing at it. She had just cleaned her plate and was looking at the buffet like a hunter in search of its prey. "Mr. Seymore, will you get me a few more of those sandwiches and several of the hors d'oeuvres, especially that crab?" Before Mr. Seymore could rise from the table, Andre stood up. "Please, allow me. Would you also like some soup and popovers?"

Mr. Seymore smiled his thanks for it was not easy to disentangle himself from the chair and table legs.

"I don't mind if I do. Vegetable soup is so healthy and I must keep up my strength. I am in delicate health, you know."

Andre took her plate and went back to the buffet table.

"Raymond, what do you think of our new President, Mr. Cleveland?" asked Jim.

Mrs. Seymore jumped in before her husband could answer. "I am convinced the country will be ruined before his term of office expires. They will regret not electing James Baine. The Republicans have been serving the country well. Actually, if the Republican Party had had the sense to nominate Chester Arthur instead of Baine, we would not be in this ghastly situation."

"Then we would have had the same situation that occurred when he took over the Presidential office upon Garfield's assassination. Arthur just died two weeks ago, and the VP would have become President," said Jim.

"Never-the-less, I stand on my convictions."

"Henrietta, those stalwarts, the Old Guard Republicans, have gone out of style. Frankly, I have had enough of Tammany Hall and all the shenanigans that went on."

"I agree," said Dr. Brown from the end of the table. "Let us see what President Cleveland can do. How did you think he did as Governor of New York, Jim?"

"I thought he did a good job. He was responsible for introducing Civil Service reform, although I did not agree with some of his ideas. We still have coolie wages- ten cents an hour- in clothing factories. He could have done something about that. Children under fifteen are allowed to work in tobacco fields for as little as twenty-five cents a day. Children slave in factories for a pittance while the owners grow rich."

"It is criminal," said Leland. "Just because Andrew Carnegie started out as a bobbin boy at age thirteen in a textile mill and ended up as the richest steel man on earth, doesn't mean that anyone else could or would do that. Legislation should be passed to protect the rights of children."

If Mrs. Seymore was bothered by being outnumbered, she didn't show it. "Truth will out," she said, glorying in clichés. She took the plate and soup Andre brought to her, politics forgotten in the higher scheme of things.

Rev. Alligood remarked, "It never works to discuss politics or religion with the intention of proselytizing. If there were only two people in a room, the two would disagree on those two subjects. Under normal circumstances, no amount of argument would change either."

"You are correct, Thomas. I avoid them like swamp fever," said his wife.

Jim steered the conversation in another direction. "Meg and I were lucky enough to see the unveiling of the Statue of Liberty, that amazing copper colossus, last month. President Cleveland dedicated it in a ceremony on Bedloe's Island and over three thousand people were in attendance."

"It was presented to the United States in commemoration of one hundred years of American independence," added Meg. "The French have always been our allies and I hope they always will be. Has anyone seen the Washington Monument yet? I have heard that it is unbelievable!"

"Stephanie and I went in October last year when it was opened to the public. It makes you feel quite insignificant," said Leland.

Andre entered the conversation at this point. "In California, I heard a rumor about a man named Steve Brodie."

"Who is that? Another politician?" asked Mrs. Day.

"Actually, he was a bookmaker who allegedly jumped off the Brooklyn Bridge into the East River, a mere drop of 140 feet."

"Was he killed?"

"No. According to the legend, he survived and afterwards opened up a profitable saloon."

"Evidently, crime does pay," remarked Rev. Day.

90

"Sad, but true," remarked Andre, drolly.

"What is a bookmaker?" Mrs. Day asked. "I assume he doesn't manufacture books."

"She's led a sheltered life," said Rev. Day, gazing at his wife fondly.

"This is a person who takes bets primarily on horse racing, or anything a person is willing to bet on," replied Andre.

"What was your occupation in California, not to change the subject?" asked Jim.

. "I speculated in growing grapes, but my investment was so small compared to other growers that I was forced out and now I am on my way to Florida. Perhaps I will be more successful with avocados or pineapples. The Indians could provide cheap labor, hopefully."

Jim didn't believe him for a minute and he was worried by the reference to Florida. He looked over at Meg who was listening intently.

"Don't get up your expectations concerning the Seminole Indians. They are a proud people and not inclined to work for a white man. Even if you had slave labor, they have a way of slipping quietly away into the everglades and swamps. Perhaps you should try your luck in the more civilized northern area with tomatoes or beans or raspberries. The opportunities are endless. Farming is a hard, backbreaking job, even with all the help you can employ. I admire your perseverance."

That was a lie, of course. Jim did not admire anything about the devious man sitting across from him.

"Somehow the prospect of tomatoes or beans sounds so prosaic. Pineapples and avocados are much more exotic, and I am inclined towards the exotic. I am a gambler, as well. In this life one needs to take a chance. Otherwise, one will never know what might have been. Do you agree, Megan?" he asked, turning towards her.

"I suppose so, to a certain extent. Of course, it is more logical and safer to do what you know has the best chance of success." Meg was mentally playing the devil's advocate with herself.

"Do you want to be logical and safe, or do you want adventure and romance?" he asked, gazing at her intently.

"Both."

"Ah, a romanticist and a pragmatist rolled into one! A rare find these days!"

Meg enjoyed their repartee. She thought he was the most fascinating man she had ever met. At the same time, she felt somewhat uneasy, not with Andre, but because she knew her uncle did not like him. Meg never wanted to displease her uncle because she loved him dearly. She was torn between fascination and loyalty.

Andre was clever enough not to press his advantage in spite of the pleasure it gave him to bait her uncle. He knew Meg was conflicted. She was so innocent, it whetted his appetite for the chase, but he had plenty of time. He would make small inroads to her protective barriers until she surrendered. He was so experienced with women that there was not one ploy Meg could use that he had not seen before. He had had plenty of exposure at an early age in the slums of Sevres watching his mother ply her trade. He had never been in love and he had known some of the most beautiful, alluring women in the world. Not one had touched that hard, cold core within him. He needed no baggage weighing him down to prevent him from getting what he wanted.

Stephanie rang the dinner bell again and everyone stopped talking to look at her.

"I believe everyone has finished eating. Let's go into the drawing room for coffee." She noticed Meg's expression. "Meg, this is good Columbian coffee and it's the first time it has been used!"

Everyone laughed for they all knew about the practice of reusing coffee grounds. They got up from the table and made their way to the drawing room. Jim felt frustrated because he had not had a chance to meet Andre's obvious challenge. Andre had already taken Meg's arm in a proprietary manner and was leading her to a chaise lounge near the window. Jim thought Meg looked like a ripe apricot in her flowing gown against the pink and blue striped tapestry. What man could resist her, especially a scoundrel like the grandson of Jean Lafitte. But could Meg resist him? Too bad dueling was outlawed. Otherwise, he would call the man out and kill him on the spot. Jim knew his thoughts were capricious, but he couldn't help it. This was his baby, about to be gobbled up by a hungry wolf. He knew as surely as the sun rose in the East that Lafitte would be on the ship with them. What could he do about it? Then he thought that maybe he could find out what the man had really done in California. He had plenty of contacts that were good at tracing.

Mrs. Seymore had ensconced herself in a Louis XV walnut chair that was upholstered in pink velvet. It clashed horribly with her puce gown.

"I found the jelly cake too sweet," she had eaten three pieces, "and the crab was overdone." She had eaten four crab rolls. "Did you not find it so, Raymond?"

"I cannot agree with you there, my dear. I found everything delicious!" replied her husband who was sitting in an armchair in which he was barely able to stuff himself.

"And her taste in décor- well, I can only say she needs a decorator." She continued in this vein with her husband looking quite uncomfortable. Fortunately, Stephanie was on the other side of the room.

A dainty French porcelain and ormolu mantel clock chimed nine o'clock.

Rev. Alligood spoke to Dr. Brown. "You know, Albert, one of the most practical things those railroad entrepreneurs did was to standardize the time zones. Most confusing thing I ever experienced traveling through seventy-five different railroad time systems. Martha and I took a trip out west in 1880 and I never could keep it straight."

"I know what you mean. Jennifer and I went to New York five years ago and had the same experience. Thank goodness they finally standardized the time zones three years ago to Eastern, Central, Mountain and Pacific. Good thing someone had the common sense to come up with that idea."

"The railroads have changed our whole way of life," said Leland. "Ten years ago there were 40,000 cowboys driving cattle a thousand miles or more over parched earth. Now the railroad is taking over that job. Many of those cowboys were Negroes and that put them out of a job. So they took on new jobs as Pullman porters."

"This is an exciting age we live in," said Jim. "My wife, Meg and I had the good fortune to see Thomas Edison light the bulb he invented in 1879. It was on New Year's Eve and thousands of people flooded Menlo Park, New Jersey, to watch the demonstration."

"Yes," said Rev. Day. "All of the big industries use electricity now. It won't be long before private homes have it. I am sure electric power will replace water power, too. No more old-fashioned windmills."

"Poppycock!" said Mrs. Seymore, using her favorite expression. "Light bulbs will never replace candles. They'll find out if they try. Rampant fires will be widespread. We will not have enough fire engines to put them out."

"But, Mrs. Seymore, Edison Electric Company is already providing power. We saw an electrically lighted Christmas tree in the home of Mr. Edward Johnson, who is a colleague of Mr. Edison. Uncle Jim says we can have one, too."

"Won't that be lovely, seeing electric lights on a Christmas tree," said Mrs. Brown.

"You will regret it. Mark my words," stated Mrs. Seymore stubbornly. "I will never allow Raymond to do such a dangerous thing in my home!" Mr. Seymore looked embarrassed, but said nothing.

The maid walked to each guest filling coffee cups from a tea caddy that she pushed around the room. Meg admired the dainty silver pierced basket.

"I also have imported Chinese tea for those that prefer tea," offered Stephanie.

"Speaking of modern inventions, besides electricity, we have got Morse's telegraph sending messages through the air. It is like magic" said Dr. Brown.

"Black Magic," muttered Mrs. Seymore.

"What about the telephone? Those 'Hello Girls' are making a profession working as operators in New York. We installed a telephone in our home last year. Many of my friends and associates have one, too," said Jim.

"Just imagine. I can actually call my friends and talk without going to their houses," said Meg.

"You'd probably have to have stock in the Comstock Lode in order to afford one," Ralph Day said .

"I am positive that in just a few years, they will be affordable for everyone," Jim said. "Lois Jean, Stephanie has told me that you play beautifully. Would you play and sing for us?"

Lois Jean blushed. "Well, I did tell Andre that I would play earlier." She looked at him almost flirtatiously.

"Will you allow me to turn the pages for you? If you know 'Jeannie with the Light Brown Hair', we could sing a duet."

"I'd be delighted!"

All the guests waited in anticipation for the performance. Andre walked over to the piano, opened it up and pulled out the piano bench.

"I don't need the music for this one. I know it by heart. Will you sing the lead or the harmony?" she asked.

"It does not matter; either one. I am like Terpsichore. I can sing in any key. Which do you prefer?"

"It is easier to sing the lead if I am playing. I only know it in the key of C. Will that be all right?"

"That will be perfect."

She played the introduction and then they sang. Meg thought in amazement to herself as she listened to their melodic voices, 'He can sing too?'

When they finished, the guests clapped loudly and called out, "Encore, encore!"

"Play some Christmas music, dear," requested her husband.

"All right. Here's a book of Christmas carols."

Andre did not know any Christmas Carols. He had learned 'Jeannie with the Light Brown Hair' from one of his paramours. All the rest of his repertoire was unsuitable for drawing room ears. "Why don't you all join in and sing. Get into the Christmas spirit." He selected a song and held the page.

Lois Jean played 'It Came Upon A Midnight Clear' and everyone joined in singing. Andre was good enough to follow along and no one noticed that he didn't really know the song. They had gathered around the piano and Andre heard Meg's rich contralto voice behind him.

After several songs, Leland said, "Meg, I understand that you are an accomplished pianist. Will you play for us, too?"

"Oh, no. I am enjoying singing while Mrs. Day plays."

"Please play. I would love to hear you," requested the minister's wife as she rose from the piano bench.

"So would I. Will you play?" Andre asked Meg, his blue eyes earnest and beseeching.

Meg could not resist his appeal. "Well, then I will." She played 'Greensleeves' 'Good King Wencelas' and 'God Rest Ye Merry Gentlemen' but her rendition sounded more like a concert performance. After a few more classical selections, Meg stopped playing.

"That's enough for now. Anyone for some Baptist punch?" Meg acknowledged their enthusiastic applause amid laughter over the punch remark. She stood up and Andre again took her arm when they went back to the loveseat.

"You are a professional. You should perform before the Crown heads of Europe," said Andre, admiringly.

"So she should," Leland agreed.

"Her music professor thought she had talent and he wanted her to continue her studies, but Meg had her heart set on being a school teacher. Her Aunt and I were disappointed because I think she has a rare gift, but that was Meg's decision and I abide by that," said Jim.

"You are indeed an understanding parent," Andre said.

"I understand Meg very well." Meg sensed the tension between them and quickly changed the subject.

"Is anyone going to the circus? It will arrive Thursday."

"What fun! I haven't seen a dime show since I was a little girl. We moved to Vanceboro and it never came there," said Mrs. Day. "Oh, Ralph, please, let's go."

"I would enjoy having the fortune teller tell my fortune. Sure, we'll go, sweetheart."

Before Andre could ask Meg to accompany him, Jim said, "Meg and I would like to accompany you, too." He turned to Meg. "You already asked to go the other day."

"If it doesn't snow, I would like to go."

Then Ralph joined in. "That's five of us. Anybody else ready to risk knowing what the future brings?"

Dr. and Mrs. Brown declined as did the Alligoods and Seymores, but Leland and Stephanie wanted to go.

"The circus will go to that clearing a couple of miles outside of town, near Safrit's sawmill. I'll get Steve Miller to drive us in his wagon. He can fill it with hay and we'll have a hayride, too," said Leland enthusiastically. "I haven't been on a hayride since Stephanie and I were dating."

"Hear, hear," said Dr. Brown. "Got mighty cold in the back of that wagon, didn't it?"

"Well, I certainly did not want Stephanie to freeze. I brought a blanket!"

Everyone laughed. "It's all arranged then. We'll meet at three o'clock on Friday in front of the Davis House dock."

"Meg, come look at Leland and Stephanie's scrapbook," Jim called out from across the room.

"I would like to see it," Meg smiled at Andre and got up.

"So would I." He arose also and accompanied her to the table.

Jim was annoyed. Andre was sticking to Meg like a leech. 'How appropriate,' he thought. 'The man is a blood-sucker.'

They looked at the full-color pictures. Many were romantic scenes.

"We will place some of those scraps on the tree," said Stephanie as she watched them.

"They're pretty," said Meg admiringly.

A clock chimed musically, playing a minuet, seemingly from a picture. Meg was intrigued by it and walked over to a picture depicting a pastoral scene. Amid forest and trees, a castle loomed in the distance, close to the spires of a church. A tiny clock was embedded in the façade of the castle.

"How utterly charming!" she exclaimed, delighted by the tiny musical clock.

"That is a French musical picture clock," said Stephanie.

"You have so many beautiful clocks."

Stephanie replied, apologetically, "Perhaps too many. I have always been fascinated by clocks- like the Spanish king of yore. One of his castle rooms was filled with nothing but a hundred clocks, all ticking simultaneously. He was quite mad, of course."

"Steph, you are one of the sanest people I know, even if you are a clock fanatic!" said her husband, who walked over to join them.

"The French have a flair for style," said Andre. "Look at this inkstand, Meg. It is similar to one I saw in Paris."

"We bought that on our last trip to Paris," said Leland who was evidently a connoisseur of French provincial furniture. "I acquired this paperweight at that time, too."

98

Meg picked up an exquisitely sculpted object in the shape of a dahlia. "Andre, this is extraordinary, isn't it?"

"Yes, it is. Stephanie and Leland, you have a lovely, tastefully-decorated home," he said, admiringly.

Jim did not like the familiarity that Andre was establishing with Meg. Already they were calling each other by their first names. It was not suitable on such short acquaintance.

"Thank you," responded Leland, stiffly. "We enjoy furniture hunting."

"Megan, my dear, it is getting late. Let's say our 'Goodbyes'."

"All right, Uncle Jim. I have been having such a good time, I didn't realize the time."

"Oh, you don't have to go yet, do you? It's not late," said Stephanie.

"You're very gracious, but we will take our leave now. Thank you for the delicious food. I enjoyed the evening so much." Jim shook hands with Leland, and kissed Stephanie on the cheek when she brought his hat. She then handed Meg her hat. The two hugged and Meg adjusted her veil.

"I had a wonderful time. You're both marvelous hosts. I'll see you at ten o'clock tomorrow," she promised, "if I have to tromp through a foot of snow!"

Andre added his thanks as did all the other guests while Leland and Stephanie handed out coats and hats.

"Brrr! It's really cold!" said Meg when Leland opened the door. The wind rushed into the cozy room causing the candles to flutter.

A chorus of 'goodnights' filled the air as the guests left the house. Andre managed to give Meg's hand a squeeze and he whispered that he would see her soon. All the guests went their separate ways and Meg and Jim hustled along the shell street against a biting, cold wind.

"Oh no! It's starting to snow," yelped Meg as a snowflake slid down her neck. They reached the boarding house, battling the gusts every step of the way.

"Goodnight, Uncle Jim. It was a wonderful party. I like all your friends!"

Jim's green eyes, so like Meg's, were warm with appreciation. "I'll come in and put more logs on the fire."

They ran quickly upstairs to escape the chilly night, and Jim added several of the biggest logs from a basket by the fireplace to the hot embers. The flames licked hungrily at the sweet-smelling cedar as he replaced the fire screen.

"That should keep you warm and cozy until morning. Goodnight, dear."

Meg hugged him. "Thank you. Sleep well."

"You do, too. Goodnight!"

Chapter Eight

Meg was awakened the next morning by the plaintive cry of a mourning dove. Her fire had lasted through the night and the room was still warm. She was eager to greet the new day and was looking forward to helping Stephanie this morning. She leaped out of bed and ran to the window that was frosted over. She rubbed a circle on the pane and looked out into a white, sparkling world. The mourning dove was pecking at holly berries, unable to find worms in the frozen ground. Meg glanced at the clock and was startled to discover that it was already eight forty-five. She must have been tired and now she would have to dress hurriedly because Stephanie was expecting her at ten o'clock. Steph had mentioned that she would have coffee and muffins while they worked. Meg knew her uncle was probably already abroad since he was an early riser. She bathed and dressed quickly, omitting bustle and corset, as well. She knew Stephanie wouldn't care and maybe no one else would see her. Well, just let them be shocked if they did! As she donned her blue flannel dress, thinking these most unladylike thoughts, her uncle tapped on the door.

"Meg, are you dressed?"

"Yes, come in."

He came in and sat down. "The most appalling thing happened last night."

"What is it?" asked Meg, apprehensively; somehow afraid it might have involved Andre.

"Rumley's Feed Store was robbed, and Horace Rumley was hit over the head when he interrupted the robbery.

."That's awful. How badly was he hurt?"

"I don't know. I saw Telford in front of the store talking to several people. I walked over and asked him what happened and he said that Horace had been taken to Dr. Brown's office. Telford didn't know just how badly Horace was injured."

"Who would do such a thing? I thought you said not many crimes ever happen here in Beaufort!"

"They don't! Maybe it was an itinerant worker or a stranger from a ship. I just don't understand. Telford said the only 'major' crime he has had in the last ten years was when Jimps Dudley went on a drunken spree and shot the 'Lewis for Sheriff' posters full of holes."

"I wonder if Leland and Stephanie know about it?"

"Probably not. Horace is in his seventies. For a man his age, that blow could be fatal."

"I hope not, Uncle Jim. Let's go see Leland and Stephanie."

They walked quickly to the Carter's home. A dozen possibilities were running through Jim's head concerning the assault. It couldn't be anyone local. Even Walter Chrichon, the town drunk, was harmless. The most he ever did was yell that the purple bugs were crawling all over him, trying to kill him. He would not have the strength or the inclination to commit violence. Poor old Horace left his door unlocked half the time. He probably remembered that he had not locked it and that is why he returned at ten o'clock that night. The police chief had said that Horace was almost incoherent when they found him this morning. He kept muttering "stocking, stocking". Someone had seen Horace walking down the street in the direction of his store shortly before ten last night. Suddenly, Jim remembered the scurvy character that had been in the dining room two nights ago. Could he have been the interrupted thief? Jim intended to do some investigating on his own.

They reached the house and Jim rang the doorbell. Stephanie greeted them with a smile.

"Come in! I was just getting out all my materials I'm going to use for decorating." Her smile faded when she saw their expressions. "What's the matter?"

"Stephanie, something terrible happened last night. Horace Rumley interrupted a burglary and was struck over the head. We don't know how serious it is," said Jim.

"Oh dear! How terrible! Leland left for the office an hour ago. We should tell him. Poor Mr. Rumley! He never harmed anyone in his life. How could anybody attack a harmless, old man?" Stephanie was distraught for she had known Horace Rumley all her life.

"I'll go to Leland's office now," said Jim.

"He will be upset. He has sat on that cracker barrel in front of that old pot-bellied stove in Horace's store, swapping tall tales with him so many times."

"After I talk to Leland, I am going by Dr. Brown's clinic and see how Horace is. I'll be back later and keep you informed."

"Be sure and let us know as soon as you find out anything," said Meg.

"I will," Jim left the house and went to Leland's office across the shell street from an open-air market. It was not far from Rumley's Feed Store. He pulled his muffler around his neck and walked into the wind that was breezy and very cold. In a few minutes, he was rapping on Leland's door.

"Come in, Jim. What brings you out so early?"

"Bad news, Leland. Horace Rumley was robbed and beaten last night," said Jim as he sank into a chair.

"What? I can't believe it!"

"Evidently, he interrupted a burglary and was hit over the head. I am on my way to Dr. Brown's clinic right now."

"Jean," Leland called out to his secretary, "I'm leaving the office for about an hour. I'll be back in time for my eleven o'clock appointment. If Mrs. Dorsey comes by, make an appointment for two o'clock. And could you have those letters ready for me to sign when I return?"

"Yes Sir. I'll take care of it."

"Thank you. Let's go," he said to Jim, tugging on his coat and hat. They left and headed for the clinic on Turner Street.

"After we talk to Albert about Horace's condition, I want to send a telegram to New York," said Jim.

"I just cannot understand why anyone would hit Horace. He would have given over the money without a struggle. It seems so vicious. The poor old man!" said Leland, shaking his head perplexedly.

"I don't either, but I intend to look into the matter myself. Telford is well-meaning, but he just is not equipped to handle what could turn out to be a homicide."

"I agree and I will help you any way I can."

"If you have time before your appointment, I want to go to the crime scene and investigate. That's after I send an important telegram."

"I have time. I'll wager they have trampled over any evidence we might have found, though."

"Maybe not."

They arrived at Dr. Brown's office and a bell jangled when they opened the door. The waiting room was crowded with patients who looked up when they entered. Dr. Brown's nurse and receptionist entered from a consulting room. "May I help you?" she asked.

Jim moved to meet her and spoke in a low voice so that the others could not hear. "We are friends of Dr. Brown and would like to speak to him privately, for just a moment."

"Doctor is extremely busy right now. If you would like to make an appointment, I'll see what is available."

"This is urgent. Just tell him that Leland and Jim are here. I am sure he will see us." The nurse appeared unwilling, but finally said she would tell him. She returned shortly.

"Right this way. He can spare you just a few minutes," she said grudgingly. She led them to a small office in the back. It was crammed with medical books and magazines on shelves from floor to ceiling. His framed medical diplomas covered one wall. She opened the door, and then closed it behind them.

Dr. Brown shook hands with both men. He looked worried. "Have a seat."

"We came as soon as we heard to see about Horace. How is he?"

"I am afraid I have bad news. He died about ten minutes ago. I have sent for Telford. Now I need to notify Horace's granddaughter. She just left a half hour ago to get breakfast and was going to return shortly. I told her I did not hold out much hope, but she didn't believe it. Poor girl."

Both men were shocked even though they were prepared for the worst. Leland was particularly distressed because Horace had been a father figure to him. Dr. Brown appeared shocked too, even though death was almost a part of his daily life.

"Now it is a murder case, not assault," said Jim. "Come on, Leland, I must send that telegram."

They left Dr. Brown's office and went next door to the telegraph office.

"I'd like to send a telegram, please."

"Fill out the form on the counter," said the operator.

Jim addressed the telegram to a private investigator with the Pinkerton Detective Agency in New York who had done work for him in the past. Jim was primarily a criminal lawyer, although he did other types of cases occasionally. He thought for a moment, and then wrote "Urgent. Stop. Need info on Andre Lafitte. Stop. Origin San Francisco. Stop. Contact immediately this address." He signed his name and wrote in the return address.

"Can you send this right now?"

"I can. That's thirteen words. That'll be $3.90. It's thirty cents a word. Eliminate some words and it'll cost you less money."

"Just send it!" Jim said as he handed over the money. The operator took the money and put it in a cash box. Then he picked up the message, turned to the machine and began tapping the words. He finished quickly.

"That'll do 'er. Your message is in New York now, but how long it will take to deliver it, I don't know."

"Thank you!" Jim and Leland left the office and headed for Rumley's Feed Store. Although Leland was a close friend, Jim decided not to discuss the telegram with him. It might prove to be a wild goose chase.

"Wonder if Telford taped off the crime scene?" asked Jim.

"I seriously doubt it. Telford's never had a crime scene before, other than shot up bottles. He did catch a horse thief once, as I recall," said Leland. By the time they reached the store, the snow seemed to be coming down in layers.

"Every winter for the past ten years seems to have gotten worse. Before that I don't remember it snowing more than a flake or two," remarked Leland.

The store was filled with people, talking excitedly about the assault and robbery.

"I knew it," exclaimed Jim. There was no sign of a policeman and if there were any clues, they had been trampled or smudged by the crowd. They made a half-hearted search, but it was hopeless.

"You go on back to the house, Jim, and tell Steph and Meg about Horace. I have got to get back for my eleven o'clock appointment. It is ten-fifty now."

They separated and Jim walked towards the Carter's home, thinking that if the snow kept falling at this rate, they would have a foot before dark.

Meg had been thoroughly enjoying herself. She had no idea that making the tree decorations could be so much fun. Their Christmas tree in New York was decorated with shining glass balls and round glass beads ordered from Paris and Germany.

"What is that wonderful aroma, Steph?"

106

"I am making sugar plums to hang on the tree. The only problem is keeping the children from pulling the sugar plums from the tree and eating them before Christmas! Nothing smells as good as sugar plums simmering in a pot on a cold December day!"

"I certainly agree with you there! Can't I taste just one sugar plum?" asked Meg .

"Well, maybe one," said Stephanie, teasing Meg. Meg blew on the steaming confection and then took a bite.

"Umm! This is yummy!"

Stephanie had mixed several cookie doughs of spice, butter, and gingerbread and brought out her cookie cutters. "I use these special cutters only at Christmas."

"Are these going on the tree too, or do we get to eat some?"

"Both! After they're baked, I'll fill the cookie jars and we'll decorate the rest."

"How?"

"I mixed up some vegetable dyes. We'll paint them. Be original. Use your imagination. You can even sign your initials and put the date. After that's done, we'll string them and hang them on the tree."

"What fun," said Meg. "I can't wait until we cut down the tree on Saturday."

Stephanie handed Meg some perfect unbroken sand dollars and various colored ribbons. "Go ahead and thread the sand dollars while I make garlands of these holly berries."

Stephanie threaded a needle with fine thread and carefully strung the berries like beads until she had several garlands. She did the same with strings of raisins.

Meg was fascinated with her sand dollar creations.

"Oh, they are pretty."

"How good are you at drawing?" asked Stephanie.

"Not bad."

"Well, draw some Christmas designs on this colored cardboard. Then cut them out and we'll hang them also, along with some of my prettiest scraps from the scrapbook."

"This is so much better than store-bought decorations," Meg said enthusiastically, as she drew and cut out sleighs and bells and angels.

Stephanie examined Meg's creations. "You are talented. I'll have to save these for next year!"

Meg dimpled with pleasure. "I love doing this!"

"Cut out some bouquets of flowers, too," said Stephanie. "I can never draw the roses. They just look like blobs of misshapen balloons!" Meg laughed and drew perfect roses.

"I think it's wonderful. It really gets you into the Christmas spirit."

"Wait until Friday night when we pop corn to string and get the candles ready to go on the tree. Leland likes to do that."

"I'll bet Uncle Jim does, too. He must have done this when he was a boy. And I guess Andre will be there, too. That is, if you invite him," said Meg.

"Your house is so beautifully furnished. You must be proud of it."

"I am, but it is Leland's fine hand that has added those perfect touches," said Stephanie.

"The two of you make an ideal pair."

"I wouldn't say ideal. We have been known to have an argument or two. Let me amend that- two hundred!"

Meg laughed. "No, really. You are suited. So are my aunt and uncle. I envy you," Meg added, wistfully.

"What are you looking for in a man? Perhaps the dashing Andre would suit?"

Meg knew she was blushing, the curse of red hair.

"Well, I hardly know him. He appears to be quite charming."

"And he's so good-looking, Apollo is probably jealous," teased Stephanie.

"Yes, and that too! But you know, for some reason, my uncle does not seem to like him. I can't imagine why."

"Neither does Leland."

"He doesn't?"

"No. Leland seems to think he's not trustworthy, maybe even dishonest. I didn't realize this or I would not have invited him to our home last night, or to join in cutting down the tree. I don't feel that way about him. I think he is absolutely dazzling, but I would never knowingly go against Leland's wishes."

"That's my problem, too. I really like him, but I know Uncle Jim dislikes Andre and I don't know what to do. It would be different if Uncle Jim was unkind or dictatorial to me, but he isn't and never has been. That is why I don't want to offend him by going against his wishes."

"We're all going to the dime show, too," said Stephanie.

"On a hayride besides!" Meg began to laugh. "I can just see Uncle Jim trying to get between me and Andre in the back of the wagon!"

Stephanie was laughing as she pictured that. "I think your uncle has met his match."

"Let's forget about men for the moment. Have I created enough ornaments?" asked Meg. "Are we going to make something else?"

"Yes. Forget the male animal," said Stephanie, tossing her cinnamon colored hair, dismissively. "Men can be so aggravating at times. I will never understand how their minds work. You've made plenty of ornaments and they are far prettier than any I've ever done. You're as artistic as you are musical! And beautiful, too! Some man is going to be very lucky. Oops! I forgot. Men! Forget them! Here is the star from last year," she said, pulling it out of a box. "This goes on top of the tree. There is one other ornament I'd like us to make."

"What is that?"

"I have boiled eggs and carefully scooped out the insides for egg salad. We'll decorate the eggshells and then fill them with comfits, lozenges , and barley sugar. Then we'll put on a coat of shellac to harden them. When we get the tree, we'll gather lots of greenery- pine cones, pine branches, holly leaves and berries.

Then we'll decorate the doors, hallways, windows, mantels and mirrors." Stephanie sighed, happily. "Christmas is my favorite time of the year. As Mr. Dickens said in his Christmas Carol."

Meg looked at Stephanie, wistfully. Stephanie was so warm and sweet. Meg almost wished that she were her mother.

Both Meg and Stephanie jumped guiltily to their feet when the front door bell rang. Stephanie ran to open the door and Jim walked in, shaking off snow. They had been so engrossed in making decorations and talking about Christmas that they had forgotten about Mr. Rumley.

"How is Mr. Rumley?" asked Stephanie.

"He died this morning," Jim announced. Stephanie sank down into the chair in shock. "I can't believe it. I was just in his store last week talking about spring bulbs."

"That means it's murder, now. Do they have any idea who did it?" asked Meg.

"No, and I don't think Telford has a notion how to solve it. Leland and I went by the store and looked around, but it was hopeless. People had trampled all over the crime scene. The only clue we have is the one word Horace uttered before he died- 'stocking'."

"Are you going to help, Uncle Jim? I've always believed you'd rather have been a detective than a lawyer."

"Yes, I will do all I can. Someone told me that he had a young fellow who worked for him. I am going to track him down and find out if any stranger or anyone acting suspiciously has been in the store in the past few days. I had better get going, otherwise I will need a sled and a team of huskies!"

"Jim, won't you have some hot coffee before you go?" asked Stephanie.

"No, thank you, but if Leland has an extra pair of galoshes, I will take those. My shoes are wet clear through, and my hose, too."

"Better than that. He's got boots." She ran to the armoire in the bedroom and came back with boots, two thick pairs of woolen hose, and some old pants.

"This is just what I need," said Jim as he sat down on the tiled hall floor, pulling off his sodden shoes and hose. "Turn your heads, ladies." They did as Jim quickly stepped out of his trousers and into the dry ones. He pulled on the hose and stepped into the boots. "Okay, you can turn around now. Lucky for me these boots fit. Meg, you stay here, that is if it's all right with Stephanie."

"Of course, it's all right. Meg would be drenched before she reached the boarding house. Come back with Leland for lunch and if this snow continues, you will certainly spend the night."

"Thanks again, Steph. We'll see you at- I'm not sure when. Don't wait lunch on us. We may not return until late afternoon."

"Okay. We'll see you when we see you!" Jim went back into the blinding snow, scarcely able to see his hand in front of his face.

Chapter Nine

Andre had not been happy when he returned from the party and discovered that Dory was not in his room. "Bloody hell! I've got to be a bloody nanny to him!" Then as he had started to go back out, Dory had returned. The seaman was wearing his stocking cap, his "pirate cap", Dory called it and he was excited and smiling to himself. The smile faded quickly when Andre came towards him and Dory was afraid.

"Wot ye doin' in me room?"

"Waiting for you. Where have you been?"

"None of your bloody business!"

"I am making it my business. Have you caused trouble? I warned you about that! If you have done anything to stir up this town, you will live to regret it, but not long!" Andre's eyes were as deadly as a cobra about to strike.

"Oi didn't mean to do it. 'e come in just as Oi emptied the till. 'e started to yell and Oi hit 'im with me billy stick."

"Sacre bleu! Imbecile!" Lafitte grabbed the shrinking Dory by the neck with both hands and lifted him off the floor. The terrified man didn't even have a chance to shriek. His dangling feet were kicking wildly as the infuriated Andre squeezed his neck. Dory's eyes were bulging with terror and when he began to turn blue, Andre dropped him to the floor. Dory gasped and choked, trying to get air into his tortured lungs. Andre watched his struggle to breathe as if he were viewing a scientific experiment.

"Who did you kill and where did it happen?"

113

"Oi don't know. Some old man who orta been dead anyway. It were in that Rumley's Feed Store," whispered Dory, pushing out the words with an effort and rubbing his neck.

"Did you wear that stocking cap any other time before last night?" Andre asked coldly, his deadly eyes pinning Dory like a butterfly to a board.

Hardly able to speak, Dory managed to croak, "No."

"Hand it to me, and your shirt, as well. Both have blood on them, or hadn't you noticed?"

Dory shook his head, looking down at the blood-spattered shirt. He pulled off his cap and shirt and handed them to his nemesis.

"And the billy club too. Now give me the money."

"It, it's moin." Avarice momentarily overcame terror and he clutched his trouser pockets.

"You have a death wish? If you do not relinquish your hoard now, you will never live to see another coin," said Andre with a smile on his angelic face. The venom in his blue eyes struck terror in Dory, and cupidity forgotten, he pulled out the money and handed it to the devil before him.

Andre took some logs and kindling from the basket beside the fireplace and added them piece by piece to the smoldering embers. He put the billy club on top. They caught fire and when the blaze was high enough, he threw in the cap and shirt.

"Me cap. It's me pirate cap. Don't burn me cap!"

"Is there a mentality lower than imbecile? Yes, there is. 'Cretin'. You are a cretin! Don't you realize that every lawman in this town will be looking for the assailant and the weapon? They will be particularly thorough in their search for strangers. When they pound on your door, and they will, they will find no evidence of a crime."

Still cowering, but aware that he hadn't been strangled to death, Dory said in a wheedling voice, "Kin Oi have me jack back after we've shunt this bloody place? Oi'll watch me step from now on."

Andre ignored Dory's request. He was still watching the flames consume the club, cap, and shirt. After the last piece was burned, he spoke without turning away from the fire. "Wash off any blood. Then get your nightshirt on and go to bed and stay there. When they come knocking on your door, you will be roused from a deep sleep. You retired early at nine o'clock. I only hope no one saw you. And you have never owned a stocking cap. Don't lose your stupid temper and arouse their suspicions."

Andre was sure that no one in the town of Beaufort wore a stocking cap unless they wore one to bed. The cap was Dory's ridiculous idea of what pirates wore fifty years ago. He wore an earring too, which made him stand out like a shark in a school of tuna. Since they had jumped ship together in San Francisco, Andre had wondered many times whether Dory's special skills outweighed the trouble that he caused. They had been run out of Galveston when Dory robbed two men and had barely gotten out of Abilene when he took money from the till in the Bad Gulch Saloon. Lafitte had almost killed him tonight. The next time he probably would.

He rose from the hearth, blew out the only candle and departed, leaving Dory trembling in his bed. He was afraid Andre would discover what else he had done.

Andre was seething with rage though no one could have told from his face. He could still feel his fingers around Dory's scrawny neck. It had taken all his self-control to stop squeezing before he killed the weasel. He gradually calmed himself as he walked through the falling snow. There was nothing more he could do tonight. As much as he wanted to go by Rumley's Feed Store to look for any traces Dory left behind, he knew that would be unwise. Someone might see him and how could he explain his presence? He walked back to the Inlet Inn. Tomorrow he would unobtrusively find out details. He went to his room. It was quite warm, as he had fueled the fire before he went looking for Dory. He pulled off his clothes and slid under the covers, naked. His thoughts now centered on the alluring, delicious Meg. She was a peach just ripe for the plucking. He smiled at the vision of her lovely green eyes, smoldering with passion. Besting her uncle would be almost as satisfactory, but not quite. Andre could never decide which was more enjoyable, seducing an innocent or defeating an opponent. 'Life has such interesting possibilities," he thought as he fell asleep.

At one-thirty in the afternoon, Leland and Jim returned to the Carter's home. Both were wet and discouraged. The snow was still falling, but not as heavily as before. Stephanie and Meg took their coats, hats, and scarves. The men stepped out of their boots and pulled off their hose in the hallway.

"Go upstairs and get out of those wet clothes before you catch pneumonia! I'll have Priscilla heat water and bring it up to you. Then you can soak in a hot bath," said Stephanie.

"Sounds great to me," said Jim.

"I closed the office for the day and sent Jean home. The snow is getting deeper by the minute." Both men headed up the stairs.

"Good. Nobody should be out in this weather. Come on, Meg. Let's go to the kitchen and heat up the soup. Priscilla already made ham sandwiches." They had been so involved in decorations that they had not eaten lunch either.

As they stirred around in the kitchen, Meg said , "It looks like we won't be able to go to the circus on Friday."

"Don't be disappointed too soon. This isn't like New York. The snow will not stay on the ground and I'm thinking it will warm up by Thursday. You'll still be able to go on a hayride with the charming Andre. Wonder if he has ever been on one before? Somehow, he doesn't look like the type, though I am sure he can adapt. He is more like the Earl of Dorchester. Don't you agree?"

"Somehow I picture him as captain on a ship flying the Skull and Crossbones, cutlass in hand," said Meg, closer to the mark than she could ever imagine.

Jim and Leland came into the kitchen. "If you're talking about Lafitte, you aptly described him," said Jim, "and include dead bodies strewn about the deck to make your visual scene more realistic."

Leland laughed. "My sentiments exactly, Jim, a true grandson of Jean Lafitte."

"I don't know why you both dislike him so much. He is a perfect gentleman and I am sure he would be shocked to know you said this about him!" Meg turned angrily away and walked to the window.

"Frankly, I don't think anything would shock him," said Jim. He looked at Meg, stiff with indignation and knew that he had gone too far. He didn't want to offend her and by so doing, push her to defend the man further. This is exactly what the wily Lafitte wanted.

Stephanie jumped in, defending Meg. "Why don't you two quit teasing Meg? The man is not the devil incarnate. He's just an extraordinarily good-looking person who probably is constantly having to prove he's more than a pretty face."

"All right. We're sorry about his pretty face. Can we still have lunch, dear? Leland said with an innocent look in his blue eyes, his sandy hair wet from his bath.

Stephanie smiled at Leland's blatantly unrepentant expression. "Okay, but I really should send you to bed without supper!"

"I apologize for upsetting you, Meg," said her uncle. Meg noticed that he did not retract what he had said about Andre, but she didn't want to quarrel.

"I accept your apology. Oh look! The snow has stopped and I think the sun is trying to peep through the clouds," she said, pulling aside the kitchen curtain. "Stephanie, your forecast was correct."

"You'll see. All that snow will be gone in two days. Let's have lunch. Everybody sit down." Leland sat down, his tall, rangy body carefully balanced on the dainty kitchen chair. The chairs were more suitable for a ladies' afternoon tea.

"Do they have any clues about Mr. Rumley's murder?" asked Stephanie as she passed around sandwiches.

"No. I went by Danny Piver's house, but he wasn't there. I wanted to find out if he had noticed a stranger or anyone acting suspiciously in the store in the last couple of days. I'll track him down tomorrow," said Jim.

"Wonder what Telford's been doing?" asked Leland.

"Not much, I'm afraid. He is out of his depth."

"Unfortunately, there is no one else who is really qualified to help either, and the snow is impeding any progress Telford could have made."

"Let's go to the library. I brought a few briefs home to work on."

"We'll leave you to your reading. Meg and I are going to take a nap." Stephanie put her arm around Meg and they went upstairs.

Both men got up and walked across the hall to the library. Two walls were lined with glass-enclosed floor-to-ceiling bookshelves. Jim scanned the titles and Leland spread out his work on a table.

"Hope I can get my mind on business. I keep thinking about poor, old Horace. The murder is so shocking. It just doesn't seem possible for such a thing to have happened here," said Leland.

"I agree. I can't believe anyone local could have done it. You are eager to work on your briefs, I know. Go ahead. I'll read this article and then begin Wilkie Collin's latest mystery, The Moonstone, which I see you have here. Maybe the snow will have stopped by then."

"That's a good one. Stephanie enjoyed it, too. I will get busy, if you don't mind."

Both men read and worked quietly, though Jim looked up from time to time thinking about the murder. Outside, the snow had stopped, but the wind still blew hard from the northeast, piling up drifts against the house.

Even as the men were discussing the murder, Andre was walking down to Rumley's Feed Store after having watched the Ocean View Hotel to see if the authorities visited Dory's room. He was relieved to observe that by mid- afternoon, they had not. Maybe he was in luck this time. He couldn't afford a second occurrence and had decided to get Dory out of town on the next vessel leaving port. He walked casually by the store noticing that the door was bolted. No one was abroad and the wind had blown the snow, obliterating any footprints. Andre glanced around carefully and saw nobody on the streets. He pulled up his collar against the biting wind and ploughed his way around the side of the building, pushing aside snow with his gloved hands. He was uneasy about Dory's demeanor. He knew him too well and Dory was hiding something. He made a path circling the building; investigating as well as he could with the snow banked up so high. It would be just like Dory to hide something, running scared, after he had killed the man. Andre had just made his tour around the back of the building when he noticed the tip of a boot sticking out of the snow. Hurriedly, he brushed away the snow covering it. After again glancing behind him to ascertain that no one was coming, he pulled on the boot. No matter how hard he tugged, it would not budge. He brushed away more snow, thinking that it was embedded in the ground. It was then that he discovered that a leg was in the boot! Further digging revealed a man buried beneath the snow.

"The devil take him! He's murdered another man!" Andre rose and frantically piled snow over the body, afraid that he would be discovered with the corpse. He turned around and walked as rapidly as he could back to his room. He had to get Dory on the very next ship leaving port, if he didn't knock his teeth down his throat first. "Why I ever brought him with me, I'll never understand," he muttered, walking rapidly through the snow.

Andre walked to the Ocean View Hotel and seeing no one about, chanced going inside. The desk clerk, sitting behind the counter, was reading a newspaper and hadn't even noticed the door ease open. Andre slipped into the lobby and quietly made his way to the stairs. He went to the first floor and tapped on Dory's door.

"'os there?"

"Open the door, now!"

"Wot toime is it? Oi went to bed loik ye told me."

"Good. You are going to stay in this room until I get you passage on a ship out of here."

"Blimey! Oi don't want to stay in this hole. Oi'm hungry." If he heard what Andre said about his shipping out, he ignored it.

"You have unmitigated gall even thinking about food. If we were on a ship, I would drop you over the side. As it is, I have to get both of us out of this bloody mess. Did you think no one would discover what you supposedly buried outside the store? I did, and as soon as the snow melts, so will everyone else. That could be as early as tomorrow. I'll bring you something to eat. You will not move from this room. Do you understand?"

"Yes, Oi want some fish 'un chips,'un vinegar."

"You will bloody well eat what I bring you." Andre knew that Dory would sneak out in spite of being terrified because he was so stupid. He seemed to forget what he had done, or what had been done to him from one minute to the next. He was like a five-year-old in intellect, but as dangerous and volatile as a rumbling volcano about to erupt.

"I'll be back with your food in a little while." Andre left with Dory giving him black looks and muttering to himself. The clerk was still engrossed in the paper when Andre came downstairs. Once again, he managed to get away without being seen.

He walked to the Inlet Inn dining room, hoping it was open. His luck held. "I'd like to order something to take to my room. Do you have fish and potatoes?" he asked the young waitress.

The waitress couldn't help but stare at a man she could only imagine in her dreams. She gulped. "We have fried spots or mullet and fried potatoes. It comes with collards."

"That sounds just like what I want. I'll have the spots. Could you add a small container of vinegar, if it isn't too much trouble, and a cup of coffee?"

"It won't be no trouble at all. I'll tell the cook. Did you want any dessert, Sir?"

"No, thank you. That will be all," Andre said, smiling at her. "Oh, I will have a cup of tea while I am waiting."

She almost melted, wishing she were the dessert, as she wrote down the order. She smiled tentatively at him and left to give the order to the cook. She returned quickly with the tea and what looked like an entire lemon sliced. Andre glanced at the few diners as he drank his tea. Most were eating soup and drinking hot coffee. No one paid any attention to him. He wasn't hungry himself, because he had too much on his mind. He would eat dinner later on.

The waitress returned with his food in a bag. The coffee was in a thermos. Andre paid her and gave her a silver dollar for a tip.

"Oh, thank you!" This was more then she made in tips all day.

"You are welcome, and thank you for such prompt service. I will return the thermos bottle later."

He left, and Sarah the cook, came out and stood beside Linda, both girls gaping at Andre.

"Didn't I tell you?" asked Linda.

"You was right. That must be the handsomest man God ever created." They sighed and returned to their chores.

Once again, Andre's luck held. There was no one at the reception desk. A sign on the counter said, "Out to lunch, Back at three'. He bounded up the stairs and walked into the unlocked room. Dory looked eagerly at the bag.

"Your order, Dory. Just what you wanted, fish and chips with vinegar." He handed him the bag and put the thermos on a small table. "Remember, do not leave this room. You'll be missing your front teeth if you try it. That is, what teeth you have left."

Andre departed, hoping Dory would heed his warning. Short of tying him to the bed, he didn't know what else to do. He didn't want to stay in the room with Dory's smarmy eyes following him around. He was afraid he'd do something he would regret, and Andre did not like to be out of control as he had been when Dory told him about the man he had hit. It was self-defense when Andre killed the lieutenant at the gaming table in San Francisco. Not that he had the least compunction about doing it, but it had cost him a lucrative business and put him on the run. Dory had compounded the situation by getting into trouble wherever they went. Andre felt sure they had left a trail any penny ante detective could follow, much less a trained Pinkerton man. And now this! Damn! If he could just get him on a ship tomorrow before the local authorities questioned him. As far as he knew, there could be wanted posters on both of them, plastered from California to New York. The only redeeming thing about it was that he had used an alias when he opened the gaming hall. He had taken identification cards from the body of a dead man he had killed in Singapore, and had been using them until he reached San Francisco. If the captain from whom he had stolen the jade and ivory had contacted the police, they would have been searching for the wrong man because he had tossed those overboard, having acquired another set in Hong Kong in a sleazy, back alley room. No one in San Francisco knew him by the name of Andre Lafitte, not even Dory. To Dory, he was Marcel Dupois. Andre had also worn a moustache and goatee, which he shaved off after they fled from San Francisco.

He went to his room, restlessly pacing like a caged cougar. He was not a man who could countenance waiting. He always had too much pent up energy, crying for release. The only outlet available to him was rum. He opened his sea bag and pulled out a bottle. There was a glass on the night table by his bed. He filled it and tossed it off in three swallows, then filled it again. He gradually drank himself into a stupor and collapsed on the counterpane, fully clothed. The shadows lengthened and he slept on, oblivious to everything.

Dory, meanwhile, had finished his meal and for once, decided to follow orders. After a swig from his bottle, he was snoring, dreaming of his lost stocking cap. The two dead bodies never even entered his dream.

Andre didn't wake up until eight o'clock the next morning. He sat on the edge of the bed, holding his head in which a fifty-pound sledgehammer was playing "The Anvil Chorus". When he thought he could stand up, he walked very carefully to the door, gradually beginning to see through the flashing lights in his eyes. He walked down the stairs to the reception desk, hanging onto the railing.

Another clerk was on duty. "Would you have the maid fill a tub with hot water, please? I'll be there in fifteen minutes. How much?" he asked the clerk.

"That'll be fifty cents. If you want an extra towel, its ten cents more," answered the clerk, holding out his hand.

"Here's two dollars. I want an extra towel and plenty of soap. When I've finished, have the maid bring hot water to my room so I can shave, and a glass of tomato juice, too. " Andre was making a supreme effort to speak concisely. Every word hurt his head.

"Yes, Sir! It'll be ready. Just go down the hall and through that door marked 'Bath'."

Andre went back to his room, pulled off the clothes he had slept in and put on a robe and slippers. He felt like he was moving in slow motion. "Merde! I have to get down to the docks."

He quickly took his bath and washed his hair. He felt a little more human, and the pounding in his head had decreased to a dull throbbing. When he returned to his room, the basin was filled with hot water and a glass of tomato juice was on the table. He drank it down, thirstily. Then he stropped his razor, shaved, and brushed his teeth. In fifteen minutes, he was dressed and running down the steps. He sped to the docks in five minutes. One steam ship and several sailing vessels were tied up at the quay. He tried the nearest one first.

A middle-aged man in a pea jacket and cap was standing in the stern rolling a cigarette.

"Pardon me. Are you the Captain?"

"Yup. Name's Skeeter Jones. What's your business?"

"Are you headed south today and can you take a passenger?"

"Yes and no," answered the captain, evidently a man of few words.

" 'Yes' you are headed south and 'No' you can't take a passenger?" questioned Andre.

"Yup," the captain replied laconically.

"I can pay you well."

"Not the problem."

"What is?" asked Andre, beginning to be exasperated.

"Short two crew members, and don't need no passengers underfoot. Got to get wheat to Gran' Bahama in ten days."

Andre was surprised that he could string two sentences together, albeit without pronouns.

"Then you're in luck. My friend is an experienced seaman. He can climb the riggings like a monkey, handle the helm, furl the sheets, swab the deck. Whatever you need done on a ship, he can do it. He could help you and you could help him. You see, his mother is dying in a town near Jupiter Inlet, and the ship he was supposed to sail on is in dry dock for another two weeks. It may be too late by then," Andre lied, in his most convincing tone.

The captain, like others before him, succumbed to Andre's persuasion. "You say he's a good sailor?"

"The best. There's not a thing he doesn't know about sailing a ship," 'or robbing the crew,' "Andre thought to himself.

"Well, get him. Casting off in thirty minutes. Guess a stop at Jupiter Inlet won't slow me too much."

"How much do I owe you?"

"Nothin'. The swabe'll be earnin' his keep."

"Thank you. I will be eternally grateful. He'll be here."

Andre hurried back to Dory's room. 'Mon dieu! He had better be there!' he thought.

Dory was still asleep. Andre shook him. "Get up! Pack your sea bag. I got passage for you on a ship that is leaving in twenty-five minutes!"

"Wot the 'ell?"

"Put on your clothes. You're going to be a sailor once again. The captain needs a crewman, and he'll drop you off at Jupiter Inlet."

"Oi don't want to go!"

"Do you want to hang? Get moving!"

"No, but where am Oi goin'? Oi won't know wot to do if you ain't there, Marcel."

"He is going to leave you at the Jupiter lighthouse. Find a place to live and stay out of trouble. That shouldn't be too difficult. Don't rob anybody and don't kill anybody. I'll be there in several weeks. Then we'll do as we planned. You have plenty of money, so that's not a problem."

"Oi'd have more if ye'd give me my jack. Oi earned it," whined Dory.

"Earned it? By killing two men? Let's get out of here before I kill you! Pick up your bag. We have to be there in ten minutes."

He pulled the recalcitrant Dory and pushed him through the door. "I just hope to get you on that ship and out of the harbor before they discover the second body."

They reached the dock and a crewman was already casting off the moorings. "Come on, get up that gangplank before they cast off!"

Dory got on board and Andre breathed easily for the first time in two days. The ship slowly pulled out of the harbor in the direction of Beaufort Inlet. He hoped Dory would make it to his destination without being tossed overboard. Or not. It didn't really matter to Andre.

The temperature had risen twenty degrees already. By noon, it would probably be even warmer. The snow was beginning to melt and drip from the rooftops and trees.

Andre stood on the pier, feeling a bit of nostalgia. The smell of the salt air, old pilings covered with barnacles, frayed lines, the sight of a full-rigged schooner crossing the bar brought back memories of the past ten years of his life. All in all, they had been hard but good years. Until he was sixteen, life had been a dogfight for survival. Left on his own, he managed to avoid the workhouses and fled to Paris where he soon became acquainted with every blackguard along the Seine. He murdered a gendarme and fled Paris shipping out as a cabin boy on an American ship. Then, by serendipity, he had discovered the siren call of the sea. He smiled ironically thinking 'It must be in the blood, the tainted blood of Jean Lafitte.' He was never happier than when he was on a tall ship, standing against the wind, or feeling the ripple of his muscles as he hoisted sail, and the salty wind drying his sweat. The sea, an uncompromising mistress, had claimed him as no woman ever would. 'Mon dieu, I am becoming maudlin in my advancing years! Ah, well, soon enough you will sail again!' he thought .

He turned from the dock, brought once again into harsh, unbending reality. His boots crunched through the snow and ice that was already starting to melt. He ambled along, as if out for a morning stroll. There was a bustle of activity along the waterfront as stores opened and people went about their various businesses. He was gradually approaching Rumley's Feed Store. Telford and two deputies were standing outside talking. Suddenly, a woman's scream pierced the air. She had been walking her dog and the feisty terrier suddenly pulled on the leash, tugging her to the side of the building. He was sniffing and franticly digging at something buried in the snow. His little paws scratched and dug as he tried to pull on this fascinating object. His mistress, a tiny lady, impeded by a long coat, had been dragged along willy-nilly. She tried to pull him away from whatever it was that had him so determined to stay. Telford and his men came running to her.

"What's the matter?" he asked.

"It's a bo-, body!" she said, hysterically.

Telford pulled the dog aside. "Joe, take Miss Mims and her dog away, please. Don't worry, ma'am, we'll take care of it." Joe led the agitated woman away, trying to quiet her fears.

"Can I walk you home?" he asked calmly.

"What is it? What has happened? Who is that man?" she asked, averting her eyes from the snow-covered body.

"I don't know, but we'll find out. Are you all right?"

"Yes. I think I will go home, but I can manage by myself. Rusty will be with me," said the little old lady. "You go on and help Telford."

Joe watched as she slowly walked towards Turner Street with her small but determined protector. He joined Telford and Ronnie, who had uncovered the body.

Telford was almost beside himself. "It's Danny, my nephew! He was just a kid," said Telford, as he looked at the eighteen-year-old face. "Oh God, he'll never see another sunrise. How will I tell his mother?"

He stood up, angrily. "If I could get my hands on the murdering slime, I'd kill him!"

"No, you wouldn't, Telford," said Joe. "The man who did this is a raving animal. You're not. Come on. Ronnie, you stay with Danny. We'll go get Dr. Brown." Dr. Brown was the coroner as well as the town's only doctor.

They walked away; Joe had his arm around Telford's shoulders. Andre watched the scene from a distance, but close enough to hear what was said.

"Sacre bleu," he muttered, thinking of Dory safely at sea. "That was a close one." He saw Jim headed towards Telford and Joe as they walked to Dr. Brown's office. They stopped and talked, pointing towards the store. Andre stepped behind some shipping crates piled on the dock where he could not be seen by Jim. Although he had nothing to do with the murders, he did not want to be found in the vicinity. Meg's uncle was too intelligent and he missed nothing. Andre had seen him glance at Dory and knew that he would not have forgotten that scarred face. He only hoped Jim hadn't made a connection between Dory and himself. At that moment, Jim had his back towards Andre, so Lafitte took his opportunity and moved quickly down the street towards the Inlet Inn. He reached his room without being detected, as far as he knew. The vestiges of his hangover still made him feel slightly queasy, so he took laudanum and slowly sank onto the bed, holding his head as he did. He thought, 'If I lie here quietly, the megrim will go away.' As the drug gradually took effect, he fell asleep, no longer worried about Dory.

Jim had not seen Andre, but he was certainly thinking about him and his possible connection to the seaman he had noticed in the restaurant. Telford was so upset, he wasn't thinking clearly.

"Jim, that was my nephew we found, beaten to death. My sister's only child. I don't know what to do," he said, trying to hold back sobs.

"Joe, why don't you take Telford to his sister's house? I'll talk to Dr. Brown."

"That's a good idea. Let's go to Lucy's house, Telford. I'll stay with you," said Joe.

"All right," answered Telford.

Jim walked on to Dr. Brown's office. He was shocked at the boy's death, and it was his only lead, as well.

He was quickly admitted to the doctor's office. "Have a seat. What's the matter, Jim?" asked Dr. Brown, noting his friend's grave expression.

"Danny Piver was murdered, too. They just found his body, buried in the snow."

"Dear God in Heaven, why? It can't be! Do we have a 'Jack the Ripper' on the loose? I'll go over and do a cursory examination, but first I'll send my nurse to get Billy Dudley to bring his horse and cart for the body. When he brings it to my office, I will have to do an autopsy on both men. Mrs. Piver won't want me to do that, but it's the law for an unnatural death," he said..

"Poor woman. I'm going with you. I want to examine the area where the body was found."

Dr. Brown put a sign on the door that said, "Sorry. Closed for the day." He turned to his nurse, who had been listening to the conversation. "Mrs. Parker, would you get word to Billy to come to Rumley's Feed Store for the body, please?"

"Another body! Who is next? We'll all be murdered in our beds!" exclaimed Mrs. Parker.

"Close up the office before you go," said Dr. Brown. Both men then left.

Mrs. Parker gave their retreating backs an accusing look as if the men were responsible. She wasn't about to walk in the slush to the funeral parlor, so she went to the apothecary shop. Her husband was the acerbic apothecary Jim had encountered earlier.

"Seth, get over to Billy Dudley's and tell him to pick up another body at the feed store. I'll watch the counter."

"Well, who is it this time?"

"That boy who worked for Horace, Danny Piver," she replied.

"Wonder what's been going on over there? Always thought there was something shady about Horace ever since he charged me extra for those bulbs he had to order from Holland."

"Sin, and ye shall reap your just reward," she said, darkly. Mr. Parker nodded his head in agreement, put on his hat and coat and departed.

By the time Albert had finished his examination, Billy was there with his horse and cart that had 'Billy Dudley's Undertaking Parlor' emblazoned on the sides. The second line read, 'Affordable rates for the Bereaved'.

"I'll ride back with Billy," said Dr. Brown.

129

"All right. Talk to you later, Albert."

Ronnie, the deputy who had remained with the body, and Billy put it in the cart, and Albert sat beside Billy in the buggy. They drove off and Ronnie said, " Guess there's nothing more for me to do here. I'm gonna' check on Telford. He looked pretty bad off."

"All right," said Jim.

Ronnie left and Jim knelt down, carefully brushing away snow from the area. As he searched, the sun glinted on something shiny. He picked it up. It was a looped, gold earring. Immediately, he remembered the scar-faced man in the boarding house restaurant. Jim's keen observant eyes rarely missed anything. He also had noticed that the man wore earrings, which was certainly unusual in Beaufort. 'He has to be the killer,' thought Jim . He couldn't figure out what Horace meant when he said 'stocking'. It had to refer to the killer. Did his killer wear distinctive stockings? He'd think more about that later. Right now, Telford needed to find the man for questioning.

First, he went to Leland's office. Leland was buried in paperwork. "Come in. What's happening? Has Telford found any clues yet?" he said, sitting back in his swivel chair.

"It's terrible, Leland. They found Danny Piver's body buried in the snow!"

"No! That's Telford's nephew! He must be beside himself."

"He is. Joe went with him to his sister's house. I don't think he's in any state to investigate, but I am almost sure I know who did it!"

Leland sat up in his chair. "Who?"

"The night we all had dinner at Miss Amy's boarding house, I saw a stranger sit down at a table by himself. He appeared to be a sailor and had what looked like a knife scar across his face. He was also wearing earrings. I found an earring near Danny's body," said Jim, holding it out for Leland to see.

"That practically clinches it, but what do you think was the significance of a stocking? Could the man have worn one over his face?"

"Possibly. I've got it!" said Jim, suddenly. "Some people wear stocking caps to bed to keep their heads warm. Maybe the killer wore one on that cold evening for the same reason!" Jim jumped up. "Where does Telford's sister live? He has to search every room in all the boarding houses and hotels immediately before the man gets away!"

Leland gave him directions and as Jim ran out to find Telford, Leland yelled, "Meet me at the house at twelve thirty!"

"Right." Jim was thinking furiously as he sped along. He hoped they weren't too late. His instincts told him that Andre was somehow connected to this man. The devious Frenchman could be implicated, too. Jim located the house with gingerbread trim and pounded on the door. Telford himself opened it.

"I know who the murderer is! You've got to search all the buildings before he escapes."

Telford's look was forbidding. "Just give me a description and we'll comb every place in town!"

"He is swarthy with a scar from his eye to his mouth, about five foot ten and about one hundred forty pounds. He was dressed in sailor's garb and he wore earrings." Jim lowered his voice as Mrs. Piver was in the next room. "I found this one near Danny's body."

Telford took the earring and put it in his pocket. Joe was still there and a neighbor was trying to console Mrs. Piver.

"Mary, Joe and I are leaving now. Will you be all right?"

Mary didn't answer, but the neighbor said, "I'll stay with her."

When they got outside, Telford told Joe to find Ronnie and George, another man who worked part-time. "I'm going to the Ocean View Hotel and then to the Inlet Inn. Joe, send Ronnie and George to search both boarding houses and you join me. Have you got your gun?"

"Yes, I have it."

"Okay, tell Ronnie and George to carry theirs. This man has already killed two people."

Telford turned to Jim. "We'll take care of this. You look like you can handle yourself, but the man is dangerous and possibly armed."

"But I can identify him."

"So can I from your description. Don't worry," said Telford grimly. "If he's here, I'll bring him in."

Joe and Telford moved in opposite directions, and Jim went to the Inlet Inn dining room for some coffee.

The Seymores were there, having a late breakfast and Jim couldn't avoid them because Raymond was already signaling for him to join them. He didn't feel like making trivial conversation.

"It's good to see you," said Raymond jovially, as Jim pulled out a chair and sat down.

"Absolutely appalling," stated Mrs. Seymore, fluttering her fan and staring fixedly at Jim.

Jim glanced down guiltily, wondering if he had left some strategic part of his wearing apparel unbuttoned.

"Murder!" she said, stretching out the syllables. "I have never been associated with murder. I warned you, Raymond. But still you will not listen to me. I nearly collapsed because of my delicate condition when I heard about TWO murders!" She paused for breath.

"The grapevine travels faster than the speed of light," said Jim, sotto voz.

"Everyone is talking about it. We heard the owner of the store was shot three times and that the poor little boy, Danny, I think they said his name was, was shot too and dragged outside leaving a trail of blood," Raymond said.

"We are getting train tickets for New York today," said Mrs. Seymore, finishing a plate of scrambled eggs and sausage. "I hope that we can leave no later than tomorrow. I have quite lost my appetite because of this dreadful mass murderer. I must be near my doctor in case my health fails completely," she murmured weakly, munching on French toast covered in syrup.

Jim was momentarily nonplused, "They were not shot. They were hit with a blunt instrument. I'm sorry you're leaving tomorrow, but glad we had a chance to get together. Under other circumstances, I think you would have enjoyed spending Christmas in Beaufort."

"I know I would. Henrietta, you exaggerate when you call this a mass murder. They say the owner interrupted a burglary, and the other man probably did, too. There is no need for us to leave. I didn't want to come here in the first place, but I have thoroughly enjoyed myself. You have delightful friends, Jim."

"How can you say that? There are probably bodies buried everywhere! I have not been able to sleep. I feel palpitations at the thought of remaining one more day!" Henrietta fanned vigorously. "Order more tea quickly, Raymond. I am quite faint!"

"Of course, my dear." He signaled to the girl as she served the next table. "Waitress, can you bring more tea please, and coffee for me."

"Tell her to bring a basket of sweet buns, too." After eating a few, Henrietta intended to put the rest in her reticule to take back to their room.

Jim drank his coffee, marveling at Raymond's infinite capacity for being henpecked. The waitress brought the buns and as soon as she left, Mrs. Seymore ate one and stuffed the rest in her reticule, drawing it closed.

"Raymond, we will leave now. I must lie down before I have an attack of the vapors and faint dead away. You make the reservations for our train trip."

Jim stood up and quickly pulled out her chair.

"So nice to have seen you again, Henrietta. I hope we meet again soon in New York."

She gave him a limp hand. "If I survive the trip. I may have to be taken off the train and taken to a hospital. I only hope

Raymond realizes how long suffering I am." Raymond certainly looked as if he were well acquainted with long-suffering.

"Raymond, have a safe trip home. It has been good talking with you."

"It's been a pleasure, Jim. Goodbye." The men shook hands, and Jim watched until they had left the room. He stationed himself outside the hotel, watching for Telford and his men. He was determined to wait until they found the suspect. Thirty minutes later, the four men came out of the Ocean View Hotel. Jim walked across from the Inlet Inn.

"Telford, did you find him?"

"No, but the manager remembered him vividly. He had been at the hotel. We went to his room, but there was no sign of him- no clothes, nothing, except ashes in the fireplace. We checked out every room- the bath rooms, the dining room," said Telford bitterly.

"He must have escaped, probably by a ship that left port early this morning."

"I want him!"

"We can check with the Harbor Master and find out which ships left port this morning, and what their port of destination was," suggested Jim.

"Let's go! Harvey should be in his office or close by." They walked to the Harbor Master and found that three vessels had left port, one bound for New York, one for New Jersey, and one for the Bahamas. He hadn't noticed any passengers boarding the ships and said that none carried passengers. They were strictly cargo ships. Jim and Telford talked to some local fishermen, but no one had paid much attention to the departing ships.

"We missed him! The bloody murdering devil got away!"

Jim felt the same way and he was sure that Andre had somehow spirited the man away. After commiserating with Telford, he pulled out his pocket watch and saw that it was almost twelve thirty. He left the docks and went to Leland's house. Leland had just arrived.

"He got away," said Jim, before Leland could ask.

"That's terrible! Isn't there any way to track him down?"

"No. Three ships left port this morning and no one saw anything. Joe checked both the Custom House and the Naptha Launch. He'll probably jump ship before it reaches its final destination." Jim berated himself. "If only I had acted on my instincts sooner!"

"You couldn't have known. Don't blame yourself, Jim."

The women joined them and over lunch, they discussed every aspect of the murders. No one but Jim had noticed the seaman in the dining room and no one but Jim suspected Andre of complicity or knowledge of the crimes. After lunch, Leland went back to his office and Jim and Meg decided to return to their rooms, with Stephanie protesting.

"Your feet will get soaked and it's still cold out."

"No, actually, the streets are dry and it has warmed up considerably," said Jim.

"We'll be fine, Steph. I don't want to impose on you any longer. I know you have many things to finish that you're too polite to do while I'm here. I need to get back to my room too. I have letters to write and clothes to wash," said Meg, putting on her cloak and hat.

"If you really feel you must. But you are not imposing."

"Thank you for a delightful time. I really enjoyed helping make the tree decorations."

Meg gave Stephanie a hug and Jim added his thanks. When Stephanie opened the door to see them off, the weather outside was almost balmy.

"You see, Meg. We'll still go on a hayride to the circus on Friday. It will get even warmer tomorrow. Goodbye!"

Jim's face tightened at the mention of the hayride, but he said nothing.

They walked solemnly back to their rooms. Jim felt emotionally exhausted and he did blame himself for not acting sooner. Meg sensed his mood and was quiet, asking no questions although she was curious. When they reached the Davis House, Jim patted Meg's arm.

"Write your letters and get some rest, dear. I'll do the same. We'll have dinner at six."

"All right. I'll be ready."

They ate dinner and the dining room buzzed with talk of the murders. Dallas Smith stopped by their table.

"Horace Rumley never did nothin' to nobody. Oi'd like to get my hands on the murderin' devil," he said.

"I think the whole town feels the same way, Dallas. Unfortunately, I believe the killer has fled."

Dallas left, clinching his hands, looking almost murderous himself.

After picking at their food, Meg and Jim decided to retire early.

On Thursday most of the snow had melted had by mid-day and Meg and Jim walked to the boatways in West Beaufort. Anson Davis was talking to one of the carpenters working on the Annie Marie.

"Good morning, Anson. How are the repairs coming along?"

"Mornin', Jim. Looks loik we'll be able to leave around the first of January, instead of the middle of the month," he replied.

"That's good news. How are Mrs. Guthrie and Davy doing?"

"They're moity grieved and Annie don't want Davy to leave. She don't want him goin' back to sea agin. They're both upset over them awful murders, too. Danny Piver was Davy's best friend.

"Does she have anyone to look after her?" asked Meg.

"Her daughter and son-in-law live next door and Belle has always took care of Annie 'cause Wade was gone so much. She's jist afroid of losin' Davy, too."

"What is Davy going to do?"

"Ye can't hold a man back when he wants to go, and sailin' is in Davy's blood loik it was in his pa's and Wade's." He looked at Jim. "Turrible thing about them murders. Oi know'd Horace all moi loif. He was a good man. And the poor boy, same age as Davy. It were a double blow for him, grievin' for his granddaddy and then his friend doin' loik that." Anson shook his head. "Don't seem roit."

Jim had seen so many cases where innocents died and vicious killers walked free that he often wondered if the so-called scales of justice were skewed.

"It isn't right. I often wonder if there is a just God or any God at all to allow such things to happen."

Anson looked scandalized. "Don't blaspheme, Jim. Ye'll suffer eternal damnation!"

"You're right, Anson. I didn't mean it," said Jim, trying to appease the old man.

Anson relaxed, "Oi know ye didn't. Well, Oi'm goin' over to tell Davy we'll be sailin' sooner than we thought."

He tipped his cap to Meg, nodded at Jim and walked away. Meg and Jim strolled back towards Ann Street.

"Guess I shocked Anson. He is a hard shell Baptist and they never question the Bible."

"We're Baptists, too," said Meg.

"Yes, but I never accept any doctrine blindly. I examine it from every angle, as I've taught you to do, I hope."

"You have taught me. I ask questions, though it got me in trouble in Sunday school."

"Think for yourself, Meg. Things are not always as they seem. Now you're going out on your own and I won't be around to protect you." He gazed intently at her. Meg knew he was not talking about religion.

"I will, Uncle." They continued their stroll and as they approached the Carter home, Meg stopped.

"Stephanie told me to stop by and get some cookies to take to our rooms. I'll be just a minute," she said, running up the steps. She knocked and Stephanie opened the door.

"Come in! Good morning, Jim. Won't you come in and have coffee?"

"No thanks. I have several things to do. I'll wait outside."

Stephanie turned away and Meg followed her into the kitchen. "I'll hurry," she said, taking a generous supply of cookies from three different cookie jars. She wrapped them and then put them in a bag. "By the way, Dr. Brown stopped in on his way to work this morning. It seems his niece will be arriving tomorrow. She's a freshman at Vassar and will be spending Christmas with the Browns. He wondered if it would be all right if Pamela went with us to the circus. I told her she would be welcome."

"Why isn't she going home to her parents for Christmas?"

"They're going to England for the holidays and evidently Pamela did not want to go."

"Oh, I see. Well, I don't want to keep Uncle Jim waiting. Thanks for the cookies. Oatmeal is my weakness!"

"You are welcome! See you later."

Meg joined Jim and they walked along the shell street towards the feed store. A 'Closed Until Further Notice' sign was posted on the door.

"Will the store just go out of business?" asked Meg as she looked almost fearfully at the murder site.

"I understand that Horace's only male relative, a nephew, might take it over, if he doesn't sell it. I hope he does keep it open because the townsfolk really need that store."

They continued walking along the boardwalk. Meg was wondering what Pamela Brown looked like. 'She would only be about seventeen years old, much too young for Andre,' she thought, from her superior age of twenty-one.

"Let's get a sandwich at the Inlet Inn. By the time we're finished, it should be around two o'clock. Then we'll go by the post office and the telegraph office."

138

They had a leisurely lunch and Meg once again ordered the tasty clam chowder. They finished and walked over to the post office, taking their place in line.

"Is Jim Styron here? Two letters for you." Jim stepped up and took his mail which he quickly scanned. "Nothing important." He checked the telegraph office, but there was no telegram for him.

"Were you expecting a telegram?" asked Meg.

"Not really, but you never know." Jim didn't actually expect to hear from the detective agency this soon.

"I'm going to visit Mrs. Day. She told me to stop by any time," said Meg. "They live at the parsonage."

"That's right across the street. I'll leave you then. I'll probably return late this afternoon."

"See you later."

Both went their separate ways.

Chapter Ten

Andre finally awoke in the late afternoon. He was groggy from the heavy dose of laudanum, but his headache was gone. He bathed and dressed. Not having eaten since breakfast yesterday morning, he felt ravenous. Andre had carried Dory's plate, utensils and thermos from the room under his coat. So he decided this would be a good time to return them to the dining room.

Linda, the waitress, was in the dining room and when she saw Andre, she rushed over.

"I brought these back as promised," said Andre, returning the plate and thermos. "You were right. The fish was delicious. Miss- uh, what is your name?" asked Andre.

"It's Linda," she said, blushing.

"Do you know what 'Linda' means in Spanish?"

"No."

"It means 'pretty' and it certainly fits you," said Andre, smiling at the flustered girl.

Linda blushed harder than ever. "Thank you, Sir. Did you want to order?"

"What's good today?"

"Well, the fried oysters is always good, or the duck. So's the clam chowder. We've got sweet potatoes, collards, field peas and really good slaw. Miss Molly Gillikin makes it for us even though she cooks for Miss Amy's boarding house. It's so good everybody wants some."

"I'll start out with the chowder. Then I'll have the oysters, hush puppies and an order of each of the vegetables. Bring plenty of tea and lemon, too."

"Right away, Sir." Linda rushed to the kitchen. She could hardly wait to see her friend, the cook. "Sarah, he told me I was purty!"

"Who told you?"

"That man who's handsomer than a speckled trout. That's who!"

"You mean that feller was in here yesterday?"

"That's him. He said my name means 'purty' in Spanish. Here, git to workin' on this order. I don't want to keep him waitin'. No tellin' what he'll tell me next!"

"Here's the chowder. Oi'll fry up them oysters. They'll be ready time he finishes his soup."

Linda took the chowder, a basket of hush puppies, freshly churned butter, tea, and lemon to the table. "Yer dinner's comin' roit up."

"Lovely Linda, a feast fit for Queen Victoria. Thank you!"

"Yer welcome. Anything else Oi kin do for ye?" She backed away, folding and unfolding her apron.

"Not right now." Andre ate his soup with gusto and he devoured four hush puppies. He also ate all the oysters and vegetables.

"That was delectable," he said as he paid the bill, leaving a generous tip. He stood up. "I'll have to run five miles now to offset that phenomenal meal. Goodbye, Linda. A pleasant day to you."

"A pleasant day to you too," murmured the bedazzled waitress.

Andre left and he wasn't making small talk about running. He was a big muscular man, but without an ounce of fat anywhere. He had broad shoulders, a flat stomach, narrow hips and powerful legs. He took off running and ran all the way to Cart Island, which was almost to the fish factory. He looked like a winged Mercury flying along.

He remembered Meg zooming down the street, her flaming hair billowing out behind her. Andre couldn't think of one woman among the pampered beauties he had known who would have run as Meg did. He liked her almost childish abandon. She was strong and healthy, yet slender and shapely- the kind of woman who really appealed to him.

He stopped at the sandy knoll and looked at the marsh grasses, now turned brown by winter's icy breath. Gulls swooped and black ducks dove in search of tasty green shoots growing under water. The live oaks were twisting in the wind and the red cedar had a variety of birds feasting on its berries. All the plants were wind-swept, clinging tenaciously to a sand dune, but the summer-loving sea oats had died back to the ground. He heard the loud, flute-like sounds of a wood thrush, followed by a softer guttural trill. Then he saw the bird perched in a tree. He moved very slowly towards it, careful not to startle the bird into flight. When he was eight feet away, he pulled out his derringer and took aim. One shot and the songster tumbled to the ground, his song silenced forever. "Good to see I haven't lost my touch."

Andre breathed in the tangy, salty sea air. At times such as this, he almost wished he were like other men, unfettered by the darkness within him. He could appreciate the majestic beauty of an eagle soaring on powerful wings, but he would feel no sadness or remorse should a hunter's bullet drop that majesty from the sky. He had never shed a tear when his mother died, though she had loved him dearly. To him, a rainbow was a harbinger of danger, not a thing of beauty. He saw men and women's weaknesses and exploited them. Andre pondered on this aspect of his self many times, but could not explain it. He was what he was- clever, charming, handsome, and deadly- the classic psychopath.

He jogged back to his room, exhilarated and almost happy. Tomorrow he would be his charming, charismatic self and wrap the exquisite Meg in his carefully woven web. He would enjoy parrying with her protective uncle, a dangerously perceptive man. He looked forward to both. That night as he settled beneath the covers, he thought, 'Even with complications caused by Dory, I will do exactly as I planned and no one will stand in my path'. He fell asleep, a smug expression on his perfect face.

Friday morning, the sun beamed down on a saddened town, as if death had sullied the landscape.

"Do you think it's wrong for us to go to the circus when two men were just murdered?" asked Meg.

"No, I don't. It was tragic, but you didn't even know them and they were not my relatives. The funeral will probably be on Monday, but you certainly do not have to attend."

"Dr. Brown's niece is arriving on the Naptha Launch at noon. I wonder what she looks like?" Meg remarked casually.

"Probably like any young woman. Pretty, enthusiastic."

"You think she's pretty?"

"Why are you so interested in someone you have never met?"

"No particular reason. Just curious."

"Well, you'll find out soon enough. Albert wants us to meet the launch. He is so tied up with the autopsies he can't get away, and Jennifer has a ladies luncheon at her house. I told him we'd be happy to meet Pamela and bring her home. We'll take her to lunch first."

"Oh. Maybe she won't want to go on a hayride this afternoon after her long trip."

"If she doesn't, she can stay home. How was your visit with Lois Jean yesterday?"

" We talked about all the Christmas parties that will be going on in between discussing the murders. She and Ralph have been invited to several church dinners and to the Brown's eggnog breakfast."

"The Brown's Christmas Day breakfast is a tradition. They have it every year. At least twenty to twenty-five people will be there."

144

"I'm going to miss being in Beaufort. There is always so much going on and the people are so friendly."

"You could stay here, you know. Your father would be disappointed, but he'd understand."

"No. I'm going to do something useful. I've gone to enough parties in my life."

Jim sighed. Meg was determined. He had openly tried to dissuade her in New York; here, he had tried subtlety. Neither approach worked. He only hoped she wouldn't be disappointed if her dream of teaching the Indian children did not turn out the way she envisioned. And after what Meg had told him about her parents' lack of interest in her as a child, he was even more worried about her venture now that he had been when she first broached the subject. Would her own father guard her as he had done? His worry was compounded by that damnable Lafitte. Jim didn't know what he was going to do when they reached Jupiter Inlet. He could not afford to remain away from his business much longer. There was no way he could remain in Florida with Meg more than a few days. He only hoped he could persuade his brother-in-law as to the importance of watching over Meg.

Both he and Meg were in deep thought as they walked back to their rooms. When they reached the Davis House Jim said, "I'll be back at a quarter to twelve with a horse and buggy. We'll drop off Pamela's luggage and have lunch at Miss Amy's dining room. Then she'll have an hour or so to get ready for the hayride and circus. If she doesn't want to go, at least we will have entertained her during her aunt's luncheon."

"I'll be standing outside."

Jim left and Meg went to her room, tossing her hat on the bed. She read a little and then freshened up and went downstairs. Jim arrived as she walked outside. He jumped down to help Meg step up and into the buggy. Then he drove down to the dock where he tethered the horse to a hitching post and helped Meg down. They walked down the pier and the launch was already tied up. Meg strained to see Dr. Brown's niece.

145

"Ah. This must be the young lady."

Meg's worst fears were confirmed. A blonde vision of loveliness, her golden tresses piled high upon her head with just a wisp of a hat tilted stylishly forward, floated down the dock. Two curls dangled artfully at each temple. Her large limpid eyes were as blue as a sunlit sea. Her complexion was creamy and her cheeks were the color of a delicate pink rose. Meg felt gigantic and gawky beside her for the ethereal vision was like a tiny, perfectly proportioned doll- petite and bosomy. She felt like Cinderella's stepsister, her feet too big for the glass slippers.

Jim held out his hand. "I am Jim Styron, your Uncle Albert's stand-in. Both he and Jennifer were unable to meet you. You must be Pamela."

"I am Pamela Brown. Thank you so much for meeting me," she said, smiling flirtatiously.

"And this is my niece, Megan Riley."

"How do you do?" she said, coolly.

"How do you do?" Meg responded, with no trace of friendliness.

"The weather is quite bracing, do you not think so, Jim?" Pamela asked, taking his arm. They walked ahead of Meg because there was not room for three abreast on the dock.

"It has been bitter cold. We had almost a foot of snow, but it melted quickly. Did you have a pleasant trip down?"

Meg was furious that this little seventeen-year-old had the temerity to call her uncle by his first name.

"Yes, I did, although several young men tried to force their attentions upon me. Maman and Papa would have been quite shocked to know that I traveled unaccompanied, but at the last minute my roommate told me she could not go with me. What could I do? I had to come see dear Uncle Albert."

Meg noticed she didn't mention her dear Aunt Jennifer. Evidently she considered the female of the species beneath her notice. 'Maman' and 'Papa' Meg mimicked silently behind

Pamela's back. 'I'll bet her roommate found some excuse not to go with her', Meg thought to herself.

They reached the carriage and when Jim would have helped her up, she pouted prettily. "I am so small I don't think I can reach that high. Would you lift me, please?" Her lashes fluttered as she looked up at him and put her arms around his neck. Jim lifted her and placed her in the seat.

"Come, Meg, give me your hand," he said. Meg did so, hardly able to control a scowl as she sat down beside the delicate Dresden doll.

Pamela leaned against Jim and away from Meg, but it was a tight fit with three on the seat.

"What you are studying at Vassar?" asked Jim, for once unaware of any tension in the air.

"I haven't decided yet. It doesn't really matter. Maman thought I should go to a prestigious finishing school before I make my debut next summer at the Cotillion Ball in South Port. All the right people will be there."

Meg thought, 'by right people she meant rich, eligible bachelors. I'll bet she hasn't a brain in her head. Oh, well. Who needs brains when you look like that?'

They had reached the Brown's house. "I'll just take your bags up to your room. Then we'll have lunch."

Jim jumped down and unloaded three traveling bags. He carried them to the door and knocked. The maid opened the door and Jim went in with the bags. The silence stretched like a piano string being tightened. Finally, Meg's sense of courtesy overcame her indignation.

"When does your second term begin?"

"You're wondering when I am going to leave, aren't you?" asked Pamela.

"Why, it never crossed my mind. You just got here," replied Meg, annoyed that Pamela had seen through her apparently innocent question.

"If you must know, the second term begins on January tenth." With this ungracious reply, she turned her head away from Meg and stared at the trees as if they fascinated her.

Jim returned and Pamela clutched his arm like a drowning person. "Your niece and I have been getting acquainted. I just know we'll become good friends. Where are we having lunch? I hardly ate a bite, I was so excited about seeing my dear relatives."

"At Miss Amy's boarding house. But just a light snack. I am sure Miss Molly has fixed a picnic that would feed a dozen people. We're going on a hayride and then to see the circus that's in town. You are welcome to come along if you like."

Pamela looked at him. "Are you going?"

"Yes. Meg and I and several friends."

'She actually batted her eyelashes,' Meg thought.

"Well, I don't want to impose, but if you think no one will object, I'll go."

"Of course not, we're happy to have you. Your uncle already suggested it," said Jim.

"Then if you really want me, I'll go." She clapped her tiny hands in delight, as if it were all planned just for her.

Meg ground her teeth. Up until now, she had been having a wonderful time.

Jim smiled, "That's all settled then. We're meeting at three o'clock at the Davis House dock."

"Oh, Could you pick me up? I hate to walk the streets unchaperoned." This from the girl who had traveled 1,000 miles alone.

Meg couldn't keep quiet. "This isn't New York. You'll be perfectly safe walking six blocks and no one will think you are a scarlet woman, either."

"Meg! Such language! What a way to talk to Pamela!"

"But we're getting to be such good friends. I know she understands I was just joking. Don't you, Pam?" Somehow, Meg knew that the blonde vision hated to be called Pam. It looks really could kill, Meg would collapse with a conjured dagger through her heart.

"I'll come by for you at twenty of three, but we will have to walk."

"With you by my side, I won't mind at all!"

They had entered the dining room and placed their orders. Meg choked on her lemonade.

"Meg, dear. Do be careful. People have choked to death on food or drink." Pamela gazed solicitously at her adversary.

"Thank you for your concern. Will you both excuse me for a moment?" asked Meg as she rose from the table. Her uncle stood up and pulled out her chair.

Meg wanted to see Molly. She hadn't seen her since she first met the little old lady and she definitely needed a respite from the poisonous air. She walked back to the kitchen and there was Molly, perched on her pillows, sitting at the table. She was busily chopping cabbage.

"Molly, how are you?"

"I been having de misery in my bones since dis ole norf wind brought de snow. I is better today," she said, continuing to chop.

"What are you making?"

"Dis is me special slaw."

"Oh yes. Someone told me that it is delicious. Some slaw just tastes like raw cabbage."

"I has a secret thing I puts in dat makes it so good."

"What is it? I'm learning to cook and I'd like to know your recipe."

"Heh, heh, heh. It be a secret! Don't nobody know but ol' Molly."

"Oh." Meg had yet to learn that cooks, professional and amateur, don't like to give out their good recipes. If they do, they probably leave out one ingredient. "Well, I had better get back to the table."

"Dat's a purty little girl sittin' der with Mr. Jim," said Molly.

"You saw her?"

"I always watches to see who is come to eat. I likes all de diffrunt peoples. Has you known her long?' Molly asked, apparently as innocent as a babe. "She be a good friend?"

"No. I mean, I just met her this morning. She's Dr. Brown's niece."

"Peers to be mighty taken with your uncle. Bet she be intrusted in all de mens," said Molly, vigorously stirring in mayonnaise.

Meg had to laugh. "How did you know?"

"Heh, heh, heh. Molly ain't lived ninety-five years fo nuthin'!"

"Molly, you are a priceless gem! May I come visit again when you're not so busy and I'm not occupied?"

"Sho can. You're purtier den dat 'un." She turned away, intent on her work.

Meg felt better. "Goodbye for now!" She returned to the table and the waitress had brought their sandwiches. "I visited with Molly. She is unique. I've never met anyone like her."

"She is that. I'll go back and say hello before we leave."

Pamela was picking daintily at her sandwich. "This chicken salad is quite good." She sounded surprised.

"We have an extraordinarily good cook. That's Molly Gillikin that Meg was talking about," said Jim, finishing his ham sandwich.

Jim paid for lunch and they walked outside to the buggy.

"Wait here, girls. I'm going to say hello to Molly."

Meg sighed, wondering how she could get through an entire day in the company of this conniving female. Jim went to the kitchen where Molly was adding the finishing touches to her special slaw.

"Molly, it's so good to see you. Still working as hard as ever, I notice."

150

"Sit yousef down, Mr. Jim. I still works 'cause I likes it. One dese days I gonna' quit and jist rock in dat good ole rockin' cher my nephew made for me. Dat be when I gits ole! Heh, heh, heh,"

"I don't think you'll ever be old in spirit. May I taste that slaw?"

"Sho nuff kin," said Molly, getting a berry dish from the counter and filling it. Jim finished every bite though he'd just had lunch.

"If you ever decide you are tired of Beaufort, will you come to New York and cook for me? I'll be the envy of Fifth Avenue!"

"You is jist like you wuz when you wuz tryin' to git mo' blackberry cobbler thirty years ago! You could talk dem fishin' worms right out de ground and den git 'em to jump in de pail, 'en you could git me to give you de whole pie! I likes it here 'en my nephew takes care of me. Molly don't want no change now. You was a purty chile, 'en now you's a purty man!"

Jim laughed. "You say I'm pretty?"

"Sho is. 'en you bettah watch dat prissy-lookin' Miss at de table with Miss Meg."

Jim looked at Molly in amazement. "You mean Dr. Brown's niece?"

"Sho does. She be a man-eating shark."

"Molly, you are mistaken. She is a lovely young girl. She and Meg get along very well and they just met this morning. And I am sure she thinks of me like a father."

"No she don't! She tryin' to spin you into de web, jist like de black spider!"

Jim could not believe that Molly would take such a dislike to Pamela. The old lady had not even seen her up close, much less talked to her. "Now Molly. You're up to your old trick of teasing me."

"Ain't no teasin'. You jist watch yousef. Miss Meg know 'bout her."

151

"I think you're both wrong. She's not much more than a child. She just needs to develop a little maturity."

"Huh! She ole alridy!"

Jim decided this conversation was going nowhere. "Well, the girls are waiting for me. Save me some blackberry cobbler," he said, grinning at Molly as he left.

Molly mumbled when he was out of hearing, "You is mighty smart 'bout most things. Hmph!"

They left the boarding house and Jim dropped off Pamela, saying he and Meg would come by later. Pamela's mouth turned down in a pout when she heard Meg would come, too. They drove off and Meg relaxed for the first time since she had met Pamela.

Meanwhile, Andre had gone to Dr. Brown's office. Mrs. Parker's dour face lit up when Andre walked into the waiting room.

"How may I help you, Sir?" she asked, for once sounding as if she really meant it.

Andre's engaging smile caused her to tidy her hair and adjust her nurse's cap.

"I'm not here to make an appointment. Dr. Brown invited me to drop in for a visit." He noticed that no patients were in the waiting room.

"The office is closed all day to patients. Doctor is doing autopsies on the two murder victims. I don't think he can talk to you now," she said, hating to disappoint such a charming man.

"Tell him that Andre Lafitte is here and that I would be most interested in watching him perform the autopsies."

"You would?" asked the nurse in amazement. She disliked having to take notes as he dictated. She had to keep her head averted from the grisly task. Being a nurse, she didn't mind the sight of blood, but the dismembering of a body was gruesome to her. "I'll give him your message." She left and returned shortly.

"He says to come on back." She led the way to his laboratory with Andre following right behind her.

152

"Good to see you, my boy. Can't shake hands right now," he said, holding up bloody gloved hands.

"Dr. Brown, I appreciate your allowing me to observe the autopsy. At one time I considered becoming a doctor."

"Glad to have you. Mrs. Parker, do you have your note pad?"

"Yes Sir." She was seated on a chair, turned partially away from the body.

Dr. Brown continued removing body parts and dictating as he worked. Andre looked on, rather interested and not sickened in the least. When the doctor paused momentarily in his dictation, Andre asked him a question. "Have the authorities made any progress in finding the murderer?"

"They are sure it was a seaman off a ship. Jim Styron saw a stranger eating at the boarding house Monday Night. He said the man was dressed like a sailor, had a scar on his face and wore earrings."

Andre cursed silently. He knew Jim had seen Dory, and he didn't miss a thing including the earrings.

"That's certainly a positive identification. Did they catch him?"

"No. Worst luck. He evidently was able to get away on an early-morning boat, but nobody saw anything. By the time Telford and his men found out he was staying at the Ocean View Hotel, he was gone and everything had been cleared out of his room."

Dr. Brown continued dictating to Mrs. Parker and Andre watched until the next pause. "Did they have any proof other than a description of the stranger that he committed the crimes?"

"Yes. Jim searched the area and found an earring near Danny's body that was a twin to the one the sailor was wearing."

'Curse the man,' Andre fumed silently. "Have they any way of finding out which ship he took?"

"The harbor master said only three ships left the harbor, but none of them took a passenger." Evidently, if anyone had seen Dory, they thought he was a crewmember, boarding at the last

153

minute. Dr. Brown continued working as he talked. "Mrs. Parker, hand me that hack saw, please."

"What were their ports of call?" asked Andre

"New York, New Jersey and Grand Bahama, but the man could jump ship anywhere. They know that he did not leave on the Naptha Launch or by horseback."

"That's unfortunate. Doctor, I know you are too busy to talk further. It has been most interesting. Thank you for allowing me to observe."

"You're welcome. Oh, by the way, Jennifer and I are having a Christmas Day breakfast. Please join us. It's an annual event and quite a few people will be there. My niece is down from Vassar, visiting us for the holidays. I'd be happy for you to meet her."

"Thank you, Sir, for the invitation. I'll be there and meeting your niece will be my pleasure. What time?"

"About eight o'clock. We like to get an early start."

"Goodbye then, until Christmas, if I don't see you before then. And goodbye to you, Mrs. Parker," he said, bowing slightly.

He left and Mrs. Parker commented to Dr. Brown, "Isn't he just the nicest gentleman? So mannerly. You don't see that too much in young people these days."

"You certainly don't. I told Jennifer he was a fine young man. Let's get back to work, Mrs. Parker. Enough chit chat."

Andre walked back to his room, deep in thought. Parrying with Jim Styron was amusing, but he had better be more discreet. The man was just waiting to catch him making a mistake. What bad luck that he had found Dory's earring. In his haste to get Dory out of Beaufort, Andre had not noticed the missing earring. That could have been a serious mistake. He must be more careful. As he reached his hotel, he was thinking about what to wear. He decided on his blue sportsman's sailing suit and a knit striped polo shirt worn with his sailing cap. The weather was almost balmy, so the clothes should be warm enough. He whistled a sea chanty as he dressed, anticipating spending this afternoon with Meg.

154

As Andre approached the Davis House dock, a large wagon filled with hay and drawn by two horses pulled up and stopped. The driver jumped down to hitch the horses to a piling on the dock. The Carters and the Days were already there waiting. Jim, Meg and a young woman were walking down the shell street headed in their direction. The people on the dock shouted greetings and Meg and Jim responded.

"Hello Andre," said Stephanie, beckoning to him. "Come join our happy group!"

"Have you ever been on a hayride before?" asked Lois Jean as Andre joined the group.

"No. Are we going to feed the horses with it?"

Stephanie and Lois Jean laughed. "Not today we won't!"

Ralph and Leland shook hands with Andre.

"The weather's perfect. I am looking forward to the circus," said Ralph.

"So am I," said Leland, as he lifted a heavy-laden picnic basket onto the cart, "if for no other reason than Molly's picnic spread!"

Meg, Jim and Pamela joined them. Meg looked so appealing in a gaily-colored print dress of green and purple with a solid purple swag around the skirt. The other young lady wore a black dress with a white pleated swag, cuffs and collar. The attire was virginal but the young, beautiful face was predatory.

Jim said, "I would like to introduce you all to Pamela Brown, Albert's niece. Pamela, this is Stephanie and Leland Carter, Ralph and Lois Jean Day and Andre Lafitte."

Pamela greeted them all with a polite but distant 'How do you do' until she saw Andre.

He smiled and bowed slightly. "Welcome to Beaufort."

For once in her young life, Pamela was dumbstruck. Never had she seen a man as handsome as this. Immediately, her plans for flirting with Jim faded. This man would be no love-smitten college boy, either. But she hadn't seen a man yet she couldn't captivate.

155

She gave him her hand and he raised it to his lips, gazing at her with admiring blue eyes- eyes as blue as her own.

"Thank you. Now I know I am going to enjoy my stay," she replied.

Meg was annoyed at this tête-à-tête. She turned to Jim and said, "Uncle, would you help me up?"

"Gladly, my dear. Up we go!" He boosted her up on the high step and into the cart. All the others began climbing aboard, the men lifting their wives into the cart. Andre started to take Pamela's arm to help her, but she threw her arms around his neck as she had Jim's, "I am so tiny, I couldn't possibly step up that high!"

In one quick swoop, Andre lifted her up and placed her in the wagon before she could enjoy his arms around her.

"Oh, my. That was fast."

Andre looked over at Meg and winked conspiratorially. She understood that he did not do it willingly, but was only being polite when he picked up the Dresden doll. She leaned back, not as angry as she had been.

"Uncle, you lost out to Andre."

Jim laughed. "Meg, Meg. She is just a child. I am old enough to be her father, grandfather almost! Your Aunt Julie would laugh at the idea as I do! Let's enjoy the hayride and circus!"

"Okay," said Meg, but she couldn't help but notice Pamela clinging to Andre like a limpet. She wouldn't have to worry about Uncle Jim coming between her and Andre.

Everyone except Meg seemed to be having a good time. They sang all the way to Cart Island. "Meg, the townsfolk gave this spot the name Cart Island because it is a favorite spot to come by horse and cart on picnics," said Jim. "Fishermen hauling nets on the southern shore dumped ballast stones into Taylor's Creek so that they could drive their carts over from the mainland. Others drove over in their carts to have picnics on Sunday afternoons. They named it Cart Island. The surveyor or mapmakers at that time were unfamiliar with the local pronunciation and they thought the people from Beaufort were saying 'carrot' instead of 'cart'. Thus the maps show it as Carrot Island. But you will never find a native calling it anything but Cart Island."

The driver stopped the horses and everyone scrambled out, the men lifting the women to the ground.

As Meg started to step down, two strong hands grabbed her by the waist and she was in Andre's arms. Her head rested against his chest and he smelled of sweet tobacco, pine forests and ocean breezes. It was such a heady mixture, her head swam. He was smiling down at her. Then Meg came out of her daze.

"Put me down!"

"Of course," he said, placing her on her feet. "You look adorable in your little hat with a- what is it called?"

"Pompom."

"Andre, there you are. We must find a good spot for our picnic," said Pamela, taking his arm and glaring at Meg.

Without another word, Meg walked over to her uncle who had been watching the scene with a wry smile on his face. His eyes clashed with Andre's. Andre was annoyed. The pretty little piece of fluff clinging to his arm did not attract him. Meg did. He concealed his annoyance and smiled ingratiatingly at Pamela.

"Where would you like to sit?" he asked.

"Over here. This looks like a nice spot." She picked a place as far away from Meg as she could find.

Stephanie, always the organizer, had brought blankets for them to sit on and oilskin cloths for the food. The snow had melted completely; not a trace remained on the ground. The wind had been blowing briskly for two days and the sun shone brilliantly, so the ground was quite dry. The Carters, Days, Meg and Jim were gathered companionably together near a small cut called Cart Island Slough, which meandered back into the woods. Only Pamela and Andre sat apart, which did not please Andre at all.

"Look!" said Meg, pointing at two little animals swimming and diving in the water near her. One popped his head up and stared at her.

"Those are otters, Meg," said Jim.

"They are darling! Those little round eyes are saying 'Why don't you give me a fish?' and his whiskers are quivering," said Meg delightedly.

"You are right. That's exactly what he wants. They are clever little thieves, too. Lambert and Joe have crab traps they set here in this cut where the crabs are so plentiful. They were getting aggravated because every time they came down in the morning to take the crabs out of the trap, there weren't any. They just knew somebody was getting there before them and stealing their crabs. So they decided to hide in the woods to watch. They intended to stay all night if they had to, to catch the crab-stealing bandit. They had hidden their horse and cart so it couldn't be seen."

Everyone was listening to Jim's tale. Leland was smiling to himself because he had heard it before.

"Did they catch the thief?" asked Meg.

"I wouldn't say they caught them, but they saw them stealing and eating."

 What did Lambert and Joe do?"

"Well, they were laughing so hard they couldn't do anything. One otter had unhooked the trap and lifted up the top while the other otter picked up the crabs and threw them up on shore. Then both of them sat there eating crabs and licking their paws."

Everyone laughed, including Leland and Stephanie who had heard the tale many times.

"They can be easily tamed," said Leland. "Wesley Paul found a baby otter whose mother had evidently been killed. The poor little thing was starving, so Wesley picked it up and took it home. He fed that otter with a bottle and gradually got it to eat ground fish. It followed him around just like a dog. Wesley had kept the animal confined until it was old enough to fend for itself.

He had that otter for four years. If it swam and fished all day, it always came home at night and slept right by Wesley's bed. One night it didn't come home and Wesley knew something must have happened. A friend of his came by later in the day, bringing the otter. It was dead. It had gotten caught in a fish net and drowned."

"How sad! Poor little otter," said Meg.

"Well, shall we have our picnic?" asked Stephanie as she began taking food from the basket.

Lois Jean and Meg helped her, distributing plates and cutlery and napkins. They laid out mounds of fried chicken, potato salad, slaw, deviled eggs, ham sandwiches, ham biscuits, pickled beets and cucumbers. "If you wade through all that, there is chocolate cake for dessert," said Stephanie.

Andre finally persuaded Pamela to join the rest of the party. He filled a plate for her and then for himself.

"What a feast! I'd like to steal the cook," said Andre .

"I have already tried," responded Jim, "and she won't leave Beaufort!"

"How about if I propose marriage?" asked Andre.

Everyone laughed. "Molly has buried three husbands and I don't think she's looking for a fourth!"

"Not even Andre?" asked Stephanie mischievously.

"Not even Andre," replied her husband.

Ralph sighed with contentment after finishing his meal. He reclined with his hands beneath his head. "That was absolutely scrumptious. Now for a nice nap."

"Oh, no you don't. I am ready to see the dime show. You did bring a dime, didn't you?" asked Lois Jean.

Sitting up suddenly, Ralph snapped his fingers. "I knew I forgot something!"

"Ralph, you didn't!"

"What I forgot was to give you a kiss," he said, kissing her on the cheek.

"Don't tease her, Ralph. She's never seen a circus before," said Stephanie, beginning to scrape the dishes.

"I know." He smiled at his wife. "I brought a pocket full of dimes. Madam Fortune awaits. She sees all and knows all! Are you ready for the gypsy fortune teller, Lois Jean?"

"Sometimes I wonder how you became a Baptist preacher. You have never acted like one. You don't really believe in fortune telling, do you?" asked his wife.

"One never knows, dear. 'There are more things in heaven and earth…' and all that sort of thing."

"He really missed his calling. He should have gone into Oriental philosophy," said Leland.

"I am firm in my religion, but it is true. I do question many things. After all, every ideology is based on interpretation. No religious beliefs can be proven. Christ said, 'Ye must be born again.' Christians interpret that to mean 'born again in Christ'. He could have meant reincarnation."

"Ralph!" uttered his wife, shocked to her Baptist foundations. "Don't let your congregation hear that. You would be thrown out of the church!"

Jim found it curious that a Baptist minister should express such beliefs. He wondered what Ralph's background had been.

"It should be interesting to have our palms read. Don't you think so, Meg?" he asked.

"Oh, yes. I can't wait!"

"Do you think she'll see a tall, blonde stranger in your life?" asked Andre, who had been listening to the conversation.

Jim quickly intervened. "But the gypsy always predicts a tall, dark stranger."

The two men stared coolly at each other.

Meg replied, "I don't really believe in gypsy prognostications, but it's entertaining to hear what stories they make up."

Pamela blinked at Meg's answer. She had no idea what 'prognostications' meant and she didn't care. Any conversation was boring when it did not center on her.

"Andre, will you take me to all the side shows? I've never been to a circus, either." She looked up at him appealingly, like a lost white kitten that wanted to be picked up and cuddled.

"With pleasure," he lied. "But you must have your fortune told also."

"I don't want to let any dirty old woman hold my hand. If she just looks in her crystal ball, I might do it," she pouted, once again clinging to Andre's arm now that she had finished eating.

"We should all have our fortunes told," said Stephanie. "I want to find out something I don't know about Leland!"

"Watch out, Leland, or she'll find out about that day you and Louise Graham went swimming and Louise lost one of her hose," said Jim.

"What?"

"You didn't know?" asked Jim innocently. "Oh, that's right. You were in New Bern, visiting relatives when it happened."

"Jim, you're the very devil himself!" Leland said, trying not to laugh.

"All I know is she wouldn't come out of the water until after dark," he replied. "Then four of us had to gather 'round her while she walked home so no one could see her bare leg."

"That was one of my more daring escapades before you lassoed me, dear. Now you know. I have harbored this dark secret for twenty years."

Pamela looked at all of them as though they were from another planet. She had absolutely no sense of humor. In that respect, she and Andre were soul mates.

"I'd be annoyed except that Louise looked like a cow with mumps!" snapped Stephanie.

"Touché, Stephanie!" said Andre.

"Thank you. I try my best! What shall I do with all these scraps?"

"We'll put them near the water. The otters and raccoons will eat them," said Leland, getting up and taking the bag of scraps. He had no sooner poured out the food than the two otters swam right up to it.

"Isn't that cute?" asked Meg. "He's floating on his back, eating a piece of ham!" They watched for a while, and then put the blankets, tablecloths and picnic baskets into the wagon.

"On to Madam Fortuna!" cried Ralph.

"How do you know that's her name?" asked his wife, always literal.

"I don't, but it is apropos."

"He's hopeless. He enjoys reading 'The Arabian Nights' too."

"So do I," agreed Andre. "Sinbad the Sailor was a man after my own heart, as was Odysseus."

"You are a seafaring man then?" questioned Jim.

"Yes. You will recall I mentioned having sailed the seven seas the first night we met."

"So you did," he said . Turning away, he pulled Meg up from the ground. "Let's go to the circus!"

Everyone followed suit and finally, the wagon rattled away. Meg looked back over her shoulder. A raccoon was tearing into the food and noisy seagulls were stealing what they could from the raccoon. She glanced beneath her lashes at Andre, wishing she were the one sitting cozily next to him. He was looking at her with an expression that told her that was what he wished too.

They drove beneath a big curved banner, hung between two trees, on which was lettered 'Silas Green Circus'. Beneath the title was written 'An Educational Experience for Children and Adults'.

Pamela snuggled even closer to Andre. She had been talking non-stop. "I think a hayride is so…."

"Provincial?"

"Yes. That's the word," she said, scratching at a piece of straw that had gone down her collar. "A horse and buggy would have been so much better. Ugh! I hope there are no bugs on me!"

162

Andre was so bored with her incessant chatter he had a difficult time masking his annoyance. He would gladly toss her off the wagon, if he could.

To Meg, it looked as though he were completely enamored by the blue-eyed, golden-haired doll. 'She was small enough to fit under his arm,' thought Meg. 'He'd have a hard time fitting me there unless I was bent like a pretzel!'

The wagon came to a stop. Pamela made sure she was holding onto Andre's arm until Jim had helped Meg down. She didn't want him holding Meg again. Pamela did not like other women, especially Meg. She hated competition, not that she'd ever had much until now.

"Let's go see 'Hernandez, the Amazing Contortionist'," said Meg, dragging Jim towards a poster that showed a man twisted into an impossible position. They paid their dime to a barker who proclaimed that Hernandez had appeared before the Crown Heads of Europe. "Step right up, folks! You'll be telling your children and grandchildren about the versatile Hernandez, contortionist extraordinaire!"

Meg and Jim walked inside a darkened tent. Folding chairs were set up in rows and the makeshift stage was lit up by several gas lanterns. They sat down and the seats were gradually filled. Meg squeezed Jim's hand excitedly. She whispered, "I wonder if he can really twist into the shape it showed in the picture?"

"We'll soon find out. Here he is!"

Hernandez walked on stage carrying a guitar, bare-chested and dressed in flaming red tights. To Meg's utter amazement, he played the guitar while putting one foot behind his neck.

Meg clapped wildly. "Isn't that phenomenal, Uncle Jim?"

"It certainly is. Great Caesar's Ghost!" said Jim as Hernandez did a backward somersault without missing a chord. He continued performing for fifteen minutes. The audience gave him three standing ovations. An emcee came on stage as Hernandez bowed, putting his head between his legs.

"Thank you, thank you! The next show will be in thirty minutes."

Hernandez stood up and walked off stage playing 'The Camp Town Races'. Meg and Jim went outside, thoroughly impressed.

"I wouldn't have believed anyone could twist his body into that shape unless I had seen it myself," said Jim.

"Wonder who else is in a side show, Uncle. Oh, here's a banner showing Blatz, the Human Fish. I want to see that!"

Jim again paid twenty cents to the barker who was claiming Blatz to be the 'Eighth Wonder of the World'. When they walked inside, they saw a glass tank filled with water. Blatz walked from behind a curtain wearing a navy blue knit swimsuit and red striped shirt with blue trunks. Leland and Stephanie and the Days joined Meg and Jim.

"We just saw the bearded lady," said Lois Jean.

"We just saw Hernandez the contortionist," said Meg. "His act is absolutely unbelievable. You will have to watch him perform."

Stephanie said, "We decided to see what we thought was a vaudeville show. After we sat down, we discovered it was burlesque. When those buxom ladies in their revealing tights started walking across the stage, I thought Leland was going to fall out of the chair."

"Yes, for once Ralph was speechless. But when the emcee started peppering his spill with blue humor, they said we'd have to leave. I wanted to stay, but Ralph wouldn't let me!"

"Lois Jean, such dialogue was not meant for your delicate ears,' he said .

"And such revealing costumes were not meant for your delicate eyes," added Stephanie, looking at Leland.

Everyone laughed at Leland's sheepish expression.

While they were talking, Blatz made his entrance. He walked up some steps and climbed into the tank. Then he submerged himself and nonchalantly ate a banana.

164

"I don't know how he does it," said Ralph. "He is a human fish! Now he's playing a trombone. It's bubbling when he blows it!"

They all gawked as Blatz apparently fell asleep while reading a newspaper. Dozens of people tried to surround the case that was on a raised platform, but the bouncer kept them back. Then Blatz woke up and stretched. He stood up and climbed out of the tank, yawning all the while. He waved to his audience and strolled away amid thundering applause.

"I saw it, but I still don't believe it!" remarked Leland. "You notice they would not allow us to get close to the tank. It had to be a magician's trick!"

They all walked outside, discussing how it could be done.

"You just don't believe he could have done it, but I do," insisted Lois Jean.

"Maybe you're right, sweetheart. What else can we see? Do they have a sword-swallower?" asked Ralph.

"Let's find out," said Jim. They were strolling along talking and listening to the barkers extol the virtues of acrobats, freaks and variety numbers and telling of the dubious educational values.

Andre and Pamela were approaching from the other direction. Pamela was not happy to see her fellow travelers. She had used every ploy possible to keep Andre to herself, from claiming she felt faint and needed to sit down to rushing him inside a tent if she saw any of them out of the corner of her eye.

Andre greeted them with relief, tired of playing Knight-errant to Pamela's every whim.

"We just saw a tattooed man. It was disgusting! He had revolting tattoos all over his body," shuddered Pamela. "I don't know how anybody can enjoy seeing these freaks!"

"If people don't enjoy the circus, they should stay home," said Stephanie.

Leland looked at his wife, surprised that she would be impolite to a guest. He too, thought Pamela was a pretty young girl, as did Jim. If she found the show revolting, it was because she led a protected life, not having been exposed to such things.

Now Pamela was staring at Stephanie, trying to decide if she should make a cutting remark or remain quiet.

Meg saved her the trouble. "Everybody, this looks interesting. 'The Great Kar-Mi' evidently swallows a revolver instead of a sword. We'll go see him and you can wait in the wagon where you can rest comfortably. I know you wouldn't want to see anything as disgusting as this!"

"That's a good idea," said Jim. "Andre, you won't mind walking with her, will you? I don't think she should sit there unattended. There are too many strangers about. After we see 'The Great Kar-Mi', we are all going to have our fortunes told."

There was no way Andre could get out of it gracefully. This day was not turning out as he had planned.

"Thank you, Jim, for the suggestion," Pamela said, giving him her dimpled smile. "But after you've seen him, come after us. I do want to have my fortune told."

"I thought you didn't want a dirty fortune teller to touch you," said Stephanie.

"I don't, but she can look in her crystal ball and predict my future."

"Very well, we'll come after you. Sorry you have to miss "the Great Kar-Mi'," said Jim to Andre.

"I am sure you are," said Andre with an unpleasant gleam in his icy , blue eyes.

Pamela once again clung to Andre's arm. "Come on, Andre. We'll make ourselves comfortable in the hay. It's starting to get chilly again and we can wrap up in a blanket," she smiled suggestively into his unresponsive eyes.

"Yes, do wrap up. I wouldn't want you to freeze," said Meg, looking coolly at Andre.

Pamela looked as satisfied as a cat with a feather sticking out of her mouth. She was almost licking her lips.

"Meg," said Andre, "hurry back. I am looking forward to having my fortune told, too."

Meg found it difficult to resist his sexy blue eyes, silently asking her to understand. But she did. "We'll probably be quite a while. So make yourselves comfortable!" She turned on her heel and walked away without a backward glance.

Pamela watched, filled with jealousy at Meg's retreating figure.

The others followed Meg, eager to see the next amazing performance. It seemed that Kar-Mi swallowed a pistol instead of a sword.

"Hurry Uncle. I really want to see this!"

"So do I," said Lois Jean, right behind her. At least twenty-five people or more were lined up buying tickets.

Stephanie remarked to Lois Jean, "Poor Andre! I don't think he has seen much of the circus. He's been too busy babysitting!"

"I know. I feel sorry for him. Too bad the little China doll had to come with us," agreed Lois Jean.

Ralph was amused at his wife. She never said anything derogatory about anyone. Pamela must have really annoyed her. To him, Pamela was a pretty, innocent girl, but not nearly as attractive as Lois Jean.

Meg acted as if she weren't paying attention to the conversation, but she was secretly glad that Lois Jean had referred to Pamela as the 'China doll' and in such a sarcastic voice.

They got the tickets and went inside, quickly finding seats. The heat from all the bodies felt good, as it had begun to get nippy again, in spite of the sun. The emcee was just announcing "The Great Kar-Mi". The drummer played a drum roll and Kar-Mi came in with a flourish, wearing green tights and a scarlet cape that billowed behind him. His black hair was shoulder length and he had a handlebar moustache. The trumpet player and drummer were seated in front and below the stage.

"Ladies and Gentlemen, you are about to behold the most spectacular, the most amazing performance you will ever witness. Have any of you ever seen Annie Oakley perform in Buffalo Bill's Wild West Show?" the announcer asked the audience. No one answered. "Well, I have, and 'Little Sure Shot' can't hold a candle to Kar-Mi. Yes, my friends, you are indeed privileged to see the greatest marksman of the 19th century here tonight. When you go home, tell your friends, tell your enemies, tell everybody what you have witnessed tonight. And now- I present the Great Kar-Mi!"

The aroused crowd clapped enthusiastically. Then a pretty, voluptuous, scantily clad girl walked up to Kar-Mi, amid whistles and catcalls. The young lady handed him a revolver. Then she walked to a table and picked up a bull's eye target. She walked about twenty paces away and held the target over her head. The audience gasped as Kar-Mi began to swallow the revolver.

"Dear me, how can he do that?" whispered Meg. He swallowed all but the muzzle. It promptly fired, knocking the target from the assistant's hand. Some of the women screamed. Then the crowd came to their feet, wildly applauding. Beaufort inhabitants had never seen anything like this. Kar-Mi pulled the revolver from his mouth, held out his hand for his assistant, and both bowed several times.

"As they say out West, 'don't that beat all?'," said Leland.

Even Jim, the cynic, was dumbstruck. They were all talking, expressing amazement as they left the tent.

"Let's go get Andre and Pamela and then find the fortune teller. I think I saw her tent all the way at the other end," said Stephanie. They reached their wagon and found Pamela shivering, wrapped in several blankets. Andre sat apart from her with no blanket. He jumped down from the wagon as if he had been counting the minutes until they arrived.

"I'm glad you are back. Pamela became quite cold, so I wrapped her in blankets. What shall we do?"

'It wasn't all that cold,' thought Meg. 'The little twerp probably thought Andre would keep her warm!'

168

"We could leave now," said Jim.

"Oh no, Uncle! I do so want to see the fortune-teller. Why can't the driver take her home and then come back for us?"

"That would be all right, I suppose. Clem is certainly reliable," said Jim.

"I agree," remarked Leland. "Dr. Brown would not object to that."

At this turn of events, Pamela suddenly stopped shivering. She had no intention of leaving Andre and Meg together. "I'm not cold now. I want to see the fortune teller, too."

Andre wished she had died of hypothermia. He said, "Do you think that is wise? The temperature is dropping and you may catch cold."

His face showed nothing but concern and Jim thought, 'He should have been onstage. He's a consummate actor.'

"No, I won't!" said Pamela petulantly. "I want to go!"

"That's settled then. We'll all go," said Jim.

Andre once again lifted the tiny but determined Pamela down. They all walked briskly to the gypsy's tent.

Madam Maria stood outside her tent in typical gypsy attire- a deep blue low-cut blouse, colorful skirt and babushka over her hair, tied to the side. She wore gold hoops through her ears and numerous beads around her neck. Many bangles encircled her arms. Her black eyes were arresting. She stared at the group, and each one felt she was looking only at him or her.

"We'd like to have our fortunes told," said Stephanie.

"Who will be first?" asked the gypsy woman. "The little one who hides behind the big blonde man?"

"Me?" asked Pamela, fearfully.

"Come. Do not be afraid, pretty little girl."

Pamela's fears vanished when she was complimented. She walked boldly into the tent. In ten minutes, she came out looking shaken.

"Well? What did she say? Are you going to meet a tall, dark stranger, and take a trip abroad?"

"No. I don't believe what she said, anyway."

"How about money? Are you going to receive riches?" asked Lois Jean.

"No, nothing like that. It was personal. She acted as though she knew me, but she doesn't. It's all a scam."

Meg thought, 'She must have said something that hit home.' Of course, a clever fortune-teller had to be somewhat of a psychologist. It wouldn't be too difficult to read Pamela. Meg was surprised that the gypsy had not flattered her and foretold all the wonderful things people expect to hear.

Leland went in next and came out laughing. "She says I have a tendency to be a dreamer, and I love my wife! But I also take care of business, first."

"She can't be all bad then," said Stephanie. "I like that part about loving your wife. Did she say you'd be rich?"

"No, but she said I would acquire a famous painting."

Leland and Stephanie stared at each other.

"How could she have known you bought paintings?" asked Stephanie.

"I don't know. It gave me a strange feeling!"

Jim smiled. "That was just a lucky guess or observation."

"I suppose so," replied Leland, but he looked pensive.

"I'll go next," offered Stephanie.

She too came out looking stunned. "She said I am practical and organized and that both my daughters inherited those traits. I will receive something I have been wanting for a long time, for Christmas. How did she know I have two daughters?"

"This is proving interesting. Wonder what she'll know about me?" asked Ralph, as he walked inside.

Ten minutes later, Ralph came out looking bemused.

"Extraordinary woman. She knew of my early days playing baseball."

"You were a professional baseball player?" asked a surprised Stephanie.

"Semi-pro. Lois Jean made me see the error of my ways!"

"I did not," replied Lois Jean indignantly. "You wanted to be a preacher. You were already planning to go to the Seminary when I met you."

"Do I dare have my fortune told? She might know about my deep dark secrets," asked Lois Jean.

"Sweetheart, you don't have any deep dark secrets. If you do, that happened before you were ten years old, because that's how long I have known you. Go ahead. It's all in fun."

"All right. Here I go, ready or not!"

"It's a little disconcerting though, how she can tell personal things about people she had never met," said Meg. "I wonder how she does it because I certainly don't believe she can see into the future, or read someone's mind."

"She is very clever at getting information from her customers without their realizing it. And she is a master at observing people. No one can read minds or predict the future," said Jim positively.

"I'm not so sure, Jim. Strange, unexplained occurrences have happened. Some research had been done on telepathy. Maybe she does have some rare gift of precognition," theorized Ralph.

"I don't believe it. When Lois Jean comes out, I am going in next, and I won't give the fortune teller any information she can use, openly or subliminally," said Jim.

Lois Jean didn't look too upset when she emerged from the tent. "I am going to have a large family and my husband and I will have a long and happy married life."

"Is that all she said to you? She didn't bring up any dark secrets?" asked her husband, teasing her.

"No, she didn't because there aren't any! So there!"

They all laughed and Jim entered the tent.

He was inside longer than anybody. When he returned, he had a serious expression on his face. But he smiled and said, "No deep dark secrets for me, either. I have a stubborn niece, a beautiful home, lovely wife, and will continue to make money."

Meg didn't think he had told all that the gypsy predicted, but she said nothing.

Andre walked over and took Meg's hand.

"Meg, let us go in together. I'll be there to protect you from the old witch, if she frightens you." He looked down at her, as if he would fight dragons, if necessary.

"No!" said Jim and Pamela, almost instantaneously.

Meg look surprised. "Why shouldn't we go in together? I don't have anything to hide, and evidently neither does Andre." Because they were both trying to prevent it, Meg was determined to go with Andre.

Jim was alarmed. So far, Pamela had prevented Andre from being with Meg. The fortune-teller had warned him of a tall, fair man who would bring danger to Meg. He placed no credence in fortune-telling prognostication, but just the same, the ominous import of her words left him shaken. Obviously, she could have seen them all together outside the tent and used her skills to weave a tale. She had certainly seen Andre, head and shoulders above everyone else. But what she had said confirmed what he felt about the man. Pamela, of course, was jealous of Meg. The young girl had a teenage infatuation for Andre, but Jim didn't think he was interested in her at all.

"Shall we face the gypsy's lair together?" asked Andre, still holding Meg's hand. "Everyone else seems to be in awe of her. I am interested in her forecast."

"Yes." She let him lead her inside, her heart beating fast.

"Especially if lovely Meg is in my future," murmured Andre in her ear.

Pamela was livid. No one ever went against her wishes, not her father or her mother, teachers or acquaintances. She had always found some kind of leverage to persuade them, if not by her looks, by other means. She would find out Meg's Achilles heel and use it against her. As for Andre, all she needed was more time to entrap him. No man had ever been able to resist her, even when she was a little girl.

Andre and Meg entered the darkened tent, lit only by a single candle. The fluttering flame cast grotesque phantasmagoria about the tent hangings and the dirt floor felt very dank beneath Meg's thin slippers. The gypsy was seated at the table and the flickering candle cast strange patterns across her face. Her large, black eyes were mesmerizing as she gazed at Meg. She felt that this ageless Rom could see into her very soul. Her hands were caressing a crystal ball that was in front of her. The orb seemed to glow from within. Meg felt no danger or animosity, just exposed.

The gypsy bent her eyes upon Andre and Meg saw a barely perceptible shudder pass through her body.

Andre reached into his pocket and pulled out a gold coin. "I cross your palm with gold, not silver. Now tell our fortunes, old mother."

The gypsy's eyes were hooded as she took the money.

"Good and evil. Light and darkness "said the crone, as she rubbed the crystal ball.

"What does that mumbo jumbo mean?" asked Andre. "Be specific or don't you know?"

She turned to Meg. "Give me your palm. The crystal is cloudy."

Meg extended her hand, almost afraid of the gypsy's touch.

"Don't be afraid of me. I am not the one who would harm you," she said, holding Meg's hand, palm up, and running her fingers over the lines and whorls. "You will meet a tall, dark man who will love you."

Meg smiled. This was the typical fortune told to young women. She relaxed, enjoying the game.

"You have known him before when you were quite young. But now, he will come to claim you. The children will love you and you will teach them many things. But you must be on your guard. I see danger all around you."

Now Meg wasn't smiling. How could she have known that Meg was a teacher? Then Meg laughed. She saw it all. Her uncle had visited the old woman before and had given her information about all of them. Just wait until she saw Uncle Jim. She'd have a word or two about this sneaky trick.

Andre was looking at the fortune-teller angrily.

"Whoever got to you first paid you well, no doubt." He too was thinking of Jim. "No dark stranger is going to claim Meg. I am!"

He stood up abruptly, causing the old woman to shrink back. She crossed herself and said nothing more.

"This has been an interesting interlude, Meg, but the others are waiting."

"Don't you want to have your fortune told?" she asked, enjoying Andre's jealousy over the tall, dark stranger.

"No." He gave the fortune-teller a steely glance and pulled Meg to her feet.

"Thank you," said Meg to the fortune-teller. "You're very good."

They left and Madam Maria muttered under her breath, "El Diablo!"

The group walked back towards their wagon and Meg noticed some long covered wagons, painted with circus logos, such as the bearded lady, and a male figure, half man and half fish. Eight or ten Clydesdale horses were tethered nearby, eating hay, their tremendous hooves occasionally pawing the ground.

"That's how the circus travels from town to town in these horse-drawn wagons. I don't doubt that one day they'll be traveling by railcar," Jim said.

"I hope they never do. Those wagons are romantic in a way," sighed Meg.

"I had a wonderful time today," said Lois Jean. "It was my first trip to the circus and I hope I get to see many more!"

Stephanie and Meg agreed enthusiastically.

"I just wish Ralph had thrown the ball to knock down those pins to win a teddy bear for me," said his wife.

"Next time, dear! I would like to have seen Andre ring the bell with the hammer. I'll bet he could have done it." Ralph didn't feel the antipathy that Jim and Leland felt for Andre.

"I'll bet he could have, too," said Pamela admiringly. "Why didn't you?"

"I didn't have the chance. We were in the cart most of the time," he replied curtly.

"Oh well. Next time I want to see you do it. With those muscles, it would probably go right through the top," she said, patting his arm.

Meg heard all this and almost gagged.

"Here we are, folks. All aboard for Beaufort," said Leland. "Are you frozen, Clem?"

"No, Sir. I been to all them shows, too!"

Everyone climbed onto the wagon and bundled themselves in blankets. The sun had set and it was cold. Andre was frustrated. He wanted to wrap his arms around Meg, but this little yapping Pekingese was by his side, preventing him from holding her.

Meg was feeling the same way and she could not understand why Andre couldn't get away from Pamela. After all, he had his own free will. Nobody was forcing him to stay attached at the hip. She didn't realize just how relentless Pamela was.

Jim knew Meg was unhappy, but he was relieved that Andre was held at bay, like the ravenous wolf he was. He had given the fortune-teller information about the others, but the old woman was uncanny in her observations. He had told her nothing about himself or about how he really felt about Andre. Yet, she knew. She recognized him for the evil man he was and warned Jim.

Trying to get Meg's mind off Andre, he said, "We saw some excellent fakery today. But P.T. Barnum was the brassiest faker of all. The Cardiff Giant was the best example."

"Who was the Cardiff Giant?" asked Lois Jean.

175

"This was supposedly the petrified remains of a primitive man. It was carved out of stone and shown in upstate New York. Thousands flocked to see it, convinced the phony was the real thing. Finally, some anthropologists proved that it wasn't. But Barnum made money. His favorite saying is, 'There's a sucker born every minute'. The circuses seem to follow that premise, but they are entertaining. People are drawn to the bizarre. Maybe they don't mind being fooled as long as it is cleverly done."

"Maybe," said Meg, looking at Jim with a knowing expression.

Jim had a wry look on his face when he met Meg's eyes. 'The clever girl knows I talked with the gypsy before the fortunes were told.'

When they rode slowly by Cart Island again, it was dark. The driver had hung two lanterns on the wagon. Meg wondered if the otters, gulls and raccoon had finished the leftovers. She was pleasantly tired and in spite of her uncle's conniving with Madam Maria, she had enjoyed having her fortune told. She was surprised at Andre's reaction, however. He seemed to have taken a dislike to the old woman, and Meg thought she appeared frightened of him. 'I must have been mistaken,' she thought. 'Maybe the shrinking in fear and crossing her heart to ward off evil were all part of the act. Uncle was right. People enjoy being fooled if it is part of the entertainment. Most people, but not Andre.'

They finally pulled up in front of the Davis House dock. "If anybody wants to take home some food, please do. There is so much left over. In another hour or two, you'll be hungry again," offered Stephanie. While everyone gathered around the picnic basket dividing the food, Stephanie took Meg aside.

"Don't forget to come to my house tomorrow at nine o'clock." She was speaking in a low voice. "I don't want that spoiled brat ruining our morning getting the Christmas tree. I hope Andre remembers. I don't dare get close to him to remind him because she is still attached to him like sealing wax and I don't want her to hear. She'll insist on going."

"Okay," whispered Meg. "Uncle Jim and I will be there. I don't think I could take two days of her in a row." Meg giggled.

All said goodbye and went their separate ways. When they reached their rooms, Meg reminded Jim that they had to be at Leland and Stephanie's house at nine o'clock.

Chapter Eleven

The next morning was a cool, crisp winter day with a radiant sun shining in an azure, cloudless sky. Meg and Jim had a leisurely breakfast of hot tea and cinnamon toast. Meg had fallen asleep as soon as she sank into the feather bed. She felt rested and happy with anticipation at the thought of seeing Andre without the Dresden doll. Meg didn't even like to say her name.

"I had a good time yesterday, in spite of your trickery!"

"Whatever do you mean?"

"You know very well what I mean. You told that fortune-teller things about us earlier," she said accusingly.

"I confess. You found me out, but everyone enjoyed it. I know I did, especially the look on Leland's face, flabbergasted that she knew about his picture buying."

"And I was shocked that she knew I was a teacher I suppose you told her to mention a tall, <u>dark</u> stranger in my life, too?"

"Guilty as charged," said Jim, not looking at all sorry.

"How did you know about Ralph's baseball career?"

"I talked to some friends of his."

"You're just too devious, by far. No wonder you're such a successful lawyer," said Meg, trying to look reproving, but failing. She smiled and patted his hand. "Uncle Jim, I am going to miss you terribly."

"I don't even want to think about it, Meg. I know fledglings have to leave the nest, but it is very difficult for the papa bird."

"But we'll see each other. I'll visit New York and you'll come back to Florida."

Jim sighed. "I know. Well, are you ready to get the tree? I hope you have sturdy boots and not those flimsy slippers you wore yesterday."

"I have on my sturdiest boots and a heavy wool dress and coat."

"Good. Let's go," said Jim, taking the last swallow of his tea. As they strolled along the boardwalk Meg noticed a dilapidated skiff, its paint almost peeled off, was pulled up on shore, lying on its side in the sand. The bottom was completely covered with a forest of seaweed. Many years ago, it may have known copper paint.

"It's sad to see a boat like that. It looks so vulnerable and forlorn as if its owner no longer cares."

"Meg, you are the only person I know who feels sorry for a boat. But I admit that I do feel some sympathy for it when it is placed in someone's yard and planted with flowers. No self-respecting boat should suffer such an indignity."

Meg smiled at her uncle as they continued their walk. He was so much fun. She enjoyed his wry sense of humor.

"We had better hurry or we're going to be late," said Jim. They walked much faster. Meg's cheeks were rosy from the brisk wind by the time they reached the Carter's house.

Andre walked up just as Meg and Jim reached the steps. Meg's heartbeat quickened. He hadn't forgotten.

"Bon jour," he said, tipping his cap. His eyes roamed over Meg.

"Good morning. Isn't it a beautiful day?" asked Meg.

"It is now."

Jim merely nodded. "Shall we go in, Meg?" he said, offering her his arm before Andre could. They walked up the steps with Andre following, a smile on his face. The battle of one-upmanship had begun.

Stephanie greeted them at the door, her neck collared almost to the ears.

"I see you dressed for the tree cutting ceremony," said Meg.

"You look charming," said Andre.

Stephanie blushed. "Thank you. Leland should be driving up any minute with the horse and cart. We'll have hot cider when we get back. Then we'll put up the tree and hang all the decorations that Meg and I made." She turned at the sound of hoof beats. "Here's Leland."

"All aboard that are going aboard," yelled Leland.

This time Andre was ready. Before Meg knew what was happening, he swooped her up in his arms and placed her in the cart, just as easily as he had the tiny Pamela. Jim politely assisted Stephanie into the seat by Leland. Andre had leaped into the wagon as nimbly as a mountain goat and was sitting on the side bench beside Meg before Jim joined them. Andre's eyes met his with a look of satisfaction. Jim sat across from them and they began their ride into the country.

With Andre beside her, Meg was happy. Pamela wasn't there to spoil a perfect day and the woods were beckoning. The steady hum of cartwheels moving, along with the rattle of the chains on the cart shafts, had a soothing, hypnotic effect. The sweet fragrance of cedar added to Meg's pleasant, relaxed feeling and she was getting sleepy. Andre smiled at her as she began to nod and gently pulled her head to his shoulder.

"Meg, look quickly, in the top of that pine tree!" said Jim, "It's mistletoe!"

Meg's head jerked up. "Oh, where?"

"That tall, long-leafed pine we're just passing."

Now Meg was sitting straight, adjusting her hat and she moved just a fraction away from Andre, embarrassed that she had been practically lying in his arms.

Andre's look at Jim was daunting. He had lost his advantage with Meg for the moment.

181

"Can we get some? That tree is so high, I do not think a monkey could climb it!"

"Leland came prepared," replied Jim. "Along with the axe, he brought a long pole with a hook on the end of it and shears for cutting greenery. You can pull the mistletoe down with that pole."

"Good. It's not Christmas without mistletoe and holly and a Yule log."

"I am sure Leland has picked out the biggest log and is saving it for Christmas Day," said Jim.

"I have never experienced a Christmas such as you have here," said Andre, managing to sound wistful.

Jim lapsed into silence. He disliked the man intensely and found it difficult to make small talk with him. He knew that with Andre, everything was competitive. Of course he found Meg attractive, but more than that, it was the pleasure of the hunt. Andre was a predator and Meg was the prey. Jim was simply part of the obstacle placed in his path. 'He will find this is one obstacle he won't get past,' Jim thought.

They finally reached a clearing after about thirty minutes and Leland drew the reins and brought the horse to a halt. Just beyond the clearing was a small lake surrounded by a grove of trees. They all got out and Leland tethered the horse to a bush.

"What a peaceful place," said Meg as they walked along towards the copse of pine, cedar and juniper.

"It is one of my favorite spots. Leland and I come here every year to cut our tree. Sometimes we bring a picnic lunch in the summer and sit here by the lake, listening to the robins sing." Stephanie had fallen in step with Meg. "Let the men go on ahead. Leland has to search until he finds the perfect tree. It will take him twenty minutes to find the one he wants!"

The men walked deeper into the woods, Leland and Jim leading the way. They were talking and Andre trailed behind them.

"I want a tree tall enough to reach the ceiling," Leland told Jim.

"How about this one?" asked Jim, indicating a tall cedar tree.

"That's tall enough, but not full enough. The branches must be spreading wide and be thick with leaves."

Andre had wandered off in another direction. He surprised a covey of quail. The mother bird was walking resolutely ahead and five tiny chicks followed in a line behind her. She squawked a warning and all the birds disappeared into the tangle of vines and bushes. Their coats blended perfectly with the foliage. Andre knew they were there, but he couldn't see them.

Other eyes were watching from afar. A red fox crouched motionless in the brush of yaupon and holly. Andre wondered what other animals lurked nearby, maybe deer or a black bear. He liked the moist, cool shade of the forest and the smell of the pine needles crushed beneath his feet. At least he wasn't bored now. He had only come on this expedition because Meg would be here. All the talk of Christmas and decorations bored him. At this moment, he would really like to be in a saloon, drinking ale, puffing his cheroot, and listening to bawdy tales with a buxom wench on his knee.

Leland called out, "I've found the tree. Bring the axe, Andre."

He walked quickly in Leland's direction and the fox scampered away. 'No quail for breakfast today,' thought Andre.

"Let me cut it down. I would enjoy the exercise."

"All right, if you really want to," responded Leland. "Jim and I will gather pine boughs and holly. We'll also find some mistletoe. Be careful that you are standing away from the tree when it falls. Call us, if you need help." Each man carried burlap bags as well as the shears and pole. They separated, Jim looking for mistletoe and Leland for holly and pine fronds.

Andre was an outdoors person. He was a big, strong man who found great pleasure in physical exertion. Though he had observed and learned the manners of a gentleman and was perfectly at ease in a drawing room, what enthralled him was standing on the deck of a ship, climbing a jagged mountain, or breathing in the heady aroma of a majestic forest. He actually looked forward to chopping down the tree. It was a physical challenge and he had not been challenged lately. He swung the axe mightily, as he might have wielded it had he lived fifty years ago, cracking bones and cutting off the limbs of an adversary on the deck of a pirate ship. The tree swayed under the assault and finally a mighty blow sent it crashing to the ground. Andre grunted with satisfaction. How he would like to be hoisting a sail right now, singing a sea chanty, along side sturdy sailors who felt as he did. He rested, leaning on the axe handle.

Jim and Leland came tramping through the woods, their sacks filled with greenery and mistletoe.

"We'll take these to the cart and then come back and carry the tree," said Leland. "Give me the axe."

"C'est bon. I will wait here."

They walked back by the lake. Meg and Stephanie had enjoyed watching the ducks and talking about Christmas, only a week away.

"My daughter Alexandria is coming home for Christmas. Leland and I are so happy because our beautiful daughter hasn't visited us for more than two years. She suffered a terrible tragedy."

"Oh. I am so sorry. What happened?"

"She was married for six years to a Spanish diplomat. They lived in Washington, D.C.. He was a rising young star on the political scene and my beautiful Alexandria was the perfect wife for him. They were desperately in love with each other, and were the toast of Washington society. One snowy night two years ago, while he was crossing the street, Carlos Cervantes, Alexandria's beloved husband, was struck by a runaway horse and killed instantly. My daughter has never fully recovered from the tragedy. For more than a year, she wandered like a lost spirit through their magnificent house on the Potomac. I could never persuade her to come home to us. But, now she is coming and I long to see her."

184

Stephanie looked so sad that Meg wanted to put her arms around her. They both looked up as the men approached.

"Hello! Are you back already?" asked Stephanie. "You usually take an hour to find the right tree."

"This time I was lucky. Andre has already cut it down and we have plenty of holly, pine fronds and mistletoe- enough to decorate every doorframe, window and table in the house!"

"Wonderful. I can't wait to get started! You mean Andre cut the tree down all by himself? Why didn't you help?" asked Stephanie.

"He wanted to do it. Likes the exercise, I guess. Let's put these sacks in the cart. Then we'll go back and bring the tree."

"Give them to us. We'll take them to the cart and you go on back for the tree," offered Meg. "Give us all the tools, too. We'll make two trips."

Meg and Stephanie took the sacks and the men went back to get the tree. The three men picked it up and made their way slowly back to the cart, Leland and Jim huffing and puffing all the way. Andre carried the tree as if it were a toy, breathing easily. They finally reached their destination. Meg and Stephanie had already put the bags and tools in the cart, and were waiting along side it.

"Oh, Leland, that is a beautiful tree. You found the perfect one," said Stephanie .

"Thanks. Okay, now for the hard part, getting it in the cart."

"Why don't you two get in the cart and pull? I'll left up the trunk and push," said Andre.

Leland and Jim looked at each other. 'Why argue?' they seemed to agree. They did as he suggested, and soon the three men had gotten the tree where they wanted it.

Meg was admiring Andre's great strength and wished she could wipe the perspiration from his brow. Stephanie's eyes were admiring, too. Finally they were on their way.

"Well, you certainly had your exercise for the day. Aren't you tired?" asked Meg.

Andre smiled. "That was a nice way to start the day. Now I am full of energy. Perhaps you would like to take a promenade along the boardwalk when we return?" he asked.

"I would love to, but I told Stephanie I would help trim the tree," she murmured regretfully.

"Too bad. How about this afternoon? We could go about four o'clock. Don't I deserve a reward for cutting down the tree?"

Meg hesitated. She wanted to go so much, but she knew her uncle would be displeased. Andre's blue eyes won out.

"Yes, I could go then."

Andre looked as though he'd won a hundred dollars in a poker game. It was enough. He would be with Meg without her uncle's censorious eyes following him every minute.

Jim could say nothing now, but he certainly planned to have a talk with Meg when they got back. The man's campaign was as insidious as a snake hypnotizing a rabbit.

They reached the Carter's home at 12:30. The men moved the tree into the house, staggering up the steps with their burden while Meg and Stephanie held the doors open.

"Take it into the parlor and prop it in that far corner," instructed Stephanie.

After catching his breath, Leland said, "I'll get a bucket and fill it with coal."

Jim went with him and they returned shortly, carrying two buckets. They stood the tree up straight and the top brushed the ceiling.

"I'll have to cut some off the top so we can get the star on." They lowered the tree and Leland clipped the top with his shears.

"Now, attach the star," said Stephanie, handing him a glittering silver star that had crowned their trees for the past ten years. "My mother made this star before she died and I treasure it."

"It's beautiful," said Meg.

Leland attached the star. Then he put the coal-filled bucket in towards the corner. "You and Andre left up the tree and place it in the bucket. I'll hold the bucket and shift the coal around."

While the men were doing this, Stephanie and Meg had gotten several bricks and a couple of flatirons. They placed the bricks on top of the bucket and then, to assure that the tree remained upright, lined up the flatirons around the trunk. Jim poured water into the makeshift tree stand from the other bucket to keep the tree green longer. Stephanie added some sugar to the water.

"This keeps the tree fresh," she said.

"I insist that you all stay for lunch. We'll have the cider and sandwiches," she said in a tone that would not accept 'No' for an answer.

They ate lunch and afterwards, Jim and Andre said they had to leave. Leland also had a few things to finish at the office, even though it was Saturday.

"Like rats deserting the ship," said Stephanie. "No one wants to trim the tree except Meg and me."

"You are correct and I'll be the first rat to leave," said Jim, picking up his hat and buttoning up his coat. Stephanie laughed and gave him a peck on the cheek.

"You see what I mean?" she asked, turning to Meg.

"Yes, but I am going to enjoy it."

Andre said to Meg, "Until four o'clock," and pressed her hand to his lips.

"What's happening at four o'clock?" asked Stephanie, full of curiosity.

"Nothing much, we're just taking a stroll on the boardwalk."

"A stroll to paradise!" said Andre gallantly. "Adieu!"

The men all left, Leland following the others. His eyes narrowed with a look of dislike, and his expression was grim as he watched Andre leave.

"You had better watch that man. He's too good-looking by far. Not that I wouldn't go in your place," said Stephanie.

"It's only a walk. What could possibly happen?"

"He could propose marriage and your uncle would have apoplexy."

"Stephanie, he hasn't even put his arm around me except to lift me from the cart."

"Yes, I noticed. He continued to hold you and Pamela was furious! That little kitten has sharp claws. Just watch out you don't get scratched!" warned Stephanie.

"Let's change the subject to something pleasant. When are your daughters arriving?" asked Meg.

"On Tuesday. You are definitely invited to help us all light the candles on Christmas Eve. My daughters and Lucy's husband will be happy to have you and Jim, so don't start telling me it's just a time for families. I am afraid I cannot invite Andre, though. Leland would definitely not stand for that. I have never seen him take such an intense dislike to anyone before. I'm sorry."

"I understand." The two spent an hour trimming the tree and Meg finally left at two thirty. She was eagerly looking forward to her walk with Andre and was trying to decide what to wear. When she reached the Davis House, Jim was sitting on the porch.

"Did you finish decorating?" he asked.

"Yes. We trimmed the tree and put up pine fronds holly and mistletoe all over the house. We even put greenery and ribbons on the banister going upstairs. It looks like a 'downeast'[4] fairyland. We're invited for Christmas Eve."

"I know. Leland already asked me. Meg, have a seat. I want to talk to you."

"I have to change clothes. It's almost three o'clock."

"This won't take long. Please sit down," Jim said with a grave expression on his face.

---

[4] Local expression for people living in Beaufort and villages east of it

Meg sat, knowing what was coming. She folded her hands primly in her lap and looked expectantly at her uncle.

"I know that you are twenty-one now, an adult. You have completed college with high grades and you have always shown good judgment, though at times a little rebellious. I understand that you must make your own choices. You are no longer my baby. But, becoming an adult does not change the fact that I want to protect you," Jim continued, looking at Meg's downcast face. "Andre is the kind of man that every female fantasizes about. He is strong, handsome, charming, debonair and has that inborn ability to make every woman believe she is special to him. But I feel with every fiber of my being that he is not trustworthy. He is a user, Meg. He will wield his considerable looks and skills to seduce you."

Meg blushed and was very embarrassed to hear her uncle say this to her.

"I realize this conversation is making you uncomfortable, but I have to say it. He would never marry, God forbid! He would take your innocence and sweetness regardless of the consequences to you. Even more than his ruthlessness towards women, I believe he is an evil person who has robbed and probably murdered."

Meg gasped and stood up. "You can't mean this! I knew you disliked him, but I did not know to what extent. How can you make such a horrible accusation when you actually know nothing about his past?"

"Meg, my dearest child, I am as sure of it as I am sure that I love you. I cannot stand by and allow him to ruin your precious life." Jim spoke, pleading, using his powers of persuasion. This was more important than any case he had ever pled in court.

"I will keep in mind all you have said. I know you spoke this way because you love me, not because you want to control me. But I don't feel any of those negative, terrible things about him as you do. I will be on my guard, however. He won't seduce me. I promise you that, though I think he is the most attractive man I have ever seen. Don't worry, Uncle Jim. I'll be safe," she said, patting him on the arm. "But nothing could convince me that he is truly evil." Then she kissed him on the cheek and went upstairs.

Jim watched her leave. He felt a slight lessening of tension. She promised to be careful, but he still worried because she could not see beyond the façade. He was not a Victorian parent who would forbid her to see the man. If she were a teen, yes he could, but she wasn't a child any more. He went to his room sorely troubled.

At five minutes of four, Andre was on the porch, waiting for Meg. He had dressed carefully for his outing. Every female eye had followed him as he walked towards the Davis House.

He stood watching the door and Meg came out. Andre caught his breath. This was a prize worth winning. She looked as pretty as a bright spring jonquil in her yellow pleated skirt. She wore a jaunty yellow hat and carried a dainty yellow polka-dotted parasol and wore white lace gloves.

Andre offered his arm to her. "You are like a breath of spring on a cold winter morn!"

"Oh," she said, smiling at him as they walked down the steps, "am I?"

"You almost made my heart stop beating when I first saw you. You are so beautiful!"

Meg continued to hold his arm as they strolled along the boardwalk. "Andre, you are well-practiced in flattery! I don't doubt that many women have heard your honeyed words, but I do thank you for the compliment," said Meg.

He managed to appear sheepish, which was quite a feat for him. "You have caught me out! I don't deny that I have known many women, but none have appealed to me like you do."

Meg glanced at him, disbelief in her eyes.

"It is true," he said quickly, as if to erase her doubting look. "I first saw you when you stepped off the Annie Marie and onto the dock, and I determined then that I would meet you. It was no accident that I went to the boarding house while you were there."

"You did?" said Meg in surprise.

"Yes, I knew I must meet you some way. After you were seated, I saw that there was one seat left at your table and I quickly took it before anyone else could."

Meg was secretly thrilled that he had connived to meet her and being the woman that she was, wanted to hear that he preferred her to Pamela.

"This was before you saw Pamela. She is lovely and apparently, quite affectionate, too!"

"Ah yes, Pamela. She is lovely and no doubt affectionate, but she is also childish, spoiled and boring. I know it is ungallant of me to say so, but I want to be honest with you, my darling Meg. She does not appeal to me in the least. Compared to you, she is dull and listless. I succumb to red shining tresses, and 'fire'" he murmured, touching her glossy curls.

Meg was desperately trying to heed her uncle's warning. Andre had called her his "darling Meg". Could she really be his darling? He looked as thought he wanted to kiss her right there on the boardwalk in front of dozens of people. Meg didn't doubt that if she gave him the slightest encouragement, he would. She tossed her head, effectively moving his hand from her curls, and said, "Look! There's a ship crossing the bar. I wonder what port she hails from?"

Andre smiled, willing her to look at him. "Probably from some faraway, romantic isle. Would you like to travel to such a place with palm trees gently swaying in the breeze and water as blue as sparkling sapphires lapping at the shore?"

Meg's eyes were dreamy. "Yes, I would. Have you been to such places?"

"Many times." Andre leaned against a railing, looking out across the water. He wanted to reveal a bit of himself to Meg. "Most of my life has been spent on a ship. I lost both of my parents when I was young, and somehow was drawn to the docks. It was a hard life at first, but soon I discovered the joy of standing on the deck of a sailing vessel, feeling the salt spray on my face, smelling the tangy air. I reveled in hoisting a sail or steering a ship through stormy seas. I suppose, at heart, I will always be a sailor, though I may not be on a ship."

Meg softened towards him. The man now speaking was not flirting with her, wearing away her defenses.

"You must miss it very much."

"I do, but I decided after eight years at sea that I needed to learn more of the world around me. I had little formal education, but I suppose you could say that I was a quick study. I learned languages easily, and I read voraciously when I had the time." He was painting a picture of a lonely boy, fighting against almost insurmountable odds, seeking knowledge. His visual imagery offered to Meg did not include rage, lust and murder. He turned to Meg. "What about you? Where did you grow up?"

Meg was impressed that he had overcome what must have been a hard life and had educated himself, in spite of adversity. So many people she knew tossed aside educational opportunities when it was handed to them on a silver platter. Her uncle, and she supposed her father too, in his own way, had stressed the value of an education, even for a woman. So she was feeling great admiration for Andre's perseverance.

"I grew up in Florida. My father was a doctor. He had a health clinic for the Seminole Indians and my mother assisted him. She died when I was ten and my father couldn't cope with a daughter on his own. So he sent me to New York to live with my uncle and aunt."

Andre noticed her sad expression and took her hand.

"That must have been difficult for you," he said.

"It was, at first. Even though my parents had never really spent much time with me because they were so involved in their work, I was hurt when my father sent me away. As it turned out, it was the best thing that could have happened to me. I really consider my aunt and uncle my true parents. They loved me as if I were their own child, especially Uncle Jim. He was my mother's brother. They didn't have any children of their own, and Uncle Jim was a successful lawyer in New York. I grew to love them dearly. I trust him without reservation." She looked directly at Andre when she said this.

Andre knew he had to tread carefully. He must not appear openly defiant to her uncle or Meg would not respond, no matter how much she was attracted to him. And Andre knew she was attracted. Her guileless eyes were so expressive and so revealing of her true feelings. She could never dissemble with him. No woman had ever been able to resist him, and Meg was no different, but she was warring with herself. He could be patient because he always won in the end. At the moment she was quite diverting to him. Besides being attracted to her physical charms, he enjoyed sparring with her. He knew this wouldn't last. It never did. Once he seduced her, he would grow tired of her clinging ways, professions of love, and entreaties to marry her. Women were all the same. He had never known one who was different.

You are smiling, Andre. Do I make you happy?"

"Cherie, it makes me very happy just to be with you. I realize how protective your uncle is of you. He sees me as a threat because he doesn't want to lose you. But believe me, Megan, I would cherish you always. I would never hurt you in any way." He gazed into her eyes.

"Well, all of a sudden we are so serious. Let's enjoy our promenade. Look, here comes Lois Jean and Ralph," she said, waving at her friends.

Andre was annoyed, but no one could have told it from the welcoming smile on his face.

"Hello. Isn't it a lovely afternoon for a stroll?" asked Meg.

"Yes, it is. I had to drag Ralph away from his study. He has been working on his sermon for tomorrow for three hours," replied Lois Jean.

"It should be a good one then," said Andre. "What is the topic? Hell and damnation for all us mortal sinners?"

"Nothing so intimidating as that. Christmas is next Saturday, and so my sermon is on the birth of the Christ child. I hope you both will come to church Sunday morning. Sunday

193

School is at nine-thirty and the church service is at eleven o'clock. If Sunday School is too early, then please come to church. The Christmas music will be beautiful. Lois Jean directs the choir and plays the piano, too," said Ralph.

Andre had never darkened the door of any church in his beleaguered life. He wondered, whimsically, if a lightening bolt would strike him dead if he did. He had no desire to walk in one now.

Lois Jean had a sudden inspiration. "Meg, could you play the piano tomorrow? I'm sure sight-reading the music would be no problem for you. Why didn't I think of it before? Could you, please? I would be free to give my entire attention to directing the choir."

Meg was taken aback. She and her uncle were planning to go to church tomorrow, but she didn't know that she wanted to play for the choir to sing.

"Lois Jean, I don't know about that," she said, unable to give a direct 'No'.

Ralph joined forces with his wife. "We would be honored and happy if you would consent to play. We can go by the church now and you can pick out some music to play for the Offertory. Also, Lois Jean can show you what the choir will be singing."

Even Andre joined in. "When you have a talent such as yours, you should let others enjoy it."

"I suppose I could," said Meg with a sigh, giving in to their persuasion. It wasn't that she was afraid to play or nervous that she would make mistakes. She was far too good a musician for that. She simply wanted to sit in the congregation and enjoy listening to the music.

"The wind is starting to pick up and it's getting too chilly to walk, anyway," said Lois Jean. "The congregation will be thrilled to hear you play, Meg. I am so pleased that you're going to do it!"

"Come inside and look over the music."

I'll stay outside and smoke a cigar, if you don't mind," said Andre.

The young minister was about the same age as Andre. Both were handsome, healthy men, but Ralph's eyes had an inner glow, in repose; when he wasn't assuming a façade, Andre's eyes were dead, cold.

By the time Andre finished his cigar they came back outside.

"Meg picked out some beautiful selections. I am going to sit back during the Offertory and just enjoy hearing her play," said Lois Jean.

The Days lived across the street in the parsonage, so they bid Meg and Andre 'Goodbye'.

"That was gracious of you to agree to play. I could see that you didn't really want to." Andre once again placed Meg's hand on his arm as they began walking towards the Davis House.

"It wasn't that I didn't want to play. It's just that I always have to perform. Sometimes I want to sit quietly and listen."

By now, it had begun to darken. The elms lining the street, planted in honor of Queen Ann, were dancing and swaying in the wind blowing in from the sound. A sudden drift of fallen leaves swirled into an arabesque, fluttering against Meg's face. By now, no one else was around. Andre stopped and turned Meg to face him.

"I have been wanting to do this since I first saw you." He pulled Meg tightly against him. His eyes were smoldering with a fierce, blue light, and he kissed her.

Meg's head spun. She really wasn't experienced with men. The few kisses she had experienced were chaste, a bare touching of lips, when some callow youth brought her home from a cotillion dance. There she was bathed in the safety of a porch light with her uncle waiting just behind the door. But now she was alone with a man unlike any other she had ever known, a man who demanded more. Finally, though she didn't want to, she pushed against him, fighting to overcome the ecstasy of his kiss. He released her immediately.

195

"I apologize," said Andre. "I should not have taken advantage of you." He appeared so contrite that Meg's spurt of indignation dissolved as quickly as it had formed.

"You didn't. I mean…" Meg didn't know what she meant. It had been exciting, exhilarating, yet she was aware that she shouldn't have allowed a man she barely knew to hold her and kiss her in such an intimate way.

"We must hurry. Uncle will be wondering where I am," said Meg with her head averted. She was too embarrassed to look at Andre because she had responded with complete abandon to his advances.

Andre gently turned her head so that he could look into her eyes. "Meg, sweetheart, what we did was perfectly natural. It's never wrong to express your feelings, but I really am sorry if I have upset you," he said smoothly, as he tenderly held her face in his hands.

Meg was confused. One minute, he was almost fierce and demanding then the next moment, he was gentle and considerate.

He took her hand. "Come on, I'll race you to the door!"

He was like a chameleon, changing from one minute to the next. Meg ran along side him, matching his strides as best she could. She wondered why he wasn't angry when she finally resisted his advances. She had heard about women who were teases. Was she one of them? She didn't dare discuss it with her uncle. He would be furious and probably challenge Andre to a fight, or have him thrown in jail. Her uncle was clever enough to do it on some trumped-up charge.

They jogged all the way. Andre was running off his frustration and Meg was running from herself. Jim was sitting on the porch waiting.

"I wondered where you were. The Alligoods have invited us for dinner. You will have to go as you are or we'll be late." He stood up, walked to Meg and took her arm.

"Goodbye," he said, dismissing Andre.

196

"Bon soir. I enjoyed our," he paused slightly, "exhilarating walk." He tipped his hat and walked away in the twilight, whistling.

Chapter Twelve

Saturday and Sunday zipped by. Meg enjoyed seeing the Alligoods again, and Sunday morning after church, everyone came up telling her how much they had liked her playing. The days were almost a blur to Meg. All she could think about was Andre. She had not seen or heard from him since Saturday night.

On Monday morning, she and Jim were having an early lunch, since they had missed breakfast. Meg had gotten up late, feeling lethargic, not really interested in beginning a new day.

"You seem far away, Meg, lost in another world. What's troubling you?" He had never mentioned her walk with Andre, and Meg was afraid if she brought it up, she'd blush.

"Nothing in particular. So many things have happened since we left New York, I can scarcely take it in," she replied evasively.

"That's true. From a life-threatening hurricane, to Wade's death, to two unsolved murders."

"Do you think they'll ever catch the man who did it?", she asked, relieved that the conversation hadn't touched on what was really bothering her.

"There's a slim possibility, but I don't hold out much hope." Jim asked casually, "How was your walk with the smooth Frenchman?" He watched for Meg' reaction.

Meg was caught by surprise. She covered her guilt by taking a sip of tea. "Oh, it was quite pleasant. We ran into Ralph and Lois Jean and talked to them. Then we went to the church. That's why we were so late getting back."

"I see." And he did see by Meg's refusal to meet his eyes that the slimy devil had probably made advances to her. But he didn't press it though he was seething inwardly. He had Meg's promise that she would be on her guard.

"We had lunch so late, it's about time for mail call. Let's go by the post office. I am expecting a telegram from New York."

They walked to the post office amid the Monday morning hustle and bustle of horse-drawn drays transporting merchandise to various businesses. Jim walked on the outside of the shell path to protect Meg from being splashed by the mud from the horses' hooves. The harbor was busy with fishing boats, sailing vessels, and steam packets dotting Taylor's Creek. Meg and Jim passed by a sign advertising a turkey and goose shoot.

"Do they actually go out and hunt down a turkey or a goose?"

"Sometimes they do. The officials fire a starting gun and the first ones to return with a bird receive a cash prize. The birds are donated to some of the poor folks for Christmas dinner. Other times, there is a bow and arrow shooting contest using a bull's eye target. The target is placed seventy-five or a hundred yards away and the men pay a dollar to shoot at the target. The one who hits the bull's eye gets the prize. Believe me, you've got to be a dead-eye shot to hit the center of the rings."

"I hope we get to see that." She was thinking, 'I'll just bet Andre could hit the target.'

A buckboard buggy came roaring by and Jim pulled Meg safely from the path of the careening carriage.

"Wonder where that fellow's going in such a hurry?" asked Jim, brushing mud from his normally immaculate trousers.

"I don't know, but if he doesn't watch out, he's going to have an accident," said Meg, adjusting her hat which was slightly askew.

200

They continued walking by a general store and a cobbler's shop.

"I'll have to bring in my shoe to get the heel repaired," said Meg.

"Do you want some candy?" asked Jim.

"Yes! I haven't had any penny candy in a long time!" They went inside and a little tow-headed tyke was concentrating on the mounds of candy behind the glass, a penny clutched tightly in his grubby little hand.

Ever the newly launched school teacher, Meg asked sternly, "Why aren't you in school today?"

"Oi told moi Ma Oi was sum sick."

"You don't look sick to me."

"Oi'm better, now."

Jim laughed. "Leave him alone. They get out tomorrow anyway, for the Christmas holidays."

"Oi'll have a candy cane," said the boy, handing over his penny to the owner who winked at Jim.

"Since it's almost Christmas, have three." He put three pieces in a bag and handed it to the grinning, gap-toothed child. "And next time, stay in bed when you're sick!"

"Oi'll do 'er," replied the unrepentant culprit, smacking his lips and sucking on the cane. He ran out the door, and all three adults smiled at each other.

"I will have some horehound, bull's eye, and chocolate," requested Meg after looking over the varied selections.

Jim paid for the sweetmeats and then stuffed them in his pocket, knowing that Meg would eat them later in her room.

They reached the post office and Jim walked over to the telegraph office.

"My name is Jim Styron and I'm expecting a telegram."

"Yes, Sir. I remember you sent a telegram to New York last week. But I've got two telegrams for you."

"Thank you." Jim tore open the first. It was from his agents in New York. The message read, 'Andre Lafitte not known in Frisco. Stop. All leads dead end. Stop. Await instructions.'

Disappointed, Jim folded the paper and put it in his pocket before Meg could see it.

"Anything important?"

"No. Just business." He opened the other telegram. It was from Sean Riley. "Meg, it's from your father."

"What does it say?"

"You'll never believe this," said Jim in amazement. "Your childhood friend, Micco Ravenwing, is coming to Beaufort."

"He is! Why?"

"It seems that Sean sent him to Harvard Medical School and Micco has just received his M.D. He is returning to Jupiter Inlet and is coming down from Boston to join us on our voyage to Florida."

"I can't believe it! Micco is a doctor! Well, he always was smart. I am so glad my father did that for him. I'm dying to see Micco!"

"So am I. Sean certainly must think a lot of him to give him such a magnanimous gift."

"Now Micco can reopen the clinic that was so dear to my father's heart," said Meg. "He was so tall and skinny. I wonder if he still looks like a bean pole?"

"Now Meg. Be kind. Looks aren't everything."

"No," said Meg aloud, 'but they come close,' she thought.

"According to this, he should be arriving by train some time tomorrow. We'll go down and meet every mooring of the Naptha Launch."

Jim felt happy and relieved. They would be so tied up entertaining Micco that Meg wouldn't have much time, no time he hoped, for Andre.

After checking with the postmaster for mail, they headed back to their rooms.

"You go on, Meg. I'm going to stop by and talk with Leland for a while."

As Meg strolled back along the boardwalk, she was remembering things about Micco. In spite of his busy schedule helping her father, he always found time to play with her, and to tell her stories about the Seminoles. Maybe that was why she was so interested in them today. Actually, she would have been quite lonely growing up if Micco had not been there to listen to her childish prattle. Funny how she had forgotten all that.

The next day, Jim found out what the train schedule was. One train arrived at 10:00 a.m. and the other at 4:30 p.m. He and Meg and Stephanie walked down to the dock at 9:50 a.m. They waited as the morning sun warmed them, and Meg and Stephanie were holding parasols over their heads to protect their complexions. Soon they saw the launch rounding Piver's Island, but there didn't appear to be any passengers sitting on the seats. They all felt a sense of disappointment. One man was sitting next to the pilot, however.

Turning to leave, Jim said, "I guess he will be on the afternoon train." As they started to walk away, Meg looked back.

"Wait! There is a tall man getting off, carrying his luggage." They all turned around and stared as he waved to the pilot and then began walking towards them as gracefully as a black panther.

"Micco?" said Meg in a questioning tone.

"Can this be my little plump, carrot-topped Meg?" asked the dark haired stranger. He dropped his bag and picked Meg up, swinging her around in the air.

"My, how you've grown, Red," he said, laughing.

Putting her down, he extended his hand to Jim. "You must be Meg's uncle. I am Micco Ravenwing. How do you do?"

They shook hands and Jim liked Micco instantly. "Yes, I am. How do you do? We're so happy to have you join us for the

203

trip to Florida. Stephanie, this is Micco Ravenwing. And Micco, this is our good friend, Stephanie Carter."

Micco bowed slightly and smiled. His pearly, white teeth shone against his reddish, golden skin. "How do you do?"

"Very well, thank you." Stephanie thought, 'The hearts of co-eds must have fluttered uncontrollably when he walked by.'

"Exactly what do you mean by 'plump'?" asked Meg indignantly. She had forgotten that he also teased her unmercifully, too.

"Well, just pleasingly so! But that was when you were five years old. You're not as plump now.

"I am not plump and don't call me 'Red'." Meg had also forgotten that he had long thick eyelashes that almost tangled in the breeze.

"I remember as if it were yesterday, your cap of curly red hair, sunburned nose, and sturdy, chubby legs," said Micco .

Meg started to make a retort when Jim intervened. "Stephanie has invited us for lunch at 12:30. Let's get you settled in your room. You must be tired after your long trip," said Jim as he and Micco walked ahead.

"I have never been so insulted in my life! Who does he think he is calling me 'chubby'?" Meg said to Stephanie, staring daggers at Micco's back.

"Meg, that is one gorgeous man! I think he's even taller than Andre. If I were you, I'd let him call me 'fatso' as long as he was talking to me. Did you notice the sun shining on his hair? It looked almost blue-black. He wears it rather short, though, just below his ears. Must be the collegiate look. If I could paint a picture of Osceola, Micco would be the model."

"You're certainly impressed with him. I think he's…he's skinny," said Meg, for lack of a better word. She couldn't think of anything insulting enough. "And he's not a gentleman. No gentleman would call me 'fat' when he first saw me. Seminole Chieftain, indeed! He probably sits around in a loin cloth, skinning an alligator!"

Stephanie laughed at Meg. "You call that sculpted, muscular body 'skinny'? My dear, you need strong glasses!"

This meeting with Micco wasn't going at all the way Meg had planned. In the first place, he seemed more interested in talking to her uncle than he did to her. In the second place, she didn't like what he said when he was talking to her. And she was going to have to be on a ship with him all the way to Florida!

Jim took Micco to the front desk and then up to his room, talking all the while. Micco apparently was entertaining him too, because Jim was smiling and looking interested in everything Micco had to say.

"I'll let you get settled," said Jim. "Just come down to the veranda at 12:15 and we'll go over to Leland and Stephanie's house for lunch."

"Thanks for your help. I'll see you then," replied Micco, again shaking hands.

Jim walked away thinking that if Sean had been responsible for Micco's upbringing, he had done an excellent job. Jim smiled to himself. Somehow, he thought Micco could handle a stubborn Meg, too. Meg was used to young men gawking at her, falling all over themselves. The exception was Andre Lafitte, who would never cherish Meg, but shatter all her dreams like so much confetti. Jim hoped the two men would never come to blows figuratively or physically because he knew that Andre was a dirty fighter who would do anything to win. He was clever enough to hide the dark side of his personality with a veneer of civility. But that's all it was, a veneer. Beneath the razor-thin mask was a barbarian. In the same way that Jim recognized a predator in Andre, he also recognized a civilized man, a good man in Micco. When he had the chance, he would take Micco aside to talk to him about Meg and about Andre. Maybe then Meg would have two protectors. He didn't know if Micco were capable of withstanding Andre's deviousness and treachery. He tried to shake off these gloomy thoughts as he walked to his room, but the gypsy's warning still bothered him. "Beware the dark angel" she had muttered. 'Foolish old woman,' he thought.

Meg called out to him, "I'm going with Stephanie now. I'll see you over there at 12:30."

Micco was tired. He had been studying day and night with little sleep for months, but he had passed the most rigorous written and verbal examinations and was watched intently by a team of doctors when he performed a delicate surgery, his brow being constantly mopped by a nurse. But now it was all over. The years of constant study, preparation, and performance were worth it. He had his medical diploma and he was a surgeon. Coming down on the train, he could hardly believe it. He kept pulling out his diploma and looking at it, over and over again. All of his life, ever since the day he began working for Dr. Riley and watched how he helped the sick and dying, he knew he wanted to be a doctor, too. And Dr. Riley saw his desire and his intelligence and turned his dream into reality. Micco didn't know how he could ever repay him, but he would find a way. He felt his mentor and friend's pain when the dedicated doctor could no longer work in his clinic. 'If you want me to take your place, then that's what I will do,' he vowed. Micco had received offers from prestigious schools and hospitals, including Johns Hopkins University, because he was the highest in his class. He turned them all down. No amount of money would have tempted him or prevented him from returning to help Dr. Riley.

He was exhausted, and he knew if he laid his head upon the pillow, he would never wake up in time for lunch. So he unpacked instead. Mr. Styron had told him there were bathtubs at the rear of the first floor, and that a maid would bring him hot water. 'Maybe I can soak away some of the tiredness,' he thought. He followed up on the bath and felt more refreshed. By the time he had bathed and dressed, it was 12:10. Micco wasn't particularly interested in the latest fashion as were his college contemporaries, and couldn't have afforded it if he had been, but the clothes, such as they were, clung to his muscular body as if they were custom-made. His proud carriage, inherited from his chieftain father, created the illusion of unquestionable taste in expensive clothes. Everyone on campus had imitated his style of dress, but they never asked him where he had them made. That would have been gauche. In fact, his clothes were tailor-made by his grandmother with her clever Seminole fingers. Sometimes he thought the colors too garish, but he wore them. And all over campus, bright reds, greens, and yellows dotted the quadrangle like Birds of Paradise.

He ran downstairs as lightly as a gazelle and met Jim on the porch. "Am I late?"

"No, you are right on time. I know you didn't get much rest, but after lunch, you can sleep all afternoon. Studying for your exams must have drained you." Jim and Micco talked amicably as they walked to the Carter's house. "Sean must be so proud of you. It's a wonderful accomplishment to become a physician. I know the long years of study and self-denial that it took. I am proud of you too, and I just met you." Jim patted Micco on the arm in a fatherly way.

"Thank you, Sir. It did, but the end result is worth so much more than missed parties and beer-drinking binges. Nothing can compare to the accomplishment!" spoke Micco fervently. "And I owe everything to Dr. Riley. I'll never forget that. That's why I am going back to Jupiter. Whatever he wants me to do, I will do."

"His faith in you was certainly justified. You'll like Leland. We have been friends since we were boys," Jim told Micco, as he knocked on the door.

"Like my friend, Gray Wolf. I long to see him. We are blood brothers."

Leland opened the door.

"Leland, this is Micco Ravenwing, my brother-in-law's protégé, and Micco, this is Leland Carter, a man with whom I share many boyhood secrets." Micco and Leland shook hands and exchanged greetings.

"Come in. I understand you have just received your medical degree. Congratulations!"

207

"Thank you." The three men walked into the dining room.

"I hate to have you sit right down to lunch, but Leland has to get back to the office," said Stephanie.

"I understand. Hello again, ladies!" Micco was looking at Meg with a friendly expression. He couldn't believe what a beautiful young woman she had turned out to be. When he last saw her as a twelve-year-old, she still had baby fat, wore Indian breeches and moccasins, and could swim and paddle a canoe as well as his Indian friends. He wondered if the probably empty-headed young debutante would ever place her dainty feet in a canoe again. He doubted it.

"Still amused by the chubby carrot top?" Meg asked .

"Miss Riley, my humble apologies," he said, making a deep bow. "You are not nearly as plump as you used to be and the green dress compliments your carrot, uh, I mean claret-colored hair."

"Well, of all the rude things to say. I had forgotten just how direct you were!"

"But Meg, I humbly apologized for saying you were plump and had carroty-red hair!"

"Shall we have lunch?" interrupted Stephanie, trying to choke back her laughter.

Jim went around and pulled out Meg's chair. Her expression was stormy. Leland seated Stephanie. The maid served a thick conch stew and cornbread.

"Did you make this, Stephanie?" asked Jim.

"Yes, I did."

"It is delicious and so is the crackling cornbread."

"I haven't had anything this good since I left home," added Micco wholeheartedly.

"That was fried possum and swamp cabbage, I suppose," said Meg.

"You're close," Micco said, smiling pleasantly. "It was snake and fried catfish with swamp cabbage!"

"Ugh!" Meg made a face.

"Micco, what do you plan to do when you return to Florida?" asked Leland, amused by their exchange.

"I plan on reopening Dr. Riley's clinic. It almost broke his heart to have to close it." He had eaten one bowl of soup and the maid refilled it. "Mrs. Carter, you must show me how you make the soup and the cornbread. I'll try it when I get home."

"Do you wear an apron in the kitchen?" asked Meg .

"About as often as you wear breeches and moccasins," he answered, reaching for more cornbread.

The meal was finally over without any bloodshed. Meg vehemently wished Micco had stayed in Boston. She excused herself and went with Stephanie to the kitchen.

"The nerve of him," she said to Stephanie. "Andre would never say those things. He thinks I'm beautiful. He called me his darling."

"Meg, Micco is only teasing you. He enjoys getting a rise out of you. Andre is another type of man altogether. He knows he is unbelievably good-looking. It probably feeds his vanity to have every woman fall at his feet."

"Why, Steph, I thought you liked Andre."

"I don't know that I particularly like him, but were I unattached and twenty years younger, I'd probably be smitten. Micco, on the other hand, is unbelievably good-looking too, but I don't think he is aware of it. He wouldn't even think of charming every female in sight just for the pleasure of the conquest."

"How do you know so much about him? You just met him. I thought you were on my side. Uncle Jim practically hates Andre, Leland dislikes him, and now you tell me he is shallow and vain. I don't care! I think he is the most attractive, exciting man I have ever met, and I know he is attracted to me."

Stephanie put her arm around Meg's shoulders. "Of course he's attracted to you. You're beautiful! What man wouldn't be? I don't mean to be cruel, but he would be attracted to any beautiful woman, and use his very persuasive skills to seduce her." Stephanie spoke to Meg as she would her own daughters.

"I'm not listening to this! I have a slight headache. I'm going home to lie down. Thank you for a delicious lunch."

Meg turned and left the room and Stephanie sighed. She didn't want to hurt Meg's feelings. Maybe she had been too hard on Andre. He couldn't help his looks.

"Where is Meg?" asked Jim, coming into the kitchen.

"She went home with the heart on her sleeve bleeding profusely."

Is she that upset with Micco?"

"Not that much. It was something I said about Andre. I just hope she's not too angry with me," said Stephanie anxiously.

"Andre! I had hoped when she met Micco she'd forget that scoundrel."

"She's infatuated and that's like being a horse with blinders. But don't worry, she'll get over it," said Stephanie, remembering her own youthful escapades. "She'll probably be wondering what she saw in him by the time she gets to Florida."

"But he's going with us on the same ship, and he is not going to give up until he gets what he wants. I am going to talk to Micco about it."

"You've just met him. You don't know what kind of person he really is. He appears to be honest and reliable, but you never know. What in the world would he think of your talking to him about a personal matter? I'd just let the situation remain as it is, for the moment. Meg may be blinded to Andre's faults, but I don't think for a moment that she would allow things to go too far."

Jim looked worriedly at Stephanie. "Do you really think I should keep out of it? You're right about confiding in Micco. How could I expect a perfect stranger to come charging to the rescue, to baby-sit Meg, or to challenge Andre?"

"It will work itself out. Don't worry. For the first time, your parental authority is being challenged. I'll never forget Leland threatening to buggy whip one of Lucy's boyfriends!"

"I suppose you are right. I can't talk to Micco. Thanks for the lunch." Jim sighed and walked towards the door.

"Ready, Jim?" called out Leland.

"Coming!"

The three men left and Stephanie wondered why Jim was so upset about Andre. He was no different from any other man, just more practiced than most, and more attractive than most. She shook her head and began clearing the table.

Things weren't exactly calm at the Brown's house either. Pamela had been frustrated since the hayride. Andre had not called on her and she did not intend to wait until her Aunt and Uncle's Christmas breakfast to see him. She had slept late as she always did, so her uncle had already gone to work when she arose. She knew where Andre was staying, but even she dare not visit a man's room alone.

She dressed quickly, went downstairs, and greeted Mrs. Brown. "Good morning, Aunt Jennifer."

"Good morning, dear. What would you like to eat?" Mrs. Brown had decided that all young people must sleep until noon these days. Pamela had certainly not risen before twelve since she had been here.

"I'm not really hungry. I thought I might enjoy a walk around town, just exploring."

"That's a good idea. You haven't seen much except the circus since you've been here. Why don't you see if Meg would like to go with you?"

The last person in the world Pamela wanted to see was Meg. "I hadn't thought of that. I'll certainly drop by her room. She's such a dear."

"She certainly is. Such a sweet girl. Perhaps after your walk you'll feel like eating something. You eat so little. I don't think that it's good for you to diet so strenuously. You are like Elizabeth Barrett Browning- she dined heartily on the wing of a lark."

"Dear Aunt, I am such a petite person, I don't require much. It would be disgusting if I swelled up like a fat toad."

"I don't think there is any danger in that. You are more likely to decline from consumption."

Pamela hated anyone telling her what to do. "You are just like my mother. She is always after me to stuff myself," she said ungraciously. "Well, I'm on my way." Pamela left. She was dressed all in pink from her tiny ruffled parasol to her beribboned hat.

Mrs. Brown tried to be charitable towards her niece, but it was difficult. If she were truthful, Pamela was the most spoiled, scheming child she had ever known. Her own children and grandchildren had never acted this way. Albert, however, thought she was perfectly adorable. 'He would,' she thought, 'he's a man!'

Pamela headed purposefully towards Dr. Brown's office. She entered the waiting room and walked imperiously over to the reception desk.

"May I help you?" asked Mrs. Parker in her usual disinterested voice.

"I wish to see my uncle immediately. It is of the greatest importance," said Pamela haughtily.

The nurse's eyebrows rose in astonishment. "I assume you mean Dr. Brown. He is very busy now. You'll have to wait like all the rest."

All the people in the waiting room were avidly watching the exchange. No one got past Mrs. Parker. If Queen Victoria had requested an appointment, she would have been told to wait.

"I demand to see my uncle! Tell him that his niece is here and must see him immediately!"

The nurse was about to deliver a blistering reply when Dr. Brown emerged from his consulting room. "Send in the next patient, Mrs. Parker," he said, handing her a chart and picking up another from the desk.

"Uncle Albert, I am so glad to see you. This person would not allow me to go to your office," she said, looking accusingly at the nurse.

"That's all right, Mrs. Parker. I will see Pamela for a moment. Come in, my child," he said, taking her by the arm. Pamela smiled triumphantly at Mrs. Parker as she walked away.

"Now, my dear, what seems to be the problem?" Dr. Brown asked as they both sat down.

"Well, you know that Andre took me to the circus and we had such a good time. I know he likes me, but doesn't think it proper to call on me without an invitation. Could you invite him for dinner tonight? Please, Uncle?" Pamela pleaded, her china blue eyes so imploring.

Dr. Brown wasn't even annoyed that Pamela had interrupted him at work. She was such a sweet, pretty child.

"You want me to track him down. Is that it?" he asked indulgently, smiling at her adorable face.

"It certainly would not be proper for me to do it," she said demurely.

"All right. I'll send an invitation over to his room."

"Oh, Uncle Albert, you are wonderful! I'm so happy!" she said, hugging him.

Enormously pleased, he mumbled, "Run along now. My waiting room is overflowing with patients. If he accepts the invitation, I'll tell Jennifer to prepare something special."

Pamela kissed him on the cheek and then strolled through the waiting room, looking at Mrs. Parker with a smug expression on her face.

Pamela wasn't the least bit interested in walking around by herself. She always wanted a man in tow. The sights didn't interest her. And so she was walking along, listlessly. 'This town is boring, boring, boring!' she thought, kicking at a cat that was purring and brushing against her skirt. "Scat!" she yelled angrily. The cat ran under a house and looked out at her accusingly. She didn't like animals, either. Nasty things. She passed by the sign

213

advertising the bow and arrow contest. 'Hmm. I'll get Andre to enter and win the prize. He's so strong, I know he can bend that bow just like Robin Hood.' She made her way back to the house, exhausted after a three-block walk. She pulled off her hat and fluffed up her blonde curls. Her aunt was sitting in the parlor knitting a tiny suit for her new grandbaby.

"Uncle Albert is sending an invitation to Andre for dinner tonight," she said, looking out of the corner of her eye at her aunt.

"He is? Why, he didn't ask me about it this morning."

"I reminded him of it when I dropped by his office this morning." Pamela paused. "I thought a clear soup as an appetizer, and roast duck with orange sauce, wild rice, and tiny peas, followed by lemon custard."

Jennifer dropped a stitch. "Is that all?" she asked.

"Well, I am sure Uncle Albert would have the proper wines for the dinner, already on hand."

"Don't be too disappointed, Pamela. We will probably have yesterday's leftover roast with boiled potatoes and cabbage."

Pamela stamped her tiny foot. "You can't do that. What would he think? That we are peasants?"

"Andre is a gentleman and I feel quite sure that he wouldn't care what I served as long as it was edible."

"You are such rubes here. My father and mother would serve only the best to a guest," she said, furious that her plans had been squelched.

"Pamela, I have tried to ignore remarks that you have made to me, but enough is enough. If you do not like it here, you can go back to Vassar early. I will call the headmistress to see if that is possible."

Pamela was staring at her aunt, dumbstruck. How dare she suggest that to her, her own niece! But Pamela was nothing if not a survivor. She knew when to back down, even if it almost killed her to do it.

"I'm sorry, Aunt Jennifer. I apologize for speaking to you the way I did.

Jennifer had no intention of sending her niece back to school over the holidays. Her sister, Pamela's mother, would never forgive her and Jennifer wouldn't do it anyway. Pamela would be unchaperoned in an empty dormitory building. But, she had successfully called her niece's bluff.

"Since you have apologized, we'll forget what I said. You had better go upstairs and lie down. You look worn out, though I don't know how such a brief walk could have tired you. If Andre is coming to dinner, you want to look your best. I hope Albert will give me some notice if and when Andre will be expected."

When Andre received the invitation to dinner, he wondered what to do. He had been deliberately avoiding Pamela. He didn't think he could take another minute of her inane chatter, but he didn't see how he could offer any reasonable excuse for refusing the dinner invitation. He wanted to keep on the good side of Dr. Brown. One never knew when he might be able to use the doctor to his advantage. He decided to accept. Perhaps during dinner, he could swing the conversation around to any developments concerning the murders. He ran down the steps and walked quickly to Dr. Brown's office. When he entered the waiting room, Mrs. Parker's eyes lit up.

"Good morning, Mrs. Parker. How nice to see you again."

"Good morning, Mr. Lafitte. Pleasant day, isn't it?" she asked, almost coquettishly.

"Quite pleasant," agreed Andre, amused by her reaction. "I wonder if I might have a quick word with the doctor? I know he is busy, as always, but if you could work me in, I would be most grateful."

"Have a seat. I am sure he can see you."

She returned with Dr. Brown following behind. "Good to see you, Andre," he said, as the men shook hands.

"I received your note and just wanted to let you know that I appreciate the invitation and would be most happy to join you for dinner."

"Fine." Albert smiled conspiratorially at Andre. "And I am sure Pamela will be delighted. Very pretty girl, my niece. Don't you agree?"

"Mais oui. She is as pretty as a Dresden doll. What time shall I arrive?"

"Let's say seven o'clock. I am running behind at the office."

"Until seven then." He turned to Mrs. Parker. "It was a pleasure seeing you again. Goodbye."

He left with Mrs. Parker staring after him.

Meg had fretted all afternoon and Micco sank into a deep sleep as soon as his head touched the pillow. He never moved until Jim knocked on his door six hours later. Micco heard the knocking as if from a far place. He shook his head groggily.

"Uh, just a minute." He sat up slowly, trying to get his bearings. Finally, he got up, feeling as if he had been drugged, and walked over to open the door.

"Sorry to have awakened you," said Jim, noticing Micco's half-closed eyes. "Maybe I should have just let you sleep. We're going to dinner next door at the boarding house and thought you would like to join us. My treat."

"Yes, of course. I'd like that. Shall I meet you downstairs in, say, twenty minutes?"

"Fine. We'll be sitting on the porch, enjoying the twilight. Take your time. We're in no rush."

Jim left and Micco poured water from the pitcher on the washstand into the basin and dashed cold water in his face. He was more awake, but still felt tired. 'I may have to sleep twenty-four hours before I am rested,' he thought. Actually, he wished Jim had let him sleep, but he was too polite to refuse his kind offer. He changed his shirt and put on a somewhat subdued green and yellow shirt with a floral design and a deeper green waistcoat. Those were his grandmother's two favorite colors, and this was probably the least lurid outfit in his wardrobe. He decided that

216

since the boarding house was next door, he would go hatless. He hoped Jim would not think that boorish of him. After a quick bath, he carefully combed back his thick, straight hair. In exactly twenty minutes, he walked onto the porch. Sleeping in snatches and dressing in a hurry had become second nature to him in med school.

Jim and Meg were rocking in rocking chairs and talking quietly. Micco took a deep breath of the crisp, fresh evening air. He could smell the salt water and suddenly, he was homesick for Jupiter. He hadn't really allowed himself to dwell on his home, his grandmother, Gray Wolf, or Dr. Riley too much. Sometimes he had longed to swim in the lagoon, to fish for trout or flounder, to confide in Gray Wolf. He had been terribly homesick when he left home at seventeen. He had never been anywhere outside of Jupiter before. He was not to return again until ten and a half years later. He had finished undergraduate school in two and a half years, going summer and winter. Then he had buried himself in four years of medical school and four years studying to be a surgeon. Now he was going home. He was startled from his reverie.

"Shall we go?" asked Jim.

"I'm sorry. I was thinking about home. I have been gone for more than ten years." He looked over at Meg as they were walking to the dining room. "Hello, Re-, Meg."

"Hello. Did you rest well?" After talking to her uncle, Meg was trying to be polite.

"Like an alligator buried in the mud, but I feel as though I could sleep all day and night. How about you? Did you rest well?"

"Yes," said Meg untruthfully.

She didn't seem inclined to talk further, so Micco talked with Jim about Jupiter. The more Jim got to know Micco, the more he liked him. They talked of floundering with a gas lantern and a gig as opposed to fishing on the bottom with a hook and line. They reached the dining room and the waitress showed them to a table. This time, they sat at a small table for three and the waitress began bringing bowls and platters of food as she had before.

"How are you, Maryanne?"

"Oi'm foin." She was staring at Micco and thought that Meg must be the luckiest person in the world to know two such handsome men as that Frenchman and this dark, tall man with the broad shoulders and eyelashes any girl would die for.

Micco was amazed at the bountiful amount of food, and Jim explained to him about family style. Meg was looking around the room, hoping to see Andre, not knowing that at this time, he was dining with the China doll.

Halfway through the meal, Meg saw Molly beckoning from the kitchen. Meg excused herself and both men rose, Micco pulling out her chair for her.

"Molly, how are you? Are you getting ready for Christmas?"

"I is. Been pourin' mo' wine on my fruitcakes. They be jist right on Christmas Day. All my chilluns 'en granchilluns, 'en great grancilluns gonna be at my nephew's house. My pound cake be jist right. Weren't no sad cake."

"What is a sad cake?"

"If it fall while it be bakin', I calls it a sad cake. Heh, heh, heh!" Molly looked sly. "Who be dat good-lookin' mans at de table?"

Meg glanced dismissively towards Micco. "That's Micco Ravenwing. He has just gotten his medical degree and is going back to Florida with us." Her eyes were still seeking out Andre.

"A doctor! I sho would like to talk 'bout medicine with him. Kin you git him to meet ole' Molly?"

"Now?"

"Ain't no betta time."

"Well. All right. I'll get him." Meg went back to the table.

"Micco, there is someone in the kitchen who would like to meet you."

Jim smiled. "Go ahead, Micco. It will be an experience you won't forget."

Micco got up obediently and followed Meg to the kitchen.

"Molly, this is Micco Ravenwing, and Micco, this is Miss Molly Gillikin."

"How do you do, Miss Gillikin?" said Micco politely.

"I be jist fine, 'un you kin call me Miss Molly. You is a doctor?"

"Yes and please call me Micco."

Quick as a rabbit, Molly asked, "What does you use to treat de ear ache?"

Micco didn't hesitate. "I get some mussels and boil them, then pour the cooled liquid into the ear."

"Lawsy, dat's right! If a mans come in and be all cut up, what does you use?"

"Pork fat soaked in turpentine," said Micco, smiling at Molly.

"Well, dey finely got a sho nuff doctor here."

Meg was listening to this exchange in utter disbelief.

"I doesn't want to disturb you alls dinner now, but if you gits de time, come back to see Miss Molly. I wants to talk 'bout my serus cases."

"I would be happy to, Miss Molly."

Molly thought to herself, 'Dis be a smart man and de best lookin' one I has seen. Dat Meg betta grab dis 'un."

"Is you and Miss Meg good friends?" she asked, her bird-like eyes darting from one to another.

"We have known each other since we were children," said Micco. "But this is the first time we've seen each other since ten years ago."

"Hmp. You betta requaint youselfs. Mr. Micco, you is 'bout as tall as a haystack. Make Miss Meg look small. Heh, heh, heh!"

Meg stood up. She and Micco had been sitting at the table with Molly. She refused to look at Micco who, she was sure, was thoroughly enjoying Molly's comments.

"It has been nice talking to you, but we have to finish dinner. Goodbye!" Meg marched back to the table.

"I enjoyed meeting you and talking about medicine with you," said Micco. "I'll certainly come back to hear about your cases."

"You is nice. I likes you," said Molly flirtatiously. "I be ninety-five years old, but I still likes to look at a purty man."

"Thank you, Miss Molly. I like you, too. Goodbye!" He smiled at the tiny old lady and went back to the table.

Molly said to herself, 'And he be a real doctor, too!"

When Micco came back to the table, Meg asked, "What in the world were you telling her about curing an ear ache and treating cuts?"

"Those are my grandmother's remedies. People who live somewhat removed from civilization must use what is available. Miss Molly and my grandmother are kindred spirits, so to speak."

Jim thought it was both clever and thoughtful of Micco to have sensed Molly's feelings about medicine. If he had given some modern medical school treatment in response to Molly's questions, Molly would have considered Micco a 'quack'. As it was, she respected him, and he respected her. 'Micco's patients will love him,' thought Jim. 'Why couldn't Meg admire him?"

They finally finished the meal and Micco's eyes were beginning to close in spite of his best efforts to keep them open.

"You are going straight to bed and sleep until you wake up. I won't wake you for breakfast or lunch either, if you're still sleeping," said Jim kindly.

"Thank you for the dinner. Sorry I wasn't better company," said Micco, stifling a yawn.

"You were great company. I haven't enjoyed myself so much in a long time. Sleep well. Good night!"

"Good night, Mr. Styron. Good night, Meg."

He wearily made his way to his room. He pulled off all his clothes and slid under the covers. Then he remembered to snuff out the candle before sleep overtook him.

Chapter Thirteen

At the Brown's home, Andre was being charming to all. He praised the roast beef and discussed Oriental art. He wondered how Dr. Brown could be both doctor and coroner. He flattered Pamela, hoping it wouldn't backfire if he had to spend more time with her. He did end up having to agree to enter the bow and arrow shooting contest.

"Are you familiar with the bow and arrow?" asked Dr. Brown.

"I do have some experience with it," said Andre. He had had experience with every kind of weapon.

"Then you must enter the contest tomorrow," cried Pamela, clapping her hands.

"Every year at Christmas time, we have a bow and arrow contest. You shoot at a bull's eye target and the one who hits the bull's eye dead center wins a turkey or goose," explained Dr. Brown.

"I see. That should be no problem. How far away is the target?"

"I believe it is seventy-five or one hundred yards. It could be farther."

"Oh, Andre. I just know you can win," said Pamela, looking at him admiringly.

"It's at five o'clock tomorrow. If you are going to participate, I will close my office a little early to watch the event."

"I'll join the party, too," said Mrs. Brown.

"Good. Andre, come by here at 4:40 and we'll go in my horse and buggy. If you don't have other plans, we could go to Miss Amy's boarding house for dinner afterwards."

Dr. Brown was starting to think that Andre might be a good prospective husband for his niece. She'd do well to get such a fine young man. He was more impressed each time he talked with him.

Andre was in a quandry. He didn't want to get more involved with Pamela even though he would be leaving in a few weeks. He had better sense than to get in bed with an all-too-willing seventeen-year-old. He had not seen Meg since their tête-à-tête on Saturday. She was probably feeling guilty because she thought she had been too forward. Andre had to laugh at that. He hadn't been able to figure out how he could see her before the Christmas breakfast. He couldn't very well go knocking on her bedroom door. Women always complicated things, especially a woman protected by a would-be avenging uncle. Perhaps she would be at the contest tomorrow. If so, he would find a way to talk to her. He wanted to see her again. Meg was very appealing and when he had kissed her, he wanted more. He would have to find some way to get rid of the clinging Pamela, momentarily.

Andre thanked Mrs. Brown for a wonderful meal and made plans to meet for the contest. He wished he were already on his way to Jupiter before things became too involved. Jim, Meg, Micco, the Alligoods, and the Days were also planning to watch the contest.

The next day Meg was sitting on the window seat, looking out the window. The bright, cool morning held no charm for her. She watched listlessly as a fishing boat entered the harbor. Its nets, piled up in the stern, were still wet from the sea and they glistened in the sunlight. A Christmas tree, trimmed with shells, painted fishing corks, and candles stood atop the cabin. Even this picturesque sight did not delight Meg. She desperately wanted to see Andre. She brightened a little at the thought that maybe he would be at the shooting contest. She thought he probably liked sports of any kind since he had told her he was an outdoor person.

She had already dressed, unable to sleep, and so decided to sit on the porch downstairs until Jim came down. It was only nine in the morning and Meg was amazed to see little Miss Priss, dressed in baby blue, mincing along.

"Good morning, Meg. Lovely day, isn't it?" said Pamela.

"It is lovely. I didn't think you ever rose in time to see it," 'How much worse could her day get?' she wondered. She tried to blot out the vision in blue.

"You are mistaken. I often stroll about, breathing in this delightful salt air. Andre likes it, too."

"Oh, really?" Meg was more irritated than ever by this remark.

"As a matter of fact, he is taking me to the bow and arrow shooting contest today. He is going to enter it and I know he will win. Will we see you there? I do hope you are going. It will be so exciting to watch Andre as he bends the bow with his strong arms."

"I am looking forward to it with great interest," said Meg .
Jim's face brightened at the sight of Pamela as he walked onto the porch.

"Jim, how are you? Isn't it a lovely day?" Pamela's smile was as sweet as a sugar plum and she swung her dainty parasol.

He thought what a charming picture she made with her saucy blue hat and a tiny boot peeping out from her full ruffled skirt.

"It is indeed. And are you enjoying your morning walk?"

"Oh, yes. Your town is so charming. I do love to explore it. I am so interested in everything."

"Have you had breakfast yet? Will you join Meg and me? Then we can all take a walk together."

"I'd love to," said Pamela, looking up flirtatiously at him.

Meg grimaced as Pamela took Jim's arm. They walked to the dining room with Pamela chattering like a monkey. Meg managed to finish her cup of tea without committing mayhem.

Then she pled a headache and retired to her room. Jim gallantly escorted the simpering Pamela back to her house.

The day dragged by and Meg remained in her room, moping, writing letters, or staring out the window. She told her uncle she didn't want lunch when he knocked on the door. Finally, at three, she emerged. Micco was awake and refreshed for the first time in weeks. Jim had engaged a carriage and by 4:15, the Days and Alligoods had arrived and were waiting outside in their carriage.

Jim was sitting, holding the reins as Meg and Micco came downstairs. Micco helped Meg into the carriage, then sat down beside her. She was surprised that he was sitting with her instead of up front with her uncle.

"Hello," the occupants of the other carriage called out to them.

Jim said, "I'll introduce you to Micco when we get there. We don't want to be late. We'll follow you."

"Okay," answered Ralph who was driving the other buggy. "Tally ho! Giddap!" He flicked the reins and the horses trotted off.

Jim followed behind them. They clopped along the shell street and the wind fluttered against the coach curtains, gently tousling Meg's curls.

"Have you ever been to a turkey and goose shoot before?" asked Meg.

Micco turned his head to look at her. His eyes were so dark they looked almost as black as his hair. 'They are warm, friendly eyes,' thought Meg. 'I remember how sympathetic they could be. I also remember how they sparked with anger. They flashed like a thunder cloud at Gray Wolf when I fell into the water.' He really was handsome with his high cheekbones and bronzed skin. With a start, Meg realized it was an aristocratic face, the face of a proud chieftain.

Now the eyes gleamed in amusement. "Remember, Meg. I was an Indian boy. We all learned how to shoot and hunt at an early age. My father, Tall Chief, taught me and he was the best of the hunters," said Micco proudly. "We had many contests among ourselves and with white men. Sometimes we used guns, but mostly we shot with bows and arrows."

"You must have really been close to your father," said Meg, feeling a little envious.

"Yes, I was. He was a loving father and a very intelligent man. I missed him so when he died, I felt that my support and my strength had been taken from me. If it hadn't been for your father, I don't know what would have happened to me."

"I never even knew that he had taken you in, so to speak. I was really surprised when we received the telegram from father, telling us that you had become a doctor."

"I can hardly believe it myself. I keep pulling out my diploma and reading it over and over."

"Are you a general practitioner?"

"Yes, but I also specialized. I am a surgeon."

"Micco, that's wonderful! What an accomplishment. Father must be puffed up like a peacock with pride."

"He told me that he expected nothing but the best from me."

"And you gave him the best." Meg felt happy for the first time in two days. She didn't know why she had been so angry with Micco when he called her 'plump' and carrot top', because she knew deep inside that he was only teasing her affectionately. In retrospect, she supposed that it was because she was no longer a little girl. She had wanted Micco to look at her and treat her as if she were a woman.

"I could have done nothing less. Not only was I grateful that he had rescued me, but I grew to respect and admire him."

They rode along in companionable silence, each thinking of the same man, but in different ways. Meg found it hard to reconcile the picture painted by Micco of a caring man. As far as she knew, her father had never really cared for her.

"Meg."

"What is it?"

"I was teasing you when I first saw you, but I couldn't resist. You always were so teasable. You are a beautiful woman, and not the least bit plump. Your hair is an extraordinary shade of red, like autumn leaves, or sparkling burgundy," said Micco, looking at Meg admiringly.

"Oh Micco. What a lovely compliment."

"Am I forgiven, my little Meg, for treating you so shabbily?"

"Yes," she said laughing.

"But you were a plump, adorable little redhead who used to follow me around like a puppy," he said, his eyes again full of mischief.

The brief moment of flirtation was over and Meg felt disappointed. What did she expect, an admission of devout admiration? This was Micco, after all, who had been like an older brother to her. Meg decided that she must be as fickle as pouting Pamela. She was swept off her feet by Andre, and yet wanted Micco to show a romantic interest in her. 'Oh, woman, thy name is vanity!' Meg thought.

They felt the steady clip-clop of the horses slow down.

"Here we are," called out Jim, bringing the horses to a halt. He jumped down and tethered the horses to a tree. Micco helped Meg down from the buggy. At least a dozen horses and carriages were there, along with horse-drawn carts filled with shouting children and men on horseback wearing ten-gallon hats. The Days and Alligoods were walking towards them.

Ralph said, "Let's find a good vantage point. What a crowd! I think just about everybody in town is here. They are having boxing and wrestling matches, too."

"They are? I have heard about them, but have never seen one," said Meg.

"You don't want to, either. They don't follow the Duke of Queensbury's Rules, believe me. That's taking place way over on the other side. It is strictly for men's viewing only, Meg. Even if it were proper for you to attend, I don't think you would enjoy seeing two men beat each other to a bloody pulp."

"No, I certainly wouldn't." Meg was walking between Jim and Micco, holding onto their arms and talking animatedly about the coming event. She was smiling up at Micco.

"Micco, do you think…" she stopped in mid-sentence. Andre was standing three feet in front of her with Pamela hanging onto him like a leech.

Andre was staring at Micco. He was filled with a jealous rage. There was Meg, his woman, holding this tall dark man's arm possessively and smiling at him flirtatiously.

Pamela, prepared to flaunt her close association with Andre, was taken aback by the sight of Micco, a man just as handsome as Andre.

"Hello again, Pamela. You look quite fetching this afternoon. May I present Micco Ravenwing?" said Jim.

Micco smiled pleasantly at Pamela and said, "How do you do?"

Pamela too, was consumed with jealousy. She had wanted to humiliate Meg, but Meg appeared on the arm of this gorgeous man. Well, she'd see about that.

She beamed coquettishly at Micco, batting her eyelashes and giving him the full benefit of her beautiful blue eyes. "I do very well, thank you, and how do you do?"

Micco was amused by Pamela. He had known so many women like her, always trying to make a conquest. "I do quite well too, Pamela."

"And this is Andre Lafitte. Micco Ravenwing," Jim continued with the introductions. He was watching both men intently. The two men shook hands and exchanged greetings, but neither smiled.

Andre turned to Meg. "How are you, Meg? You look absolutely breathtaking in green. It is your color," he said, his eyes full of admiration and something else.

Meg caught her breath. "Hello, Andre. Thank you for the compliment. I understand that you are entering the bow and arrow contest." She wondered how she could speak so calmly. She had been longing to see him for five days. Now here he was, handsome, appealing, and on the arm of Pamela, practically in her arms.

"Yes, I am. It seems that everyone else has the same idea. The competition will be tough," he said, his eyes still fastened on Meg, as if to mesmerize her.

"But Andre will win, you may be sure of that," interrupted Pamela, holding Andre even more possessively.

Jim hadn't even greeted Andre. "Well, we must find a good viewing spot. Let's go, children," he said, deliberately using a word that conveyed closeness to both Meg and Micco.

They walked off and joined their friends who had already chosen a place to stand.

"Micco, will you do me a favor?"

"Of course, Mr. Styron. What is it?"

"I want you to go over and sign up for the contest, too." Jim knew that Micco had probably grown up knowing how to shoot a bow and arrow. That would certainly have been one of the first things his father would have taught him.

"You want me to enter the contest? But why? I'm just here to enjoy watching the skills of all the others."

"Let's just say that it would give me personal satisfaction. Think of me as your surrogate father, out to enjoy his son's performance."

Micco really liked Jim. He had taken an instant liking to him and he appreciated Jim's remark about feeling fatherly towards him.

"If that is what you desire, I'll do it. But don't expect too much. You realize that I haven't picked up a bow and arrow in ten years or more." Grinning to himself, Micco walked over to the registration table.

"I'd like to sign up for the bow and arrow contest," he said to the man sitting behind the table.

"What's the name?" asked the attendant, picking up a quill pen and preparing to write.

"Micco Ravenwing."

"Oh. You're already signed up and paid for," said the man, reading the list.

"I can't be," said Micco, looking puzzled.

"Yes, you are. That man standing right over there paid the fee and gave your name to me at the Episcopal Church office yesterday." The Episcopal Church was sponsoring the event.

Micco turned in the direction that the attendant was pointing and looked into the eyes of a broadly smiling Jim.

"Well, I didn't know that. What do I do?" asked Micco.

"You got your own bow and arrow?"

"No, I don't, not here."

"We've got a selection over on that next table. Pick out what you want. Most of the smaller bows are already gone. Only the big ones, the long bows are left, and they're hard to pull, but you look like a strong fellow. Probably won't be no problem for you. You'll only need one arrow, though."

"Thanks," said Micco. He walked over and examined the bows. He picked up the biggest one, pulling the bowstring back slightly. He put that aside and then looked through the arrows carefully. Finally, he picked up one, felt the thickness of the feathers, and touched the tip. He held it up to his eye and sighted down the length of the arrow. It was straight and evenly rounded. He took that one and the long bow back to the attendant who copied down the number that had been marked on them beside Micco's name.

Andre had already made his selection and had taken his place in the line of contestants. Micco was the last one in line.

Meg and Jim, the Days and Alligoods were joined by Dr. and Mrs. Brown and Pamela. Albert and Jennifer had been talking to friends and had not met Micco. The cold, crisp air was filled with excited voices, speculating on who would win the contest.

"My money is on Andre," said Dr. Brown.

"Mine, too," said Pamela. "No one can beat him!"

Thomas Alligood said, "I think Dallas Smith will win. That fellow's arms are as big as tree trunks."

"Yes, he'll be the winner," agreed Ralph.

"You ministers stick together. He hasn't got a chance against Andre."

"Want to make a little bet?" asked Ralph. "Two dollars says Dallas will win!"

"Ralph!" said Lois Jean in a shocked voice. "You can't be gambling. What would the church members think?"

"Placing my faith in someone's ability is not a mortal sin," replied Ralph.

"He's right, dear," said Martha, the more liberal Episcopal minister's wife. "Besides, you'll contribute your winnings to the Episcopal Children's Fund, won't you?" Martha asked with a twinkle in her eye.

"You got me! The Baptist minister agrees to give his winnings to the Episcopal Church. Is that all right, Lois Jean?"

"I guess so," she said .

"I'd like to place a wager, too," said Jim. "I think that Micco will win and here is five dollars to prove it."

"Who is Micco?" asked Albert.

"You're on. I'm betting five dollars on Dallas. How about you, Thomas?" asked Ralph.

"I'm in, too," agreed Thomas. "Five dollars on Dallas."

"Oh, my. These high stakes cause my head to spin!" said Jennifer. "Our church coffers will be overflowing. I'd like to know who Micco is, too."

"I didn't get a chance to introduce you. He is a protégé of my brother-in-law. He has just completed his medical degree and is returning to Florida with us."

"I'll be looking forward to meeting a colleague," said Albert.

"He's already discussed some of his medical procedures with Molly Gillikin," Meg said.

"You don't say?" Dr. Brown remarked, looking surprised.

Pamela was extremely annoyed at the turn of conversation. "You'll all lose your money if you bet against Andre. That man doesn't have a chance against him. I am betting ten dollars." Her aunt and uncle stared at her, astonished by her wager.

"That is a great deal of money to spend for anything, much less a wager," said her aunt. "I don't believe your mother would approve."

"Maman and Papa let me do as I please. Here is my ten dollars," said the spoiled Pamela. She had no intention of being prevented from doing what she wanted.

"I suppose I'll have to up my wager to five dollars on Andre," said Albert.

"Look, the announcer has walked up to the shooting range," cried Pamela excitedly.

Meg had mixed emotions. She wanted Andre to win and yet she would hate to see Micco lose.

The announcer began speaking.

"Today we are having our annual turkey and goose shoot. As you know, the proceeds will go to pay for Christmas dinners for needy folks in our community. I am happy to say that contributions have exceeded last year. Many of you gave money who are not participating in the shoot. As a representative of our church, we all thank you, even the Methodists who contributed."

Everyone laughed. "But seriously, we are appreciative of your generosity in this Christmas season. Now we are about to begin the contest. As you can see, a target has been placed 100 yards away. Each shooter gets one shot only. The man who hits the bull's eye, dead center, will be the winner. We have two markers who will come over after each shot. They have the name of each marksman on a separate piece of paper that has a target drawn on it. The markers will indicate on the paper targets where each arrow hit. They will withdraw the arrow from the target after each shot. Gentlemen, are you ready? Number one, please step up to the line and shoot."

The crowd watched expectantly as Willie Jones stepped up. He was a small man but he had muscular arms. He lined up the target and pulled back the bowstring. The arrow hit the outside circle and the crowd sighed. The markers noted the position on their papers and then removed the arrow.

"Next," said the announcer.

The shooting continued with none hitting close to the bull's eye. Dallas Smith was number ten. He stepped up to the shooting line, full of confidence. He smiled and waved to his friends. Then he turned and lifted his bow and arrow. Carefully, he lined up the target and then pulled back the string. He released the arrow and it found its mark on the circle nearest the bull's eye. The crowd cheered and Dallas took a bow.

Ralph and Thomas were grinning and patting each other on the back.

"You see? I told you so. Dallas is the best," Ralph said, gloating to Jim and Albert.

"But Andre hasn't shot yet," said Albert confidently.

"It's a lost cause, Albert. Give it up," kidded his friend, Thomas. They got quiet as the next shooter tried to hit the mark. All failed, with none coming as close as Dallas.

Andre was next. He too, stepped up confidently. He turned and smiled at Meg and Pamela. Then, raising his bow and fitting the arrow in the notch, he took careful aim. The arrow found its mark on the outside edge of the bull's eye. The crowd went wild and Ralph and Thomas looked at each other sheepishly.

"You lose, gentlemen," said a beaming Albert. Pamela was jumping up and down. She could hardly wait to bestow a kiss on the winner.

"Not so fast," said Jim. "The contest isn't over yet."

"Jim, nobody can best that mark," said Albert.

"We shall see."

The next four shooters missed the mark. Only Micco was left to shoot. Micco stepped up to the line. He looked like a Seminole warrior, proud and assured. The crowd grew very quiet, aware that this was no ordinary marksman. The bow and arrow seemed a natural part of him. Micco sighted the bull's eye as he had deer in the forest. His powerful muscles rippled as he pulled back the bowstring until the bow was almost bent in half. Then he released the string.

Meg could hear the zinging noise as it flew towards its target. Andre was staring at the arrow's flight. Every eye was glued to the target. The arrow found its mark and quivered slightly as it struck the center of the bull's eye. The crowd roared, stomped, and whistled.

"Well, gentlemen. I don't think we need to compare marks. Number 20's arrow hit dead center. Congratulations, young man!" Ben said, shaking Micco's hand. "That was the best shooting I've ever seen. Which do you want- a goose or a turkey?"

"Thank you, Sir," Micco turned to Meg. "Which shall I choose?"

Embarrassed to be in the limelight, Meg spoke softly. "Stephanie had said she wanted to have a goose for Christmas dinner."

"The goose it is," said Micco to Ben. Micco accepted the goose, amid much clapping.

"And second place winner goes to number ten. That was mighty fancy shooting, too," said Ben, walking over to Andre. He handed him the turkey, and again the crowd clapped.

"Thank you," said Andre, taking the turkey. He had to force out the words because he was so furious that he had lost. His glance at Micco was murderous. No one ever bested Andre, especially in front of a woman he wanted to impress. He gained control of himself.

235

"I believe Dr. and Mrs. Brown would like a Christmas turkey." He presented the turkey to Albert who smiled at Andre's gracious offer, even though he hadn't won first place.

Pamela was pouting because he hadn't given her the turkey and because she didn't get to kiss him for winning first place. He didn't look in the mood to be kissed and Pamela thought she had better not try.

Jim, grinning like a schoolboy who had won at marbles, shook Micco's hand. "Congratulations, Micco. I never believed for one minute that you wouldn't win."

"I'm glad I did, since you entered me in the contest."

"Congratulations, Micco. That was an amazing shot." Meg spoke, smiling at him and held out her hand. He took it and held it.

"Doesn't the conquering hero at least get a kiss on the cheek?"

"Oh, I guess so." She looked up at Micco and turned her cheek to him.

Micco quickly ducked his head and kissed her lightly on the lips. "A kiss for my little sister," he said.

Both Andre and Pamela had watched as Micco kissed Meg. "Well, it looks like poor Meg has at last found herself a beau," said Pamela.

"Hardly. She just met him," replied Andre coldly.

"No. From what I understand, she knew him as a child in Florida."

This was news to Andre, and it complicated things. "Really. And why is he here?"

"He has just finished school and is sailing on the ship with them to Jupiter." This really displeased Andre. He was planning to use that time with Meg to plead his case, which was, of course, not marriage. Now he had this man who would not be intimidated, he thought. He had known men like him who appeared quiet and non-violent, but when pressed, were dangerous. Andre would not make a mistake with him, but when the time was right, he would

236

act accordingly. He would find a way to toss Micco to the sharks, perhaps a drug in his brandy. He would be so upset when Ravenwing was found missing. By that time, it would be too late. Andre smiled with satisfaction.

"You are smiling, Andre. I'm glad you're not angry. You almost beat him and I know if they had another contest, you would," said Pamela, looking at him sympathetically.

"These things happen. As you say, next time I will have my revenge."

Many people were leaving, but others walked down to watch the boxing and wrestling matches.

"Would you mind terribly if I stayed to watch some of the matches?" Andre asked the Browns, as they all walked back to the carriage.

"Not at all, my boy. You deserve it. We'll dine later then. Meet us at my house at 7:45 and we'll walk over to Miss Amy's dining room. Can you get back all right?"

"Yes, maybe Dallas will give me a ride. I saw him going that way." Andre wasn't in the mood to go with Pamela and the Browns at the moment. He needed to work off the rage inside him. He thought watching two men beat each other until the blood ran down their faces would help.

"Can't I go, too?" asked Pamela.

"Certainly not!" said Mrs. Brown. "That is no place for a young lady, any lady, for that matter!"

Pamela's lip curled up and she was about to say something very unladylike. Andre touched her arm.

"Pamela, it is not a sight for a well-bred young lady. Your aunt is correct."

"That's not fair!" She scowled, stamping her foot.

"Come along, my dear. You'll be seeing Andre a little later," said her uncle. They left and Jim and his friends left.

Meg again rode with Micco. She was quiet, thinking about Andre. Once again, she was frustrated, not being able to talk to him alone. The only time she knew for sure that she would see him was at Dr. Brown's Christmas breakfast, and she'd never really be able to talk to him privately. Micco interrupted her unhappy thoughts.

"How long do you intend to visit at Jupiter?"

Meg looked surprised. "Why, permanently."

It was Micco's turn to look surprised. "You're going to live in Jupiter? Not that I am trying to discourage you, but won't you be bored? Once you've explored the lighthouse, there's not much to do."

"I intend to open a school for the children in the village. I just received my teaching degree."

"Does your uncle approve of this idea? He seems so devoted to you that I'd think he would find it difficult for you to move to Florida."

"You too! Obviously, nobody thinks I am capable of doing anything on my own- my aunt and uncle, my father, and now you," said Meg, annoyed to have her thoughts interrupted, and annoyed at what he said. Maybe she was being unfair to Micco. He could just be curious or even be making polite conversation. She didn't think he actually cared. Meg didn't really understand him. On the surface, he appeared carefree, lighthearted. He was always teasing her, never serious, and yet she knew he had worked hard, never deviating from his purpose for more than ten years. Her father, and uncle too, apparently thought the sun rose and set on him.

"Meg, I don't doubt for a moment that you can make a success at whatever you do. If I appeared to be criticizing you, I am sorry. I was just under the impression that you were simply going for a short visit. Your father must be delighted that you are coming home at last."

"Ha! He wouldn't care if I never returned. He was only to glad to be rid of an inconvenience."

"That's not true. He loves you and has always loved you. He just felt inadequate to take care of a female child. He thought your aunt and uncle could provide a stable home for you, more so than he could."

"You know so much about it! You think you know how he felt. You were only a child yourself. I really know how he felt. I was unwanted by both my parents. They never had time for me because their precious clinic meant more to them than I did. They had each other and did not need a child to interfere in their lives."

"You are wrong! I know they loved you. Your father talked about you all the time. He missed you terribly when you left."

"There is no use discussing this any further. You don't know! I don't want to argue with you, Micco. I am so glad to see you after all these years. Everyone was impressed by your prowess with the bow and arrow today."

"How about you? You didn't seem too impressed. I noticed you watching that blonde giant. He was the one you wanted to win, wasn't he?"

'Micco doesn't miss anything,' Meg thought. How could he have seen her watching Andre? She thought she had been quite circumspect. "I don't know what you mean. I was watching everybody."

"Yes you do. He is something special to you, isn't he?" asked Micco.

"What difference does it make to you?"

"I'm just taking a brotherly interest in you, Meg. I might have to call him out if he doesn't behave like a gentleman," said Micco, once again teasing her.

"Of all the nerve! You are not my brother. I don't need you fighting any battle for me. Between you and my uncle, poor Andre is surely set upon."

"Your uncle doesn't like him, either?"

"I didn't know you didn't like him," said Meg, avoiding the question.

"Perhaps that was too strong a response. I don't know the man. All I can say is that we did not have instant rapport."

"Let's change the subject. I can't believe that Saturday is Christmas. Tomorrow night, Stephanie and Leland are going to light the candles on their tree and she'll be serving hot cider and some refreshments. We've already decorated most of the tree. I know they'll invite you, too."

"They already have. I'm really looking forward to it. We didn't observe much of a Christmas in my home. My father and mother had converted to Christianity, but they still clung to the old gods- spirits of the forest, the wind, the water, the sun and moon, especially the spirits of animals. Tall Chief, my father, had faith that he would go to the Happy Hunting Ground as he lay dying. He believed in the Great Spirit, a supreme being. He was the Giver and Taker away of life, and as designated by the ancient Aztecs, 'The God by whom We Live'."

Meg was interested in this approach to religion. "That is not so different from the Christian belief. We both believe in a supreme being. What did they think about the creation of man?"

"The Seminole conception of man's and woman's creation is quite unusual. Eons ago, when there was only earth, air, and water, E-shock-e-tom-isee, probably the Sun God, took many seeds and scattered them by the four winds over a fertile river valley. After a while, God saw fingers reaching up from the ground. Soon hundreds of people rose up from the sand. Some of these went to the river and washed. They scrubbed and washed for many days, too much, because it made them weak and pale. They became es-ta-chat-tee, or the white race. Others went to the river, too, but they did not wash as much. They returned full of courage, strong and powerful, the true Indian brave. These were the es-ta-had-kee, the red race. The remainder of the sand people did not wash at all and they were the es-ta-lus-tee, or black people." Micco smiled at Meg, watching her reaction to this Indian tale of creation.

"That is fascinating. I want to learn all I can about the Seminoles when I reach Jupiter Inlet. Maybe some of the children can help me in the school as you helped my father. I really am excited by the prospect of opening a school, Micco. It means so much to me."

240

"I am glad you are interested in my race. The Seminoles are a truly gentle race, an intelligent race. They rose up against the white man because of treachery and betrayal. I often mourn for Osceola, though he died before I was born," said Micco .

"But I feel the same way. Ask my uncle. He has become wearied by my constant defense of Osceola and his braves."

"You see how much we have in common, little sister. We shall get along famously, if you don't kill me before we reach Jupiter. Me big, strong brave; you little, weak white girl."

"What do you mean, 'weak'? I'll bet I'm as strong as any of your Indian girlfriends!"

"Meg, you wound me to the quick! I didn't leave any girlfriends behind. I found lady friends in Boston, but they were prone to the vapors and afraid to walk in the rain for fear of getting wet. I am sure my Indian girlfriends will be strong and hardy, as well as beautiful, when I meet them upon my return!"

Meg simply glared at him, biting her tongue to keep from making a scathing retort. By now, they had reached the Davis House.

"We're home," called out Jim. "I'm going to return the horse and carriage to the hostler. Want to come along and walk back with me, Micco?"

"Yes, I would. You can show me the sights around town. I feel rested and full of energy since I finally caught up on my sleep!"

"You certainly had strength when you pulled that longbow back. It is a wonder the arrow didn't split the target."

Micco smiled. "It would take a Hercules to do that."

He helped Meg down. She almost refused to take his hand she was so annoyed with him, but she was afraid she would trip on her long skirt.

"Get some rest, dear," said her uncle, as Micco climbed up beside him.

Meg wanted to slap Micco's grinning face. Weak white woman, indeed. She'd show him. She ran up to her room, plopped face down on the bed, and pounded the pillow instead.

Jim and Micco rode along companionably. "I'll say it again. That was a truly remarkable shot you made today. I was particularly pleased that you beat Lafitte."

"He didn't take defeat too well. Dallas and others shook my hand and congratulated me. Andre looked as though he would like to challenge me to a duel of pistols at ten paces."

"If he had, he's probably have shot you in the back before you turned," replied Jim grimly.

"I take it you don't like him very much?"

"I don't like him at all. In fact, I dislike him intensely."

Micco was startled by the vehemence in Jim's tone. He had sensed animosity between the two, but not to that extent.

"Any particular reason?"

Jim had told Stephanie that he wouldn't take Micco into his confidence, to try to enlist his aid in the campaign against Andre. He had intended to keep his worries to himself, but Micco had such an air of sympathy that it was too tempting not to enlist the young man's aid, if he could.

"To be perfectly frank, Micco, I think he is totally without conscience. I believe that he would rob or even kill, without a qualm."

"Surely not! I can sense that he is a cold man and one who is used to having his own way, but a murderer?"

"I am convinced of it. But what really frightens me is that he is after Meg, and his intentions are anything but honorable."

"Have you spoken to her about it?"

"Yes, but she won't believe me. She will not hear a word spoken against him. She has promised me that she will not give in to his advances, and I believe she means it. But the man is so fatally attractive to women and so experienced that I fear for her. He cares nothing for Meg, just the pleasure of a conquest. He could even persuade her to run away with him."

They had reached the stables and Jim turned the horse and carriage over to the hostler. They walked past the Town Creek boatways and saw men working on the Annie Marie.

"That's the ship we'll be sailing on in another week or so, and Andre will be sailing with us."

"Too bad. Is there no way we can sail without him?"

"I don't see how. He has already booked passage. I simply do not know what to do. Meg is the dearest thing in the world to me."

"The problem is that Meg certainly won't listen to me. She thinks of me as little more than a stranger who is trying to interfere in her affairs. If I get too serious, she backs off. She is as skittish as a colt around me."

"That will change, Micco. I think she is remembering more and more how you looked after her when you were children. She told me the story of your rescuing her from drowning and how you scolded Gray Wolf."

"But that was when we were children. She is a woman now and has a very definite mind of her own."

"I know, but she is very bright in spite of her stubbornness."

"I want to help you, but I don't really know what I can do. If they're together, I can't walk up to Andre and say, 'Unhand that woman!' Meg would think I was an idiot, and Andre would probably rearrange my physiognomy."

They had reached the boardwalk and were strolling by the docks. It was almost dusk and the wind was chilly, but neither man felt like going to his room.

"You can keep Meg occupied. Pamela is sticking close to Andre because she is smitten with him, too."

"What if Meg doesn't want to be in my company?"

"I'll tell her that you're feeling a little lost, homesick, maybe. You've been so buried in your books for the past ten years that you don't quite know how to respond to the world outside the halls of academe."

"You can't be serious! The only part of that scenario that applies to me is 'homesick'. At the risk of sounding pompous, I've never felt lost."

"I know, I know, but we've got to appeal to Meg's tender-heartedness. She is an ardent supporter of the downtrodden, stray dogs and cats, the unemployed, and lost causes."

"Stray dogs and cats! You want me to appear like a lost puppy?" Micco was staring at Jim as if he had suddenly sprouted horns.

"It sounds ridiculous and insulting to you, I know, particularly a man as self-reliant and assured as you are, but I don't know how else to get through to Meg." Jim looked worriedly at Micco. The last thing in the world he wanted was to insult this man, a man he greatly admired.

Micco began laughing. Several passersby turned and smiled. "I always appreciated the ability of those actors at the Broadway Theatre and wondered if I could act as they did. Now I have this wonderful opportunity to perform!"

"You went to the theatre?" asked Jim in a surprised tone.

"I wasn't completely buried in the halls of academe. A young lady of my acquaintance had box seats at the theatre, and we occasionally attended Broadway performances."

"You did? And were you serious about this young lady?"

"Not as serious as she wanted to be. She threatens to visit me in Jupiter but I have painted a picture of Indian braves in war paint, dancing around the fire. I hope she has given up the idea. Christine is persistent, though. I don't know whether I succeeded or not."

"Let's pray that Christine saw the light. We don't need any more complications. But what will you do about Meg?"

"To be a stray dog or not to be. That is the question," misquoted Micco.

"You'll try to keep her occupied then?"

"I'll try to act as downtrodden as possible. "It will be difficult because I have been teasing her unmercifully. She was itching to slap my face."

Micco, like almost everyone else, did not believe that Andre was the blackguard that Jim believed he was. He would go along with the charade because Jim was so concerned, but Micco felt that Meg could take care of herself.

They finally turned around, buttoning up their coats against the wind, and walked to their rooms.

"We'll meet downstairs for dinner at 7:30," said Jim. "See you later."

Micco went to his room, wondering how he could act humble, and also how he could resist bantering with Meg. Jim went to his room, hoping for a miracle.

Meg had decided that she would not let Micco bait her. She would be as sweet as a sugar plum. If he thought he was going to get the better of her, he was mistaken. With this resolve, she fell asleep, forgetting all about Andre for the moment.

Jim knocked on her door at 7:00. "Meg, we are going to dinner at 7:30. There is no need to change clothes. Just wear what you have on."

Rousing sleepily, she mumbled, "All right. I'll be ready."

Meg, Jim, and Micco went into the dining room and seated themselves, waiting for Maryanne to bring around the savory dishes. Micco was looking at Meg, wondering what she was up to. She was acting as demure as a uniformed schoolgirl.

"Molly was quite impressed with Micco. He made an instant hit," said Meg, "She declared him a real doctor."

"That is high praise indeed, coming from Molly. I hope she has made blackberry cobbler. I had forgotten about it until she reminded me the other day," said Jim.

Meg looked up and saw Dr. and Mrs. Brown, followed by Pamela and Andre, come in and look around. They sat down at the center table. Albert and Jennifer waved at them and Dr. Brown said something to Andre. Andre got up and came to their table.

245

"Good evening," he said politely, bowing slightly. "Dr. and Mrs. Brown would like for you to join us, unless of course, you prefer sitting here." He had looked at no one but Meg.

"We'd love to," she said . She hated the thought of sitting anywhere near Pamela, but being close to Andre would make up for it.

Jim couldn't gracefully say 'No'. Andre quickly pulled out Meg's chair and put his hand on her back, leading her to the table. Jim was angry and Micco was amused by the turn of events. Andre seated Meg on his left. Pamela was on his right, furious that he had seated Meg beside himself. There was no other chair on that side, so Micco and Jim sat across from them, next to the Browns.

"We didn't have a chance to talk today at the contest. My congratulations. That was a remarkable shot."

"Thank you, Sir. I was as surprised as everyone else. I guess luck was with me today."

He hoped he sounded modest enough to Meg. He stole a glance at her, but couldn't tell by her expression.

"I understand you just received your M.D. Did you specialize?"

"Yes, I did. I received my GP degree and then specialized in surgery."

Dr. Brown was elated to hear this. "You wouldn't consider coming in with me, would you? I'm the only doctor in town, and I have to be everything from an obstetrician to a coroner. What a boon it would be if we had a surgeon! I've been wanting to retire, but I can't."

"I'm honored that you would consider me as a partner, Sir, but I am committed to Dr. Riley, Meg's father. He is depending on my reopening his clinic. I couldn't disappoint him. You see, he sent me to college and to medical school."

Everyone stared at Micco, surprised by this revelation.

"I understand, my boy, but I am disappointed. If you ever change your mind, the offer's still open."

Maryanne was serving the platters of meats and vegetables. Andre remembered to favor her with a smile.

Micco's eyes lit up. "The cafeteria never served food like this!"

"Eat all you want, Micco. You can keep refilling your plate. It's called 'family style'," said Jim. "You mentioned seeing some Broadway shows. What was your favorite? Perhaps I saw it, too."

Micco spoke between bites of fried shad roe. "Well, I would say that <u>Hamlet</u> was my favorite. I saw both Edwin Booth and Sir Henry Irving perform at different times at the Broadway Theatre."

"So did I, said Meg. "I saw Sir Henry make his final appearance in New York. I thought he was magnificent."

"Hamlet was Edwin Booth's most famous role and I can see why," added Jim.

"It would be a difficult choice. In my opinion, both actors are unsurpassed in that role. But I felt more attuned to Booth's interpretation. He was truly a tormented man, torn between his inner struggles and his loyalties."

Meg prepared for battle, starting to falter in her resolve to remain sweet and agreeable. "I disagree. Sir Henry Irving had the air of an aristocrat, a true prince of Denmark. He bore the mantle of a hero." She had pushed her plate aside.

"Ah, Meg. You are impressed by a heroic veneer, but not by the true mettle of a man?"

"That's not true! I simply think Sir Henry is the better actor."

Pamela was bored. She didn't know who or what <u>Hamlet</u> was, and didn't care.

"Did you happen to see Gilbert and Sullivan's 'Pinafore" at the Boston Museum?" asked Dr. Brown. "Jennifer and I attended that performance. Most enjoyable. When was that, my dear?"

"That was eight years ago. It was on November 15, 1878. The reason I remember that date was because it was Julian's birthday and we took him to see it as a birthday present." She said, taking another piece of trout from the platter.

"Unfortunately, I didn't see that performance, but I did see a later one. It's absolutely amazing how they can sing so many words without pausing for breath."

"Meg, Julie, and I saw it performed several times. You know, there are more than ninety different companies performing it throughout the country. It is wholesome entertainment for women and children. No need to bowdlerize any of the material as they do with vaudeville shows."

"Andre, are you almost finished? I feel a little faint, it is so hot in here." Pamela fanned herself with her delicate Chinese fan. She had eaten nothing at all.

"My dear, are you ill?" asked her uncle .

"Perhaps, if Andre could take me outside, I would feel better." Andre had not spoken a word to her, or even looked at her. He was looking at Meg, and appeared about to ask her something.

"Meg," he managed to whisper, "meet me tomorrow morning at nine o'clock down at the dock."

Meg nodded. Andre stood up and pulled out Pamela's chair. "It is rather warm in here. Pamela and I will just step outside for a moment. Don't rush your dinner. I have finished."

Meg was thrilled that Andre had finally arranged to see her without the spoiled brat hovering around him like a bird of prey.

The Browns had noticed nothing, but Jim and Micco both saw the exchange between Meg and Andre. Meg, who had been simply pushing food around her plate, began eating as if she really enjoyed it. Jim, Albert, and Jennifer discussed their grandchildren and who would be at the Christmas breakfast. Micco ate and quietly watched Meg. 'She really is enamored of Andre,' he thought. He didn't know if he could break the spell Andre had woven or not. Actually, he wasn't too enthusiastic about the role of protector. If it weren't for Jim, he would leave Meg to her own devices. She was a grown woman, after all, not a child.

They finished dinner and the Browns joined Andre and Pamela who were waiting outside. Jim, Meg, and Micco went to their rooms.

"Goodnight, Meg. Have pleasant dreams," said her uncle, kissing her on the cheek.

"Goodnight, Uncle. You too. A 'Goodnight' to you, Micco, champion marksman in all of Carteret County."

"Sleep well, little sister," he said, his brown eyes sparkling as he kissed her on the forehead.

Meg closed the door, annoyed with Micco as usual. She was not his little sister. She didn't feel the least bit sisterly towards him. Did he actually think of her as a sister? His teasing eyes, dancing with laughter, didn't give her a clue of what he was really thinking. She was so irritated with him that she had almost forgotten her assignation with Andre tomorrow morning. But not quite. Her face became warm when she remembered his passionate kiss. This was her last thought before she fell asleep.

The next morning, she was dressed and out of the house by eight o'clock. She didn't want to run into her uncle, so she went over to see Miss Molly to get bread to feed the sea gulls.

"You is de early bird dis mornin', Miss Meg. Is you tryin' to kech de worm?"

"Whatever do you mean? I am going to feed the sea gulls if you can spare me some bread."

"I has seen dat other mans. You jist leave him with dat prissy girl. Bof is jist right for de other. I see how you be lookin' at dat debil. Dat mans is not de one for you." Molly stated this matter-of-factly as she scrambled eggs.

"How do you see everything?" exclaimed Meg . "Andre is not right for her. No one deserves her! Besides, he doesn't really care for her."

"Here be de bread. You minds what I tol' you. Dat doctor man be de one for you. Does you want some nice fry bread and scrambled eggs?"

249

"No, I don't. Thank you for the bread," said Meg, ignoring Molly's admonition.

She left, hurrying out of the house, taking a circuitous route. The coast was clear. She didn't see her uncle anywhere. She walked quickly to the end of the dock, her cape flying behind her. The morning sun sparkled on the fast-moving Inlet, making it look like a field of polished diamonds. Something soft and furry nudged up against her. She smiled in delight as a beagle puppy with a red bandana tied around her neck licked Meg's hand, furiously wagging her tail.

"You darling dog! What's your name?" Meg asked as she scratched the pup's head.

"That's Watson," said Davy. "How are you, Miss Meg?" Davy had admired Meg from afar. Now he was pleased to be able to talk to her.

"Davy, I'm so glad to see you. How have you been? How is your grandmother?"

"She's doing as well as can be expected under the circumstances. It was a terrible blow to her, losing Granddaddy like that, but she's strong. I think she'll be all right when I leave. She doesn't want me to go back to sea, but she knows that is the only life for me."

"When do you think we'll be able to sail?"

"Even sooner than we expected. I believe the Annie Marie will be ship-shape by the 28th of December."

"That's wonderful. I really like Beaufort. It's so picturesque and the people are so friendly, but I am anxious to see my father. I bet you'll hate to leave Watson. She is so cute."

"I'm not leaving her," said Davy as he threw a stick into the air. The puppy raced after it and brought it back to him, holding it in her mouth, as proud as if it were a bird.

"She'll be the ship's mascot. Watson is a smart dog. She learns so easily, and almost seems to understand what I say."

Meg continued petting the puppy, which was now lying on her back, wriggling in ecstasy. "Watson is an unusual name for a dog. Why did you name her that?"

"I always associate Sherlock Holmes and his associate, Dr. Watson, with hound dogs. That's how she got her name."

"Well, if ever you have a case to solve, I hope this Watson will prove as invaluable to you as Dr. Watson was to Holmes. At least you can squeeze and pet her," said Meg, fondling the pup's silky ear. Both Meg and Davy turned as they felt the vibration of footsteps on the dock.

"Good morning, Miss Riley, Captain Guthrie," Andre greeted them.

"Good morning, Mr. Lafitte," Davy said.

"Hello, Andre," said Meg, smiling at him.

Davy was disappointed, seeing the way Meg looked at Andre. He was a good-looking boy and the girls found him attractive, but Davy thought Meg was the prettiest girl he had ever seen.

"Watson and I have to go for our run. Good day, Sir, and Miss Meg," said Davy, tipping his cap to both. "Come on, girl. Let's go."

He ran down the dock and the puppy left Meg, bounding after her master.

"Meg, sweetheart." Andre took her hand and kissed the palm, though she wore gloves. He gazed at her as though she were a sugarplum he'd like to devour. 'It was not a tender look,' she thought, 'but a hungry one.'

"I have missed you so much," he said ardently, tracing a trail from her smooth cheek to her full lips, lightly running his fingertips over that luscious mouth.

"I, I have too," whispered Meg, thinking that was how a mere earth maiden must have felt when Apollo, the magnificent sun god, seduced her. She was not aware that interested eyes were watching the tableau from the vantage point of their moored fishing boats.

"Oh, there you are," boomed a deep male voice. Micco walked down the dock, hands in his pockets, whistling a lively tune.

Meg looked at him completely surprised..

"Good morning, Mr. Lafitte. Wonderful, brisk air, isn't it?" he asked, drawing in deep breaths. Turning to Meg, he said, "Your uncle and I were ready to go to breakfast, but when he knocked on your door, there was no answer. I told him that perhaps you had gone for an early morning walk. And I was right. Here you are looking as fresh as a dewy rose. He is waiting for us at the dining table. Shall we go?" he asked, offering her his arm.

Meg was so startled by his appearance, and by her encounter with Andre, that she curled her arm obediently through his.

"Good day to you, Mr. Lafitte. Enjoy your walk. Wish I could join you, but I'm really hungry this morning. It must be the salt air." He smiled pleasantly and strolled away with Meg on his arm.

"Good day. Meg, I'll see you later." Andre was furious. He glared malevolently, wanting to throw Micco off the dock. Meg glanced back helplessly at Andre, as she was borne along towards the boarding house.

The audience of fishermen avidly watching the scene gave Micco high marks for one-upmanship.

Micco had risen early, and had already been for a run around town. He was walking back when he saw Meg leave the house. He waited to see where she was going and when she emerged from Miss Amy's kitchen, he followed her at a distance. He felt sneaky doing this, but he rationalized that he was doing it at her uncle's request. Meg had not spoken one word to him, and he knew that when she finally did, it wouldn't be to wish him a pleasant day. They were almost at the boarding house when Meg erupted.

"How dare you practically force me to go with you? You, you kidnaper!" Meg angrily removed her arm from his. "Who do you think you are? You are not my brother; so don't try to act like it. And just wait until I see my uncle. I know he put you up to this." Meg stormed into the dining room. Jim rose from his chair when he saw her.

"Meg, I'm glad you're here. Micco and I were waiting breakfast for you. Have a seat," he said, pulling out a chair.

"I am not hungry. You sent Micco after me, didn't you? You had him follow me. And when he saw me with Andre, he whisked me away like a Victorian parent."

Micco intervened. "He did not send me after you. Just by accident, I happened to see you walking towards the docks, and I thought I'd catch up with you and we would walk back here together."

Meg was not placated. "You didn't have to be so possessive!"

"Please sit down, Meg. I apologize for embarrassing you." It seemed to Micco that he was always apologizing to her.

Jim didn't say anything and finally Meg allowed herself to be seated.

"I accept your apology, but if you ever interfere in my affairs again, I won't speak to you all the way to Jupiter Inlet," she said with poor grace.

They ordered breakfast with Meg having nothing but a cup of tea. The men talked together while Meg sat there saying nothing.

"Meg, today is Christmas Eve. We should all be in the Christmas spirit. Remember, tonight we're going to celebrate with Leland and Stephanie and their family."

"I know. I really am looking forward to it. We're going to pop popcorn and string it to put on the tree."

"That should be fun," said Jim, finishing his meal. "I'm going over to see Albert. Would you like to join me, Micco? You might enjoy seeing his office."

"Yes, I would."

"Want to go with us?" Jim asked Meg.

"No, I'll just sit here a while," she answered.

Jim and Micco left. As they were walking to Dr. Brown's office, Micco remarked, "Looks like I really made Meg angry this time. Now she's not speaking to me."

"She'll get over it shortly. She always does."

"I don't really blame her. I had no right to disrupt her meeting with Lafitte."

"But I am grateful that you did."

"You realize that I can't keep doing this," said Micco, looking directly at Jim.

"I know you can't. I had just hoped..." Jim's voice trailed off. "Here we are. If Albert's not too busy, he'll give you a tour of his office." The temperature was dropping rapidly as they walked along, and the northwest wind whipped against their faces.

"Feels like it might snow again. Leland was wishing for snow on Christmas. I think he might get his wish."

"I think so too. I just felt a snowflake hit my face," said Micco.

They entered the office, grateful for the warmth.

Meg, meanwhile, was sitting at the table, moping. She could not understand why everyone seemed to be conspiring against Andre. Even Molly, who hadn't met him, didn't like him. Jim, Leland, and Stephanie didn't like him as a suitor for her. Micco did not seem to care one way or the other whether she went out with Andre or not. She knew that he had come after her because her uncle wanted him to. She wondered if his girlfriend, Christine, would come all the way from Boston to Jupiter to see him. Oh, he was so annoying!

The rest of the day was uneventful. Meg walked around, wrote letters, and read. As the afternoon wore on, her thoughts turned to what she would wear to the tree-lighting party. Andre would probably be celebrating with "her", the China doll, on this special night. But Meg could wear something that would catch the eye of Micco who was apparently immune to her charms. It irked Meg that he insisted on referring to her as his sister. She pulled

254

out dresses, discarding one and then another. Then she found a lavender, velvet frock in the back of the armoire. 'This is perfect,' she decided. It was high waisted with a fitted bodice. The neckline was cut rather low which was de rigueur in New York. Meg wasn't so sure about Beaufort, but she decided to wear it anyway. And she had a lavender feathered hat that was most becoming against her burgundy hair. To add the finishing touch, she would wear a jade necklace and earrings that enhanced her brilliant, green eyes. A touch of rouge and more on her lips, and just a bit of charcoal on her lashes and brows would do it. "War paint to attract an Indian brave," she said aloud. 'What in the world am I thinking of? It is Andre I want to attract. It's just that I don't want Micco thinking of me as a plump, carroty-topped child, a little sister. It must be my feminine pride, that's all,' she rationalized. She decided to soak in a hot scented bath for a long time. Maybe the soothing water would dispel the divergent thoughts swirling around in her head.

Micco had enjoyed seeing Dr. Brown's office and discussing medical matters with him. He was getting more and more anxious to return home and begin his practice and to talk, as an adult, to Dr. Riley about medicine. He longed to speak to his wise old grandmother once again. There was so much that he wanted to do.

As he and Jim left, Dr. Brown reminded them again of the Christmas Day breakfast at eight o'clock. When they came outside, it was snowing heavily.

"Leland and Stephanie want us to come by around seven o'clock this evening. We'll have an early dinner before we go. As I understand it, we'll string popcorn and then attach the candles to the tree," said Jim, pulling on his gloves. "The snow is really coming down now. Looks like New York."

"Or Boston," said Micco.

The lamplighter was moving slowly from one street lamp to another, lighting the lamps under leaden skies. Each omitted a pale, watery glow through the falling snow.

255

"He is having to light the lamps early today. Do you think Meg might enjoy a sleigh ride, Micco?"

"I don't think Meg would enjoy doing anything with me. She is really angry that I interrupted her meeting with Lafitte. Let her cool off this afternoon. Maybe by tonight, she'll be in a better mood."

Jim sighed. "You're right, I suppose. Meg is headstrong, but she gets over her anger quickly."

"I have some reading I'd like to catch up on this afternoon." Micco laughed. "Miss Molly wants to discuss some of her more serious cases with me so I had better be prepared."

They parted, arranging to meet at 5:45.

Chapter Fourteen

Andre had watched Meg and Micco leave with murder in his heart. It would be even better if he could get rid of Micco before they set sail for Jupiter, but he didn't see how he could arrange it. No one could have known the murderous thoughts that were passing through his head by gazing at that handsome, almost angelic-looking face. In San Francisco, he could have picked cutthroats from among dozens along the docks, scurvy men who would kill their own mothers for twenty dollars. But here, there was no such choice. His fingers curled. Actually, it would be exquisite pleasure to do it himself. He could almost see the strangled expression, the eyes popping as he squeezed the life, slowly but surely, out of his hated adversary. He moved along and tipped his hat politely at two elderly ladies who smiled at the handsome gentleman.

He had to endure Pamela's company tonight and tomorrow. He hoped the ship would leave sooner than January. If he had to listen to her juvenile, inane chatter much longer, he didn't know if he could refrain from wringing her neck. If he could take her to bed, that would help, but he couldn't, not with her aunt and uncle breathing down his neck. Dr. Brown had actually hinted of marriage! The sooner he left this place, the better. He had found solace with the all-too-willing Maxine—willing until she found what was in store for her. He would visit her again tonight after he left the Brown's home. She would be terrified and that made it all the more enjoyable. He hummed a merry tune at these thoughts of murder and seduction, once again in a good mood. He returned to his room, cheered by the prospect of several tots of rum before dinner. He had walked through the falling snow hardly aware of it, so intense were his ruminations on life and death. He took off his hat and coat and poured himself a large glass of rum. He sank back against the pillow, savoring the strong flavor, but his thoughts were not on his midnight assignation, but of Meg. He could still feel her petal soft cheek and those delectable lips! Just the thought of kissing them made him burn with passion. The more she resisted, the more he was determined to have her.

Meg was just dabbing perfume behind her ear when her uncle tapped on the door.

"I'm coming," she called out, adjusting her frilly hat stylishly to the side of her head, so that a few feathers brushed her cheek. She gave one last glance in the mirror and smiled with satisfaction. 'The cleavage is daring,' she thought She pulled her evening cloak about her, hooking it at the neck.

She opened the door and Jim looked at her admiringly. "You look lovely, as usual," he said, taking her arm. "Micco is outside waiting. He engaged a horse and carriage since it is snowing."

They went downstairs and Jim helped Meg inside the carriage and then sat down beside her, removing his top hat. "We'll let Micco chauffeur us. Poor boy. Hope he doesn't get too wet in all this snow."

"Don't worry, Uncle. He certainly won't melt!"

"You're not still angry with him, are you?"

"Not really. I plan to enjoy myself tonight, in spite of a certain annoying person."

"Meg, don't tease him. I know he really likes you."

"Me? Tease him? It never crossed my mind!"

The horses slowed and Micco stopped them in front of the house. Jim stepped out, and then helped Meg down.

"Hurry! Go on in and after I've tethered the horses, I'll join you," Micco said. Jim and Meg hurried up the steps. She wasn't worried about her hair because it would simply curl more tightly with the dampness, but she was concerned about her feather hat.

Stephanie and Leland greeted them at the door. "Come in, quickly. Terrible weather for traveling but isn't the snow beautiful!"

"Merry Christmas, everyone," said Meg.

Micco joined them, pulling off his wet hat and coat in the hallway. Leland took their wraps. "Merry Christmas, Micco," said Stephanie and Leland.

"Merry Christmas to you, too," he replied.

"I'll take these to the kitchen to dry. Meg, you look absolutely stunning," said Leland.

"Thank you. You look pretty dapper yourself," answered Meg. Leland had put a sprig of holly berries in his lapel.

"Come into the parlor. I want you to meet our family," said Stephanie, leading the way.

A short, blonde, pretty young woman was standing by the fireplace. Standing next to her was a tall, thin, dark-haired man with spectacles that made him look rather scholarly. Two children, a boy about three sucking a sugarplum, and a girl about five, clung to their mother's skirt. The little boy looked like a wee Christmas elf. He was dressed in a long-waisted, belted green tweed Norfolk suit with a sprig of holly, just like his grandfather's, pinned to his collar. He wore green knee breeches over dark stockings and tiny black boots. The little girl's dress was a miniature fashion of her mother's dress. Both wore red velvet decorated with braid and white lace ruffles all around the front, collar, cuffs, and pockets. A red satin bow formed a bustle.

"This is my daughter, Lucy, and my son-in-law, Bob Dalton. And these are my friends, Meg Riley, Jim's niece, and Micco Ravenwing. You remember Jim Styron, of course." They all exchanged greetings, the men shaking hands.

259

"Lucy, you are just as pretty as ever. How have you been, Bob? Are the students at Carolina up to their usual tricks?" asked Jim.

"More than ever! One student pledging for TKE had to roll a peanut with his nose, completely around the quadrangle. If they spent that much time studying, they'd all be Phi Beta Kappas."

"Bob is a chemistry professor at the University of North Carolina," explained Jim to Meg and Micco.

"Chemistry and anatomy were my favorite courses," said Micco.

Before Bob could launch into a long treatise on the value of chemistry in the modern world, as he was wont to do, Stephanie intervened.

"These are my grandchildren," she said proudly. "That urchin clinging to his mama is Cicero and the little Christmas angel is Melissa." The children hid further behind Lucy's skirt.

"What do you want Santa Claus to bring you?" asked Meg, stooping down to their level.

Seeing the pretty, friendly face smiling at them, both children brightened.

"A horsie," replied the boy.

"I want a doll with real hair," said Melissa.

"I'll bet Santa will leave them under the tree tonight, but only if you are asleep. And you must leave him milk and cookies."

"Oh, no. We always leave him a slice of 'Down East' fruitcake and a glass of Harlowe 'nog'," stated Melissa. Everybody laughed.

" 'From the mouths of babes'," said Leland.

"I wonder where she learned that?" asked her father.

"Granddaddy told me that's what Santa Claus wants." They all laughed again.

"Leland, at last the truth is revealed!" said Jim.

"What is Harlowe 'nog?" asked Meg.

"Harlowe is a small community fifteen or twenty miles north of Beaufort. They are known for their special egg nog.

Leland and I have sampled it, judiciously of course, throughout the years."

"What a quaint expression, Jim. Sounds just like two lawyers arguing for the defense. A 'judicious' sample. Has a nice ring to it," said Stephanie.

She looked up as a young lady descended the steps.

"Oh, there you are, dear. This is our daughter, Alexandria," said Stephanie as a beautiful girl with a cloud of shiny black hair floated into the room. She was willowy and as tall as Meg. She wore a deep blue velvet off-the-shoulder dress and her décolletage was as revealing as Meg's. Dark blue, almost violet eyes were fringed with long, thick lashes. Her waist was unbelievably small which emphasized her generous bosom. Meg could only stare, as did Micco. 'He doesn't have to be so obvious about it,' she thought.

"How do you do?" Alexandria said in a sweet, melodious voice to Meg. "And how do you do, Micco Ravenwing? What a lovely, musical name," she said, offering him her hand.

"Thank you, the result of my Indian heritage," said Micco, shaking her hand.

Alexandria was surprised and perhaps disappointed that Micco had not kissed her hand. Any other man would have. She smiled, intrigued. This man was different. She felt a sudden shock. This was the first time she had even thought about another man for a long, long time.

"All right children, time for bed,' said Lucy, taking the children's hands.

"I don't want to go to bed." Melissa pulled away rebelliously.

Micco bent down to the child. "Suppose I read 'The Night Before Christmas'? Would you like that?"

"Yes," she said.

"Okay, up we go," said Micco, lifting Melissa and hoisting her to his shoulders. Meg watched Micco, wondering if Andre would have done the same.

"The book is in their room," said Lucy as she led the way upstairs. "It is their favorite poem." Her husband followed her, carrying Cicero in his arms.

"Where did you go to college?" he asked Micco.

"Harvard," answered Micco. The rumble of their voices faded away. Stephanie turned to Meg.

"We'll allow them to come back down and see the lighted tree."

"Let's start putting the wires through the tapers. It won't take long for them to put the children to bed," said Stephanie.

"Have you done this before?" Alexandria asked Meg.

"Yes, I have," she answered, "but next year Uncle has promised that we will have electric lights on the tree, so this is probably the last time I'll be attaching candles."

"You have such pretty hair, Meg. I envy you," said Alexandria.

"You do?" exclaimed Meg .

"I've always thought that color of burgundy hair is so unusual."

Meg looked into those startling blue-violet eyes and wondered how Alexandria could be envious of anything. They had been working long pieces of fine wire through the bottoms of the tapers.

"Hand Leland, Jim, and me the tapers after you have threaded the wires through them," said Stephanie.

"You and Meg certainly made some beautiful ornaments. Each one is unique. I think this will be the prettiest tree we've ever had," remarked Leland as he touched a delicate painted egg.

"Meg is very talented," said Jim proudly. "Not only is she an exceptional musician, but she is an artist as well. She draws and paints beautifully."

"I know," said Stephanie ruefully. "Thank goodness she can draw roses. Mine always look like globs of misshapen balloons.

Alexandria's laugh was like an exquisite tinkling bell. "Mother dear, I cherish those roses. They are unique!"

"Thank you dear, I think!" She and her daughter looked at each other fondly. Meg gazed at the mother and daughter, wishing she could have had that relationship with her mother.

Micco, Bob, and Lucy returned.

"Melissa held out until 'Merry Christmas to all, and to all a good night'," said Micco, "but her eyes were closing. Those are two nice children. I thought about specializing in pediatrics for a while."

The somewhat staid Bob clapped a friendly arm around Micco's shoulders. "You would have been a good one. Even my shy Cicero insisted on getting in Micco's lap," he told the others.

"It was my rendition of the reindeer snorting and clattering on the roof that did it," replied Micco.

Lucy was smiling at Micco as if she had known him for years instead of thirty minutes.

Meg noted all of this. 'You'd think the three of them were bosom buddies,' she thought. She also noticed Alexandria's speculative expression when she watched Micco. 'Why does she have to be gorgeous? It isn't fair to be beautiful and nice, too.'

"Will you excuse me for a minute?" asked Stephanie. "I'm going to heat the cider. Leland, add some more logs to the fire. It's getting colder."

"I'll help you, Mother," offered Lucy.

The two women left, talking about Christmas presents to be left under or on the tree.

"What do I do?" asked Micco. "I've never put candles on a tree before."

"I'll show you," said Alexandria helpfully, moving to his side. She took a taper that had the wire protruding from the bottom and carefully twisted it over the stem of a branch.

"You must make sure that there is a clear space above each wick so that nothing catches on fire."

"I see," said Micco, picking up another candle. He attached one above Alexandria's, carefully twisting the wire so that it was secure on the branch. "Is that all right?"

"It's perfect." Limpid , violet eyes met warm brown ones. Meg was jealous. Micco had never looked at her that way. His eyes had a teasing expression when he gazed at her. Andre's blue eyes were blatantly admiring, filled with desire when they met hers. Why did she want to see that expression in Micco's? She imagined those brown eyes, with lashes so thick they almost tangled in the wind, were looking at Alexandria that way. She mentally shook her head. 'How can I be so fickle? I'm as bad as Pamela!'

"This is the next step," said Alexandria, picking up a bottle filled with alcohol. She carefully rubbed a drop of it on the wick. "This will insure that the candles light quickly."

Micco followed her example and put alcohol on his taper.

"When Leland lights the candles, we'll keep a wet sponge on hand to put out fires if a candle tips over," said Jim.

Leland had spread white cotton batting that looked like Christmas tree snow, on the floor to cover the makeshift tree holder. It also would protect the floor from dripping candle wax.

Meg sniffed the aromatic scent of the freshly cut tree appreciatively. Now she could also smell cinnamon and nutmeg wafting from the kitchen. Stephanie and Lucy returned with steaming mugs of cider on a colorful tray decorated with eight tiny reindeer prancing through the sky. Lucy also had kernels of corn in a saucer and a big bowl for the popped corn.

"Gather around the fireplace while I get the frying pan to pop the corn." They all pulled up chairs around the fireplace and Leland removed the fire screen. They sat down and sipped the steaming cider.

"This is delicious," said Micco. "My grandmother makes it just like this. I wonder if she is sitting around a fire with Gray Wolf and my other friends tonight?"

264

"You will be seeing them soon, Micco." Jim noticed the look of wistfulness on the young man's face. Even Meg sensed homesickness in Micco. She touched his hand sympathetically.

"I want to see Gray Wolf, too. I wonder if he changed as much as you have? Maybe he won't be so cowed by your lordly behavior now!" said Meg.

"Lordly?" asked Micco with a puzzled look. "What do you mean?"

"He always looked at you as though you were Osceola resurrected. If you told him to jump off the lighthouse, he would have done it."

"You are mistaken, Meg. Gray Wolf was always my best friend. We even went through the blood brother ritual when we were eight years old. He hardly thought of me as Chief of the tribe."

"You may have been his best friend, but he still thought of you as the leader."

Jim saw that Micco was a little annoyed with Meg.

"Are we ready to pop the corn?" he asked Stephanie.

"Yes, and I have a needle and thread for everyone to string the popped corn. That way we'll have eight strings. Oh, the tree is going to be beautiful with all those candles and wonderful decorations. Here Micco, you shake the pan."

The pan had a long handle and was really more of a pot with a lid. The fire was blazing and Micco held the pot over the flames, shaking it constantly. In a minute, the corn began to pop. Micco moved it from the heat and poured the popped corn into one of several bowls. He added more corn and kept repeating the process until four bowls were filled with white, fluffy popcorn.

"I think that's enough, Micco. You did a great job," said Stephanie. "Here everybody, take a needle and make strings of popcorn."

"My grandmother and I used to pop corn, but we ate it. I've never decorated a tree with it. That was not an Indian custom."

Meg noticed that no one seemed in the least prejudiced that Micco was an Indian. She was surprised because none of her friends in New York would have accepted him as they did. She prided herself on being modern and unbiased, and now discovered that she wasn't unique in that respect. Her uncle had warned her about trying to become too involved with the Seminoles. She had thought he was prejudiced, but she suddenly realized that perhaps he thought the proud Seminoles might not respond to her friendly overtures. She had no way of knowing that Micco had been tops in his class and that his charm, leadership, and personality had won him many friends and the respect and admiration of his professors. She also didn't know that Christine, his lady friend, was from a wealthy Boston family.

Meg watched Micco as he strung the popcorn, fascinated by his strong, capable fingers as they easily handled the needle. Leland and Bob were both muttering.

"Ouch! Darned needle! I never could get the hang of this," said Leland.

"Nor could I," agreed Bob.

"Neither one of you is cut out to be a seamstress or a surgeon," said Stephanie.

Leland carried his string of popcorn over to the tree. He pulled up a straight chair, placing it beside the tree, and then took off his shoes. He stood on the chair and placed his string around the topmost branches. Stephanie handed him hers, and he placed it on the branches just below his. Lucy's was next and then Leland stepped down from the chair. Each person continued placing the strings until all eight were hung.

"Everyone go into the hallway," instructed Leland. "I'm going to light the candles." They all obediently left the room and Leland closed the double wooden doors to the parlor, while they all waited impatiently outside.

"This is always the most exciting time," said Lucy. "I used to think Daddy deliberately drew it out to make us anticipate it more. Shall we bring the children down now?" she asked her husband.

"No. Let them sleep. We'll light the candles again early in the morning when they start to wake up."

Meg was aware that Alexandria was standing quite close to Micco. 'He didn't even notice my dress,' she thought wistfully. Then Micco turned his head and looked directly into her eyes. He had the sweetest expression on his face, and his eyes were filled with admiration as he gazed at her. Meg's heart fluttered. Maybe he had noticed her after all.

Suddenly the doors swung open and Leland called to them. The parlor was completely dark except for the glittering tapers and the warm glow of the orange flames in the fireplace. An aromatic scent of the candle-lit tree filled the air. The whole effect was breathtakingly beautiful.

"Ooh, this is the prettiest tree ever," sighed Alexandria.

They all gathered around the tree, the flickering lights reflecting on their faces. Micco thought Meg was like a delicate Christmas poinsettia with her red hair, sparkling green eyes and porcelain complexion bathed in the softly glowing candlelight. Lovely Alexandria could have been a model in the latest fashion magazines, but Micco found Meg's fiery beauty much more appealing. He had to smile at her serious face though. She was so easy to tease. Yet somehow, he felt something for Alexandria, too. What was it? Sympathy? Micco was a sensitive man, and he sensed sadness within her.

Meg thought Micco looked like a handsome and proud Indian Chief, the warm lights reflecting against his honeyed skin.

Leland had placed a doll for Melissa in the branches. It was dressed like a princess, in purple velvet with a crown sparkling on her real blonde hair. Cicero's horse and cart appeared to be prancing on a bough. Meg could see the glitter of a thin gold chain with a miniature heart, suspended from a branch. Toy soldiers were stationed among the lowest branches waiting for a tiny hand to clutch them. Beneath a throw cloth, dozens of brightly wrapped packages tied with gaily-colored bows, were piled high on the under cloth surrounding the tree. Meg and Jim had put several packages under the tree for all the Carter family. Stephanie had added more decoration to the tree including tiny American flags of gay ribbons, stars and shields of gilt paper, whistles, round balls of colored paper and painted nuts. The candlelit tree in the darkened room looked like a magical tree in fairyland. Meg almost expected green-elves with curled, up-turned shoes to peep from the branches.

Stephanie had not put her presents to Leland under the tree yet. She planned to give him new waders, a clam rake (the handle had broken on the old one), and a new lantern. Of course, she had ordered new clothes from his New York tailor. They had arrived last week. Leland placed a small package wrapped in shining gilt paper and a green bow on the top branches of the tree. Inside was a ruby necklace and matching earrings. Stephanie had exclaimed over them when they were in a jewelry store in Paris a year ago, and unbeknownst to her, he had bought the gems.

"Stephanie and Leland, this is the most beautiful tree I have ever seen, even on Times Square," said Jim.

"Yes it is," agreed Micco, "and look at these stockings filled with tiny treasures." They all glanced at the mantle where six Christmas stockings were hanging.

"The children would be so disappointed if we didn't have the stockings, too," said Stephanie.

"So would Father," said Alexandria, smiling at Leland.

"Well, that's true. He's still a boy at heart," said his wife affectionately.

Meg felt the closeness and love surrounding the family almost enviously. She had known that love from her aunt and uncle, but not from her parents, when she was a child.

"You three are invited to Christmas dinner tomorrow at three o'clock. We're having a real 'down east' meal of clam chowder, oyster fritters, conch soup, charcoal mullets, ham, wild goose (courtesy of Micco, our champion archer), and Christmas pound cake. I won't take no for an answer, so don't even try to refuse the offer," said Stephanie.

"My dear Stephanie, the thought never entered my mind. Once you said 'charcoal mullet', I was doomed to stuff myself on Christmas Day," said Jim.

"Well, don't stuff yourself at Albert and Jennifer's breakfast, or you won't be able to enjoy dinner!" said Leland.

"That's true, my friend. I'll merely imbibe a tot or two of Harlowe nog."

"That's the custom here, Micco," said Leland. "Eggnog is served before breakfast as the first food on Christmas morn. After breakfast, we all go to church, and then have dinner at three o'clock."

"You couldn't keep me away," Micco said fervently. "You do have unadulterated eggnog, too, don't you? You know how 'firewater' affects us Indians," he said, tongue-in-cheek.

Micco had seen too many of the adult men in his tribe drunk and out of control. It was a fact that they could not handle alcohol, and Micco had vowed never to put himself in that position. He wanted to be in control at all times.

"Of course we do. The children and many adults drink eggnog without spirits added," said Stephanie.

"Leland, will you read <u>A Christmas Carol</u> to us? It doesn't seem like Christmas without it. And then we can sing some Christmas carols. I don't think the carolers are coming around tonight because it is snowing so heavily." Even as she spoke, they heard the clear, lovely sounds of "Hark the Herald Angels Sing" floating on the cold night air.

"Oh, they are out caroling! I can't believe it! In all this snow," said Lucy.

They all went to the door and opened it. The porch lights were already on and the snow was falling heavily on the caped and hooded singers standing on the porch.

"Come in, come in!" urged Stephanie and Leland. "We have hot cider and Christmas cookies for you." The bedraggled singers stepped into the foyer pulling off their capes and hats. There were eight singers, four young men and four young women with red cheeks and noses, and wet hair. Leland took their wraps and Stephanie, Lucy and Alexandria led them to the fireplace.

"Sit down and warm yourselves by the fire," said Lucy. Stephanie came in with the steaming cider and a plate full of cookies.

"You are dedicated souls to come out in this weather," said Jim. "I hope you don't catch cold. How many houses will you visit?"

"I think yours will be the last," said one young fellow sipping the cider. "We've made a complete circle around three blocks. We started at six o'clock and it's almost nine now."

"Can I give you a ride back home? I have a horse and buggy outside. I think six of you could squeeze inside and two ride up front with me," offered Micco.

"Well, we don't want you to have to go out in this weather. We're already wet," said the same young man who seemed to be the leader.

"I'm used to snowy weather. I've just come from Boston, and believe me, this is like a gentle rainfall in comparison. After you've filled up on cider and cookies, we'll go," said Micco decisively.

All the girls looked relieved, and they were eyeing Micco as if he were a tasty dessert. One pert young lady with blonde hair and big, blue eyes said, "I'll ride up front with you. It'll be less crowded." The other girls giggled.

"If you really want to do this, we gratefully accept your offer," said the young man.

"My name is Micco, and this is Meg and Jim. You probably know the others."

"I'm Kilby Garner," said the youth as he and Micco shook hands. "And these are my friends- Jenny, Sue Ann, Becca, and Rachel. And this is Josh, Brondell, and Decater."

"We'd better be going then. Our parents will wonder if we've fallen in a snow drift!"

Everyone bid the intrepid youngsters goodnight as they pulled on their coats and hats and once again went out into the whirling snow. Micco bundled up and ran out into the snow. He unhitched the horse and Kilby helped Sue Ann onto the seat by Micco. She sat sandwiched in between the two men and felt quite cozy sitting so close to this handsome stranger in spite of the falling snow. The rest piled into the carriage, laughing as they fell over each other. They shouted merrily, and sang "Jingle Bells" as the horse slowly walked down the snow-banked street.

"That was so unselfish of Micco to do that," murmured Alexandria, watching as the horse and carriage moved away.

"He is one terrific guy. I'll say that about him. Some girl will be very lucky to catch him. Not only is he considerate and charming, but he's so good-looking," said the usually reserved Lucy. "Alexandria, why don't you bat your violet eyes at him?" she asked her sister.

"I have been batting," laughed Alexandria, "But he seems to be impervious to my charms."

"I've never seen a man yet who wouldn't fall for you," said her mother, looking a little anxiously at her older daughter.

"That's true," sighed Lucy. "All the boys in Beaufort practically salivated when she walked in the room."

Alexandria smiled at her sister and gave her a hug. "Lucy, you exaggerate as usual! But I'm so glad to be home. It feels warm and wonderful!"

Leland and Stephanie looked at their beautiful daughter, and Leland had to turn away to brush aside and errant tear. Maybe the icy shroud that had encased their beloved daughter had started to thaw.

"Shall we wait for Micco to return before I read <u>A Christmas Carol</u>?" asked Leland.

"Yes, let's wait. I know he would want to hear it, too," said Alexandria.

"Meg, will you play for us again? The girls and Bob haven't heard you and I could listen all night," asked Leland persuasively.

"All right," agreed Meg. She seated herself at the piano and played a selection of Christmas music. Leland had lit several oil lamps so that she could see. The light from a lamp near the tree shimmered on ribbons and sand dollars. Meg's audience listened, enthralled by the artistry of her playing. The lilting melodies filled the room and no one spoke as she played. No one was even aware of the musical clock's chimes, and Micco had returned and was standing quietly in the doorway watching Meg and listening appreciatively as she played.

Then Meg lifted her hands from the keyboard and it was if a spell had been broken. For a moment there was a reverent hush, and then they clapped.

Micco walked over to her. "Meg, your playing was exquisite."

Meg flushed with pleasure at this compliment from Micco. "Thank you. Did everyone arrive home safely?"

"Yes, we did not end up in even one snow bank," he said, smiling at her.

"That was considerate of you to take them home."

"Not at all. I enjoyed their singing and chatter. They never stopped the whole way there. They all live fairly close to each other, so it didn't take that long."

Bob, Lucy, and Alexandria came over to the piano. They all complimented her.

Alexandria lightly touched Micco's arm. "We waited for you to return, so that you could hear father read Charles Dickens' A Christmas Carol, too." He looked into her beautiful blue-violet eyes and saw a lingering sadness there. He wished he could take away the hurt. He was so moved, he took her cold hand and held it in his warm one, as if he could give her some of his warmth.

Meg saw this and felt a quick stab in her heart. 'They were so right for each other,' she thought, with such a sense of loss that she felt bereft.

Still holding her hand, Micco led Alexandria to the sofa, and then seated himself beside her.

Jim said, "Leland, I am eager, once again, to hear your reading filled with pathos and suspense, joy, and sorrow," Jim spoke innocently, egging him on.

"Hear, hear," said Stephanie, "Can you rise to the occasion, husband mine?"

Leland arose, book in hand, trying to look humble, but failing entirely. He was a born 'ham', as were typical trial lawyers the world over. "I shall do my best," he said, clearing his throat.

Leland really was a clever actor. They could all see the greedy, miserable Scrooge, without a benevolent bone in his body, gradually transformed into a joyous, caring human being. He ended the story to enthusiastic applause.

"Tiny Tim was such a dear boy," said Stephanie, dabbing her eyes.

The clock struck eleven and Jim turned to Leland and Stephanie. "It has been a wonderful Christmas Eve. I am so happy to have spent it with you and your dear family."

"I had such a good time, too," added Meg. "You made me feel so at home. I'm glad to have met everyone. What a warm, friendly family you are."

"We loved having you with us, dear," said Stephanie, hugging her.

Leland gave her a kiss on the cheek, as did Lucy and Alexandria. Even the reserved Bob smiled at her and patted her on the shoulder.

Micco shook hands with Leland and Bob and thanked them all for including him in their Christmas celebration.

While Leland went for their wraps and the others were talking among themselves, Micco pulled Meg gently over to the doorway.

273

"You're standing under the mistletoe, Carrot top!"

"What?"

Micco tilted up her chin and looked searchingly into her brilliant green eyes with his incredible brown eyes as dark as a raven's wing. He gently kissed her parted lips. "Merry Christmas, dear little Meg. Hi-yi-tee-e-chaw."

Meg had closed her eyes when he kissed her. They fluttered open at his words.

"What does that mean?" she asked, almost in a daze.

"'Morning star'. Your eyes are as bright and shining as the morning star that greets me when I rise," he said, gazing at her without a hint of laughter in his eyes.

"Your language is so musical. I like the sound of it," Meg said, bemused by his look. She felt as if he could sense her innermost thoughts and feel her emotions.

"This is for you," said Micco, handing Meg a small, gold package, tied with a green bow.

"Oh, I didn't expect a present! I have nothing for you. "

"I didn't want you to give me a gift. My grandmother made this and I wish you to have it."

Meg unwrapped the package and opened the box. Nestled inside was a delicately etched necklace of beaten silver.

"It is so lovely," breathed Meg as she lifted it from the tissue wrappings.

"Here, let me fasten it," offered Micco. Meg turned around and Micco placed the necklace around her neck and fastened it. The silver gleamed against Meg's throat, bathed by candlelight, and Micco thought it complimented her alabaster complexion and burnished, copper hair.

"It suits you perfectly as I knew it would. You look like a Celtic princess of Tara."

Meg laughed. "An Irish princess? My great grandfather probably dug potatoes! Besides, shouldn't this be adorning the neck of your Indian sweet heart?"

274

"I told you, Meg. I have no Indian sweetheart. That can be easily remedied during the Corn Dance, however," said Micco, appearing thoughtful.

"Corn Dance? Whatever is that?"

"I'll tell you all about it when we get to Jupiter."

Jim's voice broke into their conversation. "Time to go, Meg and Micco. Stephanie is politely trying to stifle her yawns."

"No, you don't have to go," protested Leland.

"Yes, we do. Tomorrow's a busy day for you. We'll see you at three o'clock. Thanks again for a wonderful Christmas Eve."

Micco once again ran outside to bring the horse and buggy as close to the steps as he could. Jim held onto Meg's arm to help her down the now slippery steps, and Meg held onto the railing with her other hand. They reached the carriage safely and waved goodbye to their friends. It was snowing so hard that they could hardly see them. Jim helped Meg into the carriage and the two sank into their seats, gratefully.

"I don't know how Micco can even see to stay on the street. Thank goodness it's not far to the Davis House," said Meg .

"It's difficult, but Micco will get us there," replied Jim confidently.

"You really like him, don't you, Uncle Jim?"

"Yes, I do. I think he's a fine man in every respect. He is dependable, honorable, and trustworthy."

"That's quite an endorsement, coming from you," said Meg, knowing in her heart that he was comparing Micco to Andre.

Jim looked directly at her. "Meg, I don't pretend to know the true mettle of a man just by looking at his outward appearance, or to judge him by his behavior after a brief acquaintance, but I have spent my entire adult life observing men and women in and out of the courtroom. I have observed human nature at its worst and its best, and I think I am a pretty good judge. Though I have only known Micco for a few days, I am convinced he would never cheat, lie, or steal, or knowingly hurt anyone. He has a compassionate nature. That is why he will make a wonderful doctor."

"And Andre doesn't? Is that what you are saying?"

Before Jim could reply, the carriage came to a stop. Micco jumped down and opened the door.

"Meg, let me help you," he said, lifting her to the ground. He put his arm around her waist and held her tightly when her boots slipped on the icy ground, preventing her from falling.

"This dratted hoop skirt and bustle was not made for walking in the snow,." she said.

Micco chuckled. "Meg, you're still a hoyden. I suppose you'd prefer to wear breeches like a man?"

"It would make a lot more sense in certain circumstances," she said, trying to blow the sodden feathers on her hat from her eyes. They reached the door with Jim right behind them.

"I am going to return the horse and buggy to the stable," said Micco, opening the front door for them.

"You can't do that, Micco. It's too far. You'll have to walk back a half a mile in this blinding snow and ice," said Jim in a worried tone. "Just tie up the horse and wait until morning to take it back. The owner will understand."

"I can't leave that poor horse out all night in this storm. He's already suffered patiently for five hours. He deserves a warm stable and some hay and water."

"Micco, you could get pneumonia, or slip on the ice and break a bone! Please wait until morning," pleaded Meg.

"Sorry, Red. I'm a strong, healthy male. A little walk in the snow is not going to disable me." 'Oops,' he thought, 'I am supposed to appear downtrodden to Meg!'

"Tell you what. If I become ill or injured, you can bring me hot soup and bathe my fevered brow. How's that?"

"You are so hardheaded, Micco Ravenwing. You always were and you always will be," retorted Meg. "I'll be standing at the foot of your bed saying 'I told you so', while a big fat nurse spoons soup in your mouth."

"Big fat nurse! Please, Meg, not that!"

She gave him one final blistering look and turned and trounced upstairs to her room.

"You see, Jim? I can't win with Meg. I'm trying to appear humble, but all I do is ruffle her feathers."

Jim smiled sympathetically. "I know what you mean. Sometimes I have the same effect on her. Well, be careful, Micco. It is getting quite icy. I'll be listening for your return. Goodnight!" He gave Micco a pat on the back and walked upstairs to his room.

He stopped Meg on the stair steps. "Meg, wait! I have something for you- your Christmas present. It's in my room. I bought it before we left New York." Jim walked into his bedroom and came back with a gaily-wrapped, oblong package.

"I have yours, also," said Meg, pulling a large box from behind her back. "I purchased this in New York, too, right before we left."

"You first, Meg." She opened her present eagerly. "Oh, Uncle Jim. The Pegasus!" Meg cried.. She picked up a small gold figure of Pegasus, its emerald eyes sparkling in the gaslight. Semi-precious stones adorned its mane.

"Thank you so much," said Meg, hugging her uncle so tightly he almost stumbled. "I wanted it, but I never dreamed I would have it!"

"I'm glad you like it, dear."

"Now, open your present! It won't compare to this, though," she said, gazing at the golden horse in awe.

"I'll treasure it just as much because you gave it to me," answered Jim, unwrapping his gift. It was a red vest, hand embroidered with gold and silver threads.

"Meg, it is magnificent! I'll have to hobnob with the Vanderbilts to show them what the well-dressed lawyer wears to one of their soirees!"

"I'm glad you like it. Look what Micco gave me. I was so surprised!" She showed him her necklace.

"That's lovely and it matches your coloring perfectly," said Jim .

"That's what Micco said." Meg laughed. "He compared me to a Celtic princess!"

"The man is definitely a connoisseur," said Jim, smiling. "Go to bed, Meg. It's been a long day. I'm going to wait up for Micco."

"All right. I am a little tired." Meg gave Jim a kiss on the cheek.

Outside in the blizzard, Micco was having a difficult time. Everything was a blur. He couldn't really see where he was going, but the horse seemed to know, so Micco let him make his way back to the stable. He spoke soothing words to the animal who understood the tone of his voice. Micco loved horses. He had ridden bareback so many years that he still preferred it to a saddle. Slowly but surely they approached their destination. Micco's hands were wet and cold in spite of his gloves. He was relieved to see the stable door, and the horse whinnied in anticipation of warmth. He jumped down and took off the harness though it took him a while because his fingers were so stiff. Micco led the horse to the barn, murmuring in his ear. He lifted the latch and took the horse to an empty stall. Three other horses whickered a greeting.

"Good boy," he said, rubbing the horse's mane. He found a blanket and threw it over the animal's back because even though it was bitter cold, the horse was sweating from exertion. Micco stayed in the barn for a little while, huddling close to the horses, until his frozen fingers and nose started to become warm. He talked to the horse.

"I never was introduced, so I don't know your name, fella', but I do know you are a good horse. Feel like listening to an Indian boy's story?" The horse looked up from munching his hay as if to say, 'Tell me all about it. I'm a good listener.'

"Well, thanks old fellow, for lending an understanding ear." Feeling warmed, Micco went back outside. He hoped the buggy would be safe left unattended. No human was around at this hour of the night, so Micco latched the door and began his trek through the snow. He could still see wheel marks and followed those back to the house, hoping the snow wouldn't completely obliterate them. After about thirty minutes of hard trudging, he finally saw the glow of gaslights in the distance. Jim had left the porch lights on, as well as the hall light, and a light in his bedroom window. Micco moved towards the welcoming lights. He certainly appreciated Jim's thoughtfulness. Finally, he reached the house and went inside, thankful he was back in one piece. True to his word, Jim was waiting.

"Come into the kitchen, Micco. Sit down. I made some hot tea." Micco had never been so happy to have a cup of steaming hot tea.

"Thank you. I didn't think I was ever going to be warm again." He drank the tea gratefully, warming his frozen fingers on the cup.

Jim watched Micco, thankful that he had returned safely. He had never felt such familial closeness to any man before. Micco was almost like the son he never had.

"Did you get there without any mishaps?"

"Yes, lucky for me, the horse knew the way home, so I just let him take the lead. I had to leave the carriage outside, though. I hope nobody steals it."

"I don't think you have any worry on that account. People in Beaufort leave their doors unlocked. We seldom have any crime. That is, until last week," said Jim, thinking with sorrow of his old friend and the young boy who had been murdered.

Micco sensed that Jim was upset about something. "What happened?"

"Two men were ruthlessly murdered, and they haven't caught the murderer. They don't even know who did it, but I have a strong suspicion who it was."

"If you know, why can't they arrest him?" asked Micco, disturbed that such a crime could have been committed in Beaufort.

"Because he escaped on a ship before we realized he was the one. It was a stranger, a scurvy seaman with a knife scar across his face. Two deaths and all for a few paltry dollars. It was so senseless. Horace Rumley, owner of a local feed store, was an old man who would have given him the money with no resistance. And Danny Piver was only eighteen. He worked part-time in the store. If only I had acted sooner," said Jim..

"I know you did all you could. The man was clever enough to get away before he was found out."

"I don't think he was clever. I think he had help," Jim spoke grimly, thinking of Andre.

"Then why didn't they bring the man who helped him in for questioning?" asked Micco.

"It was only a suspicion that I alone had. There was no concrete proof that he was involved."

"Is this man still here, or did he follow his accomplice out of town?"

"No. He is still here and I am afraid for Meg." Jim experienced a sense of relief that he had finally expressed aloud what he felt to be true.

"Meg!" Micco jumped up, knocking over the empty teacup. "How is she involved?"

"I am convinced that it is Andre Lafitte. I believe him to be totally without conscience. I have no proof other than my instincts, which have always proved to be reliable. I've told you that he is trying to seduce her, but much worse than that, I believe he is a killer."

Micco sank back down into his chair, shock and disbelief on his face. "How can you be sure?"

"I can't prove it. I have no evidence. Meg would be horrified if I suggested such a thing. I have simply told her that I don't like him, that I don't trust him, and that he will take advantage of her and then leave her. She thinks I am trying to run her life, to dictate what she must and must not do. I am at my wit's end. If we were going to leave here and never see him again, I

280

would be relieved, but he is sailing to Jupiter with us." Jim put his head in his hands and Micco felt a mounting rage.

Micco was a product of his upbringing. The Seminoles were inherently a gentle and trusting people. They were honest. Unlike most native societies, women were accorded the same respect as men. But once the trust was violated, the Seminole could prove an unforgiving foe. Micco had all the gentle qualities of his forebears, but the blood of his father, Tall Chief, and his uncle, Chief Tallahassee, and his long distant cousin, Micanopy, coursed through his veins, too. At that moment, Jim thought he could have been a warrior, riding beside the intrepid Osceola and the fiery Wild Cat.

"Andre Lafitte will not harm Meg. I believe in your instincts. I will protect her." Micco's eyes flashed with an inner fury, and his hands were clenched as if he were choking something. His voice was ominous.

For the first time since Lafitte had appeared on the scene, Jim felt a lessening of his fears. He trusted Micco completely, and he had seen a side of him tonight that he never imagined existed. Micco could be as ruthless as Andre if he believed the cause was just.

"Micco, we'll talk further in the morning. You must go to sleep. This has been an exhausting night for you."

Micco looked at Jim with glazed eyes, almost as if he didn't hear him speaking.

"Come on," repeated Jim. He got up and went over to Micco, putting his arm around his shoulder. "Let's go to bed. There is nothing you can do now."

Finally, Micco's eyes registered the fact that Jim was speaking to him. He rose from his chair. "You are right. We must sleep on this, but have no more fears, because I will be Meg's amulet, her protective talisman."

Jim smiled at Micco. "I believe you will. Together, we will protect her."

They walked upstairs, neither man speaking further. Jim's thoughts were relief that he had a powerful ally. Micco's thoughts were of a cold fury: something he hadn't felt since he was a teenaged boy and discovered the senseless slaughter of a bald eagle. When he found out who had killed the eagle, he beat the man senseless and then banished him from the tribe. That anger was nothing compared to the fury he felt now against one who was a threat to innocent Meg. When he reached his room, he pulled off his wet clothes and put on his sleeping garment. As he slipped under the covers, exhaustion claimed him, and his last thoughts were of his little red-haired Meg pursued by a white devil with the face of an angel.

Meg had been awake too, unable to sleep until Micco returned. When she finally heard him come upstairs and enter his room, she closed her eyes and slept.

Just before dawn, when the snow finally stopped falling, a foot and a half covered the ground. At six o'clock, Jim tapped lightly on Meg's door. Hearing no response, he opened the door. Meg was sound asleep, so he quietly put more logs in the fireplace. He placed paper underneath and rekindled the fire. Once the log began to burn, he replaced the fire screen and left the room. He couldn't go back to sleep though it was two hours until the Brown's Christmas breakfast. Last night as they were leaving, Leland had said that he would pick up the three of them in his own horse and buggy. Lucy and Bob decided not to go since the children were too young to enjoy the adult affair and would rather stay home and play with their toys. Jim put on his robe, built up his own fire, and then went downstairs to the kitchen to make a cup of coffee. He sat down at the table, pondering the situation. It seemed inevitable that there would be a confrontation between the two men. Micco was a civilized man, a man dedicated to saving lives, and Jim hoped he could resolve the conflict without physical violence, yet he saw a fierceness lurking beneath the polished veneer, too. He wondered how his brother-in-law would react to the situation. Sean Riley was an idealist who existed in his own

282

little cocoon. He had been consumed with his wife, his clinic, and the immediate problems of the Indians he attended. It was almost as if he weren't aware of anything beyond that. He did not even know that people like Andre Lafitte existed. Jim shook his head as if to dispel the myriad thoughts racing through his brain. If only he and Meg were safely back in New York- but they weren't. The problem was compounded because Meg was so much like him. In his youth, before he met Julia, he had been enamoured of an older, beautiful, but empty-headed woman. His father had warned him repeatedly, that she was unsuitable , and that he was too young, but Jim would not listen. They eloped when he was sixteen and she twenty-one. His father tracked them down and offered her money to leave. She took it and a heart-broken Jim returned home to his parents. Three months later, they learned that after a drunken mid-night spree, she had ridden her horse into the woods and was killed instantly when she was thrown into a tree. Jim reflected on this, wondering how his life would have turned out if she had turned down the offer. He probably never would have become a lawyer. For a while he was bitter, but finally he realized his parents were right. Who was he to tell Meg what to do? No one except his parents, not even Julia, knew of his youthful indiscretion. He arose, washed out his cup, and went upstairs to dress. It was almost time to wake up Meg and Micco. Leland had said he would be here at seven forty-five. Jim sighed. He hoped he could be strong for Meg.

By seven thirty, the sun was shining brightly. Micco was already downstairs and had cleaned the snow and ice off the porch and steps, and Meg was almost dressed. She came down five minutes later.

"Uncle Jim, thanks so much for lighting my fire early this morning. It was warm and cozy when I got up." She walked over and kissed his cheek.

"You are welcome, dear. Are you ready to meet the rest of the Beaufort citizenry? Many people will be there."

283

"Yes, I look forward to it. Everyone I have met here is so nice." She turned to Micco. "I don't notice any splints. Evidently, you didn't break anything. I hope the horse appreciated it," she said .

"He certainly did! We talked about it in the barn. He told me that he hates to stand around in the snow for hours. It's all right if he's galloping: it's just that standing around that bothers him!"

"I see," said Meg, trying not to smile.

"Uh, thank you for your concern about my health," said Micco, attempting to look humble.

Meg looked at him suspiciously, about to make a rejoinder. Then they all heard the jingle of bells outside.

"That must be Leland. Let's go," said Jim. They put on their coats, hats and gloves and went outside. Leland and Stephanie were seated on the buckboard seat up front and Alexandria was inside the coach. All were exchanging greetings and saying 'Merry Christmas'.

Jim, Meg, and Micco walked down the steps and before Meg could put her foot into the snow, Micco picked her up and carried her to the carriage. Jim opened the door and Micco placed her on the seat.

"What are you doing? I'm not crippled. I can walk."

"I know. I just didn't want you to get your shoes and skirt wet."

"Oh, thank you," she muttered with poor grace. 'He still thinks of me as a helpless five-year-old,' she thought resentfully.

Jim sat down by Meg and Micco climbed in beside Alexandria.

Meg thought, 'How can anyone look so gorgeous this early in the morning?' She was dressed in a deep rose frock trimmed in fur with a rose fur hat dyed to match the dress. Rose quartz earrings sparkled in her ears and those magnificent eyes looked like deep blue sapphires.

284

"Merry Christmas, Meg. How are you this lovely Christmas morn?" she asked in her clear, sweet voice.

"Merry Christmas! I'm fine. It is a glorious day, isn't it? Did the children like their presents?"

"They were ecstatic! Melissa kept saying, 'My doll has real hair' and Cicero wouldn't release his 'horsie' even to eat breakfast!" She spoke to Jim, "You are looking quite elegant today, straight out of a Fifth Avenue drawing room."

"Thank you, Alexandria. That dress is most becoming. It makes your eyes look like jewels."

Meg noticed that Micco had been staring at Alexandria ever since he sat down beside her. 'Who wouldn't stare,' she thought

"Micco, you are quiet this morning. What are you thinking?" Alexandria asked.

"I am thinking how lucky we all are to have so much to be thankful for on this Christmas Day in 1886," he said, his face quite serious.

Alexandria looked at him, her sad eyes searching his face. "Yes, you are right," she said at last. "I do have many things to be thankful for, though many times I have thought I had nothing, nothing at all."

Again, as he had done the evening before, he took her hand and held it, giving her his warmth.

Meg turned her head away and looked out the window. 'Why am I even bothered? Micco means nothing to me except as a friend, a friend who torments me,' she thought, but poor Alexandria needs his comfort.

"Here we are," called out Leland, pulling the horse right up to the steps. Dozens of carriages were already lining the drive. The gentlemen all helped the ladies down and Leland drove off to tether the horse.

They entered the house and exchanged joyous greetings with friends and neighbors. A wonderful aroma of freshly baked bread, sizzling bacon, ham, and sausage tantalized their noses. The room was filled with people dressed in all their finery.

Albert and Jennifer were standing at the door greeting guests, and Pamela and Andre were next to them. Meg tried to be nonchalant. She hadn't seen Andre since Micco unceremoniously dragged her away from their meeting on the dock. He was so unbelievably good-looking. His blue waistcoat, stretched across his chest and broad shoulders, matched his blue eyes perfectly. A diamond stickpin twinkled in his perfectly tied cravat. He smiled at Meg and she gazed at his lips, remembering his passionate kiss.

Pamela looked like a shimmering Christmas fairy, dressed all in white lace and satin. She even wore a shiny tiara nestled in her blonde curls. Tiny white satin shoes peeped from beneath her voluminous skirts. Diamond earrings sparkled and dangled from her dainty shell-like ears. She smiled, looking up at Andre adoringly, clutching his arm even more tightly when she saw Meg.

"It's so good to see you all again. Jennifer, don't Meg and Alexandria look absolutely stunning?" asked Albert.

"Yes, they do dear. The three most beautiful ladies in Beaufort are standing right here!"

Meg felt gauche and dowdy as she always did around the petite Pamela, but now, standing between her and the exquisitely beautiful Alexandria, she felt positively homely. Her green satin dress that fit her flawlessly, seemed colorless, and she wished that she had caught her hair up in a sophisticated chignon, instead of letting it float like an uncontrolled fire around her shoulders. She could not know that all the men in the room gazed at her appreciatively, admiring her vivid coloring. She was aware of Andre's eyes almost devouring her. Micco was behind her so she didn't know where he was looking, probably gawking at Pamela while holding Alexandria's delicate hand.

"Everyone, please have some eggnog. Remember, it's the first nourishment taken on Christmas Morning," invited Albert. Two maids were serving the eggnog, one with alcohol, the other without.

"Meg, you look gorgeous," said Andre.

"Thank you." Their eyes were locked in silent yearning.

"Yes, she does, as always," agreed Micco, coming up behind her and putting his arm around her waist as though they were lovers. He murmured in her ear, "Come on, Sweetheart. Let's get something to drink."

Meg's mouth dropped open in shock as he propelled her into the parlor.

"What do you think you are doing?" she said , trying to pull away from him.

"Hush, dearest. People will think we're having a lover's quarrel."

Meg looked around her and noticed the interested glances in their direction. She saw that Alexandria had walked on ahead, her hand resting on her father's arm.

"I don't want any eggnog. Will you let me go?" she whispered angrily.

"It's tradition. You can't fight tradition, Meg," Micco replied cheerfully.

"Is this non-alcoholic?" he asked the maid.

"Yes, it is." He took two glasses and handed one to Meg.

"Merry Christmas to you and a Happy New Year," he said, touching her glass with his.

"I told you I did not want any, and if I did, I'd want it with alcohol."

"It's bad luck not to drink it and insulting to your host and hostess, besides."

Meg took one quick sip and then put the glass on a nearby table. She turned away from him, crossing her arms in front of her, trying to see Andre.

"Meg, can't you tell? He's completely enamored of the little fairy princess."

"I don't know what you are talking about."

"Yes, you do. Forget about him. He's all tied up with a silver bow. Your uncle is signaling us to come over. We must mingle, dear. It's the thing to do at these little gatherings."

"Don't you 'dear and 'sweetheart' me. I am neither to you."

"Ah, but you are, dearest. I've had to restrain myself from calling you my little Chickadee!"

"Chickadee?"

"It's the highest compliment I could pay you. It expresses my innermost feeling towards you."

"You think of me as a small, insect-eating bird?"

"Well, not an insectivore exactly, but quick and flighty, darting here and there, your inquisitive eyes staring curiously at the world around you."

She had completely forgotten about Andre and Pamela and was preparing to give him a withering reply when Jim walked up.

"Come on over, you two. I want you to meet some of my friends." Meg had to go along, unwillingly, because Micco had his arm around her again and she had to go with him or be dragged by him.

Jim introduced them to so many people that Meg's head was swimming, trying to remember the names. Micco charmed them all. They were fascinated by whatever he said. Meg would like to have tossed her eggnog in his beaming face if she'd had any. She muttered something distinctly unladylike.

"What did you say, Dear?" asked Micco , leaning his dark head towards hers.

She debated whether to kick him but decided she couldn't get enough leverage with her long skirts hindering her. He had the audacity to keep his arm around her waist, and she could see that he was using supreme effort to keep from laughing at her.

An elderly couple smiled at them. "Have you two known each other a long time?" asked the gray haired matron.

"Too long," answered Meg, staring daggers at Micco as she tried to detach herself from him.

Micco held her closer. "She means that we have known each other since we were children, and have only recently met again after years of separation. It was Kismit," he sighed. "Fate brought us together once again."

"Oh, how romantic," said his questioner. "Don't you think so, Roland?"

"Yes, my dear. Fate and all that."

Micco was laughing now though he tried to hide it behind a fit of coughing. The whole morning continued like this. Micco was attached to her like a sucker on a fish. When they finally sat down to eat, she wondered if he was going to spoon-feed her. Everyone was talking at once and seemed to be enjoying themselves tremendously. If she hadn't been so annoyed with Micco, she could have enjoyed herself, too. "He is the life of the party," she thought . Every female from eight to eighty was hanging on his every word, ogling him like a piece of prime beef.

Jim watched the expressions on Meg's face, warring with each other. She tried to remain furious, but sometimes she couldn't keep from smiling at one of Micco's outrageous stories. So far, Pamela had kept Andre away from Meg. Jim was happy that there were fifty or more people there to prevent any unpleasant encounters. Just as he was exhaling a shaky breath of relief, Meg excused herself to go upstairs. Micco could hardly accompany her to the bathroom, so he stood and pulled out her chair and watched her walk away. Meg had finally caught Andre's eye and he watched as she left the table and headed for the stairs. After a few minutes, he excused himself from Pamela, who could hardly accompany him to the bathroom. Jim had turned his head and was talking to Micco, and the two men did not see Andre follow Meg up the stairs.

Meg stood waiting in the shadows, just the faint glow if one wall lamp illuminating her. In long strides, Andre reached her. He pulled her into his arms and held her tightly against him, feeling the softness of her body. He was aroused by the enticing scent of her perfume, as intriguing as Meg herself.

289

"Mon Dieu, how long have I waited to hold you?" he breathed in her ear. Andre was not used to being thwarted in his pursuit of women. He had never had to wait until now. This made her more desirable than ever. He felt her trembling against his body. He knew she felt the same as he did.

"Cherie, it seems like an eternity since I've held you. I have missed you so. Did you miss me a little, too?" he asked softly, nuzzling her ear.

"I, ooh, yes," she said breathlessly. She looked into his eyes that were gazing so ardently into hers. "Every time I tried to see you, you were with Pamela, or I was with my uncle or Micco." She felt him stiffen at the mention of Micco's name.

"What does he mean to you? Is he your lover?"

Meg rejoiced at the jealousy in his voice, but was shocked by his question. "What do you mean, 'lover'?" she asked.

Andre realized he had made a tactical error. He also realized they were too exposed in the hallway. Anyone could walk upstairs, looking for a bathroom.

"I merely meant, Mon petite chou, has he declared his love for you and you for him?"

"Certainly not! He thinks of me as his little sister."

"And you? Do you think of him as a brother?"

"I, I..." Meg hesitated. She didn't think of Micco as all as a brother. What did she think of him? "When we were children, he always played with me and looked after me, as a brother would," she temporized. Getting on safer ground, she asked, "What does 'Mon petite chou" mean?"

"Come in here and I'll tell you," said Andre, as he turned the knob on a door behind him.

"What are you doing?" asked Meg in confusion as he pulled her with him into the bedroom. Closing the door behind him in the darkened room, he picked Meg up and carried her to the bed.

"We can't stay in here," said Meg .

"Don't worry, beautiful Meg, I won't hurt you. I just want to lie beside you and hold you." Meg tried to pull away, but Andre had her pinned down.

"I insist you let me up immediately. This isn't proper. What would my uncle say if he knew?"

"But he doesn't know. This is natural between men and women, Meg. It is nothing to be ashamed of, believe me. I wouldn't do anything to blemish your reputation."

Meg couldn't see him clearly in the semi-darkness and was shocked when she felt him slip the thin material of her dress down her shoulders.

"No! Stop, Andre! I don't want you to do this!" By now, Meg was really frightened that he wouldn't stop. She felt the material rip.

Suddenly the room was flooded with light, and Andre was plucked backwards as if he were a bag of meal and flung across the floor and into the wall. Terrified, Meg sat up, pulling her dress back up over her shoulders. Micco was crouched over a dazed Andre, his hands around the Frenchman's throat.

"If you have touched her, I'll kill you," said Micco, his voice cold and deadly.

"No, Micco. He didn't do anything. Please..." Meg pleaded. "Let him go." She thought Micco looked like a savage about to scalp his victim. She couldn't believe he could be this fierce. Her words finally pierced that film of rage that had blotted out all reason. He stood up slowly, watching his foe as he would a poisonous snake.

"Get out!" If you ever try to touch her again, her uncle will have you behind bars for assault and attempted rape. I heard her cry out and tell you to stop!"

Andre got up, his face convulsed with hate. "This is not over between us. I would not have harmed Meg. She knows that." He turned towards her, looking so contrite, that she almost believed she had not seen the look of pure hatred moments before.

"You heard what I said! Don't come near her again."

291

Lafitte walked out the door, and spoke venomously, "Watch your step, Indian. You won't catch me unawares again!" He left, and the air was thick between Micco and Meg.

"We'd better get back downstairs. Your uncle will wonder what has happened to you."

Micco waited for Meg to precede him. Meg didn't know what to say. Somehow she felt that Micco was disappointed in her. And she had seen a side of Micco that she didn't know existed.

When they returned to the dining room, Andre was nowhere in sight and Pamela looked furious. Jim walked over to Micco, a questioning look on his face.

"What happened?" he asked in a low voice. "Andre left, looking like an angry hornet. He barely paid his respects to his host and hostess and Pamela."

"I don't think we'll be bothered by him anymore. I told him to stay away from Meg or you would have him thrown in jail for assault and attempted rape."

"What? By God, I'll kill him!"

"Wait, Jim," said Micco, restraining him. "I have taken care of it. He didn't hurt Meg. We'll go to Davy tomorrow and tell him not to allow Lafitte passage on the ship."

"Yes, you're right, but when I think that he had his lecherous hands on her, I want to go after him."

"Be calm. We'll handle it without violence. I can't believe I almost tried to choke him to death. I thought myself to be a civilized man, and I almost became a savage," said Micco, still shaken by the remembrance of the rage that had consumed him.

"Perhaps there is a violence, a dark side in all of us that has to be overcome. I too, felt a momentary murderous rage. We both felt it when someone dear to us was threatened. You know, Micco, I think I should speak to Albert about Andre. I believe he actually thinks the slimy devil would be a good catch for Pamela. The girl is besotted by him. Just look at her. Minutes ago she was furious, now she has run from the room weeping."

292

Dr. Brown looked bewildered. He didn't understand why Andre had left with barely a civil word, or why Pamela was crying. Mrs. Brown was trying to explain to him that it was probably a lover's quarrel, easily mended.

"Jim, I don't think that right now is a good time to talk to Dr. Brown about Andre. Arrange for a casual chat tomorrow, perhaps lunch somewhere," suggested Micco.

"You're right. That's what I'll do."

Meg had collapsed in a chair, still disturbed by both Andre's and Micco's actions. Davy, seeing her alone for once, walked over, glad of the opportunity to talk to her.

"Hello, Davy. How is your adorable puppy?"

"Watson is just fine. She's already learned to sit up and shake hands. Except for her, it would be paws!" Davy looked at Meg admiringly. How beautiful she was. He came out of his reverie with a start.

"Miss Riley, may I get you some eggnog or some tea? You look a little flushed."

"Yes, thank you, Davy. I would love some eggnog with alcohol."

Davy looked surprised, but walked over to the punch bowl. He came back with two glasses.

"May I fix a plate for you, too? The food is awfully good , especially the scrambled eggs and fish roe."

Meg smiled at him, thinking what a truly innocent face he had. "I'm really not hungry. I'll just drink my eggnog."

She took a sip and choked. She began coughing and Davy became alarmed and pounded her on the back. Her coughing finally subsided, much to Davy's relief. He was afraid she was going to have an apoplectic attack.

"You can stop hitting me now, Davy," gasped Meg between coughs.

"Oh, I am sorry. I was afraid you were choking, or that you might swoon. Hope I didn't pound too hard."

293

"Not at all. You see, that was my very first taste of liquor, and now I know why they call it 'Demon Rum'. I don't think I'll ever try it again. Ugh! That was horrible tasting!" She made a face just as Jim and Micco walked over to them.

"What an expression, Meg," Jim uttered in astonishment.

"I think Meg just tasted the eggnog. I told her she wouldn't like it," said Micco, smiling at the flustered Davy sympathetically, and studiously avoiding looking at Meg.

"How would you know? I'll bet you've never tried it yourself."

"Oh, but I have. My grandmother, Shontee, used to make it once a year at Christmas time; she called it 'sylabub'. A family from England settled in Jupiter and befriended her and taught her how to make it. I never cared for it, even though it is not as strong as whiskey."

"I'm sorry. It was my fault because I got it for her. I should have known better." Davy appeared quite downcast.

"Don't give it another thought. It was Meg's choice entirely," said Jim kindly. "Davy, Micco and I were going to talk to you about the trip tomorrow, but since you're here, perhaps we could talk now?"

"Sure. We'll be able to leave on Tuesday."

"Let's take a stroll around the room while we talk," said Jim. They walked off, discussing the trip, and Meg thought she heard Andre's name mentioned. She scowled mutinously after them, annoyed by everything in general, and particularly by not being invited to join them. She was also thinking long and hard about Andre. Would he have continued if Micco had not stopped him? She was still attracted to him, in spite of what had happened, but she didn't like that violent side of him. Alexandria came over and began talking animatedly about the breakfast and Meg momentarily forgot about Andre.

Jim had decided to take Davy into his confidence to a certain extent, as the three men drank eggnog and casually talked, speaking to acquaintances.

"Davy, I have a great favor to ask of you," said Jim as they paused in a corner of the room, away from the other guests.

"What is it, Mr. Styron? If it is in my power to do it, I will."

Jim looked at Micco as if for support, and then turned to Davy. "Uh, this is embarrassing for me to discuss, and I wouldn't talk about it with you unless I thought that it was necessary and important."

Davy was puzzled by Jim's demeanor. "I understand. What you are about to tell me is in confidence."

"Yes. You see, Micco discovered Andre about to assault Meg."

Davy's face became blood red. "The bastard! Excuse my French! Where is he?" asked Davy, glancing around the room.

"Hold on, Davy. He is gone. The favor I am requesting is that you not allow him to sail with us to Florida. It is your ship, and you alone can prevent it. I don't want him anywhere near Meg."

"You don't have to worry, Sir. He will not be on my ship when we leave on Tuesday. I will find him tomorrow and tell him so, and if he tries to board, my men will have orders to prevent it."

"Don't discuss the reason with him. Think up some other reason why it would not be feasible to sail on this voyage."

"You can depend on my discretion, Sir, though it will be hard not to knock him down," said Davy, his young face etched with righteous indignation.

"Thank you. This relieves my worry." They left Davy and rejoined Meg who was now talking to the Browns.

As Andre walked through the snow-covered streets back to his room, his thoughts were murderous. If he had hated Micco before, it was nothing compared to his state of mind now. He envisioned every kind of torture to be inflicted on him, ten ways to slowly kill him including feeding him to the sharks or barracudas. Every time he remembered how Micco had tossed him against the wall, he was almost blinded by fury. He was angrier than he was at sixteen when he killed a gendarme on the streets of Paris—a man who had dared to arrest him. The ship would sail in a few days and he would bide his time until then. He would take care of this man who had thwarted him at every turn. He knew that he had frightened Meg, but he had been so eager that he lost control. That had been a mistake. He realized he would have to regain her trust. She was innocent and inexperienced. He should have been more patient. She was not like the light skirts who expected to be taken quickly. But this prize was worth waiting for, wasn't it? But if she teased him too long, she would regret it. All these thought assailed him. When they were at sea, Micco would die. And when they reached Jupiter and he had seen the last of her uncle, Meg would be his to do with as he wished. He reached his room with thoughts of murder flooding his mind.

Davy was troubled too. He hadn't particularly cared for Andre from the little that he had seen of him, but now he was angry that the man had treated Meg as he had. He decided to compose a message to Lafitte, requesting that they meet at the Town Creek Marina at noon the next day. Davy was young and somewhat shy, but he was not one to back down from a confrontation. He intended to tell Andre face-to-face that he would not book passage on the Annie Marie.

Meg, Jim, and Micco left the breakfast after thanking the Browns for a wonderful get- together.

"How will we ever eat again at three o'clock?" asked Jim. "I over-indulged."

"So did I," said Micco.

Meg was silent and neither man mentioned the incident with Andre. Jim knew Meg too well, and decided not to embarrass her further.

At the dinner that afternoon, they did find room for Stephanie's famous Christmas goose, and her rum-soaked pound cake. Meg tasted one bite and decided she had had enough alcohol for one day. After exclaiming over the children's Christmas gifts, and enjoying conversation with their good friends, they bid farewell, promising to see them later.

The next morning, Davy dressed and then walked over to the Inlet Inn, letter in hand. It was only eight o'clock, but the receptionist was already behind his counter.

"Good morning, George," said Davy.

"Well, good morning to you, too, Davy. What brings you out so early on the day after Christmas?"

"I want to leave a note for one of your boarders."

"Sure. Leave it with me. I'll see that he gets it."

"Thanks, George. It is very important. Merry Christmas to you!" Davy left, feeling relieved.

When Andre walked downstairs fifteen minutes later, George greeted him and called him over to the desk.

"Letter here for you, Sir."

Andre took the envelope and tore it open as he walked away. 'Wonder what he wants?' he thought, stuffing the note in his pocket.

He had composed a letter to Meg early this morning, apologizing profusely for his behavior. He had to keep on Meg's good side. He realized he had made a serious mistake, but he could appeal to Meg's compassionate nature. She was the type who was always willing to forgive anyone if she thought that person was sincere. He knew Meg wanted the chance to forgive him because she was attracted to him. Now he had to find a boy to deliver the letter. He didn't dare go to the Davis House where her uncle and the accursed Micco would prevent him from seeing Meg. He ate a leisurely breakfast, once again dazzling Linda, the waitress.

"Do you know of someone who might deliver a letter for me?" he asked.

"Well, Marlan's in the kitchen washing dishes, but he could take off long enough to do it, if it's not too far," said Linda, eager to please this handsome man.

"It isn't far, only to the Davis House."

297

"That's all right then. I'll get him for you." She went quickly to the kitchen and returned with an older man who was wiping his hands on his apron.

"This here is Marlan."

"Hello, Marlan. Could you deliver a letter for me?" asked Andre, showing the man a silver dollar.

"Yes Sir!" said Marlan, his eyes lighting up. "Where to?"

"The Davis House. Give this letter directly to Miss Megan Riley. Can I trust you to do that? Give it to no one else, understand?"

"I'm your man. She'll have it in her hand in the next fifteen minutes."

"Good," said Andre, handing him the money.

Marlan took off, moving quickly for an oldster. His skinny legs flew out of the restaurant and he appeared to be a man on a mission.

Andre left and headed for Dr. Brown's office. He needed to apologize to the Browns and Pamela, too. He wanted to stay in their good graces, even though he would be leaving in two days. One never knew when they might be useful. Andre's plans for revenge against Micco had put him in a better mood. He was actually whistling as he strolled down the street. He was looking forward to being at sea once again. Andre didn't think he was capable of being nostalgic, but he was today. Never for a person or a relationship though, just the beautiful, treacherous, beckoning sea. This was the mistress that claimed him, body and soul.

By the time Andre had appeased the Browns and Pamela, it was almost noon. He had promised Pamela he would see her that evening, and she was no longer pouting. He went away leaving everyone in a good mood, winding his way to the Town Creek Marina.

Davy had apprised his crew that Lafitte would not be sailing with them, and under no circumstances was he to be allowed on board. He was standing on the dock talking to Anson

298

when he saw Andre approaching. Davy felt a hot anger towards the Frenchman, almost hoping to get into a fight with him.

Andre walked up to Davy. "I received your note. What's the problem?"

"When I spoke to you earlier about booking passage on the Annie Marie, I did not realize that my grandfather planned to take on additional passengers in Beaufort. Unfortunately, there won't be room for you. I'm sorry I didn't know this sooner." Davy was about as sorry as a fox with a rabbit. "You won't have trouble getting a berth on another ship, though. Many ships frequent Beaufort harbor on the way to Florida or the Bahamas."

Andre stared at Davy in amazement. "You cannot be serious! You assured me I could sail on this ship. It is imperative that I reach Jupiter as soon as possible. I will not brook a delay!"

"Mister, I'm afraid you will have to! There is no room for you on my ship. I suggest you talk to the harbor master about other ships and when they will be entering port." Davy turned away to continue his conversation with Anson.

Andre was livid with rage. Who did this fresh-faced kid think he was? He grabbed Davy's arm and jerked him around.

"You will find room!" he yelled in a threatening voice.

"Take you hand off me, or you will take an early morning swim," said Davy, ready to throw Andre into the swirling tide.

Samese and Joey walked over to the two men. "What's going on?" asked Samese, pushing up his sleeves from his brawny arms.

"Nothing," said Davy, jerking his arm away. "This man is just leaving."

Andre gave Davy a malevolent glare. "You'll be sorry you did this."

"Just be on your way, Mister," said Samese as he and Joey stood on either side of Andre.

With a final glare, he turned on his heel and left.

Chapter Fifteen

M arlan made his way quickly to the Davis House in spite of slipping and sliding on the snow and ice. He asked at the desk which room was Meg's and then walked up to her room. He knocked on her door.

"Who is it?" asked Meg.

"I have a letter for you, Ma'am."

"Oh, just slip it under the door."

"I was told to hand it to you personally," replied Marlan.

"Who gave you the letter?" Meg did not intend to open her door to a stranger.

"It's from a big blonde man who gave it to me at the Inlet Inn dining room and he told me not to let nobody get this letter but you," said Marlan.

When Meg heard this, she opened the door, and Marlan handed her the letter. "Thank you," she said, happy that Andre had contacted her in spite of their unfortunate last meeting.

"Is there a reply?" Marlan asked, thinking he might get another tip.

"No, goodbye."

Marlan turned away, disappointed. Meg eagerly ripped open the envelope and read Andre's apology.

"Mon petite chou (My little cabbage),

This is a French term of endearment, by the way. Can I find the words to tell you how sorry I am for my behavior yesterday? I was boorish and ungentlemanly. I am so sorry to have treated you in such an unspeakable way. Can you ever forgive me? My only excuse is that I am so attracted to you that my strong emotion overcame my better judgment. I do think of you as a lady and should have treated you as one. Can you find it in your heart to let me express my regret to you personally? I want to tell you, tête-à-tête, how I feel. Have no fear. I will not touch you if you do not desire it. Can we rendezvous in front of the Duncan House at five o'clock? I will be there waiting to reveal my heart to you. But if you do not meet me, I understand, though mon coeur will be breaking.

Toujours,
Andre"

Meg clasped the letter to her bosom. 'I will meet him. He sounds truly sorry for his behavior. And this time, I'll make sure that Micco is nowhere around,' she thought. Someone knocked at the door.

"Meg, are you ready for lunch?" asked Jim.

"Yes. I'll be right out, Uncle Jim."

"All right, Micco and I will meet you downstairs." Jim felt relieved at Meg's cheerful voice. At least she sounded in a good mood. He didn't know what to expect after the encounter with Lafitte and the eggnog episode. He only thanked whatever gods there were that Andre would not be on the ship with them.

Meg gave a quick glance in the looking glass, ran a comb through her hair, dabbed perfume behind her ears, and put on the silver necklace Micco had given her. If Alexandria weren't around, maybe he would deign to look at her. She ran lightly down the steps. Jim and Micco were waiting on the porch.

"Good morning, Meg," Micco greeted her pleasantly. "Did you sleep well?"

"Like a baby bear in hibernation," she said , smiling at him.

Micco thought he would never understand Meg. She was almost flirting with him, and she was wearing his necklace. He was prepared to withstand an attack about his behavior with Andre and his remarks about the eggnog. Her beaming smile caught him off-balance. One thing for sure, being around Meg was never boring.

"You are kind of furry! Wrong color fur though, more like a red fox cub," said Micco, staring at her hair.

Meg's smile faded. "Well, I didn't mean for you to take me literally!"

"You know me, Meg. Literal to the bone," said Micco.

Meg glared at him and Jim intervened before she made a scathing remark. "Wonder what delicious food Miss Molly has prepared today? I hope she has blackberry cobbler again."

"No doubt she'll want to consult with the witch doctor," said Meg.

They had reached the dining room and found a table. Fortunately, Andre was not there.

"Miss Molly is knowledgeable about home remedies. Many of the natural materials she uses are quite helpful in curing or relieving symptoms of some illnesses."

"I am glad to hear you confirm what I thought to be true," said Jim. "I know she cured my croup one time. The medicine was awful, but it worked."

They sat down and ordered lunch, which Meg ate sparingly.

"You don't eat enough to sustain a chickadee," said Micco. "Pretty soon, you won't be able to dart here and there, you'll be so malnourished. This chowder is quite delicious. Here, taste mine, my small chickadee." Micco held out a spoonful of soup to Meg.

"I told you before I am not your chickadee to spoon feed or a worm-eating bird and I don't dart. I have finished my lunch," said Meg, rising from the table. "Miss Molly has been signaling to me ever since we arrived. Excuse me." Both men had risen when Meg did.

"I think she's been signaling to me, too. Jim, will you excuse us?" asked Micco, holding onto Meg's elbow.

"Certainly. I'm going to have dessert. You two run along. After I finish, I plan to visit with Leland and Stephanie. See you later."

Micco escorted a stiff Meg to the kitchen. When they reached it, Meg flounced around. "Will you stop treating me like your younger sister? I don't feel the least bit sisterly to you!"

"Heh, heh, heh. You sho doesn't," chimed in Molly.

The somewhat flustered Meg said, "What I mean is, I am not a juvenile, for your information, Mister Ravenwing. Or should I say 'Doctor'?"

"You'll have to pardon her, Miss Molly. She drank alcohol for the first time yesterday, and I don't think she's fully recovered," said Micco, unable to resist the opportunity of further teasing Meg.

"I doesn't believe it be de alcohol. You has her dancing de juba, Doctor Micco. Heh, heh, heh," chuckled Molly, her sly old eyes darting from one to the other.

Meg was furious. "I came here to see you since you were waving at me from the door. He came with me uninvited, and believe me, I am not dancing over him!"

"I was waving at de doctor. I needs to discuss one of my serus cases with him, but I is happy to see you too, Miss Meg. You is welcome to stay while we be talking 'bout medicine."

"No, thank you. I have other things to do." She turned to leave; really annoyed that Molly wanted to see Micco instead of her.

"Meg, please stay. We're leaving day after tomorrow and you won't have a chance to see or talk to Miss Molly again. Please? We both want you to stay." Micco's expressive eyes pleaded with her, and she knew deep inside that he simply liked to tease her.

"Well, if it won't be a bother."

"You is no bother to me, and de doctor's heart be broke right in two if you leaves." Molly grinned at Micco, the light from the lamp glinting on her gold teeth.

Micco grinned right back at her. "Miss Molly, I am going to miss you."

Meg stared at both of them. Molly was as bad as Micco about teasing.

"I be old and bossy. Dat pretty red haired girl be young and bossy. You soon be forgettin' dis 'un and fallin' in love with dat 'un."

"I won't forget you, Miss Molly, believe me!"

Meg noticed that he ignored the part about falling in love with her. Evidently, she just wasn't his type. He liked the sweet, but exotic Alexandria. She couldn't wait until five o'clock to see Andre, who did find her attractive and who could fall in love with her.

"Well, Molly, how can I help you?" asked Micco.

"I has a patient who has a misery in de bones. She be aching all de day 'un night. I has mixed some goosefoot, 'un wort, 'un bittersweet, den heated dem in my curing kettle. Does you think dis be de right medicine?"

"In Florida, where I was born, not far from the Everglades, during the Corn Festival, our medicine men gather a plant they call 'hot root'. They make an infusion from this and rub it like a liniment on aching joints. I believe what you are using would work the same way. Add a little mint and boneset to it to hasten the healing. Many of my people have been healed by these brews of herbs."

"Thank you, Doctor. I has some dried mint and boneset in my herb bags," said Molly . "Dis be a sure cure."

"You're welcome. We doctors have to share information."

"That is the second time you have mentioned a 'Corn Dance'. It sounds interesting. What is it?"

"It is an inherent part of Seminole life. You will understand its significance when you actually attend the celebration. It will be difficult, but not impossible, for you to attend. White people are not welcome at this festival because it is sacred as well as enjoyable to the Seminoles."

"I understand, and would certainly consider it an honor if I am allowed to attend," said Meg.

"Now dat is right. You is going to learn all 'bout de Indians 'fore you marries one," stated Molly positively.

Micco laughed and Meg sputtered indignantly. "You don't know anything about it. It is true that I want to learn all I can about the Seminoles because I am going down there to teach the Indian children. I am certainly not interested in marriage to Micco Ravenwing whom I consider as a, a," she paused, almost unable to say the word "brother".

"Stay away from dat white debil. He be a Jonah and he got a cloud all 'round him," warned Molly. "Dis be de man for you."

"That is ridiculous! Cloud indeed!" Meg said angrily.

"I think she means an aura," suggested Micco.

"You're both witch doctors! He is just an ordinary man. He has no nimbus of evil encircling him!"

Micco wasn't teasing now. He was deadly serious. "Meg, can't you see what kind of man he is? He is dangerous. I am only trying to protect you from him." He looked at her intently, hoping to convince her of his sincerity.

Meg was no longer angry, but she was unconvinced that what they were saying was true.

"I know you are, Micco. You always had my best interests at heart. I know your intentions are good too, Miss Molly, but can't you see? I have to make my own decisions, to judge people for myself. I am not a child anymore," Meg spoke earnestly. She really didn't want to quarrel with them because she knew they truly were her friends.

"I likes you, Miss Meg. You is nice," said Molly. Meg realized this was the closest Molly would ever come to apologizing.

"I consider you my friend. I understand your concern and I thank you for it," Meg said.

"What about me? Do you consider me a friend, too?" asked Micco.

"Yes. Let's don't argue anymore. We're leaving Tuesday, so I may not see you again, Miss Molly. I shall miss you. The people of Beaufort are lucky to have you around for your medical advice and for your marvelous cooking." She gave the tiny old lady a hug. "Take care of yourself." Meg felt sad because she knew she would probably never see Molly again.

"I be baking some pies for you to take on de boat. Dat way you be thinking of ol' Molly when you eats 'em. I gonna send Maryanne over with 'em late dis afternoon."

"Thank you." Meg had to turn away because she was about to cry.

"And, Doctor Micco, I has my special herbs I wants to give you." Molly scuttered over to her herb cabinet and took down a bag of asafetida. "Here it be. I has cured most de peoples in Beaufort with dis medicine," said Molly as she handed Micco the stringent-smelling bag.

"Thank you. I consider it an honor to be given this special gift. My grandmother will appreciate it, too." Micco took the old lady's gnarled, work-worn hand and kissed it.

Molly simply couldn't resist flirting with this handsome young man. "If you doesn't take him, I will. He be the bestest-lookin' man and he be smart, too!" Micco and Meg both smiled.

"I must be going now. I want to say goodbye to all the wonderful people I have met and then I need to pack," said Meg, trying to control her tears.

"I too, must pay my respects before we sail. Goodbye, Miss Molly. Keep healthy!"

"Goodbye, Miss Meg and Doctor Micco. You bof watch de signs. I sees danger in the future."

"Goodbye" was all Meg could manage to say.

They left, looking back at the little wisp of a woman, sitting on her pillows, her elfin brown face peering up at them. As they walked outside, an errant tear slid down Meg's cheek. "Oh, Micco, we'll never see her again!"

Micco pulled out his handkerchief and gently dabbed her face. "That's true, honey, but our lives have been enriched by knowing her. Think of it that way."

Meg felt comforted by his words. She wondered if he realized how his tender action and term of endearment affected her.

"I'm going to run up to my room and freshen up. Uncle Jim said that we're invited to a farewell dinner at Leland and Stephanie's house at seven o'clock. I'll see you then," said Meg.

"All right. Until seven, then." Micco watched as Meg walked up the steps. Then he turned and headed to Dr. Brown's office to bid him farewell. It never occurred to Micco that Meg would even entertain the idea of meeting Andre again.

He felt lighthearted as he strolled along. The sun was shining gloriously in an incredibly azure sky and he could hear the raucous cries of seagulls as they circled overhead. Tomorrow he would be sailing for home. Home! It was strange, but he almost felt more homesick now than he had ten years ago when he first left his native village. He was excited about returning, anticipating reopening Dr. Riley's clinic. His friend, mentor, and benefactor had written him a long letter several weeks ago telling Micco how he had longed for and dreamed of the day they would once again treat patients. The doctor's health had improved and they could work together. Micco had enjoyed those years at Harvard in spite of the grueling hours of study and preparation. He had learned about an entirely different world, a sophisticated world far removed from his Indian society, and Micco had been an apt student. Not only was he a brilliant student, but he observed the

308

manners and mores around him, and had gradually become urbane and sophisticated. That had a certain appeal, but never for one moment, had he considered remaining in that upper crust society. Christine's father, an influential banker, had tried to persuade him to remain in Massachusetts and be a surgeon ministering to the wealthy Bostonians. Micco knew that Christine had cajoled her father into pressuring him about practicing in Boston. Christine was a determined lady who did not want to lose Micco. It really wouldn't surprise him to find her in Jupiter, waiting for him. She didn't give up easily, though he had told her that he would never practice medicine in Boston. Oh well, he'd handle that situation if it occurred. Right now, he was happy. Soon he would be home, walking in the forest, talking with Gray Wolf, consulting with Dr. Riley.

The bright December sun was melting the snow, but the North wind was blustery. Micco didn't care. He seemed oblivious to the biting cold. He heard a catbird trilling a joyous tune. Micco spotted his gray plumage amidst the branches of a holly tree, his black-capped head busily plunging among the shiny red berries. Micco laughed and whistled a response. The catbird cocked his head curiously, as if to say, 'I didn't know another bird was around,' and then warbled again. Micco could imitate any bird's song that he had heard. He was as clever at imitation as a mockingbird. As a young boy, he had often lain quietly in the tall grass communicating with hoot owls, robins, larks, laughing seagulls, or mourning doves. He had sat near the shore, as motionless as a heron waiting for a fish to swim by. He could caw just like a bad-tempered blue heron disturbed by some man-made interruption. All these images were crowding in on him while he approached the doctor's office. Was the uncivilized man still lurking within him? He was surprised to recall these things that had nestled dormant for so many years. Suddenly, he longed to glide noiselessly in his canoe across the Loxahatchie River. He could almost feel the smooth paddle in his hands. He shook his head. What a strange metamorphosis. When he stared at the holly tree, the catbird had flown and the air was mysteriously quiet. He was once again a young man calling on a fellow doctor.

When he reached the door, a note was attached saying the office would be closed until the 28th of December. In case of emergency, contact the doctor at home.

Micco turned away, disappointed and reluctant to go to Dr. Brown's house. There was a possibility that Andre might be visiting Pamela, and Micco had no desire to encounter him again before he left. Oh well, he'd risk it because he did want to see the doctor one more time.

He strolled back up Turner Street. As he walked past the stagecoach stop, several young passengers stepped down from the coach, laughing and talking. They were apparently college students returning home for a late holiday. The students were met by loving parents who bestowed hugs and kisses on them. Micco felt even more wistful as he watched their happy reunion. He had no parents, but he had a grandmother and close friends who would welcome him, too.

He trilled a little whistle as he walked along lightheartedly, and a hidden warbler answered him. Micco laughed with the sheer joy of being alive, and in anticipating his life ahead. He reached Dr. Brown's house, took the steps two at a time, and rang the doorbell.

Mrs. Brown answered the door. "Micco, how nice to see you! Come in!"

"How are you, Mrs. Brown? I wanted to come by and say farewell before I leave for Jupiter tomorrow. Is your husband here?"

"Yes, he is. Have a seat," she said, leading him into the parlor. "I will get him."

Micco sat on a delicate needlepoint chair, lowering his long frame very carefully. He let out his breath slowly when the chair didn't break. A highly polished mahogany table, covered with a beaded cloth, held family portraits. 'Good looking family,' thought Micco. A handsome young army captain, looking like a younger Dr. Brown, stared confidently at the world. An attractive woman, perhaps ten years older, dressed in evening clothes and bearing a strong resemblance to Jennifer, had the same confident expression. A glamorous picture of Pamela in furs and jewels completed the family portraits. Seeing Pamela's portrait reminded Micco of Andre. He worried about what to do. If the Frenchman was involved in murder, Dr. Brown should be warned. On the other hand, this was a serious accusation without proof. As Micco sat mulling these thoughts, wishing Jim were with him, Dr. and Mrs. Brown entered the room. Micco rose quickly.

"Hello my boy. How are you?"

"Fine, Sir. We are sailing for Jupiter tomorrow and I wanted to tell you how much I enjoyed meeting and talking with you."

"I wish you would reconsider practicing in Florida. You could come in as a full partner with me. I want to retire soon, but I can't until I have someone to take my place."

"Dr. Brown, if there were any way I could help you, I would, but my loyalty and obligation is to Dr. Riley. He sent me through college and through medical school." Micco paused. "You know, I do have a friend who might be interested," he said thoughtfully. "He is an internist and wants to practice in a small town. I don't know if he would consider the South since he was born and bred in Vermont, but it's worth a chance. If you'd like, I'll send him a telegram today."

"Yes, yes. Send it. Perhaps my prayers will be answered."

"If Dennis should be interested, he would fit right in here. He's well qualified and he has a sympathetic manner. He had no desire to practice in a metropolitan area. I will include your name and address so that he can contact you. Uh, by the way, is Pamela here? I'd like to say goodbye to her, too."

"Poor girl. She is in her room, quite devastated." Dr. Brown looked a little embarrassed. "Yesterday, Andre told her that he was leaving today. She thought that he was, well, rather serious about her. Dear child. She is so in love with him, and we thought he felt the same way."

"Fiddlesticks!" said Mrs. Brown, uncharacteristically unladylike. "She is distraught because she finally encountered a man who didn't fall for her big blue eyes and helpless air!"

"Jennifer, how can you say that about dear, sweet Pamela? She is just a naïve child, unused to the manner of a sophisticated man like Andre. I had hoped he would return her ardor because she needs a strong man to love and protect her." He turned to Micco as if surprised to find him there. "I do apologize for our little tiff. We have been concerned about my niece. She has refused to come out of her room, even to eat," said Dr. Brown .

"I apologize too, Micco, for exposing you to our family argument. I do feel that when Pamela gets hungry enough she will emerge from her room. Teenage heartbreak is so dramatic, but she'll soon forget when the next available male makes his appearance."

"Please don't apologize. I understand family concerns perfectly. My grandmother loves me dearly, but she never misses an opportunity to set me straight. I expect she'll continue to do it when I'm doddering around with a cane. Give my regards to Pamela and tell her that I'm sorry to have missed seeing her."

Micco shook hands with Dr. Brown, and surprised Mrs. Brown by kissing her hand when she offered it.

"Goodbye. Come back to visit us soon," she said, smiling at him.

"Goodbye, Micco, and good luck to you," Dr. Brown said.

"Farewell, my friends. I'm going to the post office now to send that telegram."

He left after deciding to say nothing about Andre. After all, the man was leaving, and why should he cause more heartache for Pamela and the Browns by suggesting the Frenchman was a scoundrel. Much relieved, Micco ran to the post office to send the telegram.

Andre, meanwhile, had controlled his rage, and being the resourceful man that he was, immediately began scheming his next step. He could easily have decked Davy, breaking his nose and spoiling that rosy, childlike complexion. A knee to the groin of one seaman, and a flat-handed punch to the throat of the other would have incapacitated the one and probably killed the other, but he had fought down the urge, knowing he'd end up in jail. He knew too, that the Indian and Meg's uncle had been responsible for keeping him from sailing on the Annie Marie with them. They thought they had won, but they hadn't. This was just a momentary setback of his plans. He had gone straightway to the docks, looking for passage on another ship, but he found something even better. A vessel had come into port the night before with a drunken captain and scurvy crew of eight disgruntled sailors, looking for trouble. These were just the kind of men Andre had sailed with and he knew how to handle them. He went on board and asked in a commanding voice, "Where's the captain? I want a word with him."

A tall, burly fellow with arms as big around as pilings answered.

"He's in his quarters, tipsy as a lord, startin' on the fifteenth verse of 'Blow the Man Down'," said the mate, pointing toward the cabin.

All the men laughed and watched Andre curiously. No one challenged him, not even the muscled hulk whom he questioned. Something about the stranger made them stand back.

"He shouldn't be hard to find then," answered Andre, moving in the direction of a booming, bass voice issuing from the forward deck area. Andre didn't bother to knock, but walked boldly into the captain's quarters. He found the captain half sprawled in a chair, waving his cup around as he sang the next verse. Pausing only to pour rum from the half-empty bottle on the table, the captain was startled to see a blonde giant with the face of an angel before him. Squinting through his alcoholic haze at the apparition before him, he asked, "Are you the Angel Gabriel come to take me home?"

Andre laughed evilly. "No, I am Beelzebub, come to take you to hell!"

The frightened man dropped his cup, covering his eyes. "No, no! I ain't been that bad! I just like me rum!"

"My good man I'm just joking. Mon dieu, I have no wings. Look at me. My name is Andre Lafitte, and I have come to make you a proposition. A very favorable one, I might add."

The captain looked at the interloper through his fingers which he still held over his eyes. "You want me to sell my soul to you," he whispered in a terrified voice.

"Not at all. I want you to sell your ship to me. You may keep your soul. I have no use for it."

"My ship? You want my ship? What would I do? It's the only life I know." By now, the captain had lost some of his fear.

"For a thousand gold pieces, you could live quite well, provided you don't spend it all on rum. What do you say, my good fellow? What is your name, if I may be so bold?"

"I am Captain John Cavendish, commander of the Osprey out of New York. Did you say one thousand in gold?"

"I did. Do we have a deal?"

"If you ain't the devil, we do."

"Rest assured, I am not, though many have accused me of it. Come, drink up. I'll return shortly with the money," spoke Andre as he poured the rest of the rum in the cup.

Captain Cavendish grabbed the cup greedily, spilling part of it on his doublet. He drained it and sank back in the chair, his eyes glazed.

Andre left to get the money. He spoke to the crew before he departed, promising them ten dollars more than they were getting and suggesting the possibility of wealth if they were willing to do anything to get it.

314

"Mister, if you come back here with the money, you've got a crew." The others murmured agreement as they hadn't received last month's pay.

Andre had read them well. All had planned to jump ship in Beaufort and leave the besotted captain on his own, in a perpetual state of oblivion. Andre had enough money with him to pay each crewman his back wages.

"I will return within the hour."

"Aye, Sir, but what about the captain?" asked the mate.

"I'll take him off the ship when I return," answered Andre, jumping onto the dock.

He ran down the street, eager to get the money to buy the Osprey. He felt excitement coursing through his veins as he sped along. At last, he would have his own ship. This was turning out even better than he had planned. When he reached his room, he got the money from where he had hidden it, packed up all his belongings, and then picked up his luggage and sea bag. He gave a final glance around the room, making sure he had missed nothing. Satisfied, he made his way back to the ship. He took his luggage into the captain's quarter, and roused the sleeping Cavendish.

"Come on, man. You'll be a landlubber now. Here is your money. Count it before we leave," Andre said, putting the bag of coins on the table.

The groggy captain reached for the bag, spilling the coins on the table. "I ain't never seen this much money," he said, eagerly counting the coins.

Andre waited impatiently as the captain counted. Finally, Cavendish began shoving the money back into the bag.

"It's all there," he said.

"Up you go," ordered Andre, as he pulled the man to his feet. "Put that bag away. Where's your sea bag?"

"It's under the bunk," said the captain, finally on his feet. Andre found it and quickly put the money in the bag.

He escorted the captain, half carrying him off the ship and down the street, to his own room at the Seaview Hotel. He deposited him on the bed, and placed the sea bag under the cot. He was half-tempted to take back his gold from the recumbent man, but decided to avoid the possibility of pursuit by the authorities. They were close enough on his heels as it was. He left the sleeping captain and went by the reception desk.

"I shall be leaving," he told the clerk, "But a friend of mine, Captain Cavendish will be staying in my room. I believe I am paid through the week; however, here is an additional week's rent, and something extra for you."

"Thank you, Sir. I'll be sorry to see you go, Mr. Lafitte. You've been a quiet boarder, and I always appreciate that," said the clerk.

"De rien," replied Andre, shaking hands with the obviously admiring George. "I am sailing for New York this evening," he lied glibly.

"Good luck, Sir. Come again."

"If I return some day, I'll certainly stay at the Inlet Inn."

Andre left and quickly returned to the Osprey which was now his ship. He had inspected the vessel and found it to be in good condition. He explained to the crew that they would be leaving at sundown, heading for Jupiter, Florida.

"Go into town and have a good dinner on me, and get whatever supplies we may need," said Andre, handing money to the first mate who appeared to be fairly intelligent.

"Aye, aye, sir," responded Anderson eagerly. "We'll be ready."

After they left, Andre set about cleaning his quarters. In spite of his expensive tastes and acquired veneer of wealth and sophistication, he didn't mind hard or dirty work. He was used to it. Of course, they needed a cabin boy. If one could be found in Beaufort, he'd hire him before they sailed. As he worked, scrubbing the floor, throwing out bottles, and changing the bed linens, he savored thoughts of revenge and of claiming the delectable Meg. Soon he would meet her. When he finally finished cleaning to his satisfaction, he found a barrel filled with

316

stored water for drinking and bathing purposes. There was a tin bathtub that he partially filled. He lit a gas lantern for its feeble warmth, stripped and then quickly bathed and dressed. There wasn't much time before his meeting with Meg, and he wanted to find a cabin boy first. He left his ship and decided to talk to the harbormaster to see if he knew an available boy.

While Andre was making his preparations, Meg was anxiously anticipating her rendezvous at five. She was excited because her uncle and Micco would be more than disapproving. They would be furious! She hated to go against her uncle's wishes, but she was fascinated by the dashing Frenchman and did not believe he was dishonest or villainous. In spite of his cavalier behavior at the party, she was physically attracted to him. He was so handsome, his blue eyes so appealing. She dressed in her most becoming apple-green dress with matching hat, parasol, and white kid gloves. Last night, she had told her uncle that she was going to visit friends, and so he left her on her own while he too made last minute calls. At quarter to five, Meg took a final look in the mirror, dabbed perfume behind her ears, and left her room, glancing about cautiously. She went quietly down the steps and out the door. No one was about. She almost expected to see Micco behind one tree and Miss Molly behind another, waiting to catch her. As she hurried towards the Duncan House, she was glad she had worn a cloak over her woolen dress. The air was quite chilly though most of the snow had melted. She made her way rapidly to their appointed spot. He was not there yet, so Meg brushed off the bench with her handkerchief and sat down to wait. She had agreed to meet him alone one more time because his note sounded so penitent. Meg was softhearted, and if he wanted to apologize in person, she would let him. Just as she began to get really cold, she saw him running down the street towards her. She stood up as he approached, and he clasped both her hands.

"Cherie, have you frozen? I'm sorry if I am late, but I had some business I had to take care of." He gazed at her, warming her gloved hands between his big ones.

"No. I haven't been here long."

"Let's walk over to the side of the house where you'll be more protected from the wind," said Andre, putting an arm around her waist and leading her across the street.

Meg went willingly because she was chilled by the wind. They stood under the shelter of the western wing of the house.

Andre stared soulfully at Meg as if willing her to believe what he was going to say. "My beautiful one, can you forgive me for forcing myself upon you? I would never do anything to harm you. I apologize with all my heart for offending you. Can you forgive me?"

"Yes, I know you were just, uh, impulsive."

"Thank you," said Andre, kissing her wrist. "Now I am going to tell you something that must be kept between us. You cannot reveal it to anyone. Do you agree to that?"

"If you want me to, yes."

"Let me keep you warm then, while I talk." He put his arms around her, shielding her from the biting wind. "I will not be sailing with you tomorrow."

"Oh, why not? I thought you were going to Florida with us," said Meg.

"Are you sorry I am not?"

Meg couldn't meet his eyes. "Well, I thought we might start our acquaintance over again."

"We are, ma petite."

At this, she looked up into his admiring blue eyes. "But if you're not going, how can we?"

"I have purchased my own ship, the Osprey, and will sail tonight on the full tide. I shall arrive ahead of you and be waiting. I won't contact you until after your uncle has left to return home."

"Why did you suddenly decide to do this? I don't understand."

"The young captain, Davy, I think his name is, told me he had no room; that unexpected passengers would be sailing. I think that your uncle and Indian friend persuaded him to refuse me

318

passage. I had to make a quick change of plans. Already I am missing you, but we won't be parted for long."

"I can't believe they would do that, although both of them were quite angry when they thought you... tried to take advantage of me. My uncle is as protective of me as if I were a baby bird, still in the nest."

"And he is right to protect you, but you are no longer a child, are you?"

"No."

Andre laughed. "Yes, you are, at least in the ways of the world. When we are together in Florida, I will take over that job and be your protector, dear sweet Meg. Now, let's go. It is too cold for you. You must return to your room before you catch pneumonia. Remember; do not tell your uncle, Micco, or a friend about this. Everyone must believe that I left for New York. I told the desk clerk at the Inlet Inn that that was where I was going. You know nothing, of course, because you haven't seen me at all."

"I understand," said Meg.

"I'll leave you here so that no one will see us together. Au revoir, ma Cherie," said Andre, kissing her cheek. "Go now, quickly."

"Goodbye, Andre, until we meet again in Jupiter."

Meg turned and walked back to the Davis House, hoping she wouldn't meet her uncle on the way. He would certainly question her. She saw no one and slipped unobtrusively into her cozy room. A maid must have added coals to the fire, for it was blazing brightly. She took off her cloak, hat, and gloves, toasting her frozen fingers over the orange flames. She thought about her meeting with Andre. She was more attracted to him than ever. He was so gentle with her and caring and said he wanted to protect her. Could he be in love with her? Meg was thrilled at the thought, but at the same time, she was not a devious person. It disturbed her to be at all dishonest with her beloved Uncle Jim. She couldn't enjoy her duplicity, though she longed to see Andre again. Feeling depressed, she took off her shoes and dress and slipped under the covers, enjoying the warmth of the blankets piled high on her bed. They weren't going to dinner until seven thirty, so she would just get warm and think of what to do. She began to get warm and cozy as she snuggled under the covers, and soon drowsiness overcame her, and she fell asleep, forgetting her problems.

Andre watched until Meg went into the building, and then he walked briskly along the boardwalk back to his ship. He was pleased, even happy, at the turn of events. He had found a cabin boy after talking to the harbormaster. The boy's parents had died and he was temporarily living with a neighbor who was glad to be free of the responsibility of his care. The boy was delighted at the prospect of being one of the crew on a sailing vessel. Andre had charmed him with tales of adventure at sea. Now, if Anderson had gotten all the needed supplies, they could sail. When they arrived at Jupiter Inlet, he would lure Meg away from the accursed Indian, and then take care of him permanently. He soon reached his ship and leaped on board, eager to depart on the flood tide. He found Jamie on the deck, huddled against the blustering wind, his threadbare coat a small comfort against the relentless gale.

"Are you all settled in, Jamie?"

"Yes, Sir. I didn't know what you wanted me to do, and the other men acted like I was in their way," answered the boy anxiously, as if afraid that Andre would send him back to Mrs. Barnhill, who had never wanted him.

Andre had never felt tenderhearted towards any living creature, but he did feel a slight empathy for Jamie, remembering when he too, had been twelve years old, parentless and friendless. There was a difference though, between the two. Jamie's uncertain eyes were guileless. He was an innocent boy. Andre's eyes had never shone with innocence, even when he was a small child. By the time he was sixteen, he had murdered his father and another man. Andre knew that Jamie would instinctively abhor violence and dishonesty, but he also knew that Jamie would be fiercely loyal to anyone who showed him kindness. Andre intended to cultivate that loyalty, so much that it would overpower his doubts. He needed the loyalty of every member of the crew to accomplish what he intended to do. He would gain the loyalty of the men by bribery, sheer power of command, and by striking fear into their hearts if they failed to follow orders. Andre was an adept judge of character. He had an uncanny ability to read men's and women's souls. His angelic face caught them off-guard, but many had learned, to their sorrow, of the devil within.

Andre smiled at the boy and saw relief flood his face. "You don't need to start your duties just yet. There will be plenty of time for that when we're underway. Have you eaten dinner?"

"No Sir."

"Good. Then you and I will dine together. I just happened to have brought conch chowder and oysters from the Inlet Inn restaurant. Do you like that?"

"Oh, yes Sir, I do!"

"We'll eat after we're underway. Come. I'll take you to my cabin. You look cold." Jamie followed Andre to his quarters.

"Put some more wood in the stove, and sit by the fire. I'll be back shortly. That is, unless you'd rather stay on deck and watch as we leave the harbor."

"No. I don't care about it and that fire feels mighty good," said Jamie, putting more wood in the stove.

"C'est bon. When I return, we'll eat and then look through whatever clothing the former captain left and find you some warm clothes."

Andre left Jamie curled up by the fire, already a look of dawning adoration glowing in his eyes. In his short, loveless life, he had no heroes.

Andre found Anderson on the bridge, looking out over the harbor. "Is the boson knowledgeable about these waters?" asked Andre.

"McGuire? He's sailed up and down this coast from Massachusetts to Cuba for twenty years; ever since the end of the war. He knows every shoal and buoy between the two. You couldn't ask for a better navigator. His only problem is rum. Right now, he is three sheets to the wind."

"Get him up here along with the rest of the crew. I want to leave on this full tide."

"Aye, Sir. I'll see what I can do, but he may be in sailor's dreamland by now," said the mate, a cunning look on his face.

Andre turned to the man, fixing him with a glare that erased the smile from his countenance as effectively as a frigid winter wind.

"Maybe I can persuade him. Lead me to him."

"They walked down the stairs to McGuire's bunk. The man was sprawled across the bed, snoring with his mouth opened. Andre walked over and jerked him up to a sitting position.

"What the devil." McGuire shook his head, trying to focus.

"Get up. You have a new captain now."

"And what if I don't want to get up? Are you going to make me? Said the man as he tried to shake off Andre's hand.

With another jerk, Andre pulled McGuire to his feet and then struck him hard across the face. McGuire went down and rubbed his jaw, a frightened look in his eyes.

Anderson said. "Why did you do that? He's just a little drunk."

Andre turned to face him and his expression was murderous as he pulled out his knife and backed Anderson up against the wall.

"Maybe you'd like a taste of it, too?"

"No. I'll get him up on deck."

Have them all on deck in five minutes. No later," he commanded, his eyes deadlier than a cobra about to strike.

Anderson took off as if pursued by the devil himself. In five minutes, all the crew were mustered, including a bleary-eyed McGuire.

"Gentlemen," said Andre authoritatively, "we will be casting off immediately. It is extremely important that we leave now and take advantage of the fair tide and wind, and reach our ultimate destination, which is Jupiter Inlet, in Florida, as soon as possible. I understand we have a cargo of grain bought and paid for by the captain, to be delivered to the Port of Savannah, Georgia."

The men sullenly nodded agreement.

"I expect every man jack of you to handle his own job, or any other, without being reminded of it. I have paid you well, and will continue to do so. When we arrive in Florida, you'll have the opportunity to earn more gold than you ever dreamed of. So we understand each other?"

All the crew looked at him, burly hard-bitten men, some murderers, all petty thieves, with greed gleaming in their eyes. "Aye, Sir!" each man answered.

"Then I don't expect you to run us aground. Cast off, Mr. Anderson."

The mate took over. "Lenny, Stoker, cast off lines. Brondell, Gully, hoist the sails."

Anderson took the helm and the Osprey fairly flew down Taylor's Creek, her sails puffed by the north wind, past Piver's Island and headed towards the Beaufort bar. Two crewmen had hung lanterns from the port and starboard stern, and one swung from the bow.

Andre stood by the helmsman, breathing in the cold salt air. At last, he was at sea again.

Andre thought of his past. As a boy, his drunken father's tales of Jean Lafitte's exploits had enthralled him. Andre determined that one day he, too, would go to America and make his fortune. And now he was on his way, captain of his own ship just as he had dreamed so many years ago. He was especially fond of his grandfather's slogan, 'Dead men tell no tales' and thought it quite clever that no one was left alive to identify the pirates or testify against them. He savored the stories of chests of gold, silver and jewels buried in the dense jungles of a wild and desolate place. Satisfied, he gave a quick backward glance at the disappearing harbor lights, glad to see the last of them. As they crossed the bar, the swelling ocean waves made the ship dip and rise, and Andre adjusted to the motion with a rolling seaman's gait, making his way to his quarters.

He could almost see the buccaneers soaking their sails in alum so they wouldn't catch fire so easily.

A sudden motion of the ship startled Andre from his reverie. He said aloud, "I'll have to make sure Anderson got plenty of alum."

As the ship, with its ungodly crew, moved away from the little fishing village, Meg paced back and forth in her bedroom, filled with guilt about concealing Andre's plans. She wondered if he had sailed yet, and if she would ever really see him again. She kept remembering the look on his face as she walked away. It was loving and tender. She couldn't be mistaken in that, could she? A knock interrupted her thoughts, and she opened the door.

"I'm ready, Uncle Jim. It will be sad to say farewell to our friends tonight. I visited Lois Jean and Ralph this morning and they are so disappointed that I won't remain here and be the church organist."

"I know. I stopped and had coffee with Albert and Jennifer. We had a good, long talk. Maybe we can persuade Leland and Stephanie to accompany me when I make a return trip next year."

"Oh Uncle, don't talk about leaving me now. That will happen too soon as it is."

"All right. Let's enjoy our last visit tonight and look forward to our trip to Jupiter."

Micco met them downstairs. "Meg, will you be warm enough walking to Leland and Stephanie's house?" he asked.

"Yes. I'll enjoy the walk. I haven't been getting enough exercise in all this snowy weather."

"Very well, then. We're off!"

Meg walked between the two men, holding onto their arms. They jogged along and reached the house in less than ten minutes.

Leland greeted them at the door. "Come in! Stephanie's in the kitchen helping Priscilla," he said, taking their coats and hats.

They moved into the cozy parlor, appreciating the warmth of the crackling fire. Lucy, Bob, and Alexandria, who were seated close to the fireplace, all rose when they entered. The two children were on the floor, playing with their Christmas toys.

"Sit by the fire," invited Lucy. She came over to Meg and kissed her on the cheek, as did Alexandria.

"Hello, Jim and Micco. It's so good to see you again," said Lucy.

"Yes, indeed it is," agreed Alexandria. "We've talked about how enjoyable it was to have you help us trim the tree." She looked directly at Micco as she spoke.

Meg saw this and again felt a stab of jealousy even though she sympathized with Alexandria's loss. This evening, Alexandria wore a frock of deep fuchsia and she wore her thick, curly hair loose. The ebony tresses were so long that they reached past her shoulders. Her earrings were small clusters of diamonds that glittered in the gaslight, and she wore a matching diamond necklace.

'Surely Micco would bask in those unbelievable violet eyes,' thought Meg when she saw him kiss Alexandria's hand, never taking his eyes from hers.

"Hello, Micco and Jim. We're so happy to have you join us your last night here," said Bob, shaking hands with them.

Cicero and Melissa jumped up and ran over to Micco. "Micco, Micco! Tell us a story," cried Melissa.

"Melissa," reprimanded her mother, "you address him as Doctor Micco. You do not call an adult by his or her first name alone."

"Please Lucy. Don't scold them. It's my fault. I asked them to call me 'Micco."

"Well, all right," said Lucy doubtfully," as long as they understand that this is an exception."

"If you prefer, they can call me 'Uncle Micco'."

"Uncle Micco," chorused Cicero. Everyone laughed.

325

"I guess that's settled then. 'Uncle Micco' it is," said Lucy smiling.

Meg thought unhappily, 'If he marries Alexandria, he will be "Uncle Micco" for sure!'

Micco said to the children, "Who wants to hear some Indian stories?"

"I do," said Cicero.

"Me, too." Melissa said.

"Come along then." Micco took them into the parlor.

Stephanie and Priscilla walked in bearing hot, steaming cider. " Here's something to warm you up." said Stephanie as she and the maid passed around the drinks.

"The town is in a state of shock over the murders," said Leland. "I've had people calling me all day. Not only are they upset about the deaths of their neighbors, but they are afraid a killer is stalking the community. I can't get it out of my mind either."

"We're going to the funeral on Monday," said Stephanie. "I almost start to cry when I think of it. It would be sad enough if Horace had died of natural causes, but to have been struck down so brutally is unthinkable. And poor Danny, just a child. They're having Horace's funeral in the morning and Danny's in the afternoon. I've made several casseroles to take over to Mary's house."

Bob said, "Don't the authorities believe that the man who did it escaped by ship?"

"Yes," said Leland, "but stories abound. It will be a while before the furor dies down."

Alexandria, still grieving for her husband, wanted to dispel the unhappy atmosphere.

"Meg," she said, what exactly do you plan to do in Jupiter. I understand you're a teacher."

"My hope is to establish a school for the Indian children and any others who would like to attend. I know Uncle Jim and

326

Aunt Julie are disappointed that I didn't pursue a career in music, but this is what I want to do."

"It will certainly be a challenge, especially since you'll be opening up a new school," said Lucy.

"I know, but that's part of the excitement- creating something on my own. Uncle Jim has given me more than enough money to buy supplies, including desks and chairs, and with Micco's influence, I am sure he can persuade the parents to allow their children to attend school. This is a welcome added bonus for me. I was so surprised when my father wrote that Micco had become a doctor and would be going to Jupiter with us."

"I'm sure that was a pleasant surprise," said Alexandria. "You are indeed lucky to have him for a friend. With his help, I know you'll reach your goal. He is kind and understanding."

Meg noted a tone of wistfulness in Alexandria's voice.

"He is that, but he's also a tease! He makes me so angry sometimes. It's as if he doesn't take me seriously, or that he thinks I'm immature. At times, I almost want to slap his grinning face!" said Meg .

Stephanie and Lucy smiled at this outburst, but Alexandria seemed shocked.

"Surely not! Micco is such a gentleman, so understanding. I'm sure he appreciates your abilities."

Meg blushed. "I know he is a gentleman, and I wouldn't really slap him. I don't know why he provokes me so."

Stephanie patted Meg, as she would have Lucy or Alexandria. "Don't worry, dear. You're a little confused, and I don't blame you. Here you have two absolutely gorgeous but different, men vying for your attention. Who wouldn't be confused?"

"What do you mean, two men? Micco thinks of me as his kid sister, and for all I know, Andre, and I'm assuming you're referring to Andre, seems to be involved with Pamela."

"You must know he is not interested in that little... in Pamela. She's hanging onto him like a barnacle, but I'm positive it is not mutual," said Stephanie. "Incidentally, I heard Jennifer say that Andre is not going with you to Florida."

"Oh?" said Meg, trying to look surprised. "He's not?"

"No. According to Jennifer, he left for New York today. Didn't he even say goodbye to you?"

Meg felt like she was walking on baked meringue. "Why do you think he did that?" she answered, evasively.

Stephanie replied, "I have no idea. Evidently, Pamela has taken to her bed with an attack of the vapors. How do you feel about it?"

Meg avoided looking at Stephanie. "I'm disappointed, of course."

"Disappointed. Yesterday you couldn't wait to see him"

"Now you'll only have Micco pursuing you," added Lucy.

Meg noticed that Alexandria looked unhappy. "I repeat- he is not interested in me, nor I in him. I understand he has a girlfriend in Boston," said Meg.

"Men!" exclaimed Stephanie. "He probably has a girlfriend he left behind in Jupiter, too. And no doubt, Andre has left languishing maidens in every known and unknown village in the Western world!"

Meg couldn't help blurting out, "Andre is not like that! He told me..." and then she caught herself.

"He told you what?" asked Stephanie .

Lucy interrupted. "Meg, pay no attention to Mother. She always tried to trap us, too!"

"That's not true! I merely made it easy for you to confess," said Stephanie, trying to appear contrite, without success.

"Mother dear, you are incorrigible!" said Alexandria, giving her a hug. "But we love you anyway!" Meg watched the three, envying their closeness.

"Come on, everyone. Dinner is ready. Leland, bring Jim and Micco along." They all sat down and Priscilla began serving.

"Did you know that Andre left for New York today?" Stephanie asked Jim, not for one minute about to leave the subject alone.

"Yes. I visited with Albert and Jennifer earlier and they told me."

"And you didn't tell me?" asked Meg angrily.

Before Jim could answer, Stephanie jumped in. "Don't you find that surprising? He was supposed to sail with you to Jupiter, wasn't he?"

Jim glanced at Meg, expecting her to express regret, but she remained quiet.

"Maybe he decided he'd be better off investing in cranberries and corn instead of avocados and pineapples, even though they're not nearly as exotic."

Meg still said nothing, though she was annoyed with her uncle. She wanted to defend Andre, but didn't dare express her true feelings. She glanced at Micco, who was watching her intently. Well, they may have thought they had won, but they hadn't. She was going to see Andre, her love, again.

"It's a shame he left today because he certainly made things lively around here," Stephanie said.

"I wish I had had the chance to talk to him. He sounds interesting," said Alexandria.

"He's interesting, all right, and he's a suave Frenchman with a charming accent who looks like a Greek sun god," added her mother.

Leland looked disgusted. "He's gone now and best forgotten. Pass the peas, dear."

Stephanie smoldered like a volcano about to erupt. "Of course, honey," she replied sweetly, her expression belying her words.

Jim rushed in to prevent a family squabble. "Has Telford gotten any more leads on the two murders?"

"Nothing. That gold earring you found and Horace's last word, 'stocking', led to a dead end. The scar-faced man disappeared without a trace. It's really affected Telford, too. He left Ronnie in charge while he scoured the area for two days, looking for anyone that might have seen the stranger. He can't rest or sleep. He was really close to his nephew."

"Who is Telford, Daddy?" asked Melissa, walking in from the kitchen where Priscilla had set up a little table in the corner for the children.

"No one you know, sweetheart," said Bob. "Now go back and finish your dinner. It's almost bedtime. I'll read 'Cinderella' to you." The little girl left without arguing.

"I believe everyone has finished dessert. Let's have coffee in the drawing room," offered Stephanie, rising from her chair. Leland leaped to pull out her chair.

"I'm sorry," he whispered in her ear. "It's just that I can't stand that guy. Let's don't argue."

Stephanie took his arm, smiling. "I know you don't like him, and we won't argue."

She believed that old adage 'Never go to bed angry' was an integral part of their marriage.

Everyone sank into the plush chairs, replete with good food.

"Ah, Stephanie, that was a wonderful meal," said Jim.

"It was indeed," agreed Micco. "But more than that, I have enjoyed your warmth and friendship, and feel privileged to have met you all."

"The pleasure was ours," said Alexandria. "I'm going to miss you." She gazed at him with sadness in her violet eyes. The others were talking among themselves.

Micco rose and went over and sat down by Alexandria. He held her delicate fingers in his big hand. "Alexandria, you will be happy again. I sense that you are terribly unhappy. Perhaps you have suffered a great loss, and it seems that the good part of your existence has passed you by. You'll never forget that part of your life, but the rest of your life is beckoning. Respond to that call, dear." Micco spoke as a reassuring physician might speak.

330

Alexandria felt comforted and even more, she believed this kind, understanding man. "Thank you. I will respond. I know your life as a doctor will be fulfilling, and that so many people will be touched by you."

Jim walked over. "We will be sailing at six in the morning, so reluctantly, we have to say farewell."

Meg hugged everyone, promising to return some day. "You must come down to visit me. Uncle Jim said you might join him next year. Please do! I already miss you!"

"Stephanie and I certainly will," said Leland.

"We'll all try to come, too. I've never been further south than Charleston," said Bob.

"Oh, Bob, could we? I want to see Meg again soon," asked Lucy.

"That's a promise!"

They were gathered in the hallway and Leland brought their coats and hats. Jim, Micco, and Meg left feeling sad. They would miss their friends.

"It's freezing," Meg said, shivering.

"Let's run," offered Micco, grabbing her left hand. Jim held her right hand and they sped down the shell street to the Davis House.

"I'm not cold anymore!" gasped Meg, panting for breath.

"I'll knock on your door at five o'clock," Jim told Meg. "We'll have breakfast on the ship after we've crossed the bar and on our way out to the open sea. Let me check your fire."

They walked upstairs and Micco went to his room, tired and ready for bed. Jim added logs to the smoldering fire in Meg's fireplace.

"That should do it," he said, brushing off his hands. "Sleep well, dear." He left, thinking that Andre was on his way to New York. He could sleep easily tonight. There was no further need now to investigate his past. All three fell into a deep sleep.

Chapter Sixteen

The morning dawned misty and very cold as Jim, Meg, and Micco stood on the deck near the stern of the Annie Marie. The ship moved swiftly towards Gallents Channel, pushed along by the blustery north wind. The docks looked ghostly in the fog as the sun peeked above the horizon. They passed Piver's Island, just a faint outline in the heavy fog, and heard the moaning of the bell buoy as they crossed Beaufort bar.

"There's Shackleford Banks to our left. It looks like a faint shadow rising from the sea," said Jim.

"I remember when we sailed by it. It seems so long ago, and so much has happened since then. You told me about Diamond City and the whalers."

"I can't see Beaufort anymore," said Meg regretfully.

"You'll return some day," Jim told her.

"Look Meg, the fog is beginning to lift and a rainbow is forming," pointed out Micco. "It's the bridge of the gods, their pathway from earth to Olympia."

"I didn't know you were a romantic."

"Oh, I can be very romantic," responded Micco, smiling at Meg.

Before she could reply, Davy called out, "Breakfast is ready." By now they could no longer see land. They were fairly flying along and Meg felt the gentle rolling of the waves. Gradually the fog was lifting and the rainbow began to dissipate. Meg looked back as she walked towards the dining table.

"Micco, now the gods are stranded."

"They'll manage. I'm starved. Let's eat!"

"So am I," agreed Jim. "Come on, Meg," he said, taking Meg's arm. They walked below into the dining area and Meg was glad to get out of the cold wind. They seated themselves and she had a sense of 'déjà vu', except that the stalwart captain, Wade Guthrie, wasn't there. Priam Jones, Anson Davis, Davy, and Tom Midgett, who was now first mate, were standing around waiting for them. Other members of the crew including Tim, Samese, and four others Meg didn't know, were at the far end of the table. The cook had fixed sausage and eggs along with Miss Molly's clabber biscuits and Ham. This time the gentle swelling of the waves didn't affect Meg and she enjoyed her breakfast. She remembered her earlier trip from New York sorrowfully, thinking of Captain Guthrie and his untimely death. So much had happened since she had left her sheltered world. It seemed so far away. Micco was engaged in conversation with her uncle, so Meg turned to Davy, who was seated at her right, at the head of the table.

"What cargo are you carrying now?" she asked. "I don't smell the salt fish anymore!"

"Luckily, I was able to sell our cargo to another ship's captain who was heading out to Charleston, two days after we arrived in Beaufort. Otherwise, it would have been a complete loss. I bought peanuts, sweet potatoes, and dried fish roe that we should be able to sell in Savannah."

"Yeh, toimes was bad. Confederate money was worthless. Near everybody in Beaufort lost everything," chimed in Anson. "But now things is almost normal."

Jim looked at Meg who had said little. She had been unusually quiet for the past two days and Jim felt he was in disfavor. She would have no way of knowing that he and Micco were responsible for keeping Andre from sailing with them. Davy and the two crewmembers were sworn to silence. So why did he have the feeling that she knew?

"If you have finished Meg, let's go topside. I could use a stroll around the deck after this breakfast."

"So could I," said Micco.

"All right." Everyone left at the same time.

"Samese, relieve Joey at the helm. He and Blondell can get breakfast now," ordered Davy.

Micco pushed open the cabin door against a brisk northwest wind, and Meg hung onto her hat as they stepped onto the deck.

"I'm enjoying this. I took the train all the way to Boston when I left Florida, and of course, I rode the train to Morehead from Boston. This is the first time I have sailed on a vessel this size. It's exhilarating!"

"Once I traveled to Canada by steamboat. Now, that's traveling!" said Jim enthusiastically.

"One day, we'll probably have boats powered by electricity or gasoline," said Micco. "The world is changing before our eyes. We already have a hydroelectric plant producing power for businesses." He gave Meg a sideways glance, but she seemed lost in thought. "Look meg, at that flock of ducks. The sky is dark with them!" Micco observed, pointing towards the faint outline of the western shore.

"Gracious, I have never seen so many!"

"Fishermen say flocks of ducks seven miles long have been seen on Bogue Sound."

"That may be, but if hunters slaughter so many of the birds for profit, they can become extinct," said Meg, a staunch conservationist. "We'll no longer see the sky filled with beautiful birds. The white plumed egret is fast approaching that unfortunate distinction because the feathers adorn ladies' hats. When I reach Jupiter, I shall dispense with my hats and will never buy a new one."

"Meg, you cannot mean that. Ladies in all societies wear hats," replied Jim.

335

"I am changing my society. Of course, I'll have to wear a hat to church or a very formal occasion, but other than that, no. And I do not intend to wear a bustle ever again, or a corset!"

"Meg, you shouldn't be discussing so delicate a subject in mixed company," said Jim .

Micco laughed. "Jim, I am a doctor. No subject is considered 'delicate' to us hardened physicians. Besides, Meg is a progressive-minded young lady like Mary Wollstonecraft Shelley, or Amelia Bloomer. You must reconcile yourself to this tide of change."

"You are right, I suppose, but sometimes Meg would try the patience of St. Peter himself."

"I'm right here, Uncle Jim. You two are discussing me as if I were a lab specimen."

Jim was secretly glad to see Meg responding. "You're right, dear, but please don't discuss corsets, bustles, or bloomers in polite society. Uh, not that Micco isn't polite."

Meg looked at Micco's grinning face, just waiting for his response. "I don't consider him 'polite society', so no subject is verboten." The wind was whipping her flame-colored hair across her face, and she stood tall against the blustery gale. Micco thought she was magnificent, Junoesque.

"That's my little girl. Stick to your principles."

"I am not your 'girl', big or little."

"Of course not. It was just a figure of speech, Red. I remember so well how you cried for days when Lazy Bear killed a deer with his bow and arrow,"

"That was horrible, and don't call me 'Red', either."

Jim sighed. This was not going to be a peaceful trip. He tried to divert further argument. "Remember when we were discussing The Voyage of the Paper Canoe? I think we're approaching the South Carolina line, near the Nickerson plantation and one of the amusing tales the traveler told was about being met by a group of hogs that greeted him with friendly grunts. As it grew dark, they trotted across the field, conducting him to the very doors of the plantation home. "

Meg smiled picturing the friendly hogs escorting the stranger. She was no longer annoyed with Micco, for the moment. By now they had been sailing for six hours and it felt warmer, too. The ship had veered in closer to shore, and Meg was enjoying the sight of swooping birds and the smell of the briny air. She noticed an estuary where dozens of seagulls were gathered along the shore.

"At the rate we're traveling, it won't be long before we'll be docking in Savannah. It will be good to see Sean again. I haven't seen him since your mother's funeral, though we've kept in touch, of course. He's known about every phase of your life since the day you came to live with us. Meg, he hated to send you away, but he thought having you live with us would be the best thing for you. He was only thinking of your welfare."

Jim was concerned about what Meg had told him earlier that she was merely an inconvenience to her parents. He knew this wasn't true and hoped that father and daughter could reconcile and have a loving relationship.

"Don't worry, Uncle Jim. I'm not going to berate him about sending me away. I wouldn't have had you and Aunt Julie and your love. You gave me something I never had before. Everything will be all right."

"Yes, Jim. I'll see that she behaves herself!" said Micco.

"You'll what?" sputtered Meg. "You, you- Oh, I'm going to my cabin!" She spun around and left, running in spite of her long skirt.

"Whatever happened to 'acting humble'?" asked Jim.

"I don't know. I'm just not good at that role. I thought we were getting along well. It's so difficult to stay on an even keel with Meg. One minute we're friends. The next minute we're in a sparing contest. I thought with Lafitte gone that the conflicts would end," said Micco .

"I can't figure out Meg's behavior either. Like you, I thought everything would resolve itself with that accursed

337

Frenchman out of the scene. Somehow I feel that she knows or suspects that we're responsible for preventing him from sailing with us."

"But how could she?"

"I can't figure it out. Let's just hope she forgets about him when she gets to Jupiter and becomes involved in her work."

"She will because this is what she has chosen in life. Meg has disdained the soft life where she would be pampered and safe without having to work or worry about money. She'll be too involved in organizing a school and teaching the children to mourn Lafitte for long," Micco said confidently.

"I hope you are right. We will just have to endure her annoyance until we reach Florida."

"I'll apologize. That is if she will listen to me."

Both men stood at the taffrail, enjoying the gentle rolling of the ship as she crested the waves and then swooped down as the Annie Marie glided effortlessly through the ocean. The repairs had made her as good as new.

"Going to sea on a sailing vessel does have a strong attraction, doesn't it?" asked Jim. "I can understand why Wade and Anson, and now Davy were drawn to it."

"Yes. The sea gets into your blood. I have only paddled my canoe, but I've always felt an affinity for the ocean. 'For men may come and men may go, but I go on forever'. Tennyson said it best- speaking of the mystical, eternal sea."

Davy joined them, coming down from the bridge, followed by the boswain with a spyglass in his hand.

"At the rate the tide is running and the wind is blowing, we'll be in Savannah by tomorrow night," said Davy, skimming the horizon. "We're making better time than I anticipated."

"That's good. Maybe three more days after that to Jupiter, do you think?"

"Easily, unless we hit a slick calm," replied Davy. "Anson, check out that choppy sea ahead."

"Aye, Sir."

To Jim and Micco's amazement, the sixty-five-year-old Anson climbed, as nimbly as a monkey, up the ratlines to the crow's nest. He put the glass to his eye and scanned the ocean lane ahead.

"Drop the sounding line," he yelled.

Tim, who had straddled the bowsprit, dropped a weighted, knotted line overboard.

"Three fathoms, Sir," he cried when he felt the line touch bottom. Davy ran quickly to the wheelhouse.

"Tack, Joey. We're heading into shallow water." Joey made a hundred and eighty-degree turn of the wheel, and the ship answered the helm, turned seaward and slowed, almost stopping, and her canvas momentarily flapping.

"Two fathoms. Shoaly water ahead."

"Head her for the blue water, Joey." The Annie Marie leapt forward as the wind filled her sails and she sped towards deeper water, leaving the shoreline behind.

"It gets shoaly in a hurry off this area of the South Carolina coast. This ship draws eleven feet of water, and I sure don't want to run her aground."

Meg had felt the changing motion of the ship and returned to the deck to see what was happening.

"Why did the boat, I mean 'ship', almost stop?" she asked.

"We were getting too close to shallow bottom and so Davy headed her back out to deep water. We're really making good time, though; Davy says that if we keep this up, we should reach Jupiter within the next three or four days.

"That's wonderful, although I am enjoying the trip. In spite of our terrible experience before, I really do like sailing. Just the smell of the salty air and the breeze whipping my hair makes me feel rejuvenated. Don't you feel it, too?"

"Yes, I do. It must be our inheritance from a sea-faring captain," replied Jim.

They remained on deck, savoring the brisk, tangy air. The Annie Marie almost seemed to fly over the water. Fair tide and fair wind propelled her towards her destination. Soon the day faded into night and the sky looked like an endless black velvet cloak encrusted with myriad twinkling diamonds.

Davy joined them. "We've got a bright star to steer the Annie Marie by. The weather couldn't be better."

Jim laughed. "That reminds me of a tale my grandfather told me."

"Well, tell us," urged Davy.

"Marlon Salter had a sharpie that he'd load with cantaloupes and watermelon. Every year, he'd take them to Norfolk to sell. He had a thirteen-year-old son who'd been begging to make the trip with him. Finally, Marlon gave in and agreed to take his son along, but on one condition- the boy must help with sailing the boat. The lad was so excited that he agreed to do anything. Finally after loading the cargo, they set sail. They sailed all day, and the boy did just as his father instructed. Then about six o'clock, as the sun was setting, the father called the boy over next to him.

"Jethro, you see that brightest star up there?" he asked, pointing to it.

"Yes Sir, I see it."

"That's the North Star. All you have to do is keep her bow headed towards that North Star. I'm going to get some sleep. Here's my pocket watch. At midnight, you come and wake me up. Okay?"

"Yes, Sir."

Marlon went to his cot and stretched out. He hadn't been sleeping for more than an hour when Jethro rushed in and woke him up. The father was really annoyed.

"What are you waking me up for? I told you to call me at midnight. It's only seven o'clock."

"But Pa, I had to. We done passed by that star. You'll have to pick me out another one!"

They all laughed and Davy was really tickled.

"Oh, look at the phosphorus," said Meg. "The sea around the ship is luminescent!"

"It is a non-metallic element of the nitrogen family," said Micco.

"You are so knowledgeable, Doctor Ravenwing," said Meg.

"We physicians know a bit about chemistry."

"You seem to know a bit about everything!"

"Well, not everything, Meg. For instance, I haven't been able to figure out how a woman's mind works."

Jim intervened, sensing another of Meg's flare-ups. "I couldn't agree more, Micco. After all my years of married life, I am still constantly intrigued by the mysterious machinations of my wife's logic."

"I suppose you think we aren't logical?" asked Meg, ready to leap into the fray, swinging.

Davy, being smitten with Meg, didn't like to see her upset.

"They didn't mean that at all. Why, you're logical and smart, and uh, pretty, too." Davy blushed when he said it.

Meg gave him a dazzling smile. "Now here's a man who understands women."

Davy blushed even more. "I came up to tell you that dinner is ready. We have some of Miss Molly's chicken and dumplings and I can't wait to eat them!"

He offered Meg his arm and Jim and Micco glanced at each other with amusement.

The dinner was delicious and Jim was touched that Miss Molly had included blackberry cobbler.

Meg, Micco, and Jim went to bed early, pleasantly tired. The next day they were approaching Savannah, accompanied by a pod of frolicking porpoises that were swimming, leaping, and diving around the ship.

"I see now what the voyager in the paper canoe meant when he wrote about being chased by playful dolphins," said Jim, marveling at the cavorting fish.

"The animals appear to be intelligent and I almost feel that I can communicate with them," said Micco.

They heard a cry from above. Anson was perched in the crow's nest, scanning the horizon with his spyglass.

"Land, ho," he yelled. Davy came out of the wheelhouse.

"We should be docking within thirty minutes. Unless you want to spend the night at an inn and explore the area, we can take care of business in a half day and then continue on our way." He looked questioningly at Meg.

"No, I am eager to reach Jupiter unless Uncle Jim and Micco want to explore." She turned to her uncle.

"I'm eager to reach our destination, too," said Jim.

"So am I," echoed Micco. "The closer I get, the more I want to reach home."

"That's settled then. We'll off-load the cargo, get our money, take on some supplies, and then continue our journey."

The ship moved quietly into the harbor, a gentle breeze nudging her along. Meg could see indications of sub-tropical foliage. Occasional palm trees lined the shore.

"Palm trees," she cried excitedly. "I'm seeing a palm tree again after ten years."

"Wait until you reach Jupiter. You'll view the most beautiful tropical plants imaginable," Micco replied, with nostalgia and pride in his voice.

"I remember, but this is a beautiful town. Many houses are nestled along the water as they are in Beaufort."

"It is. Some day we'll take a trip back here and explore it," answered Micco with complete assurance.

Meg looked at him thoughtfully. He had stated that as a fact. What did he mean? That she and Micco would be together in the future? But that couldn't be. She would become Andre's wife. Wouldn't she? Suddenly, she felt bereft at the thought of losing Micco. What was the matter with her? The man was incorrigible and so annoying. She could never live with him. She was truly confused, but she was convinced that as soon as she saw Andre, everything would resolve itself.

Micco watched the emotions warring in Meg's transparent face, that expressive face that he had observed so often when she was a child. If only he could take care of her as easily now as he did then. Unfortunately, she was still mesmerized by Andre's physical magnetism. At least the devil was gone.

They felt the gentle brush of the bumper guards as the Annie Marie edged into the dock slip. The crewmen quickly secured her lines to the piling. Davy jumped to the dock, looking for the harbormaster, eager to off-load his cargo and find supplies. He found him in his office in a small building at the end of the pier. The man who would buy some of his merchandise was also there. Davy took care of business and returned to the ship. Samese and Blondell had tied a gantline, which was roped through a block aloft the ship, around three crates.

"Let 'em go, Samese. We're in business," called out Davy.

"Aye, Sir." The two men hoisted the crates and two other crewmen who were on the wharf, untied them.

"Take it away," yelled Tim.

Workmen from the buyer's company began loading the crates on a dolly. Meg, Jim and Micco, who had walked down the gangplank, watched the process with interest.

"I hope those crates are secure," said Meg nervously. "If they fall, someone could be seriously injured or killed."

Davy, who had walked up with the harbormaster and another man, said, "Don't worry, Miss Meg. Those men are as experienced in handling cargo as they are in sailing a ship. There's a soda fountain on Main Street. It's not far from here for some light refreshment, or if you'd prefer, the Palms Hotel. They serve a very nice lunch.

"I'd like a strawberry soda," said Meg.

"A strawberry soda it is then," said Micco. "Will you join us, Davy?"

"Maybe I can join you later. Right now, I must oversee the cargo and make sure what goes and what remains on board."

"How about you, Jim?"

"No, thanks. You two run along."

Jim left and Micco and Meg continued their stroll.

"Oh, no! Watson has followed us!" The puppy, wearing a red bandana proudly, was trotting along beside them, tail wagging happily.

"How did you get out, you bad doggy?" Meg's tone was not censorious, so the pup gave a joyous bark.

"I see. You waited until the coast was clear and then made your move. All right. You can go." She picked up the dog's leash, which was dragging in the dust. "Come on."

They had to stop at every interesting tree and bush to satisfy the pup's curiosity. They found the soda fountain and Meg indulged herself and enjoyed the strawberry soda. When they went back outside, Watson, who had been tied to a tree, was fast asleep. Micco picked up the tired puppy and carried her back to the Annie Marie. She didn't even wake up and slept on peacefully in Micco's arms. Davy met them on the dock and took the sleepy puppy back to her basket in his quarters.

When he returned, he found Meg and Micco talking excitedly about Jupiter and what they would do when they arrived.

"We're ready to cast off, if you are," Davy said to them.

"I think if we wait any longer, Meg and Micco will start swimming to reach Florida," said Jim, amusement in his voice.

"Hoist the sails, boys, and cast her off," ordered Davy.

Within minutes, the ship was under sail, headed for the ocean lanes, moving gracefully into the wind. Meg leaned against the rail and felt the spume from the running tide gently caress her face.

"If I had been born a male, I would have been a captain on a sailing vessel," she said joyously. "I would have been a vagabond leading a vagrant life, sailing on a ship to see the world."

"And would you have enjoyed weevils in your bread, not being able to take a warm bath, and being at sea for three or more months at a time?" asked Micco.

"It would have its downside, I know, but the adventure and excitement would certainly make up for it." She walked along the deck, holding onto the railing, the breeze ruffling her hair as she made her way to the prow. Micco walked beside her, smiling at her enthusiasm. The seagulls flew above them, swooping and gliding on downdrafts.

"Look," Meg said, "They're free to soar wherever they want, whenever they want."

"That's how you'd like to be, isn't it? Unrestrained, with no physical or mental fetters."

"No. You make me sound childish! I simply want the will to be responsible to myself, to be self-sufficient."

Micco took Meg's hand, looking deeply into her eyes, and Meg felt vulnerable, as if he were searching for some truth she didn't want him to discover.

"I know you do, Red, but you have to realize that others care for your welfare. Others love you and want to protect you, in spite of yourself. I know you are capable of doing great things; you are capable of doing whatever you want to do, but can't you include a friend in your plans?"

His pleading, brown , velvety eyes were so appealing that Meg's resolve to spar with him melted.

"Yes I can."

"Good. That's settled. Now remember that friends confide in each other. If ever you have a problem, come to me and we'll solve it together. I'm an accomplished listener. I've had lots of practice listening. After your uncle leaves, you'll still have me, and once you really get to know him, you'll have your father, too."

Meg felt bathed in his warmth and friendliness. She had such ambivalent feelings towards him, though. Right now, he was looking at her as though she were a lost puppy. She shivered involuntarily, awash with conflicting emotions.

"Are you cold?" Micco asked .

"No. I like the brisk air and already its much warmer than it was in Beaufort."

"Let's continue walking then," he said, and tucked her arm beneath his. They circled the deck watching the seaman do their chores.

Jim was talking earnestly to Davy, but his eye was on the young couple. How perfectly suited they were to each other. 'If only Meg could be won over,' he thought, sighing to himself. Davy, too, watched as they strolled along, envying Micco his spot by the beautiful Meg.

"When do you think we'll reach Jupiter Inlet?" asked Jim.

"If this fair wind continues, and with a little help from the Gulf Stream, we should arrive day after tomorrow."

"Excellent. I really need to get back to New York. The long layover in Beaufort totally disrupted my schedule. All my clients have probably given me up for lost and availed themselves of the services of my competitors."

"I don't think you have to worry, Sir. They'd be losing the best lawyer around if they did," said Davy loyally.

"Thank you, my boy, but lawyers can be sharks among mullet, when they sniff blood. Anything is fair game, and I'm not there to coddle my clients."

"The tide and wind seem eager to help us. I believe the weather is on our side." Davy glanced at the sails. Every inch of canvas was stretched to capacity. They were making amazing time as the Annie Marie dipped and rode each wave like a lively porpoise.

Chapter Seventeen

The days and nights passed rapidly, and at twilight a day and a half later, Anson yelled from the crow's nest, "Green water ahead!" They had reached the waters of the Loxahatchee River, which would flow into Jupiter Inlet.

"Are we there?" asked Meg excitedly.

"We're here," answered Davy, "but we'll have to anchor for the night. This is a dangerous inlet. The tide, currents, and shifting sands are unpredictable. There are no charts of the area, and many a ship has foundered on a shoal. Grandfather had the greatest respect for these waters. He would never have entered the harbor at night, even with the lighthouse's beckoning light. Do you see the flashing light, Meg?"

"Where? Oh yes, I see it. We must be close by."

"The light is deceiving at night. We can be eighteen or twenty miles away and still see it, the candlepower is so bright. And the Gulf Stream is tricky. Sometimes it comes in as close as a mile from shore. Other times, it may be forty-five miles off shore. This is the closest place it comes to land, but the riptides make the area dangerous."

"How can there be such a variance?" asked Meg.

"I don't know. It's just one of those strange things in nature. It's a..." Davy tried to think of a word to describe it.

"You mean an anomaly?" said Jim.

"Yes, that's the word. The waters in this location are almost as unpredictable as those between Cape Lookout and Cape Hatteras. There are treacherous reefs as well. Many ships filled with treasure, in the past, have disappeared beneath the waves here. That's why we're going to wait until sunup to sail into the inlet."

"I understand," murmured Meg, disappointment in her voice.

"I remember some of the white settlers searching for buried treasure when I was a boy," said Micco. "I've climbed up those lighthouse steps many times. It was a fascinating view from the top. You could see all around our village, the forests, the ships coming in the harbor."

"Just a few more hours, Micco, and you'll see your home again," said Jim.

"After ten and a half years, I guess I can wait for a few more hours. They always had three men to run the lighthouse, the Head Keeper and two assistants. I know it was constant work to keep it going. I used to run all the way to the top of those 105 steps because the mosquitoes and fleas couldn't fly that high. They were voracious at the bottom. We kids would yell because the sound would echo inside. It made the men working inside so angry, but it wasn't worth the effort to run after us," Micco chuckled, remembering. "The lighthouse is built right by a midden."

"What's a midden?" asked Meg.

"I guess you could say it's a junk heap. Your father told me this one had been used around 950 A.D. by my forebears. They just threw all their junk, or dung, into the ground and kept covering it up. Tomorrow when we arrive at the lighthouse, you'll see that it's a hill. The lighthouse itself was finished in 1860."

"That was just six years after Cape .Lookout was built." said Jim .

"I can't wait to see it again," said Meg . "For some reason, I never walked inside the lighthouse."

"Your chubby little legs couldn't have made it," teased Micco.

Determined not to be provoked, Meg said, "Well, now my legs are long and I'm going right to the top!"

"In that long skirt? You'd trip before you went five steps, much less one hundred and five!"

It was too much for Meg. "I'll just wear buckskins and we'll see who gets to the top first!"

Micco laughed. "What is your father going to do with you? Even as modern as his ideas are, I don't think he'll approve of his daughter wearing men's pants!"

"Too bad, because that's exactly what I'm going to do!"

Davy looked shocked at this revelation, and Jim looked resigned.

"Miss Meg, you wouldn't really do that, would you?"

"You just bet I would. Davy, we are not in the dark ages. Women everywhere are revolting against these strict Victorian ideas." She relented a little bit, seeing his disbelieving face. "Maybe I wouldn't do it in New York, or even Beaufort, but here it's different. This is a new frontier and I'm going to be a part of it."

Davy had never met a girl like Meg before. None he knew would be so daring as she. He was more smitten than ever in spite of being somewhat shocked. Maybe she was right. He wouldn't mind seeing her in leggings. The ship had been moving steadily towards the light and he came out of his reverie abruptly.

"Samese and Tim, throw over the anchors, fore and aft," he shouted. The men obeyed their orders and the Annie Marie slowed, dragging her anchors until they caught. She finally stopped and rocked gently on the waves while the crew quickly furled the sails.

"We'll have dinner and after that, get a good night's rest. Then as soon as it is light, we'll sail. Too bad we don't have any more of Miss Molly's good food. I picked up plenty of supplies in Savannah, though."

"I ate the last of her blackberry cobbler," said Jim regretfully.

349

"I think dinner's ready. Shall we go?" Davy led the way and they all followed. After a filling, if not delicious meal, they went back on deck to enjoy the warm night breezes. Meg leaned over the railing, looking at the waves lapping against the ship's hull. Micco stood beside her, staring at the blinking light of Jupiter lighthouse.

"I'm a little nervous about seeing my father after all this time," said Meg.

"Don't be. He's probably more nervous than you are, but I know he's anxiously waiting to see his beloved daughter."

"How can you say that? He sent his 'beloved daughter' away. Besides, he and my mother hardly knew I existed when she was alive. You were closer to me than my own parents," Meg said with a note of sadness in her voice. She had held herself in control, but now the time was fast approaching when she would face her worst fear- rejection, again.

Micco turned her to face him. "You are wrong. He is lonely, Meg. He talked of you constantly, and he will be so happy to have you with him again. Give him a chance."

"I know you are right. Uncle Jim has said the same thing. Okay, I will give him a chance."

"Good girl." Micco put his arm around her shoulders and they stood there, companionably.

It rained early in the morning and when Meg awakened, she looked out the porthole and saw the sun shining through the raindrops. A magnificent rainbow stretched across the inlet. "Ah, it is Iris, the messenger of the gods. Does she have a message for me, I wonder?"

Meg smiled at her fancy and quickly dressed, eager to view her old home, and if she admitted it, more than eager to see her father, too. With a start, she realized that she had pushed the thought of seeing Andre into the recesses of her mind. But now, she felt a spurt of excitement and just a little apprehension. Would he really be here? And could she see him without her uncle or

Micco knowing? She went outside and tapped on Jim's door, but he didn't answer. Evidently, he was already up and about.

It seemed everyone was on deck. She saw Micco and Jim talking to Anson and Davy. The sailors were raising the anchors and hoisting the sails. Several of them were singing a sea chanty, "The Whaling Song", and their voices were strong and melodious in the fresh morning air. Suddenly Meg felt very happy. She was embarking on a new adventure, and only the capricious gods knew the outcome.

"Good morning, Meg. Did you sleep well?" asked Jim.

"Oh yes ,Uncle Jim, even though I was excited."

"Hello, Meg. Good to hear no hobgoblins disturbed you," said Micco with a friendly smile.

"Hello to you, too. Hello, Davy. How are you, Mr. Davis?" she greeted everyone joyously. "I can't even see the lighthouse. I thought I'd be staring at it this morning."

"Oi am foin," Anson replied as he squinted through his spyglass.

"Remember I told you the lights are deceiving at night," said Davy. "We're still about fifteen miles away. But you'll enjoy cruising through the inlet, seeing all the tropical foliage and animals. Tom'll take us through this estuary. He's had enough experience doing it. See that sand bar off our port side? It's easy to run aground here because the sands are constantly shifting due to the converging tides." Even as he spoke, the Annie Marie bounced up and down like a bobbing buoy, buffeted by the swirling, contradictory tides.

"Those are mangrove islands and grass flats off against the starboard bow. Coon oysters attach to the mangrove roots, and it's a haven for immature fish like sea trout, snapper, grunts, flounder, barracuda- you name it. It also harbors shrimp and crabs."

"That's fascinating. It's like a marine nursery."

"I never thought of it in those terms, but I guess that's a good name for it."

351

Jim and Micco joined in the conversation. "Those mangroves also help build up the coastline and are a buffer, to a certain extent, from storms," said Jim. "See that dark area over there? Those are oyster bars. I don't think Florida oysters are as good as oysters found further north, though. In my opinion, oysters need a spell of cold weather to give them outstanding flavor."

"I agree with you, Jim, and I'm a Seminole who has eaten oysters since he was a papoose. I didn't realize the difference until I tasted oysters in Long Island."

"Well, I remember eating them as a child in Jupiter, and I thought they were good," said Meg, ready to defend her early home.

"Oh, they are. I'm not disagreeing with that. It's just that they have more flavor in colder waters. We'll go out in Gray Wolf's canoe with a burlap bag and pick some Loxahatchee oysters and have an oyster roast."

Determined not to allow Micco to dominate the conversation with Meg, Davy pointed out other interesting spots. "If we took a tour up through that slough, you'd see a cypress swamp. Harvesting that lumber is a lucrative business. I've seen some of the carvings done by these local inhabitants and they are real craftsmen. They smooth and sand that wood and create pelicans, turtles, manatees, or dolphin that are truly beautiful. Grandmother has several pieces at home on the mantel that Grandfather brought back to her." Davy's voice was sad, as he remembered the beloved parent he would never see again.

"What's a manatee? I don't think I ever saw one when I was here," asked Meg.

"They're gentle, tropical, plant-eating mammals. Some people call them sea cows."

"Today, people think that the supposed mermaids sighted by sailors of yore were actually manatee," said Jim. "They must surface to breathe, and at a distance to the superstitious seamen, they must have looked half fish and half human."

352

Micco listened to Jim's tale of the manatee as he stared across Jupiter Narrows at the meandering stream called Lake Worth Creek, relieved to see that the inlet was open. As a child he remembered it closing periodically. Then local residents would dig small canals with their shovels. Evidently, the fall rains had filled the river until the small, hand-dug ditch became a half-mile wide, pouring brown muddy water into the Atlantic Ocean.

He turned to Davy. "We'll be able to get through to the lighthouse because the river is up."

"Yes, they must have had a good rainy season this fall. We're lucky. Sometimes the creek is only a few inches deep."

"Oh, I'm glad we won't have to wait another day or days. I can see the tower now," said Meg.

"Yes, we're less than five miles away," said Davy.

Micco was as excited as Meg and he was overcome with nostalgia. Soon he would see his beloved grandmother, Shontee. For a moment he was transported to his boyhood, remembering carefree days and his friends. It was as if he had never left, and had never become a respected surgeon, graduated from a prestigious school. He felt his Seminole blood surge through his veins and he wanted to put on loose clothing, clothing that would not bind him as he slid silently through the Everglades. He shook his head slightly as if to release himself from the thrall of his imaginings.

They were rapidly moving closer to the lighthouse and the brick structure stood tall against the morning sky. Now they could make out the dock and the keeper's coquina shell house.

"What is that flat, funny-looking boat tied up at the pier?" asked Meg.

That's a scow," answered Davy. "They load those flat-bottomed boats from an ocean-going buoy tender anchored out in the ocean. The tender draws too much water to navigate the inlet. Then the scows come in on a high tide and when there's enough rainwater in the river to reach the quay, they'll unload cargo such as oil, paint, and anything else needed by the lighthouse keepers.

Once a year the U.S. buoy tender anchors off the inlet to deliver these supplies."

"How interesting. That must be quite an undertaking. It's incredible they can do that out in the ocean."

"These buoy tenders are equipped to lift and clean the buoys so they're able to off-load supplies to the lighters or scows. On the occasion when the inlet is open, they send the supplies in on scows up to the dock. When the river is so low that it's closed to boats, and even a scow can't get through, they just unload the cargo and leave it high up on the beach. Then it is carried across the beach and ferried to the lighthouse by skiff."

Davy had listened to his grandfather talking about Jupiter lighthouse many times though he had visited it only once.

Micco said nothing, just absorbing remembered sights and sounds. By this time, the Annie Marie was approaching the dock. The lighthouse loomed 105 feet into the sky behind it.

"Just imagine the time and prodigious effort it took to build this lighthouse," said Jim.   "It's amazing that they were able to build it with all those obstacles," said Meg.

"I understand Captain Armour has been the lighthouse keeper for quite a few years. Sean said that he and Mrs. Armour are nice folks. They live in the keeper's house and you'll meet them and some of their children. I'm sure they'll probably insist we stay for dinner, but remember, Micco's grandmother is expecting us.   I wrote to Sean about a week before we left Beaufort, and he sent me a telegram in reply."

"Oh, you didn't tell me about that, either," said Meg in surprise.

"I'm sorry, but there were just so many things happening that it completely slipped my mind."

"It's all right. We're here now and soon I'll see him in person."

The Annie Marie, with lowered sails, slid smoothly towards the pier. In no time, Blondell and Samese had tied the ship to the dock pilings. Meg was as fascinated by Jupiter Inlet as she had been by the Port of New York. Scrub pine along the banks mingled with the red berries of the dahoon holly. Willows swept their fronds gracefully, almost touching the river. Sitting on the half-submerged roots of a mangrove tree, a curious raccoon observed all the activity serenely. A little bridge led to the newly built two-story keeper's house that was shaded by a banyan tree.

The seamen carried Meg, Jim and Micco's trunks into the yard while the three trod carefully as they descended the swinging rope gangplank to the dock. Davy followed them down and then took Jim aside.

"I'm not going to spend the night here. No telling what this tide'll do. We're headed out to the Bahamas to pick up a cargo of sugar and rum. If conditions are right, we'll return for you in about ten days and then sail to Savannah, where you can catch the train north."

"I really appreciate this, Davy. I must get back as soon as possible. I will pay you extra, of course."

"I can use the money, for sure, but I would not do it for just anybody. Normally, we would sail straight back home with the cargo." He turned to Meg. "Miss Meg, I certainly enjoyed meeting you and maybe we can meet again the next time I come into Jupiter Inlet." He blushed when he looked at her.

Meg held out her hand. "It has been a pleasure knowing you, too, Davy. I think you are a terrific captain. You would have made your grandfather so proud. Somehow I have felt he was here all along, guiding you over every wave."

"Thank you. I've felt his presence, too."

Anson and the rest of the crew bid them farewell, saying they would see Jim and Meg again soon.

Micco shook hands with Davy. "A pleasure to have met you, Davy." Lowering his voice, he added, "And thank you for keeping Lafitte off the ship."

Davy had a grim expression on his face. "I'd like to have blackened his eye." The two men shook hands and Davy ran nimbly up the gangplank. Turning around, he pulled it up behind him.

Jim, Micco, and Meg watched as Samese and Tim cast off the lines and pushed the Annie Marie from the quay with a poling oar. Blondell and Tom hoisted the sails and the stalwart ship coasted down the inlet, heading for the ocean. They all waved goodbye.

"I am going to miss those fellows," said Jim.

"So am I," agreed Meg as she turned to face the keeper's house and lighthouse. She watched as supplies from the scow were taken to the foot of the steep steps at the base of the lighthouse. Both keepers had a yoke across their shoulders with a five-gallon metal can hooked on each end. They walked carefully up the steps and were met by Captain Armour who had a cloth in his hand.

"What are they doing?" Meg asked Micco.

"Captain Armour has saturated that cloth with linseed oil. He'll wipe all the cans to make sure there is no salt water on them before they are placed on the shelves. It is a constant job maintaining a lighthouse. Besides painting and maintaining the masonry, they have to go up all those steps every day to light the mineral lamps and wind the weights. The illuminating apparatus moves on ball bearings and they have to be greased regularly. As you discovered, the flashing light can be seen eighteen or more miles away."

They had gradually walked down the dock and across the bridge and were standing in the yard. Meg tilted her head back and stared at the tower. "I want to walk on that balcony and look at the surrounding countryside."

"You'll never make it in that skirt," observed Micco. "You would trip and I'd have to catch you and we would probably both end up at the bottom of the stairs!"

"You mean you couldn't hold me? I thought you were a big, strong , Indian brave."

"Ah, Meg, our exploits are greatly exaggerated. Now, if you weighed less, I might manage to keep us from falling."

"Micco Ravenwing, I hope you end up marrying a fat tub who feeds you mush, and that she sits on you when you try to sneak out of the house!"

Micco only laughed, making Meg more annoyed. He winked at Jim and ran up the steps to greet Captain Armour.

Meg and Jim turned as someone called out their names.

"Meg, Jim! I can't believe you are here at last!"

"Father?" asked Meg haltingly. The father she had known had dark brown hair and piercing blue eyes. How well she remembered those eyes. As a little girl, when he had looked at her, she always felt guilty. Now as Sean Riley drew closer, she could see those deep- blue ,intelligent eyes. She remembered how they slanted down at the corners, but now she saw something else within those blue smoky depths. She saw an expression she had never recognized before- sadness.

"My dear daughter, my grown-up girl. How are you?" He spoke lovingly and held out his arms.

Meg hesitated and then flew into the waiting arms. He hugged her tightly and she felt how thin he was. His hair was completely white; his skin was as translucent as alabaster, and she could see faint blue veins at his temple. She hardly knew what to say. He was somehow different from the father she remembered. He was frailer for one thing, and less overpowering for another. He held her off from him and looked searchingly into her eyes.

"You are so much like your mother."

"Am I? I remember that she had red hair."

"And trusting green eyes just like yours."

Jim walked over. "Aren't you going to greet your long lost brother-in-law, Sean?"

"Jim, how wonderful to see you again." The two men shook hands. "It's been so long; ever since you took my Megan with you to New York. How is Julie? I wish she could have come, too."

"Her mother is quite ill and Julie did not want to leave her."

"I am so sorry. I would like to have seen her. Jim, we have years of catching up to do. But where is Micco? He did come with you, didn't he?" Sean's voice was tinged with disappointment.

"He came. You couldn't have kept him away with a Union army. Here he comes," said Jim as Micco bounded down the steps and ran across the yard.

The doctor's eyes sparkled with happiness as he watched his protégé approach. Micco's eyes were filled with affection as he greeted his mentor and benefactor.

"Doctor Riley!"

"Micco!" The two men were emotional and seemed at a loss for words. Then they embraced as a father and son would.

"Micco, what a big strong man you are. You were a gangly teenager, all arms and legs when you left."

"And you, Doctor. How are you? You said in your letters that your health had improved," Micco asked .

"It has, I may look a trifle sickly, but I am greatly recovered since my bouts with malaria. Now that you're back, we'll open the clinic again. That is, if you want to practice here. I wouldn't blame you at all if you decided to practice medicine in a big city where you could make money and lead a luxurious life."

"Never! Here beside you and among my people is where my place is."

Dr. Riley looked relieved. "Let's talk shop later. Come, Meg, and Jim, and meet the Armours and their children."

Two dogs of indeterminate heritage ran out to meet them followed by an orange cat with perfectly symmetrical markings.

"Our canine-feline welcoming committee," said Dr. Riley, as he patted a dog's head .

Meg had picked up the cat and it was purring in contentment as she rubbed its glossy coat. She was drawn to all cats and most dogs.

A slim , graying woman stood at the doorway of the house, a smile on her face. They walked to the house and Sean made the introductions.

"Mrs. Armour, may I present my daughter, Megan Riley, and my brother-in-law, Jim Styron?   Meg and Jim, this is Mrs. Armour."

"Welcome to Jupiter Inlet and to my home," said Mrs. Armour, extending her hand.

"How do you do?" said Meg . "Your yard is breathtaking! Everything is so lush."   Huge yellow and vermilion-striped morning glories ran rampant along the fence. Orange tiger lilies tossed their heads in the breeze. "All these flowers and trees in bloom! Back home, snowdrops and crocus are just beginning to thrust their leaves up through the snow. Oh, look at those purple orchids on the tree limbs! How beautiful they are! That banyan tree is spectacular with its twisted air roots dropping to the ground. What a unique tree!"

"Thank you, but I can't really take credit for it. In Jupiter everything grows on its own. I just kind of direct it. I've gotten used to it, but it really is amazing how plants seem to grow overnight. That Royal Palm over there in the corner of the yard grew six feet in one year."   She pointed to a stately tree that towered above the house.

"That banyan tree is indeed unusual. So nice to meet you, Mrs. Armour," said Jim, shaking her proffered hand.

"Come in, come in. I have lemonade and some fresh-baked ginger cookies. Captain Armour will be along in a moment when he finishes his work in the oil storage house."

"Remember me?" asked Micco.

Mrs. Armour looked at him, uncertainty on her face. "Why, it can't be! Land sakes! It's Micco Ravenwing, a grown man!" She walked over and gave him a hug, craning her neck to look at him. "You're taller than my Sabal palm tree. Let's go sit down and you tell me what you've been doing these last ten years or more."

"If your ginger cookies are as good as they were when I used to filch them off the counter fifteen years ago, just hand me the platter right now!" said Micco, grinning like a ten-year-old.

"That's Micco, all right. You haven't changed- always teasing." They walked past a pump just outside the front door, and then entered the quaint coquina rock home. They also had a well inside the house. This had been essential in earlier times when the keepers were under siege by hostile Indians.

"Sit down, everyone. I'll bring out the refreshments."

The two dogs and cat, Salty, Pepper, and Rusty, followed them into the house and waited expectantly, by the rough-hewn oak table. Meg, Jim, Sean, and Micco sat down; talking among themselves while Mrs. Armour went into the kitchen. She returned shortly, bearing a tray laden with a pitcher of lemonade, glasses, and a large tin platter of cookies.

"Oh, you three, always waiting for a handout," she scolded. "Well, you don't get anything 'til you ask for it properly. Sit!" The three animals obediently sat back on their launches, front paws in the air, though Rusty's stance managed to imply that she did it condescendingly. Mrs. Armour broke a cookie in three pieces, giving each pet a piece. "There now, that's all you get. Go lie down and don't bother me anymore."

The three moved over in front of the fireplace and plopped down on the planked wooden floor, which had been built from the hull of a wrecked ship.

"That's amazing," said Meg. "How in the world did you train them, especially the cat? I've never seen such well-behaved animals except in a circus."

"Just about any animal can be trained, even cats, if you have the patience to do it. If they're going to come into my house, they'd better behave!"

She served the lemonade and cookies, and Micco took four cookies, smiling unabashedly as he did it.

Captain Armour entered the room, apologizing for his tardiness. Again, Dr. Riley made the introductions. After they

360

exchanged greetings, Mrs. Armour offered her husband refreshments. Meg noticed that she adhered to her strict Victorian upbringing and never addressed her husband by his first name. It was always, 'Mr. Armour'.

"Did you have a good trip? Any rough seas?" asked Captain Armour.

"Fortunately, we had clear sailing from Beaufort. And after our encounter with Racer's Storm from Hatteras to Cape Lookout, we were eternally thankful," said Jim.

"I heard about that hurricane. You were lucky to have survived it. The Carolina coast has been hit pretty hard in recent years. We've had some bad ones off the coast here, too. The area around Jupiter Inlet is treacherous to ships. There's been many a shipwreck hereabouts. The government's built some Life-saving Stations to rescue and help out the survivors. Actually, in our little settlement here, we've acquired a lot of things that have floated up on shore from the wrecks."

"We sure have," agreed Mrs. Armour. "Salty and Pepper are the sons of Storm and Wreck, two of three dogs that Captain Armour helped rescue from the Victor, a steamer that was wrecked just south of the Inlet in 1872. Then seven canoes of Indians paddled up from Fisheating Creek. When the Victor began to break up, they joined in the salvage. They were as eager as we were at what we might find."

That's when Mr. Pierce, our assistant keeper, was standing on the lighthouse dock. He noticed a packing case floating by and so did an Indian standing beside him. They both ran down to the shore to get the case. When Mr. Pierce read the description of contents on the box, he claimed it. The Indians wouldn't have had any use for it anyway because it was a Wheeler and Wilson sewing machine. Mrs. Pierce has sewn many a garment on that machine. She says it's the best gift she's ever received," said Captain Armour.

"I was talking to Billy Bowlegs some time ago and he sure appreciated the case of Plantation bitters his tribe brought home, along with the useful canoe loads of salvage," added Mrs. Armour.

"That must be exciting to find a treasure right in your own backyard, so to speak," said Jim. "I'm sure you've given comfort and shelter to the survivors, though. You must have made many friends."

"Yes, we did," said Captain Armour. "And Dr. Riley gave them medical aid. We welcome travelers too, coming down the Indian River by sailboat. They always enjoy climbing those spiral stairs to the top of the lighthouse to see the view of the ocean and forests."

"Those shipwreck survivors and travelers must certainly appreciate your hospitality," said Meg .

"We're happy to help. Besides, we enjoy hearing the news about what's happening elsewhere."

Dr. Riley joined in the conversation. "Believe it or not, Meg, we've even had earthquakes here."

"Really? I thought you just had those in California."

"No. We had a bad one here eight years ago. It shook the lighthouse so hard it sent the two keepers on watch tumbling down the stairs."

"That's awful. Thank goodness, it didn't destroy the lighthouse. Were the keepers badly injured?"

"Not really. They had some cuts and bruises, and were shaken up a bit, but no serious injuries. Fortunately, this lighthouse is sturdily built. It was shaken from the top to the bottom, but held up against the force of the tremors.

Captain Armour spoke. "Actually, I had a close call myself, and it wasn't even during the earthquake. I was coming down an iron ladder from the dome of the lantern. I had propped the ladder against the railing of the balcony and when I stepped on it, the rail broke."

"Great Caesar's ghost! You could have been killed, falling down all those stairs," exclaimed Jim.

362

"That's true. I was just plain lucky. I was able to catch hold of part of the railing that didn't break, and pulled myself back away from the stairs. I landed full force on the platform and was dazed, momentarily. Then when I looked down those winding stairs and realized I could be lying on cold, hard stones a hundred or more feet below, I knew I had a guardian angel!"

"Amen!" said Mrs. Armour.

"Absolutely amazing," said Jim. "I notice you have photographs on the wall of some huge fish. Were they caught here?"

"Yes, Right off the lighthouse dock. That's a 360-pound jewfish. I brought a steelyard down to the dock to weight it. President and Mrs. Grover Cleveland were visiting here last year and Mrs. Cleveland caught a tarpon. Wish I'd gotten a picture of that, but I didn't. There's a steamer, moored out across from the lighthouse. It's like a floating hotel and we get some fancy guests that stay on it and go fishing."

"That must have been thrilling to have met the President of the United States."

"It was. When we found out they were coming, my wife made herself a new dress, all the children were spruced up with new shoes, and I got a new hat."

Jim smiled and continued walking around looking at the pictures. "This is a good picture of the lighthouse, too. Whoever took these photographs has flare for photography."

"That's Mr. Spencer's work. You'll meet him later on. He does have an artistic eye. Look at those photographs of that big manatee. And that one's a picture of a twelve-foot panther that I shot. I potted him from the tower."

"I imagine that keeping the lighthouse in good running order is a twenty-four hour job."

"It is. The lamps must be kept lit. A keeper must be on the balcony at all times to watch for ships in distress, and maintenance is constant. But it can be a boring job, too. I try to keep 'em busy painting, unloading supplies, and taking care of the grounds. So fishing and hunting is a favorite pastime. We even have stories of pirate treasure buried around here, and some of the young fellows spend their spare time digging for it."

"Did they ever find any treasure?" asked Meg.

"No big treasure, but occasionally, a gold doubloon will wash up on shore from a Spanish galleon wrecked 350 years ago. But you know something that concerns me is that we've got modern-day pirates right off the coast here raiding ships. It has just been happening recently. There have even been a couple of murders. And those beach combers are a rough bunch, too."

"You have pirates in this day and age? I thought they disappeared seventy-five years ago. Who are the beach combers?" Meg asked.

"We've had two reports of vessels being boarded and pillaged. In one instance, the captain of the crew put up resistance and he was shot and killed."

"How horrible. Can't the authorities do anything?"

"By the time the raided ship reaches safe harbor to report it, the pirate ship is long gone. And on land, we've got scoundrels that live on the beaches, roaming from Jupiter to Lake Worth and south to the settlement of Miami. They prey on innocent people traveling along the beaches. Our mailman faces danger from them as well as from the weather, alligators, and sharks."

"Your mailman? You mean he walks the beaches carrying the mail?"

"There are several of these U.S. mail carriers, but James Hamilton is the one we see most often. He is unique because he never wears shoes on his mail route."

"He doesn't wear shoes! How could he possibly endure the burning sand, sharp objects, and sand spurs?"

"He says it's easier walking that way. I don't know how he does it. He carries letters over 100 miles between Lake Worth and Miami. It takes him three days each way. He ought to be arriving at the lighthouse shortly. He usually gets here in the early afternoon from Lake Worth. A sharpie brings the mail from

Jacksonville there, and James picks it up and brings it to Jupiter and then on to Miami. There's talk that Flagler is going to build his railroad all the way to Key West. It ends at Titusville now. I guess that will put the mail carriers out of a job."

Jim had been listening intently. "When that happens, the whole eastern seaboard of Florida will open up to businessmen and tourists," he observed.

Mrs. Armour, noticing that everyone had finished drinking the lemonade, asked if they wanted more. None did.

"If you won't have more lemonade, please let me fix lunch."

"No, thank you. We're going to go on over to my house. I know Micco is eager to see his grandmother and friends. The lemonade was delicious," said Dr. Riley, rising from his chair.

"It certainly was," agreed Micco. "I'll just take a few more cookies with me to fortify me on the way home, you understand!"

Mrs. Armour had been busy putting the rest of the cookies in a container. "I figured you might. Here. This should last you 'til you reach the house. Are you sure I can't persuade you to stay for lunch? It wouldn't be any trouble and I could have it ready in ten minutes." Visitors were limited and Mrs. Armour enjoyed gossiping with whomever arrived.

"No, we really can't, but thank you for the kind invitation, and for the lemonade and cookies," said Jim.

"Yes, thank you for your hospitality. I'll be back to visit you soon," added Meg, realizing that the lady longed to talk.

"You are most welcome. Come anytime!" said Mrs. Armour in a disappointed voice.

They all walked out into the sunshine and were touched by a gentle breeze as they moved towards the lighthouse, past the two-story keeper's dwelling. Meg noticed an iron wash pot in the Armour's backyard. She felt a wave of nostalgia remembering Miss Molly and Maryanne washing clothes in Beaufort. 'I wonder how they're doing, and all the other friends we made there,' she thought.

Micco noticed Meg's wistful expression. "Are you missing Beaufort a little?"

Meg never ceased to be amazed at Micco's perceptiveness. Sometimes she thought he could read her mind.

"Yes, I am. I was remembering how Miss Molly bossed poor Maryanne around. But Maryanne didn't really seem to mind."

Micco had put his arm around her shoulders as they strolled along. Dr. Riley, even as preoccupied as he was, noticed this and wondered if there was more to their relationship than friendship.

"We'll forge a new life here, a wonderful fulfilling life, and some day we'll go back to visit our friends. I feel that they are my friends, too."

Again Meg wondered exactly what he meant by that. She was unable to fathom his meaning because he did not treat her as a sweetheart. Now Andre...ah, Andre, who was so romantic, showed his feelings. She knew that he was as passionately attracted to her as she was to him. Micco showed no sign of that. If he truly felt that way about her, wouldn't he demonstrate it? Wouldn't he crush her in his arms as Andre did? Meg blushed at her thoughts, horrified that Micco might read them.

In spite of his considerable experience with women, Micco was kept off-balance by Meg, and in spite of what she imagined, he really didn't understand her thought processes. To him, it was obvious that Andre was a scoundrel, and yet Meg couldn't see that even after the way he had treated her. Instinctively, he sensed that she still longed for Andre. He could only hope that gradually she would forget him. Now she was blushing. What had he said to cause that? She was an enigma, but then he enjoyed solving puzzles, especially beautiful, redheaded ones.

They caught up with the others. Captain Armour was talking about the new building. "We added a new kitchen in 1875 and completely renovated the house, but it was just too crowded with three families living in it. We finally convinced the government to build another house for the two keepers and their families. It was completed just four years ago, praise be. Now we've all got plenty of room. What with seven children, we sure needed it. Of course, most of them are out on their own now."

"Sean, what is that small structure near the lighthouse?" asked Jim.

"That's our telegraph building."

"You have a telegraph office here?" Jim asked .

"I told you we were real modern," said Captain Armour with a twinkle in his eye.

"It was installed just a month ago, in spite of government bureaucracy. They brought the Western Union cable over from Nassau, but the crewmen couldn't take it ashore until they telegraphed Washington from the lighthouse for permission," Dr. Riley said. By this time, they had reached the small bridge that led to the lighthouse.

Captain Armour squinted his eyes in the brilliant sun. "Ah, here comes our mailman right on time. I don't know how he keeps such a schedule."

A young, slender man walked across the sand from the direction of the Indian River. The beach itself was traversed from one village to another since there were no roads. His trousers were rolled up past his knees, and his skin was burned to a deep bronze color. He wore a cap emblazoned with the words 'U. S. Mail', and he carried a haversack with canvas straps across his shoulders. When he came within hailing distance, Captain Armour called out.

"James, you made pretty good time today. Must have been outrunning those pesky flies and biting mosquitoes."

"Yes, I did, didn't I? The conditions was right. Didn't have many sand flurries blinding me, or rain squalls. Wish I could outrun those flies! Sometimes my face is pure covered with 'em. I did encounter some sharks chasing a school of mackerel. They chased those fish right up to the shore, and I picked up some big ones when they jumped up and landed on the beach. I roasted them in coals on the fire, along with some yams and biscuits. It was mighty good."

"Couldn't have a better meal than that," agreed Captain Armour. "How did you get around those sharks, though? When they are in a feeding frenzy, you better steer clear."

"Lucky for me, somebody had found my skiff where I'd hidden it beneath some branches, and rowed it over from the other side. I wouldn't have wanted to swim across like I usually do to get it. But don't you know, one of them sharks took a bite out of my oar when I was sculling her across the cut. They're about as bad as the alligators in the Loxahatchee River."

"I've got some extra oars you can have, James. When you make your return trip from Miami, take them with you. One of my sons can help you carry them."

"I appreciate that, and I'll take you up on the offer."

Captain Armour introduced the mailman to his guests and they all continued to the oil storage room. When they reached it, Jim noticed a flat, rectangular woven bamboo basket on the counter containing several letters.

"Our telegraph office is so new, we're not completely organized yet. So we still use the storage room as a mail room," said Dr. Riley.

James had walked up the stone steps at the base of the lighthouse, his calloused feet impervious to shingles and tiny sharp-edged stones. He dropped his canvas mailbag on the floor. The bag was shackled with a padlock.

"Let me get the key," said Captain Armour. "We have a couple of letters going to Miami, and there's some letters and a package going to Juno and Lake Worth for your trip back."

James unlocked the mailbag. He removed the package,, and took out two letters, placing them in the basket.

"This one is for you, Mr. Styron," said James, handing him a letter. Jim took it, surprised to have received a letter. It was from his wife. He tore open the letter, a relieved expression on his face as he scanned the contents.

"Meg, your aunt's mother is much improved, and listen to this- 'Mrs. Henrietta Seymour called on me today. She said that she had met you all in Beaufort, and that she was nearly murdered in her bed when a notorious killer went on the rampage. Her doctor is seriously concerned about her health and recommends bed rest and a healthy diet.'

"Ha," said Meg. "A diet intended for a herd of tigers! Uh, do tigers come in herds?"

Jim continued, with a smile. '...so that she may regain her strength after the terrible ordeal she went through. Ah, she also says that young ladies who do not wear bustles are contributing to the decline of Western society. She gently hinted, with the delicacy of a charging buffalo, that Meg needed more parental guidance. Quoth she, 'I fear for the very tenor of our society.'

Jim laughed. "Well, Meg, you certainly made a lasting impression on Henrietta. It is a good thing that Julie knows her only too well. Otherwise, she would be terribly upset to hear of a 'notorious killer' stalking Beaufort citizens."

"I hope I shocked the old harridan. What a pious busybody," said Meg.

"Meg, you should not talk about Mrs. Seymour that way," Jim said, half-heartedly, since he felt the same way about her.

"And poor Mr. Seymour. He is such a fine man. Too bad he has to put up with her. A swift kick in the..."

"Meg!" interrupted Jim. "He loves her in spite of everything!"

"Humph! If that's the case, 'love' is not only blind, it is deaf and dumb as well!"

"Some day you'll understand. That is, if you ever fall in love."

"Not much chance of that, Jim. Meg is a liberated woman," said Micco.

"Is that so? How sad. I never knew." Jim shook his head, despairingly.

369

Meg fumed and Micco laughed at Jim's doleful expression, while they were talking.

James took the mail intended for Miami, placed it in the oilcloth, and then locked the bag. He returned the key to Captain Armour, who placed it in its hiding place.

"Come on over to the house and have some lunch and a cool drink of lemonade. Mrs. Armour is dying to hear if Bonnie Russell had her baby and any other gossip you can tell her."

"You don't have to ask me twice! Seems like it was especially hot out in that sun today. Hope she has some sour orange biscuits to go along with that lemonade!"

"She's got that and fried snapper, besides."

Meg, Micco, Jim and Dr. Riley bid them goodbye and watched as the two made their way across the bridge. Mrs. Armour was waving from the doorway. They waved back.

"My horse and cart is not too far from here. If you can walk a quarter mile, Meg, we'll get it and ride over to the house," said Dr. Riley.

"I'm fine. I'll enjoy the walk."

"Those heels are not made for walking in sand," said Micco, looking down at her shoes. "Why don't you let me go get the horse and cart and come back for you all?"

"No, thank you. I can manage," Meg replied, annoyed that Micco thought she couldn't do it.

"As you wish," he said. "At least you're wearing a hat to protect your complexion from this Florida sun. You can't be too careful, Meg, with that red hair. Your skin is not meant to bake in the sun."

"Why don't you save your advice for your patients who will listen to you."

"Most of my patients probably won't have to worry about it since they have black hair and dark skin."

Meg said nothing to this, but tossed her hair and forged ahead. Micco caught up with her and took her arm, none too soon it appeared, since she caught her heel on a rock and stumbled.

370

She didn't try to shake his arm off after that episode. That's all she needed to do, fall flat on her face with Micco looking down at her, his expression saying 'I told you so'.

After five minutes, her thin shoes were filled with sand, and she was hot and wet with perspiration. If Micco dared to make one comment, she'd never speak to him again, at least not for a day.

Micco knew better than to tease her at this point. Her eyes were flashing fire; her hat was drooping to one side; her blouse was stuck to her back, and she was noticeably limping. He decided not to say anything at all to her.

"Dr. Riley, is the clinic all set up?"

"Yes, Micco. I have medicines and instruments. It's bigger than when you helped me and my wife. There are five patient rooms, and I've increased space in the waiting room. I've decided to give up my job as bookkeeper at the lighthouse. With you taking on most of the burden of patient care, I want to work exclusively in medicine again."

"But are you able to do it?" asked Micco .

"I believe so. I'll do the bookwork, primarily. If I feel tired, I can go lie down. This is the advantage of having the clinic in my home. I also want you to live here, too. Would you consider that? I know you wish to be close to your grandmother, but it would be such a relief to me to have you close by in case of emergencies."

Micco looked at his mentor and benefactor. He owed this man so much. It seemed little enough to ask, and he knew Shontee would be disappointed, but she would understand.

"I will live at your home and be there if you need me. My grandmother is a wise woman and an unselfish woman. She let me go eleven years ago, though I was her only child."

Dr. Riley clasped Micco's hand in gratitude.

"Thank you, my boy."

Jim observed this and saw the strong bond between the two men. He could understand it because he felt the same way towards Micco, almost as if he were a son.

"There's a small house and stable up ahead," he said. "Is this where you keep your horse?"

"Yes, this is it. I'll stable him in a barn behind the house now. I recently bought the horse and cart when I knew you were returning and I hired a man to take care of the horse until you arrived. Now we'll have transportation. Maybe I can find a carriage somewhere. That would be more comfortable for Meg."

"Good planning, Sean," said Jim. "As I recall, your house is several miles from here."

"Yes, about three miles from the lighthouse. When we arrive, I'll send Chotskee back for your luggage. I had supplies brought in by boat from a general merchandise store in Lake Worth several weeks ago. I also hired a housekeeper because I thought taking over household duties might be overwhelming to Meg."

"You're right there. I suppose you could say that Meg had been sp..., um, she has led a sheltered life. Doing household chores was not one of her duties. As a matter of fact, I don't think she's even boiled water. We have always had servants. Meg developed social skills and educational skills. She's a wonderful musician, and she paints beautifully, and as you know, she graduated with honors from college, too."

"Jim, you and Julie did a fantastic job training my child. I couldn't ask for a more perfect daughter. That's why I sent her away; so that she could have all the advantages I could not give her here. She can learn to cook and sew, if she wants, but I certainly do not expect her to run my house. She is going to set up her school and that pleases me. I admire her determination in coming back here when she could have had an easy life in New York." The doctor looked at his daughter affectionately. "But right now, she's probably wishing she were back there. We're almost at the stable, Meg, just a few more yards."

Meg had half listened to the conversation, too miserable to take it in. She had cursed her stupid pride a dozen times as she

372

trudged along. Why, oh, why hadn't she agreed to wait for the horse and cart?

"Here we are at last. Chotskee is coming to greet us."

"Chotskee, it's Micco."

The elderly Indian stared at the tall man before him. "You Micco?" he asked in astonishment.

"Yes, I am. How's that misery in your back?"

"Back bad."

"I'll have to do something about that. Come by Dr. Riley's house when you can. We are opening up a clinic there. I have just the thing to ease your pain."

"Umh," he replied noncommittally.

Jim introduced everyone They exchanged greetings that consisted of a grunt on Chotskee's part. Micco helped Meg into the cart and the others climbed aboard. They followed a barely discernible, rutted wagon wheel road in the sand along the edge of the forest and beach. The passengers were jounced, up and down though the wagon moved along fairly slowly.

"It might be easier to travel by horseback," gasped Meg, when they hit a deep rut that almost dislodged her from the buckboard seat.

"I agree with that. How well do you ride?" asked Micco.

"I am no equestrian, but I can learn to improve," she said, hanging on to the side of the wagon.

Jim too, found the ride an endurance contest. Surprisingly, Dr. Riley seemed to suffer least, along with his stoic driver.

"We're almost there. The house is directly ahead." He pointed to a two-story Bahamian-style house with wide verandas facing the Indian River. Spanish moss hung from salt cedar trees left growing in the yard, and a twisted gray cypress spread its wrinkled toes towards the beckoning water. Meg had never been so happy to see anything in her life. She could not decide which was more miserable, trudging through the sand or bouncing on the seat. The wagon finally came to a halt and Meg stared at the house before her. This would be her home now, far removed from the

Georgian mansion in New York City equipped with indoor plumbing, running water, a telephone, and even electricity. Meg moved forward, almost in a daze, towards her new life, with Micco at her side.

Chapter Eighteen

Andre made excellent time on his trip to Florida. He didn't stop until he reached Lake Worth. McGuire had sailed these waters many times and was familiar with the quirks of the tides and the locations of hidden shoals. He had learned to respect Andre, though he did not like him. Anderson and the rest of the crew felt the same. Not one of them would have crossed him. Besides, he had promised them wealth and they did not care how they acquired it. Under Lafitte's tutelage, the crew was well organized. Each man accomplished his task with speed and efficiency, and Jamie did his chores willingly, for unlike the others, he admired Andre tremendously. The Osprey proved to be a fast, sturdy ship, cresting the waves easily and plunging into the troughs like a flying fish. Andre was actually happy. This was the life for him. He had despised his weak, drunken father, but felt a strong affinity for the grandfather he had never known, the notorious Jean Lafitte. The same love of the sea coursed through Andre's veins, as did the ruthless disregard for others. Both were born to command; both were relentless in their pursuit of self-gratification; both were murderers.

He had brought the ship safely through a stiff gale, running the vessel under lower topsails, with her lee rail awash. He had ordered Anderson aloft on a black, starless night, sixty-five feet above deck to spread the canvas that was stiff with salt, and the man did it without a murmur of dissent, though he rocked back and forth, holding onto a shroud and the masthead. When he finished his job on the precarious perch, he quickly descended the ratlines and joined Lafitte for a shared watch. They casually strolled the deck, smoking cheroots.

Anderson was an intelligent man, though he had little formal education. Andre had discovered that his first mate was smart enough to be counted on in any tight situation, and little ruffled him. 'A good man to watch my back,' thought Andre. They passed the navigator, ensconced on the stern with a sextant at his eye, observing the celestial bodies to determine latitude and longitude. Andre had deliberately kept the Osprey far out in the ocean, except when they went into Savannah to sell their goods, avoiding land until they neared their destination, and so he needed a competent navigator. The two men continued their watch around the deck. Amazingly, even in the vast reaches of the ocean, ships had been known to collide with other ships, and even with whales.

"How about a hand of poker?" Andre asked. " I'll have McGuire take an hour's watch."

"Okay by me. Gully and Brondell like to play."

Andre was nonpareil in taking men's money and making them feel they were unlucky in cards, but lucky in knowing such a charming fellow. His crew, of course, did not think he was charming. They thought he was the devil incarnate. He remembered that night in San Francisco a year ago when a lieutenant in the army accused him of cheating. He had drawn a pistol but Andre was quicker and Lt. Guilford topped with a hole in his forehead. Andre and Dory fled the scene before the police arrived, gathered up their money plus a few belongings, and disappeared before the local constabulary broke down the door.

Andre smiled as he dealt the cards, remembering Guilford's astonished look as he fell forward on the table. He easily took the men's money since he knew every possible way to cheat. They glared at him but were afraid to say anything.

"Well, that's enough for tonight. Come on, Anderson. We have much to discuss."

They went topside and relieved McGuire.

Andre said, "We'll go into port at Lake Worth and pick up supplies. We'll be plying our trade, so to speak, along the well-traveled sea-lanes. But we also need to find a secluded island with a deep water creek somewhere here along the coast where we can hide out, if need be, and careen the ship when necessary."

"Hide out? Why would we want to do that, Sir?" asked Anderson.

"Because when we plunder merchant ships, we'll need a get-away, a hide-out. We'll sell what the captains so graciously give us, prodded by a gun placed convincingly against the temple. I am going to see if I can find a buyer or a middleman for selling our goods in Lake Worth. There are always those who will do anything for a price. Don't you agree, Anderson?"

"That I do. Every seaman on this ship will do anything for the right price," responded Anderson, almost licking his lips.

"Anything?"

"Aye, Sir," responded the mate with a knowing look.

"I knew I could count on you all. Get some sleep. I will finish the watch. Relieve me at ten bells."

"Aye, Sir," said Anderson as he turned to disappear below deck.

Andre continued his watch around the ship. White-capped combers licked against the rails. He heard the thudding rataplan of halyards against the spars, the creaking of the rigging, the booming of the surging surf against the beach they were now approaching. All were integrated parts of a symphony that delighted his ears.

He passed seamen engaged in various jobs, even on their night watch. All wore woolen jerseys and bell-bottom trousers. 'They'll need to get lighter clothing for this semi-tropical weather,' he thought.

Even as they approached Lake Worth, dawn was lighting up the shoreline. He saw the shadowy figures of coconut palms silhouetted against the skyline. 'Jupiter Inlet is not far from here,' he thought, 'but I cannot afford to be seen there yet. Soon, Meg, soon I will hold you in my arms.'

They glided into the harbor as the sun was rising, reaching port before Anderson was to relieve him. Andre talked with the harbormaster, and then found directions to the general store. He wouldn't have to worry about getting hardtack and other canned goods that had a tendency to spoil at sea, or rancid butter since they would be living on the coast except when in pursuit of merchant ships. They could easily supplement their supplies at any time. He took two crewmen along with him to help carry the goods. They found the store and ordered barrels, nails, sailcloth, bandages, a new deck lantern, along with a gallon of lamp oil and alum. He also got fresh vegetables, flour, lard, and freshly caught grouper.

"I think that should do us for now. Oh, by the way, you don't happen to sell Jamaican rum, do you?" he asked the green grocer.

The proprietor was quite happy with the large order and he wanted to keep a new customer happy, too. "Well," he said, looking around to see who was in the store, "I just happen to have two bottles under the counter here. I was saving them for somebody else, but I reckon I could sell 'em to you."

"Sir, I would be most obliged if you would, and my men would be eternally grateful."

The grocer thought Andre a most polite fellow and was glad to accommodate him. "Here you are," he said, wrapping the bottles. "That'll be two dollars for the rum, plus twenty dollars for the rest of the order."

Andre paid him and they gathered up the supplies and headed back to the ship, but not before Andre assured the grocer that he would be a steady customer.

They unloaded the supplies and later that night, Andre allowed the men to spend the night in town, drinking and carousing in a local tavern. He knew these hard-bitten men needed a release or they would revolt, in spite of promises of wealth. They also knew what would happen to them if they failed to return. He did not join in the revelry, but found a room for himself and Jamie.

The landlady was thrilled to have such a handsome, charming boarder.

"And is this your son? He is a lovely boy," she said, batting her forty-year-old eyelashes at Andre.

"You could say he is my adopted son."

"How unselfish of you to take in a poor lost boy. God will reward you."

"I am sure he will," said Andre .

Jamie's heart swelled with devotion when he heard Andre say these words, because this man was just the kind of father he wished he had had.

It amused Andre to play the role of father.

"Have you had dinner? You must be hungry. I could fix us all a nice meal," asked the landlady.

"That is a kind invitation, but we would not want to impose on you."

"You wouldn't be. I'd be only too happy to cook dinner for you. Besides, I would enjoy the company," she said coyly.

"Well, if you really do not mind, we accept."

"Why don't you two just rest in your room while I fix dinner. There are two cots and a wash basin."

She flew to the kitchen, mesmerized by Andre's smile and sexy blue eyes. And that accent! She could almost swoon when he spoke.

Thirty minutes later, they sat down to dine. She had prepared fried mullet, grits, sweet potatoes, and biscuits. After the meal, Jamie's eyes were starting to droop.

"What a wonderful repast. Merci, a most delicious dinner," said Andre. "I see Jamie can barely keep his eyes open. Let me go put him to bed."

Andre had never put a child to bed. The only people he had performed that service for were women and drunken sailors. It was strange, but he found Jamie's innocent devotion unsettling.

"After you do, perhaps you'd join me for a cup of coffee?"

"It will be a pleasure, Sally."

As he spoke, he wondered how long it would take to get her to bed. He needed a woman, and though this one was a little long in the tooth, she was pretty. He did not think it would take long. He also thought she might be the 'middleman' he was looking for. This was even better because he could always manipulate a woman. She would be only too willing to do anything he asked.

The next morning Sally looked at the man sleeping beside her. She touched his hair, hair as golden as the sun. In all her life she had never seen a man as handsome as this. Her own dead husband had been a good man, but he was no lover to compare with this one. Sally sighed in drowsy satisfaction. She had not known lovemaking could be like this. But now she began to worry that he might leave right away. What could she do to keep him around? She would promise anything at all.

Andre opened his eyes and smiled at her. "You're just as lovely this morning as you were last night. Ah, Cherie, you were wonderful."

Sally blushed. "You must be hungry."

"I am, but not for food." So saying, he pulled her down and kissed her passionately.

"Oh, but I heard Jamie moving around," she sighed breathlessly.

Andre appeared disappointed. "I must arise then."

Sally dressed quickly and went to the kitchen. After a hearty breakfast that Sally insisted on making, Andre and Jamie departed with Andre assuring the bedazzled Sally that he would return in a week. He needed to find Dory, if the idiot hadn't been killed before he reached Jupiter Inlet. He also wanted to scout the Jupiter area. Mulling over this, he decided to take Anderson in his confidence, especially since he himself could not afford to be seen there. Andre and Jamie walked along the oyster shell path down to the docks where the Osprey was moored.

"Mrs. Marlow sure is a nice lady, isn't she?" asked Jamie.

"Very nice. We'll go back to visit later on. Right now, we need to check on the crew."

"Yes, Sir."

When they jumped on deck, all was silent. Only the gentle creaking of the lines could be heard when the wind rocked the ship. He found McGuire sprawled over the hatch in a drunken stupor. Evidently, the entire crew had passed out sometime during the night. He hoped none of them had fallen overboard and drowned. Not that he cared, except that it would be an inconvenience to replace them. He and Jamie counted heads as they passed by recumbent bodies. Anderson had made it to his bunk, but had knocked over a lamp, scattering broken glass everywhere. A table was overturned, and Anderson's prized chess pieces of wood and goony bones had fallen in a broken heap.

"Looks like they had quite a party, Jamie. Clean up this mess, will you, and everywhere else that needs it? I'll let them sleep it off for another hour while I finish some entries in my log."

"Right away, Sir."

"Jamie, I don't mind if you call me Andre, but don't say it in front of the others. While you are around them, I am Captain Lafitte, but when we are alone, we're friends. C'est bon?"

"Uh, yes Sir. I mean, Andre."

"Tres bien. Now we must work."

Jamie began his chores, willingly. He idolized Andre whom he had begun to think of as his father.

Andre went to his quarters and pulled out his Atlantic Chart and logbook. Like all good captains, he kept accurate records. He had entered the time of departure, distance and bearing from the land and when it was taken. Now he entered arrival time. He adjusted the sperm-oil lamp, and its golden glow lighted the pages of the open logbook. He checked the chronometer to see if his pocket watch agreed with it since the chronometer kept precise time. After he made a few more entries and comments concerning the trip, he took a tour of the ship to see what repairs, if any, were needed to the spars, sails, and rigging. He had purchased an extra supply of canvas and rope for that purpose. Everything appeared to be ship-shape. Jamie had finished cleaning the mate's cabin and had started working on the deck where beer bottles were strewn from bow to stern.

Andre went to the mate's bunk and shook him awake, none too gently.

"Anderson, wake up, man!"

"Ooh, my head," he groaned.

"Get up! I have something for you to do. The sun's already over the masthead."

Anderson sat up and staggered over to a small table with a basin and a pitcher of water that had miraculously escaped being broken. He poured the water over his head, blowing like a right whale surfacing for air.

"After you change clothes, join me in my quarters," ordered Andre.

He left the mate sitting on the side of the bunk, staring blearily into space. Fifteen minutes later, Anderson joined him in the cabin, amazingly wide-awake.

"I want you to take the gig and sail up the Indian River to Jupiter. You'll have to go into the Loxahatchee River at Juno and then come in through Jupiter Inlet to the lighthouse. I'm looking for a man called 'Dory'. He has a scar from his eye to his mouth, and he always wears a stocking cap. He is supposed to have arrived in Jupiter a week ago. Bring him back with you. Also, is there a man we can spare for a week or two? I want him to remain, temporarily, in Jupiter. I am expecting a ship, the Annie Marie out of Beaufort, to arrive there at any time. I want to know when it arrives. And exactly when one of the passengers, a Jim Styron, will be returning north. I want to know for sure, that he is on an out-going ship."

Anderson thought for a moment. "Well, we could probably spare Gully. He's the carpenter, and he has a way of getting information without appearing too nosey."

"Bon. Get him on his feet and take him with you. It shouldn't take too long to sail to Jupiter. Then find Dory and bring him back here. Leave Gully there to spy until you return for him. Dory has special skills that we can use on our forays. I can't go myself because I don't want to be recognized. Do you understand?"

"Aye, Sir. I'll take care of it."

"Thank you, Anderson. I will expect to see you before the week is out."

Anderson left, and a half an hour later, Andre saw him with Gully, with the aid of the windlass, lowering the gig into the water. They got in the boat, hoisted the sails, and headed south. Andre knew that Anderson was familiar with the area, though he hadn't sailed in a small craft up the river before. Andre felt completely confident in Anderson's navigating abilities. He was an experienced seaman.

Jamie walked up, wiping his hands on his pants. "All finished, Sir, I mean, Andre."

"Let us stroll over to the general store, then. I want to talk to the proprietor again."

A week later, Anderson sailed into the harbor with Dory sitting near the bow. They tied the gig to a mooring line on the Osprey. Andre had seen them enter the harbor and jumped onto the dock to meet them.

Dory looked sullen, as usual. "What's 'e calling you Captain Lafitte for, Marcel?" Dory asked when Anderson greeted Andre.

"Never mind that," was the annoyed reply.

"I'm lucky I found him, Captain," said Anderson.

"I don't doubt that. Where was he?"

"In Juno."

"Juno! Sacre Bleu! What were you doing there? I told you to stay put in Jupiter."

"Oi got mixed up when they was talking about Juno and Jupiter. Oi got off that rum ship in Juno. Bloody bastards, they was. Almost tossed me over the side 'alfway out."

Anderson was looking as if he had considered it also.

"There are only three families living in Jupiter, the lighthouse keepers. So I tried to find out, in a roundabout way, if a stranger fitting Dory's description had been in Jupiter lately. No one had seen him, but the mailman had just walked up, and he had noticed him walking around the wharf in Juno. I left Gully there and sailed up to Juno on the chance Dory would be somewhere in the vicinity. It was pure sailor's luck that I found him."

"What happened with Gully?"

"He's sharing a room with a hunter in a hunting camp. It's not much bigger than a duck blind. Told the man he was looking for a hunting guide. He sure don't need lessons in shooting. I've seen Gully plug a man's eye out at twenty-five yards."

"He's just the kind of man we need," agreed Andre.

"And he'll find out what you want to know. He has a knack for gaining people's confidence."

Both men looked surprised when Dory spoke. They had almost forgotten he was there.

"Oi kept mostly to meself," Dory said slyly, looking out of the corner of his eyes. "Just like you told me."

"You did not kill anyone or steal from anyone?" Andre asked, staring at Dory until the seaman's eyes shifted to his boots.

"Oi didn't kill 'im, just cut 'is bloody face a little when 'e wouldn't 'and over 'is jack."

"That is why you were in hiding, isn't it? Is the sheriff after you, or a posse?" It was all Andre could do to keep from squeezing Dory's scrawny neck.

"No. Oi wore a cloth on me face, and cut out two holes for me eyes. They don't know who done it."

"You better be right. Mon Dieu! The devil protects his own! Come, let's talk to the crew. We have plans for tonight."

384

Andre walked down the dock to the ship and swung himself over the rail, leaping onto the deck. The others followed suit.

"Mr. Anderson, muster the crew in my quarters."

"Aye, Sir," he said, giving Dory a murderous look as he departed.

Dory trailed after Andre, muttering to himself. "Oi don't like that mate. 'e told me to shut me trap or 'e would feed me to the alligators."

"I would not cross him if I were you. He will not think twice about slitting your throat like a pig," warned Andre.

"Blimey! Oi'll slit 'is first!"

"Don't try it or you will regret it. I don't want any trouble among my crew. We have more important things to do than squabble among ourselves. Do you understand me?"

"Yes."

"Come on then. We have business tonight."

The crew were gathered in his quarters, all staring curiously as he and Dory entered.

Andre sat down at the table and picked up several papers. "I have made three trips to the House of Refuge called the Orange Grove Station.

The men looked at each other, wondering how this affected them.

Andre continued. "Besides telling me tales of ship-wrecked mariners whom he aided, he told me about his other duties. Not only does he put the tide gauge on record every day, but he writes down what vessels pass by and makes a monthly report."

Seeing the men still looked mystified, Andre explained his plans. "I expressed a strong interest in becoming a House of Refuge keeper myself, and the man was only too happy to let me copy down whatever information I wanted. I now have the voyages mapped out of certain merchant ships. I know generally when they will pass by this area. They'll be loaded with goods for sale in Cuba when they are headed south, and rum and sugar cargo when they are headed north. We will lie in wait and relieve them of their cargo."

The crew's eyes gleamed with greed at this revelation.

"When do we strike the bugger?" asked Dory, bloodlust in his expression.

"Tonight. There is a sailing vessel coming from Cuba that will be passing by about midnight. We'll take them by surprise, then board and breach her. You all have been acquiring your weapons?"

"Aye, Captain," said Anderson. "We're ready to take on the British grenadiers with our arsenal. Right, men?" he asked, looking at the hard-bitten sailors.

"Aye," they all said together.

"C'est bien. We will leave port at ten o'clock tonight, and lie in wait for the Petrel. Go into town and have a good dinner, but don't get drunk." He exchanged glances with Anderson. "You'll need all the cunning you have for this venture."

The crew didn't need a second invitation to leave. They intended to go straight for the tavern. Andre only hoped Anderson could keep them sober. Even though he was a hard drinker himself, the first mate realized the importance of their foray tonight.

After the men exited the cabin, Andre turned to Jamie who had been sitting in the corner, away from the other men. The boy feared them and sensed that they were wicked men who would commit unspeakable crimes. His whole attention and devotion had been focused on Andre, and now his idol had fallen, shattered into a thousand pieces. He looked at the man who had been like a father to him with dazed, unbelieving eyes.

Andre saw disillusionment on his face. "Jamie, let's go to Sally's house. She is expecting us for dinner."

"I don't feel very hungry. I'll just stay here."

"No. You are going to remain with her tonight."

Jamie stared out of the porthole, unwilling to meet Andre's eyes. "Why are you doing this? Stealing is wrong."

"Years ago, when I was a boy your age, I felt friendless and alone. I left my home in France after my parents died, and became a cabin boy like you. I did not speak English, and the crew were a rough lot. I understand exactly how you feel." What Andre didn't say was that he was as ungodly as the crew he joined. More so, for he had already murdered a man. "The difference with you is that I am your protector. I will not allow anything bad to happen to you."

"But you're going to rob a ship and maybe hurt somebody."

"Not if I can prevent it. These are well-to-do men who own these ships. They can easily afford the loss. I need the money. Right now, I don't have it to buy a cargo to sell," Andre lied easily. "I must have your loyalty, Jamie. Won't you trust me? We are alike, you and I."

Jamie was torn between his morals and his devotion to this man. "I guess so. Will this be the last time you do it?"

"Probably. It depends on what the Petrel is carrying."

Jamie's misgivings were stilled somewhat because he desperately wanted, more than anything, to believe in Andre.

Andre read the changing expressions on the child's innocent face as clearly as if Jamie had spoken.

"Bon. We will go see what Miss Sally has fixed for our dinner." They left the ship with Jamie walking trustfully beside Andre. Sally was thrilled to see her lover. She had pined over him since the morning he had left her a week ago.

"Sally, my pretty flower, how have you been? I have missed you so."

"I missed you too," she murmured; drowning in his deep, blue eyes. "How are you, Jamie? Are you ready for some sweet potato pie?"

"Yes, ma'am!"

"I have collards, biscuits, and ham, too."

"You see what I told you, Jamie? We are going to have a feast," said Andre, looking at Sally as if she were the main course.

After dinner, once again, Jamie's eyes were closing, though he tried to stay awake. He had worked hard, swabbing down the decks, polishing the brass, emptying chamber pots, and filling water buckets.

"You don't mind if Jamie spends the night with you, do you, Sally?"

Sally didn't mind anything as long as Andre stayed. "No, of course not. Go on back to the room you used before," she told Jamie.

After the boy had left, Andre pulled the willing Sally into his arms. He made passionate love to her again and again during the next two hours. Sally lost count. What stamina! How could he do it? She felt like she was drifting among the stars.

"Cherie, I must leave now," said Andre, pulling on his trousers.

"So soon? You've only been here three hours."

"I know. I wish I could spend the night with you in my arms, your soft body next to mine, but I have business to attend to. Which reminds me, I wonder if you can help me?"

He leaned down and tipped her chin up, kissing her lightly.

"Yes, of course. Anything you ask," answered Sally, still in the rosy throes of lovemaking.

"I will be taking on cargo tonight, and I need someone to act as sort of an agent for me. I don't know anyone here and you do. Perhaps you can find buyers for me, ma petite?"

"I do know several businessmen who might be interested. What is your cargo?"

"Rum and sugar, possibly fine Cuban cigars," answered Andre.

"When will you have the merchandise available? I can talk to one man in the morning."

"How about noon tomorrow?" asked Andre, thinking they could get back into port by dawn and be organized by noon.

"I'll arrange it then, my dearest Andre," she said, sitting up and putting her arms around him as if to pull him back into bed.

"Not now. I really must go." He moved out of her embrace and finished dressing.

"Oh," she sighed, disappointment in her voice.

"But I will see you soon, Cherie. Au revoir," he said, raising her hand to his lips. He left and made his way quickly to the ship. He would just make it a few minutes before ten. The men were ready to cast off when he arrived.

"Is everything prepared?" he asked Anderson.

"Aye, Sir. All men accounted for, except Gully, of course, who is still in Jupiter."

"Bon. As soon as we have cleared the harbor, we'll blacken our faces and arm ourselves."

The moon was hidden by squally clouds and no one was abroad as the ship slipped silently away from the dock. They sailed about five miles out, nearing the Gulf Stream.

"Drop anchor here," ordered Andre.

Lenny lowered the hook and it played out rapidly. Gradually, it caught on the sandy bottom. The ship swung around, buffeted by a strong southwest wind.

"We'll wait here. According to the keeper's log, the Petrel, out of Boston, makes a regular trip to Cuba and back once a month. She should be coming through tonight. When she's sighted, we will send up a distress signal, and when she comes to our rescue and pulls up alongside, we'll board her."

The men murmured agreement, and Dory licked his lips in anticipation of a blood bath.

"Remember. No violence, if we can avoid it. We'll move quickly and take them by surprise."

Dory scowled when he heard this. He wanted violence. They waited, watching towards the southeast, for a glimpse of the masthead lantern. It began to rain and the sea became choppy.

McGuire said. "Those clouds gave us cover, but they're going to make that ship hard to see until she's right on us."

"That's true," agreed Andre, "but we all know not to expect the sea and sky to accommodate us. We simply have to adjust to nature's whims. She is a changeable mistress."

"She is that," said McGuire.

"Light off the starboard quarter," called out Stoker, who was in the crow's nest with his spyglass.

When Brondell heard this, as arranged he sent up a distress signal that he had at the ready. Now they all could see a faint pinprick of light through the rain. The ship was heading directly towards them.

"Send up another flare, Brondell," ordered Andre. He did so and the oncoming ship responded with a flare of its own. Inexorably, the ship moved closer to them, as if drawn by the devil himself.

"Ahoy there," hailed the ship's captain. "What's the trouble? Can we help you?" The voice echoed eerily across the waves as if from a netherworld.

"Praise be," shouted Andre. "We are taking on water fast. The hold is flooding. Can you take us onboard?"

"Aye. We'll come alongside you."

Andre's crew watched as the ship materialized from a ghostly outline to a two-masted schooner, not twenty-five yards off the stern of the Osprey. They waited quietly until the ship drew next to them.

"Here, catch these lines," said someone on the Petrel.

"Right, mate. Toss them over. We'll tie 'em off," answered Lenny. He caught the lines and quickly lashed the two ships together. Both vessels were rocking on the waves, and the squall had intensified. The crew of the Petrel could not see the Osprey crew clearly through the sheets of rain.

"All secure, Sir," called out Lenny.

"Come aboard, then," said the captain.

The masthead lantern shone into the stygian night, a faint beam, but enough to light up the deck. The motley crew with blackened faces, black pants and shirts and bandanas tied around

390

their heads, poured over the rails like a school of barracuda with razor-sharp teeth.. All brandished weapons. Each man wore a bandolier over his shoulder filled with ammunition, and carried a pistol at his side, and a knife in his pocket. Dory led the ungodly swarm, eager to let the first blood. Andre followed the last man over the rail, a sharp knife clenched in his teeth as he swung easily onto the deck.

The crew of the Petrel stood immobilized at the sight of armed brigands standing on the deck, but the captain was infuriated.

"What is the meaning of this? Why are you pointing guns at us?" he asked, enraged by their actions.

"We 'ave come to relieve you of your cargo," replied Andre. "'and it over peacefully and there won't be any bloodshed."

The crafty Frenchman had mimicked a cockney accent. His blonde hair was completely covered by a bandana, and his face blackened beyond recognition.

"I'll do no such thing. This is an outrage! The days of piracy are long over. You'll never get away with it," the captain replied angrily.

"Yes, we will, ye bloody bugger," cried Dory. He raised his pistol and calmly put a bullet between the captain's eyes.

"You fool!" yelled Andre. "Quickly, start moving the cargo to our ship. You men 'elp them!"

He pointed his pistol at the terrified crewmembers who were staring unbelievably at the dead body of their captain whose blood ran in rivulets along the planks. Shocked, they moved to the black hole of the after-hatch. Some descended into the cargo hold and began handing up the portable cargo. When this was done, others on deck turned the crank of the windlass, lowering the rope with the hook attached into the hold. Two men slowly cranked the handle hoisting crates to the deck, while Andre's crew lifted them over the rails onto their own ship.

In less than an hour, the Osprey was loaded with all the stolen cargo. The crew hauled in the anchor and cast off the lines from the Petrel. Andre knew timing was essential. He wanted to get out of the area quickly, especially since Dory had killed a man. They caught the wind and the racing tide bore them towards a peninsula on the coast between Lake Worth and Juno. Andre had scouted the land and found a secluded deep-water inlet that would allow passage of his ship inland and afford a hideaway. They made good time, propelled by the tide, and the rain began to abate. By six o'clock, as dawn was beginning to break, they approached the mouth of the inlet. The men were jubilant over their successful plunder of the Petrel, but they were avoiding Dory like a particularly virulent disease. Even they, criminals that they were, did not condone a senseless murder. Dory stalked around the ship, mumbling to himself and giving the crew dirty looks. Anderson wondered why a man like Lafitte kept him around. Andre couldn't have explained it himself, except that the man felt slavish devotion to him. Dory had never forgotten that Marcel, as he knew Lafitte, had saved him from being whipped or worse. No one else had ever done anything for him in his miserable life. Andre figured such devotion could be profitable to him, so he kept Dory around.

The crew washed the black paint from their faces and changed into lighter jerseys and pants; Andre went over the cargo with Anderson. He found an official manifest of the cargo among the crates. He made a duplicate list of the merchandise.

"That should do it. Lucky for us that the manifest was not in the captain's quarters."

"Aye, the devil's own luck," agreed Anderson, looking intently at Andre. He almost believed that Lafitte was the devil's advocate. Dory was a thoroughly detestable human being, but Lafitte sent shivers up Anderson's spine. His eyes were chilling, deadly. Anderson had not lived the life of a saint, but he had some morals. He knew instinctively that Lafitte had no scruples or morals. If he had been a religious man, he would have crossed himself, but he believed that events were preordained- what would happen would inevitably occur. He was caught up in the whirlwind enveloping the diabolical Frenchman. So be it.

At eight o'clock, they sailed from their hideaway. By eleven, they were docked in Lake Worth. Gully came down to meet them.

"What news, Gully?" asked Andre.

"The man you were asking about, Jim Styron, left Jupiter on a sailing vessel called the Annie Marie three days ago."

"You are sure of this?"

"Yes. I talked to the lighthouse keeper. He had met the man several weeks ago and said that Mr. Styron was returning to New York."

"Good man, Gully. That's just what I wanted to hear. And the girl, his niece, Megan, what of her?"

"She is living with her father who is a doctor. A Seminole Indian who is also a doctor lives there, too. Seems she's set up a school for the Indian children. It's a strange thing that a white doctor would let a redskin live in his house, and let his daughter teach them Injuns."

"Living away from civilization can give men strange ideas. Well, enough of that. Come see our 'inventory'. We had quite a successful night. You will get your share of the booty, of course. Go take a look. I have business to attend to."

Andre walked to Sally's house, the manifest in his hand. He met the buyer there and a satisfactory monetary arrangement was made. This was to be just the beginning of many such deals. The buyer asked no questions and Andre offered no information.

Two days later, Andre and Jamie were in the general store buying supplies. The townsfolk were shocked by the news of murder and piracy on the high seas. Andre appeared to be as shocked as anyone.

"Why haven't the authorities captured these pirates?" he asked indignantly.

"They tried, but by the time the ship came into port, those murderers were long gone," said Hobart.

The proprietor shook his head despairingly. "I just can't believe such happenings in this day and age. The crew said the captain was shot for no reason at all. After that happened, they were forced to help load the cargo onto the pirate ship."

"I reckon when word of this gets out to the shipping companies, they'll require the seamen to carry arms. They'll probably tell them not to respond to a distress signal," said another man, standing at the counter.

"Maybe," agreed Hobart, "but how can you pass by a ship in distress?"

"I don't know. It's a bad situation."

Andre had been listening intently to the conversation. "A terrible thing," he said, turning to Hobart. "How much do I owe you? I think that's all I need today."

Hobart totaled the bill. "That'll be fifteen dollars."

"Here you are, Sir. Here is a twenty. Just keep the change. I'll be back soon. Come Jamie, let's gather up our supplies. Good day to you all." He tipped his cap politely, and he and Jamie carried out the boxes.

"Goodbye and thank you," said the proprietor. "Now that's what I call a real gentleman."

"Yep, he is that. Most folks coming off these ships are pretty rough, but he's as nice a fellow as you'd want to meet," agreed one of the patrons.

As they were walking back to the ship, Andre turned to Jamie. "Lad, we are going to take a trip to Jupiter lighthouse. You'll enjoy walking up to the top. After we store these supplies, we'll sail up there in the gig. Would you like that?"

"Yes, Sir, I would. I've never actually been close to a lighthouse. Just saw Cape Lookout light blinking in the distance. I always wanted to go there, though."

Chapter Nineteen

Memories washed over Meg as she stepped up onto the porch. Two rocking chairs swayed slightly in the brisk southeasterly breeze. She had lived in this house with her mother and father, but it seemed so long ago. She breathed in the sweet fragrance of orange blossoms from several trees growing in the back yard. Wide jalousie windows were open upstairs and downstairs, and she could see the curtains behind them billowing. A tall jacaranda spread its lavender-blue flowers over the upstairs veranda, and branches of fuchsia bougainvillea climbed the walls.

"I had forgotten how beautiful it is," said Meg.

"Your mother was so fond of plants and flowers. I planted that Flame tree a year before she died."

Meg looked at a magnificent, gloriously red tree growing near the riverbank. "How she must have loved it. An artist's palette could not have captured that vivid color."

"Yes, she did," said her father with a faraway look on his face. He turned to Micco. "Come in. I had so hoped you would live here too, that I prepared a bedroom for you."

"I'll get my suitcase and bring it in. Just a moment."

Chotskee had brought their luggage to the porch, and he and Micco together had lifted down Meg's heavy trunk.

While Chotskee and Micco were bringing in the luggage, Meg gazed around the front room. She gave a gasp of surprise when she saw a piano in the far corner.

"Oh, Father, you have a piano!" It was a small upright. She walked over and touched the gleaming rich patina of rosewood and admired the beautifully carved legs. The case was covered with a lovely blue Spanish shawl that was held in place by a 'piano baby'. The bisque figurine was lying in a basket, playing with her toes.

"Your uncle told me a long time ago that you were a talented pianist. When I found out that you really were going to return here to live, I ordered this from New York. It was sent down by steamer and you cannot imagine what it took to get it here from the lighthouse dock. Four of Micco's friends carried it from the ship to the cart. They had piled layers of blankets inside and all around the sides to protect it from jouncing, and three of them sat with it, holding it so that it would not slide. Gray Wolf said that was the most nerve-wracking trip he ever made!"

"Father, I don't know what to say! What a wonderful gift. Thank you! Thank you so much!" She threw her arms around his neck and kissed him on the cheek.

Dr. Riley looked pleased and embarrassed at the same time.

"I'll play it later," Meg said .

"I'm glad you like it, Dear."

Meg walked around, remembering little things. She smiled at the bust of Hippocrates placed on a ledge over the dining room door.

"Wait a minute. Don't I get a hug and kiss too, for telling your father about your talent?" asked Jim, who had been staying in the background.

"Yes, you do, my darling Uncle. Did you know about the piano?" asked Meg as she hugged and kissed the man who had really been a father to her.

"Well, yes. I didn't think he could do it, but you Rileys are very determined," said Jim, smiling at Meg's happiness.

Meg walked over to an oil painting on the wall. "I remember this. I was always concerned because the ship had run aground." It was a painting done in blues and greens by Fitz Hugh Lane called "The Dream Painting".

The furniture was eclectic, mostly bamboo and rattan. A fruitwood table was in the corner of the room. Surprisingly, there was a stone fireplace with a fire screen in the shape of a fan. The desk and bookcase were of oak. On the desk was a gold, pearl, and turquoise caduceus.

"How lovely," said Meg, picking it up and examining it.

"That was payment for my services from a sea captain who had just returned from the Orient."

While they were talking, Micco and Chotskee had returned with the trunk, and then Micco and Jim went back for the other suitcases.

"Come Meg, I'll show you your bedroom. It is at the end of the hall now, not next to your mother's and mine." They ascended the oaken staircase, leaving the morose Chotskee below, and strolled down the airy corridor. Meg's bedroom was on the east side, facing the Indian River. She could feel a cool breeze wafting through the window as it ruffled the pink, lacey curtain. An embroidered rose counterpane graced the four-poster bed, and a vase of pink zinnias was on the night table beside it. A built-in ledge along one wall contained seashells- a perfect, unbroken sea fan, its inner shell glowing with mother of pearl; a smooth tan and brown olive shell, several scotch bonnets, a small conch, a whorled chambered nautilus, a large sand dollar, and a scattering of tiny coquina clam shells. Meg turned to face her father.

"My shell collection! You saved my shell collection after all these years? And the room is so beautiful!" Meg was overcome with emotion realizing that her father had saved her childhood treasures.

"Well, your mother liked to dress you in pink, and I thought it would be appropriate. She embroidered that bedspread herself."

Meg had tears in her eyes, not knowing what to say to her father. He had never forgotten her. How wrong she had been.

Dr. Riley cleared his throat. He felt emotional, too. "Do you like this Cheval mirror?" he asked.

Meg walked over to a large mirror on a stand. It was in a high frame made of wicker, and could be swiveled to allow the viewer to see both shoes and hat. "It's perfect," she said.

"I saw it advertised in a magazine and thought it looked practical."

Jim walked in then. "Sean, you amaze me. I never knew you were even aware of feminine fancies."

"It is true I am decidedly of a scientific bent, usually encased in my own little cocoon, but your sister was such a beautiful, loving woman, I couldn't help but be aware of her femininity and what she wanted. After she was gone, I sorely missed her womanly touches."

"I can certainly say that her womanly influence on you has made your daughter happy today," replied Jim.

They heard Micco and Chotskee struggling to come upstairs with the trunk. The men entered the room carrying it as though it contained rocks, and placed it in the corner of Meg's bedroom, against the wall.

"Is this where you want it?" asked Micco.

"Yes, that's fine."

They brought in her other suitcases and put them on the floor.

"Come along, Micco and Jim, and I will show you your bedrooms." They followed him down the hall, and Chotskee plodded downstairs, and waited patiently outside.

Meg whirled around her room happily. She felt so at home. Then she noticed a door on the far wall. Curious, she walked over and opened it. She was amazed and delighted to see a porcelain tub on clawed feet, a basin, and a commode in the room. The house had running water! How had he done it? When she had lived there before, they had an outdoor privy.

Micco's room was at the west end of the hall, and Jim's right next to it. The house had five bedrooms upstairs and one downstairs, for the Rileys had had many overnight guests. Dr. Riley's bedroom was downstairs, saving him from walking the steps everyday. He had added a partition to the house for his clinic. He lived comfortably with his father's inheritance and he planned to pay Micco a handsome salary as his partner whether they made much money or not in their practice. Micco was not aware of this and expected to subsist on very little. Dr. Riley had also made sure that while Micco was gone, his grandmother had all she needed.

They heard whoops outside, and Micco bounded down the steps and out the door, whooping in return.

"Yohoeehee!" Micco answered with the Seminole war cry they had shouted as children, pretending to be great warriors.

"Gray Wolf!" he yelled. "Echockotee!"[5]

Meg ran down the stairs in time to see three men, riding bareback down the path, their horses prancing and whinnying. A horse-drawn buckboard, driven by a gigantic man, precariously balanced on the narrow buckboard seat, with a stately Seminole woman sitting in the back, followed way behind.

The young Indian in the lead slid off his horse, and he and Micco embraced, grinning like Cheshire cats, and pounding each other on the back.

Gray Wolf was tall, thin, but muscular, and copper-skinned. He was almost as tall as Micco, well over six feet, and his lively black eyes indicated a cheerful disposition. He wore deerskin moccasins, buckskin leggings, and a long-sleeved shirt with a short vest. His hair was cut close to his head, except for a traditional scalp-lock, which was plaited and hung down his back, and he wore a turban.

"You weren't any bigger than a walking stick when I saw you last. What happened? Did you drink too much black tea?" asked Micco.

"It must have been the same thing you were drinking because you looked like a jack rabbit, all arms and legs," answered Gray Wolf.

---

[5] Seminole word meaning 'brother'

The other two men slid off their horses, tethering all three animals to a low-hanging tree limb. They waited quietly while Micco and Gray Wolf talked. Then Micco turned to greet them.

"Little Fox, are you still catching gopher with your gopher stick?"

Meg had walked up by then, followed by Jim. She couldn't imagine how the slight, fragile-looking young man could pull a struggling gopher turtle out of a hole. She would have been very surprised to see his moccasin-clad feet springing from tuft to tuft in the cypress swamp as lightly as a falling pine needle. He was both swift and strong, in spite of his size.

"Me still best, Echockotee," said Little Fox as he too gave Micco a hug; though he was so short he was staring at Micco's chin.

Still smiling as though he would never stop, Micco greeted his other friend, a tall handsome man of dignified demeanor with charcoal-black eyes. He was dressed in a tunic with a bright red sash and leggings of deerskin decorated with delicately cut thongs that hung gracefully from his waist to his ankles.

'He is certainly a Seminole chief,' thought Meg, for he wore a turban made from gaily-colored handkerchiefs, secured by a band of beaten silver. He, as well as Gray Wolf , and Little Fox, wore several brightly colored bandanas loosely knotted about their necks.

"Echockotee, Spotted Dear, how is the hunting?" asked Micco, noting the buckskin belt from which hung a hunting knife, revolver, a pouch made from a pelican's bill that carried ammunition, and other miscellaneous articles necessary for hunting game.

"I bring dinner home everyday," said Spotted Deer. Then, he too, embraced Micco.

"Jim, I want you to meet my best friends. We are all blood brothers, including Lazy Bear. You'll meet him too, if he ever gets here with my grandmother. That is why I address them as

'Echockotee" which means 'brother'. This is Gray Wolf, Little Fox, and Spotted Deer," introduced Micco, so proud of his friends.

"It is nice to finally meet you. Micco has been singing your praises ever since we left Savannah. Of course, he also told me about your pranks," added Jim with a grin on his face.

"And this is Jim Styron, Meg's uncle," said Micco. They shook hands and all smiled, showing incredibly white teeth.

"We are most happy to meet you, too," replied Gray Wolf, while the others nodded in agreement.

"Meg, I know you remember Gray Wolf, though you probably wouldn't have recognized him."

She held out her hand. She wanted to hug all three of them whom she remembered very well, but decided the reserved Seminoles might be offended by a woman acting so unrestrained. "It's true I wouldn't have recognized any of you, you're so changed since we were children, but I have fond memories of our childhood when we played together. Of course, you probably hated to have a little pesky kid along, cramping your style!"

All three men were staring unabashedly at this beautiful woman with hair like a blazing campfire.

"You no look same either," said Little Fox, his tongue finally coming unglued. Then all three laughed and eagerly shook her hand.

"I remember when you fell into the water from my canoe. Micco saw you from the shore and came leaping like a porpoise after you. He was so angry with me for taking you out on the lake, I thought he was going to scalp me," said Gray Wolf, glancing sideways at Micco.

"I wasn't hurt at all. At least I gained something from the experience. You taught me how to swim after that," said Meg.

"I had to. My Echockotee threatened me with bodily harm if I didn't."

Meg was surprised that Gray Wolf spoke English so well. She did not realize that both he and Spotted Deer had attended an English school in Lake Worth. Their fathers were chiefs and had some money to send them there. Little Fox and Lazy Bear had remained in their Indian village, and their English- speaking ability was limited, though they understood it quite well.

"At last! Here comes Lazy Bear and my grandmother," said Micco excitedly. They all watched as the horse-drawn buckboard slowly approached and finally came to a stop in front of them. A dignified, older Seminole squaw sat erect in the buggy, her uncovered hair fashioned into a bang and psyche knot. Meg noticed that her hair was still jet-black. She wore a long checked, straight full skirt and, as was the Seminole custom for women, her feet were bare. The upper part of her dress had long sleeves with a large, separate collar. The lower part of her ensemble had a loose-fitting waist. She wore silver breastplates, made from quarters and half-dollars, which had been beaten into various designs, along with three strands of beads. When Meg saw this, she fingered the delicate filigree necklace around her neck. It was the one Micco had given her on Christmas Eve. Micco had told her that his grandmother had made it. Meg felt somewhat intimidated. Shontee was a direct descendant of the legendary Micanopy and had regal bearing. Micco had inherited her good looks and her beautiful honey-colored skin.

"Shontee! Hilipputkashaw?" he asked, as he reached up and lifted her from the carriage. He swung her around and around.

"Put me down. You were asking how I was. Well, I was fine until now," she protested, though Micco knew she didn't mean it. He put her down but continued to hug her.

"I have missed you so. Are you well?" he asked.

"Ho[6]. I am well and so happy to see you, Soppochee."[7] She reached up and took his face in her hands, looking searchingly into his eyes. "You have turned into a fine strong man, and now you are a doctor." Micco's grandmother had been brought up by

---

[6] Seminole for yes

[7] Seminole for son

missionaries when her parents were killed in a skirmish between soldiers and Indians, so she too, spoke English fluently.

"And I am back home to stay. Mmm! What is it that smells so good?" he asked, looking at many containers and pots in the back of the cart.

"I have a big bowl of safki, your favorite stew."

"Quickly, we had better move it to the kitchen before Lazy Bear gets to it!" said Micco when he saw his friend finally get down from the buckboard. Micco was only kidding about Lazy Bear, who was lumbering over to greet him, but Shontee scolded him soundly.

"You must not insult your friend. He cannot help it if he is nihittuschay[8]. He was a big baby."

Micco managed to look chastised, though he was really tickled at the mental picture of Lazy Bear as a baby. They must have used a hoist and tackle to get him out of bed. He ran over to Lazy Bear. The man was gargantuan, at least six feet six, and as big around as a banyan tree trunk. It must have taken fifteen yards of cloth for his shirt, and Micco figured five deer had been skinned to make his pants. Three average Seminole feet could have fit into one of his moccasins. The feather on his black cap swayed from side to side as he walked.

"Echockotee!" said Micco. "I am glad to see you, Lazy Bear!" He put his arms around his friend, as best he could, hugging him.

"You, brother, come home," spoke Lazy Bear, his voice rumbling like thunder. He almost squeezed the breath out of Micco, and then lifted him into the air as easily as he would a five-pound sack of coonti flour.

"Lazy Bear, put him down!" ordered Shontee.

"But he my brother," objected Lazy Bear.

"He won't be much longer if you don't let him breathe."

---

[8]Seminole for fat

"Me do." Lazy Bear put Micco on his feet and Micco was laughing so hard, he couldn't speak. "You okay, Echockotee? Me no hurt?" Gasping for breath, Micco assured Lazy Bear that he was all right.

Jim was staring in amazement at the gigantic Indian's display of strength. Micco was no ninety-pound lightweight.

"Whew! I'd never want to arm wrestle with him!"

It was all Meg could do to keep from calling out. She thought Lazy Bear must be killing his friend until she saw how hard Micco was laughing. "Well, I must say they play childish games for grown men," she said primly.

Shontee turned to Meg and surprised her by saying, "You are very pretty. Your hair is like the flaming sun, but you need more beads around your neck." She was looking at the silver necklace that Meg was wearing. Seminole women sometimes wore as many as three or four pounds of beads around their necks. On festive occasions, they wore twenty-five or thirty pounds. Nothing was so valued as their beads. It was a badge of distinction, and no squaw would ever appear in public without them. The beads represented good character, usefulness, and social position. Even the babies wore them.

"You are looking puzzled. To the Seminole woman, beads are her vanity, and an essential part of her life. Oh, by the way, I am Shontee. Micco has forgotten his manners and failed to introduce us."

"How do you do," said Meg, rather startled at the abrupt change in conversation. "I am Megan Riley and this is my uncle, Jim Styron."

Jim politely tilted his hat and said, "How do you do. Micco is a fine young man. You did an excellent job in training him. We all think highly of him."

"Thank you. I am so proud of him. He was always a good boy. I never had to worry about him. And now he is a doctor, one who will be able to heal the body and comfort the soul."

She turned to Meg. "I am happy to see you again. You probably do not remember me, but one day Micco brought you into our camp. You sat on my knee and I told you stories about our chiefs, of Osceola, and Micanopy. Later, I will tell you more about the Seminole woman and her legacy of beads."

Meg nodded. "I would appreciate that. There is so much I want to learn about the Seminoles and their way of life."

Micco came over and took his grandmother's hand, looking really chagrined. "I am sorry, Shontee. You all had to introduce yourselves. That was impolite of me."

"Not at all, my boy," Jim said soothingly. "We understand this is your homecoming. Your mind is not on civility at the moment."

Micco looked at Meg and saw that she was a little intimidated by his grandmother. Shontee had that affect on people, but he also saw that Shontee liked Meg. He was glad because he knew that Meg would be an important part of his life. However, he also knew that Shontee would not approve of his marriage to a white woman, if it ever came to that. That was verboten in Seminole society. But this was a problem to be tackled in the future. Perhaps Meg felt the same way. Perhaps her father did, also.

"What are we waiting for?" asked Micco. "Let's get the food into the house. It has been more than ten years since I have tasted my grandmother's safki. Come on, Gray Wolf. This is one time all of us are going to eat together."

The Seminole custom did not allow members of one clan to eat with members of another clan. Gray Wolf was of the Wolf clan while Micco was of the Tiger clan. Little Fox and Spotted Deer belonged to the Deer clan, and Lazy Bear to the Bear clan.

"We are not going to eat in the house. Take everything to the shore in front of the house. How do you expect to have a camp fire inside?" asked Shontee. "And while Spotted Deer, Gray Wolf, and Micco are carrying the food to the beach, Lazy Bear and Little Fox can gather logs for the fire. I brought some wood, but it may not be enough." Shontee ordered everyone around, and no one seemed to think it unusual.

Sean had been standing by watching the reunion, like Jim, trying not to intrude. He watched Shontee directing the activities like a medicine man at the Green Corn Festival.

"At long last, Shontee, you have your Micco back to attend to your every whim. What chores do you have arranged for him to do tomorrow?" he asked.

"You act as though I ever forced him to do anything," she said, keeping a vigilant eye on each person. She was sitting in a rattan porch chair, one of eight that Micco had brought from the verandas.

"Gray Wolf, be careful with my safki! I spent all day yesterday making that!"

Sean watched as the obedient Gray Wolf stepped carefully through the thick scrubby vegetation carrying the huge kettle as easily as if it were an empty wiregrass basket.

Little Fox emerged from a clump of palmetto palms embracing an armload of split logs. Lazy Bear followed him, his arms so filled with logs that only the tip of his turban could be seen.

"That's more than we need. You have enough wood to light five fires. Now go ahead and clear the brush and then arrange the logs for my cook fire," ordered Shontee; pointing to the spot she had chosen.

The soft cadence of her Seminole voice, so like others of her tribe, held no harshness of tone, yet it carried authority. Little Fox and Lazy Bear dropped their burden on the ground and began arranging the logs in a circle, the Indian way, leaving an open area in the middle. They struck their flints and soon had a fire blazing as the ends of the palmetto logs began to burn, catching fire from the kindling in the middle.

Both Sean and Jim had dragged chairs over beside Shontee. Micco knew that Meg, Jim, and Sean would be more comfortable sitting in chairs rather than on the ground, and so would his grandmother, who would never have admitted it.

"I know you are preparing a marvelous dinner," said Sean as he watched Micco and Spotted Deer bring more and more food to their campsite. Gray Wolf had put a huge flat stone, probably ballast from a wrecked ship, in the center of the fire, and then placed the kettle of safki on top of it. This would keep the stew hot all day. Such was the Seminole custom. In their chickee, or wigwam[9], the family gathers around the cook fire in the morning and again in the evening.

Meg had gone into the house to freshen up and had returned, sniffing appreciably at the aroma of savory stew. Shontee invited her to join them. "Sit down, Meg. It won't be long before we eat."

"Oh, what a heavenly smell!" said Meg. "What is in it?"

"This I made with beef and thickened it with grits and corn meal. I added squash, palmetto cabbage, peas, beans, and potatoes. In every camp, the cook fire is burning from early morning until late at night, and a pot of safki is there for anyone to dip into. When the braves go hunting, they may eat nothing from dawn to dusk. So when they return home, the safki is waiting for them, nice and hot."

Micco and Spotted Deer brought in a cooked saddle of venison. A wild turkey and duck were placed on spits and were roasting before the fire. Sweet potatoes were placed in the smoldering embers, along with corn in the husks, and already Meg could smell the sweet fragrance of the yams as the skins popped open and sizzled with juice.

"Come," invited Shontee. "We will share the safki while the turkey and duck are roasting."

They all gathered around the kettle. A large wooden safki spoon rested in the pot. The safki ladle was carved with the design

---

[9] Seminole for house

of a tiger, indicating Shontee and Micco's clan. In each camp, the safki spoons were highly decorated, often embossed with silver.

Shontee dipped into the savory stew with the ladle, taking a single mouthful. Then she passed the spoon to Micco, who was beside her. Micco dipped the spoon into the safki, also taking a single mouthful. Meg was sitting on the other side, trying not to look appalled. Micco glanced at her, knowing what was going through her mind. He smiled encouragingly at her, as he passed the spoon to Gray Wolf.

Meg wondered what she would do when the spoon reached her. It was obvious that all the diners were going to eat from the same spoon, dipping each time into the stew. She could plead a digestive upset and leave the campfire. "No," she decided. 'I will close my eyes and taste it.' She knew Shontee would be both offended and insulted should she leave. Sean, of course, was quite familiar with the ceremony, and as a doctor, he certainly would not approve of a communal eating pot, but he showed not the slightest sign of disapproval. Even Jim bravely partook of the stew, exclaiming how tasty it was. Meg could do no less. When the spoon was passed to her, she resolutely dipped into the safki, and slipped the spoon gingerly into her mouth. She swallowed, almost choking, and then quickly took sips of cool, fresh water from a wooden cup that had been hollowed out by burning and scraping. This was done by means of a blowpipe.

"What do you think, Meg?" asked Micco, knowing exactly what she thought. "Isn't it tasty? Want more? The spoon will come around again. As a matter of fact, we could be eating safki for another hour." He just could not resist kidding Meg. She was so teaseable.

Meg knew perfectly well that Micco was once again deliberately provoking her. She thought he would get over that once they reached Jupiter, but he hadn't. Well, Micco Ravenwing could go squat with a squaw in a chickee eating safki all day long, as far as she was concerned.

"Thank you, but no. If I keep on eating this delicious stew, I will not be able to eat anything else. I'll just wait for the turkey and vegetables." She smiled sweetly at Shontee, refusing to look at the smirking Micco.

"Too bad, but I am aware of your delicate constitution, and understand perfectly. We will probably have scrambled turtle eggs, too, and bear meat. Can you at least try those?" he asked, his expression as innocent as a papoose's.

"No!" she almost shouted. Then, lowering her voice when she noticed the startled looks of those around her, she said, "I really need to watch my weight. I won't be able to fit into any of my clothes."

"That's true," agreed Micco, glancing at her twenty-three inch waist. "I had not thought about that. Why, you'll be waddling out the door like Lazy Bear's pet duck in just a few weeks!"

"Me like big squaw. You eatum more," said Lazy Bear, trying to compliment Meg. "You no be eheseeko."

Shontee was looking from Micco to Meg, puzzled by their conversation. She had little sense of humor, and never really knew when Micco was kidding or serious.

"What does he mean by 'eheseeko'?" Meg asked Shontee, ignoring Micco, though she would like to have wiped that smirk off his face.

Before Shontee could reply, Micco answered. "He says you will be an old maid if you don't eat more. He appreciates a strong, healthy squaw."

"What?" exclaimed Meg, looking venomously at Micco.

"He admires you, and is paying you a compliment, uh, kind of like calling you 'chickadee'."

"Don't you 'chickadee' me," sputtered Meg.

Shontee looked even more puzzled by the conversation. He was referring to her as a bird? And Gray Wolf, who was as bad as Micco, was staring at the safki spoon, trying not to laugh. Sean, too, was at a loss.

"You don't have to eat more stew if you don't want to, Meg," he said, solicitously. "Just wait for the turkey and vegetables. Besides, we have a wonderful dessert- sweet, fresh pineapple and guava."

Jim sat there wondering, as they ate their delicious dinner, how it all would end between Micco and Meg. Meg was as volatile as a firecracker. The least spark from Micco set her off.

Lazy Bear spoke again. "We eat plenty soon. Big wind come," he predicted, looking around him. When the pollen of the saw grass is seen floating in the air, Seminoles always seek higher ground, sensing that a storm is approaching. As he spoke, raindrops began to fall. Fortunately, by this time, everyone was 'stuffed' except Lazy Bear, who appeared as though he could finish off the half-rack of venison that was left.

Spotted Deer, Gray Wolf, Little Fox, and Lazy Bear began gathering up the kettle, pots, and food, running back and forth to the wagon, quickly loading it. Micco and Jim were taking the chairs back to the house. Meg was contributing by hanging onto her hat that threatened to be ripped off her head by the increasing gale.

"You had better put those chairs inside, Micco. This looks like it might be more than just a light wind," said Dr. Riley. "Shontee, you all stay here until this blows over. That sky is ominous."

The cloudless blue sky that they had enjoyed during their dinner had suddenly changed to a threatening gray.

"No. We will go back to our camp. I must be home before dark. I promised Stemolakee I would be there. She is afraid when night falls."

Stemolakee was a child whose parents had died of fever during the night, and Shontee had taken the little girl into her own chickee since Stemolakee had no other close relatives.

"But you could be injured or worse when this storm hits full force," said Micco.

"Shontee go now. Me take 'em," said Lazy Bear confidently. "Me drive quick."

"I hope he drives quicker than he did getting here," muttered Micco worriedly. He knew better than to insist on his grandmother's staying. When her mind was made up, nothing short of the Great Spirit descending and asking her in person could persuade her.

Micco helped her up into the wagon, and Lazy Bear urged the horse on in the rising wind. It was not raining hard yet, but soon the squalls would pound across the saw grass and scrub pines. The men mounted their frightened horses, following behind the wagon, ready to help if the buckboard became stuck.

Meg, Jim, and Sean stood on the veranda watching as the wagon moved down the unmarked path, rocking slightly as it was assailed by the northeast wind. Micco had followed the procession, watching anxiously as it made its precarious way into the forest. The camp was about three miles away, located near a small lake. He walked behind until they pulled far ahead of him. Gray Wolf turned around and waved confidently, and Micco reluctantly returned to the house. By now the rain was beginning to get stronger.

"I should have ridden with them," he said unhappily to Dr. Riley.

"Micco, you should know how they have weathered many storms. Of all people, they know how to take care of themselves."

"I know they do. I would trust Gray Wolf and the others more than anyone else to take care of Shontee, but no one can withstand the force of nature."

"How do you think you could help, then? She is in the Great Spirit's hands. Trust in that," advised Sean.

"You are right. I have been away too long. Civilization has dulled my perception. Let's go inside. It is starting to rain harder," said Micco, taking Meg's elbow and ushering her into the house.

They all trooped inside as the wind began to howl menacingly, and a sudden deluge of stinging rain pricked their faces. Meg took off her sodden hat, the feather drooping dejectedly. In just those few moments, her blouse was soaked.

"I'm going to run upstairs and change my clothes," said Meg.

Micco was wet as if he had been swimming in the Loxahatchee River, so he, too, went to change clothes. As he climbed the stairs, divergent thoughts were darting through his mind. He was being pulled in two directions. When he had left Jupiter, so long ago, he had been an untutored Indian boy, completely innocent, almost unaware of a society outside his own. Of course, he had seen the difference in Dr. Riley's lifestyle from his own Seminole way of life, but he was unprepared for the shock of 'civilization'. He was astonished by New York and Boston society, the modern conveniences, mode of dress, transportation, and annoyed by cavalier attitudes. In his society, there was a high sense of honor. They did not lie, cheat, steal, or use profanity, and the children were taught this from infancy. They abided by this code until the Great Spirit summoned them to the Happy Hunting Ground. The Seminole had no oath in his language, or any irreverent word, and Micco's ears were bombarded by curses all around him. Being the extremely intelligent boy that he was, and determined not to disappoint his benefactor, he gradually adjusted and submerged his disappointment at what he perceived as a decadent society. His high moral standards were never tarnished, but he enjoyed all the accoutrements of a fast-developing urban society. It would be difficult to go back to an impoverished and naïve society to live. He had made a promise to Dr. Riley to return, and the proud Seminole never broke a promise. Now he was once again in the place of his birth, as out of sync as a panther at the seashore. He had been so eager to return home, and he did love his grandmother and friends dearly, yet he remembered that wave of apprehension that touched him when he looked back from the train, taking in the wondrous sights of the city for the last time.

Was ever a man so perverse? Now he longed for Boston and New York. Maybe when he was absorbed in the demanding duties of a physician, he would forget the glorious lights of the skyline, the unbelievable thrill when Edison lit his electric light. He needed to be near Shontee now too, for she was getting old. He had been shocked by how much she had aged since he had left, though her prickly disposition had not changed.

Perhaps he could make trips from time to time revisiting his haunts in New York and Boston. He had a burning need to see Europe, too. None of this changed his desire to be a good doctor, and to administer to his people, but he had other ambitions as well. He could never go back to his native way of life. He admired and believed in the innate honesty and integrity of his Seminole brothers, but he could not be as they were again. Yes, it would be wonderful to slip through the woods on moccasined feet, to pole his canoe quietly on a calm lake to briefly recapture his heritage, but to change back into that native he had once been, he could never do. He had become a red man in a white man's world.

While Micco's head was spinning with these disturbing thoughts, Meg too, was contemplating her life and the choices she had made. She pulled off her sodden clothes, put on a dressing gown, and plopped down on the bed, watching the gathering storm through her window. The palm trees outside were arching with the force of the wind, their leafy heads flopping like gigantic dust mops being shaken, while the driving rain pelted against the windows like a fusillade of pebbles. As she watched the storm intensify, Meg hoped Shontee and the others were safe, and had pulled into a sheltered area.

She looked around the room her father had so thoughtfully prepared. She had so wanted to prove to him that she was worthy of his devotion. She was a crusader and a champion of the underdog, but what made her think that she, insignificant Meg, could make a difference? From the little she had seen, the Seminoles appeared to be quite happy, the few that were left, that is. She was a little depressed watching the water run in rivulets

413

down the jalousie windows. Maybe no one would attend her school. And where was Andre? Was he really waiting for an opportunity to see her? If he was, where could she arrange to meet him without Micco knowing? It was so isolated here, and she didn't have her own transportation. Tomorrow, she would ask her father about getting a horse for her.

She didn't have the inclination or the energy to move from the bed. She was still there three hours later, thinking about her childhood here in Jupiter and of her teenage years in New York. She had been so pampered by her Aunt and Uncle, and now she was on her own. Suddenly, she felt bereft, for she dearly loved her Uncle Jim.

Someone knocked on the door.

"It's Uncle Jim. Are you all right?" It was if he had mental telepathy.

"Yes, Uncle. Come in." She sat up on the bed as he entered the room.

"When you didn't come down after an hour, I was afraid you were sick," Jim said, as he sat down on a delicate cane chair.

"No, I'm not sick, just a little depressed. I am dreading the day you leave. I have been thinking about so many things. What if no one goes to my school? What if I can't teach them if they do attend?"

"Meg, everything will work out. They will come to your school. I am sure Micco can talk to the members of his village, and when they do arrive, you will be a wonderful teacher. You know too, that if things should not work out, you can always return home to Julie and me. We are going to miss you terribly, but your aunt and I want what makes you happy."

Meg almost cried because he had such a loving expression on his face. "I know, I guess the gloomy weather is depressing me."

"This is a tremendous undertaking. Your whole life is changing, but I have faith in you and your dreams. You are not

414

alone. You have your father, and you have Micco. I couldn't ask for better security for my little girl."

"Thanks, Uncle Jim. You've cheered me up."

"Good. Micco told me that he had asked his friends to build your school for you. I will pay them, of course. They're coming over tomorrow to discuss it. This storm should pass through during the night, so that won't present any problem. They'll actually be able to make your chairs and desks too. The Seminoles are very industrious, and some are quite skilled in carpentry."

Meg's expression brightened. "That's wonderful. Do you think they are having trouble getting back to their camp?"

"I wouldn't worry about it, Meg. They are quite resourceful and have, no doubt, lived through many a hurricane. The housekeeper didn't make it before the storm hit, but your father is preparing a light meal."

"Uncle Jim, I could not eat another bite. I don't think I'll be hungry at breakfast time. Would it be all right if I just stay in my room?"

"It is perfectly all right just as long as you don't brood about things that haven't even happened. Is that a deal?"

"Yes. I'll think happy thoughts. You have encouraged me, so I'll encourage myself, too."

"Goodnight, dear. Sleep well," said Jim as he kissed her on the cheek.

"Goodnight. I still don't want you to leave, though."

Jim smiled at her and left the room. He went downstairs and found that Sean had made sandwiches and brewed some tea. There was also a bowl of grapes and bananas on the table. Micco came down at the same time, dressed in fresh clothes. They both pulled out chairs and sat at the kitchen table.

"Meg is fine. She's just not hungry and says she doesn't think she will be at breakfast, either. She hopes you'll excuse her if she stays in her room."

"Of course. She's probably tired too. That was quite a trek from the lighthouse here," said Dr. Riley.

Meg mentioned horseback riding yesterday. Maybe you could get her a gentle pony, so that she would be free to go as she pleases," suggested Micco.

"Good idea. I'll ask Chotskee about a horse tomorrow."

"Ah, Sean, I see you have gastronomic skills as well as medical skills," remarked Jim, eyeing the sandwiches.

"Wait until you eat it before you make that statement. Being a widower so many years, I have learned to make do. Of course, the housekeeper is usually here, but when she isn't, I don't starve." They all ate the sandwiches and some fruit and drank several cups of tea.

Micco said, "I didn't think I could eat anything after that dinner Shontee made. She really went all out. I hope she and my friends are home safely by now."

"Don't worry, Micco. They are okay. As I assured Meg, they have weathered many a storm," Jim assured him.

"I suppose so, but Shontee is too old to go riding around the countryside, especially in a storm. I can't help but worry about her."

"Don't let Shontee hear you say that she is old. She is still wearing three strands of beads. When she gets down to one, then you can start to be a little concerned," said Sean.

Jim had a questioning look on his face. "What is the significance of three strands of beads?" he asked.

"Beads are all-important to the Seminole woman. When the papoose is one year old, she is given her first string of beads. This string has a first year bead that is always larger than the rest, and is of a different color. She is allowed a string of beads each year until she is married. Then, at her marriage, her mother gifts her with many strands, and if she is a chief's daughter, she is allowed two strings for each child that is born."

"I remember the custom now," said Micco. "When the squaw reaches middle life, she begins taking off her beads, one string at a time, for many moons, until finally only one string is left. She is now an old squaw, too old to work, and the single strand that she wears is made of the life beads and is buried with her." Micco looked sad. "My grandmother wears only three strands now. In a few more moons, she will wear but one."

"That doesn't mean she is going to die then, Micco. She is quite strong and healthy. She is only following the custom of her tribe," said Sean, patting Micco's hand.

"You are right. I will have my Shontee many more years."

They continued talking, listening to the howling wind rattling the shutters and the sudden bursts of rain bouncing against the house.

"Welcome to the semi-tropics, Jim."

"Oh, I don't mind the storm. As a matter of fact, I rather like both the wind and the rain. Julie hates the wind, and Meg doesn't like the rain. But this is mild compared to the hurricane we encountered on our ship. We were lucky to get out of that alive."

"You mentioned that in your letter. The Captain died during the storm, didn't he?"

"Yes. It was tragic. He was an old friend of mine. His grandson is now Captain of the Annie Marie and I will probably be sailing back as far as Savannah with him, where I'll board a train for New York."

"He said he would be back within ten days," added Micco. "I asked Captain Armour to let us know when Davy returns."

"Jim, I wish I could persuade you to stay longer," said Sean. "We have much catching up to do, and I am so happy to see you again."

"I know. I hate to leave this soon, but we were delayed so long in Beaufort that my law practice has suffered. I must get back as soon as possible," said Jim regretfully. "You look sleepy, Micco. I know I am. Let's go to bed."

"I won't argue with that," agreed Micco. They all got up from the table.

"We need to get started early, Micco, to look over equipment, and arrange our office and patient rooms to your satisfaction," said Sean. "Have a good night's sleep."

"Goodnight, I'll be down bright and early, Dr. Riley."

"The housekeeper should be here in the morning, so we'll have a good breakfast." Jim and Micco walked upstairs, eager to fall into bed.

Just as the dawn was breaking, Micco bounded downstairs. A gentle breeze was wafting through the open window and the air had a fresh clean smell. Dr. Riley was standing at the parlor door.

"Eat your breakfast quickly. It's on the table. But take a look outside first."

Micco opened the door curiously. Five young squaws stood there, waiting patiently. One held a papoose in her arms; the others had papooses strapped to their backs. On the ground near them, was a cage with two chickens in it and a large sack filled with corn. Two old squaws were sitting on the porch, holding a sack of coonti flour, and three old braves stood by with arms folded across their chests. One of them grinned at him.

"Me have ojus money," he said, patting his jacket.

One of the other braves pulled out a beaded pouch. "Me have pouch. Much beads."

The other said nothing, but a finely woven wiregrass basket was at his feet.

"It appears we won't be able to check everything as I had wished. Our patients are already here. I'll take the first one while you have breakfast," offered Sean.

"All right. I'll be just a minute," said Micco in a dazed voice. He wondered how long they had been standing there.

The day continued like this. Every time Sean and Micco thought they had a breather, another patient stopped by. Even one of the Armour's teenage boys was there. The ailments ran the gamut from broken bones and stomach cramps to croup and fever.

Neither doctor had time to eat lunch. Finally, at four o'clock in the afternoon, the procession stopped.

"I certainly could have used Miss Molly today," said Micco with a grin.

"Who is that?"

"Someone I met in Beaufort with a knowledge of medicine."

"Oh. Well, I am starving. How about you?" asked Sean. "Sheyokee has been signaling to me for the last hour that dinner is ready."

"I could eat that whole rack of venison we had last night. Lead me to the table."

Meg finally woke up at ten o'clock. She had not been able to sleep while the storm was raging. Finally, when the storm passed through and out to sea around midnight, she fell asleep. When she woke up, sunbeams were shimmering on the wall. She felt refreshed and in a happy frame of mind. 'What a joy to have running water! I never realized how wonderful it was until I didn't have it. If the ancient Romans could do it, so could Father,' she thought. She bathed and dressed quickly.

"And no hat! The Seminole women never wear hats, so why should I? When in Rome..." she spoke aloud.

As she tripped lightly down the steps, she thought, 'Since Micco is so concerned about my delicate complexion, I will carry a parasol when I go outdoors.'

When she reached the hall, she was amazed by the anthill of activity. People were standing around talking in soft Seminole voices; others, both men and women with children, were coming and going from the patient rooms. Chickens were squawking, and mothers were crooning to their papooses. Meg was even more surprised to find Gray Wolf, Spotted Deer, Little Fox, Lazy Bear, and four other men waiting for her in the hallway.

"Good morning, Meg. My friends and I have come to build your school house," Gray Wolf said, as if this were an everyday occurrence.

Meg was dumbfounded. "You have? But where is the lumber, and where are you going to build it?"

"Me bring ojus[10] wood. Me make 'um chair. Me make 'um table," said Little Fox.

"There is a clearing in the woods about a hundred yards from this house. I think it would be a good place for your school," said Spotted Deer.

"You come. Me show," offered Lazy Bear.

"Well, all right," said Meg uncertainly. "Uncle Jim, are you in the kitchen?" she called out.

A huge woman appeared in the doorway. Her flaring, gaily-colored skirt had enough cloth to sail a johnboat. Her jowls rested like puff pastry on a wide collar, and she wore at least twenty strings of flashing glass beads.

"Me Sheyokee. You eat."

Meg gazed in astonishment at the amazing figure before her.

"That's Lazy Bear's sister. You'd better do as she says or she will lock us all in the kitchen until you do," said Gray Wolf, who was really tickled by Meg's expression.

"Meg, come in and sit down. Sheyokee is a fantastic cook. You have an experience waiting for you," said Jim, who was standing behind the cook. Jim looked dwarfed and he was over six feet tall.

"But I'm not hungry," said Meg. "Uh, maybe just a bite," she murmured, cowed by Sheyokee's unwavering expression. Meg and Jim went over to the table and sat down.

"I'll bet that sister and brother team have sunk a lot of canoes," Meg muttered mutinously, under her breath.

"Just eat a little, dear. Sheyokee is really very nice. You'll hurt her feelings if you don't.".

---

[10] Plenty, more than enough

"I certainly wouldn't want to do that," Meg said. Grudgingly, she put a spoonful of scrambled eggs, a half a piece of toast, and a dollop of blackberry jelly on her plate. Under the insistent cook's formidable gaze, Meg took a bite, chewed, and swallowed. Her expression changed.

"This is very good," she said in a surprised voice.

"I told you so," replied Jim. "Now clean your plate and she'll be happy."

Meg finished what food was on her plate and even took a little more. "That was quite good, delicious, in fact."

Sheyokee's face was transformed. She smiled at Meg happily. "Now go. Lazy Bear make chickee for papoose."

After again thanking Sheyokee for a wonderful breakfast, Jim and Meg exited the kitchen.

"I can't get over how many people there are in and outside this house. Are they all patients? If they are, my father and Micco must be overwhelmed."

"Yes, they are patients. Evidently word spreads like brush fire on the Indian grapevine," remarked Jim as they stepped around a papoose crawling on the floor. The baby was trying to touch a squealing porker in a cage.

Meg noticed that the Indian babies never cried, and the older children were well behaved. What the mother said do, they did, no questions asked.

"Will you go with me to see where Gray Wolf and friends want to build the school?" Meg asked.

"Of course. I wouldn't miss it. They don't waste any time, do they?"

"No. Whoever referred to Indians as lazy, never met a Seminole." Meg picked up her parasol and they went outside into the bright Florida sunlight. Several palm fronds were scattered on the lawn, and the ground had absorbed the water like a sponge, almost as if it had never rained at all. Everything was lush. The leaves and grass were emerald green with touches of chartreuse here and there, indicating new growth. Micco's friends were waiting in the yard.

"We go," said Little Fox, smiling at Meg admiringly.

Meg was wearing a lavender dress with long sleeves and a high collar. She also wore high-topped boots. She didn't know what kind of terrain she'd be traveling and didn't intend to suffer with sand and pebbles in her shoes as she had on the way from Jupiter lighthouse. The boots were hot, though. As they walked away from the pleasant breeze blowing in from the sea and approached the woods, the wind stopped blowing and Meg began to perspire. She swatted at a black fly buzzing around her head, and swung at a bumblebee attracted by her perfume as she stumbled doggedly onward.

The Indians were gliding almost effortlessly through the leaf-carpeted path that was interspersed with tangled vegetation weaving chaotically over underbrush, Indian rubber trees, palmetto, and pine trees. Meg couldn't understand how they did it. She was determined not to fall, and she welcomed her uncle at her side.

"All I need is a mangrove swamp filled with moccasins from tree limbs, and alligators basking on the roots!"

Jim patted her arm encouragingly. "Meg, it's not so bad. You will just have to get some proper shoes and clothing for this climate. You are dressed for New York. "

"Right," she muttered. "Is it far?" she asked.

"No, we are almost there," said Gray Wolf.

She heard the croaking of a bullfrog, and the twittering of birds. Something slithered across her path and she didn't want to know what it was. They passed a hammock of myrtle and cypress clumps where snowy, white herons and some other migratory birds were vacationing in their winter homes, resting on the branches. Two ibis hunted casually in a small pond, their long curved beaks skimming the translucent water for fish.

Suddenly, they came to a clearing that was flat and sandy. Before Meg could step forward, she saw Spotted Deer raise his rifle. He aimed at a tree some twenty-five yards distant and fired. Meg fully expected a bear or panther to tumble from the branches. Instead, a vine with several large pumpkins fell to the ground. Spotted Deer's well-directed rifle ball had neatly cut the stem. The fruit of the climbing pumpkin vine is a Seminole luxury and he did not intend to pass this one up.

"You like 'um? Good place?" asked Lazy Bear as he picked up the pumpkins, his mouth watering.

"What? Oh, well it looks all right, but isn't it rather far in the woods?" asked Meg, wondering how she would ever travel this path twice a day.

"We can cut a trail for you and put down flat stones to walk on. You'll see. It will be easy for you," said Gray Wolf.

Meg didn't look very enthusiastic, but she said nothing as they walked back to the house. When they emerged from the woods, she welcomed the cooling breeze as it dried the perspiration on her face.

When they reached the veranda, Jim turned to Gray Wolf. "I appreciate your scouting the land for me, Gray Wolf, but even if you blaze a trail making walking easier, I think it would be too hot in that clearing. There is little breeze in the enclosed area and Meg is not used to the heat. Why couldn't you build it a little ways down from the house and closer to the shore? I realize you would have to clear out quite a few trees, but I would pay you well for it. Meg is having a hard time adjusting. She has never known anything like this, and if I could make her physical surroundings comfortable, that would be one less obstacle to overcome." Jim was trying to be tactful. He didn't want to insult or offend Gray Wolf in any way by disagreeing with his choice of a plot for the school, but he knew Meg would be miserable if they built it there. He need not have worried, for Gray Wolf was 'cut from the same cloth' as Micco.

"I understand perfectly, Jim. Let's walk over and look at the area you have suggested," offered Gray Wolf.

"Thank you for understanding. Meg, why don't you go in and have something cool to drink? I saw Sheyokee fixing lemonade this morning. You might talk to her about making you some clothes, too. I understand from Sean that she is a skilled seamstress."

Meg gladly agreed. She was so thirsty she could drink the whole pitcher. She went into the house, grateful for the shade. Then Jim and the other men walked to the area that Jim had suggested might be suitable. There was a ridge about a hundred yards from the shoreline, dotted with palm trees. The breeze blew even harder here than it did at the house. There was a small clearing just beyond it.

"What do you think?" asked Jim.

Gray Wolf and Spotted Deer were talking, and then they conferred with the other men. "It will take some time to clear those trees out of there, but we can do it. You are right. This will be a nice, cool place for Meg and the children."

Gray Wolf smiled, "They won't have the excuse of falling asleep from the heat."

"When can you get started?"

"Right now. We brought axes and machetes and other tools in our cart. I think we can get the cart up here, if we don't get stuck in the sand."

They all walked back to the house, talking among themselves. The men went to get their horse and cart that they had left about fifty yards from the house and Jim went inside. Meg was sitting at the table looking less flushed, and Sheyokee was hovering over her like a mama bear with her cub.

"Meg, we have picked out another spot that is cool and breezy. It's not far from the shore, and Gray Wolf and his crew are going to begin cutting down and clearing trees right now."

Meg was so relieved she could have gotten up and danced a jig in spite of her sore feet. "Thank you!" she said fervently. "Uncle Jim, you are my guardian angel!"

"Well Meg, I'm not dead yet, just plain old flesh and blood. Besides, if your Aunt Julie could hear you refer to me as an angel, she'd think the Florida sun had gotten to you," Jim said.

"Well, you may not look like one, but you are one," Meg insisted.

Jim turned to Sheyokee. "I see you are taking care of my niece. I appreciate that. I won't be here much longer and it is good to know that she'll have you when I'm gone."

"Me take care, you no worry," Sheyokee assured him.

"I wonder if the clinic will be filled with patients like this every day. If so, Sean and Micco are going to have to set up a schedule. They can't continue to work from dawn to dark and after, without a break. It is just too much. Sean is already looking fatigued, and that means the full burden will fall on Micco's shoulders. They will simply have to have specific office hours, with no exceptions, except in the case of an emergency," said Jim.

"Let's work out a schedule for them. Maybe I can act as receptionist until my school is built," suggested Meg.

"That's a good idea. We'll talk about it over dinner. That is, if they get away for dinner."

Sheyokee was standing nearby listening, arms akimbo, disapproval stamped on her face. No one should miss dinner! She would have a talk with Dr. Riley if he continued to do this.

At eight that night when the last patient had finally left, Micco came into the parlor. He had insisted that Dr. Riley go lie down at three that afternoon. He was alarmed at the ashen color of the older man's face. Meg and Jim were sitting on the sofa, talking about the situation.

"Is Dr. Riley still resting?" asked Micco, sinking into the armchair wearily.

"I believe he is getting up. Sheyokee is in his room talking to him. Scolding him, I believe is the most descriptive word," said Jim. "Micco, Meg and I have been talking, and we both believe that you must set up a strict schedule of office hours. Neither of you can continue this way. Not only is it exhausting for you, but eventually, your patients will suffer."

Meg spoke up. "Until my school is ready, I can set up a schedule and act as receptionist. You explain to them in their language exactly when they may come back, and that no one may just appear without an appointment." Meg thought she could impress upon Micco the seriousness of her suggestion.

"It is called 'Hitchiti'," said Micco.

"What?"

"That is the name of the language two-thirds of the Seminoles speak." Micco was massaging his forehead as he spoke. "I admit that this has been an exhausting day, but I will adjust to it. It is just that I am not accustomed to a constant procession of patients requiring immediate care. My residency in the hospital at times was grueling, but it was so different in that setting. I am physically strong and healthy. I can handle it, and I cannot ignore a person's medial need at any time. It is my responsibility as a doctor. I took the Hippocratic Oath and I intend to abide by it."

Meg was startled by the determination in Micco's voice and didn't know how to argue against it. 'Not that he would listen to me anyway,' she thought resentfully.

Jim understood Micco's attitude and wouldn't have expected anything less of him. But he also understood that in spite of Micco's superb physical condition and unconditional commitment, he could not continue this way for a long period of time. If he did, his own health would break down. Jim realized that he needed to talk to Sean privately. He knew that his brother-in-law would certainly realize that it was not only expedient to limit patient hours, but vital, if they wanted to continue the clinic. Micco might go on in this way for a year or two, but he couldn't keep it up. No one could, no matter how good their intentions.

"Here comes Sean," he said.

The doctor walked into the parlor, followed by a determined Sheyokee. "Meg, will you play for me while Sheyokee is getting the dinner ready?" asked her father.

426

Micco noticed that Dr. Riley's color had improved, but he still did not look well.

"Of course, Father. What would you like to hear?"

"Whatever you wish to play. I do enjoy Chopin, though." He settled back expectantly, prepared to listen to restful melodies.

Meg seated herself at the piano, eager to play. Her fingers fondled the keys lovingly, as she played the hauntingly beautiful Chopin etudes. Both Dr. Riley and Micco felt soothed.

After thirty minutes, Meg lifted her hands from the keys and turned, smiling at her father.

"Meg, that was wonderful. Your uncle is right; you are truly talented. You could have been a concert pianist. I never realized you had such ability."

"Thank you, father. I hope you enjoyed listening as much as I enjoyed playing."

"I could compare you to the Pied Piper of Hamlet," said Micco. "The animals would be charmed by your magical music; the children would be charmed by it, and I am charmed. Where do you want to lead me? I will go! I can't resist your magical music."

Micco smiled at her and it was such a sexy alluring smile that Meg felt that he, not she, was the mystical Piper luring her to an enchanted place with him. The blood rushed to her face, and she arose, glancing down, smoothing her skirt, to avoid looking directly at Micco. She didn't want him to see how he affected her.

"I think Sheyokee wants us to come to dinner now," said Meg, noticing the housekeeper standing in the doorway.

"Excellent. All I've had to eat today was a banana at four this morning," said Dr. Riley.

"No wonder you're so thin, Sean. Sheyokee needs to fatten you up with her safki and cornbread," Jim said, as they were walking to the dining room.

Micco had offered Meg his arm. She rested her arm on his, but she still kept her eyes downcast. Micco, as usual, was confused by Meg's behavior. If he teased her, she became annoyed. If he tried to carry on a normal conversation, she became argumentative. If he flirted with her, she seemed to take offense. He just could not understand it. He had never had trouble attracting a woman in his entire life. Maybe they were just so opposite in temperament that they could never be truly compatible. He'd still keep trying, though. What was her Achilles heel?

They all sat down to a delicious dinner and everyone ate heartily, except Meg, who picked at her food. She was confused. Micco had made her so angry because he would not listen to her suggestion, and then he was blatantly flirting with her. Men were all the same, except her uncle, of course. Micco thought he could get around her and ignore what she knew was best for him by charming her. She wouldn't fall for it, no matter how good-looking and sexy he was. Besides, his grandmother probably had an Indian maiden with soulful doe eyes already picked out for him.

At nine o'clock, Micco declared that he was ready for bed. They all got up from the table, Micco pulling out Meg's chair for her.

"Sean, do you feel like talking for a little while?" asked Jim.

"Of course, I would enjoy it. We haven't had much opportunity to chat since you've been here. I am feeling much more rested now, just pleasantly tired."

"Well, if you'll all excuse me, I am going to sleep. I just hope I can get my clothes off before I fall in bed. Good night," Micco said as he headed for the stairs.

"I think I'll go to my room too, and pull out the books from my trunk and start preparing lesson plans."

Meg's voice was enthusiastic. She was going to put the annoying Micco out of her mind and concentrate on her project. She walked over and kissed her father and uncle, each on the cheek.

"Good night, dear," said Jim, giving her a hug.

"Thank you again, Daughter, for playing the piano. It is true that 'music soothes the savage breast', and it also soothes the

428

fevered brow. Good night, sleep well," Sean spoke affectionately. Meg left them to their conversation, hoping her uncle could get her father to convince Micco that he needed a definite schedule.

In just four days, Gray Wolf and his seven friends had built the schoolhouse. It was large enough to accommodate twenty students. They had struggled getting the cart carrying the tools through the sand, but perseverance and muscle finally prevailed. They had worked from dawn to twilight, not even taking a break for lunch. That didn't bother them though, because they had hunted many times all day without eating until they went home at night and dipped into the waiting safki kettle.

Gray Wolf came by and asked Meg and Jim to come look at the building. They walked over to inspect the new schoolhouse, and Meg was hardly able to contain herself. When she saw it nestled among the palm trees, she was thrilled. It was constructed of cypress logs and poles and was floored with split logs of cabbage palm, elevated about two feet above ground. The roof was thatched with the fan-shaped leaves of the palmetto palm. There was a doorway in the front and in the back allowing air to circulate.

"Oh, it is absolutely wonderful! How in the world could you build it this quickly?"

"We are wonderful guys," agreed Gray Wolf.

"The fact is," continued Spotted Deer, "Micco threatened to force a pelican's pouch of the Black Drink down our throats if we did not finish it within a week."

"Yeah. With a threat like that, what else could we do?" asked Gray Wolf, mimicking a look of fright.

"Now make 'um chair," said Little Fox.

"Me make 'um big desk," offered Lazy Bear.

"Yes, Now we will make twenty chairs and desks. Lazy Bear wants to build your desk and chair himself," said Gray Wolf with a grin. "He likes your pretty red hair."

Meg smiled happily. "Thank you so much. I couldn't ask for a better schoolhouse if I were in New York City."

429

"It is indeed a work of art and I am amazed that you finished it so quickly, even with the threat of the Black Drink," Jim added with a smile. "Come back to the house, Gray Wolf. I want to pay you right now."

"That is not necessary, Mr. Styron. We can wait until the chairs and desks are finished."

"I absolutely insist. I want to pay you now for the building. When you finish everything else, I'll pay you for that then. Let's go."

"You go ahead, Uncle. I am going to stay here and look around more. I want to examine every inch of my schoolhouse."

Gray Wolf and Jim left, and Spotted Deer, Little Fox, and Lazy Bear showed Meg around, explaining how they had built it.

In five more days, everything was complete. Twenty student desks and chairs were ready, waiting for the young occupants, and Meg's desk was a work of art. It was made of cedar, and was as beautifully carved as a Victorian side chair. It had three drawers on each side. The top had a place for a recessed ink well, and Lazy Bear had placed a quill from a white plumed heron beside it.

Meg was so touched she hardly knew how to express her gratitude. "Oh, Lazy Bear! It is so beautiful!" She rushed over and hugged him, her arms barely reaching halfway around his massive chest. She didn't care this time what they thought. She could not believe the care that had gone into it.

Lazy Bear looked so pleased and proud, and the other three looked as if they wished that they had been the ones to receive a hug.

"You better watch out, Lazy Bear. Micco will remove your hair when he hears that Meg hugged you," teased Gray Wolf.

"Me no care. First he catch 'em Lazy Bear."

'Whatever are they talking about?' wondered Meg. Micco certainly couldn't be jealous of her.

"All of you are wonderful! Thank you so much. I only hope the students will come to school."

"They come. Parents send. Ojus papoose," Little Fox assured Meg.

And they did. Meg spent the afternoon bringing over books and supplies. The next morning, the children were waiting outside the schoolhouse, fifteen pairs of black eyes staring at her expectantly.

It was daunting because although most of them understood a little English, few spoke it, but Meg found she was up to the challenge. Meg was a 'natural born' teacher. By the end of the day, she knew she had made the right choice. She truly loved teaching. The only dark spot in her world was that Jim was leaving the next day. He had received word that the Annie Marie had arrived. Meg only kept the children for a half-day for now, fearing that too long a day at first would discourage them. So she planned to accompany her uncle to the ship tomorrow afternoon.

Everything had fallen into place. Sean had convinced Micco that patients must be scheduled and not be allowed to drop in at will. He had even convinced Micco to allow him to hire an Indian girl as a receptionist. She spoke English quite well and would be invaluable in the office. Shontee had brought the girl in after consulting with Sean.

The next day after school, Meg walked to the house with a heavy heart. Chotskee was waiting out front with a horse and buggy. He had already put Jim's luggage inside.

Meg ran into the house. Jim was saying goodbye to Micco and Sean. "The best of luck to you. Your clinic is thriving and will continue to do so thanks to your skills. I feel privileged to have met you, Micco. You are a fine man in every way. And Sean, you take it easy. Micco can handle it. You take care of the bookkeeping."

The men shook hands. "Well, Jim, we're going to miss you. Come back soon," invited Sean.

"Jim, I am really going to miss you and your valuable suggestions and advice. And I have enjoyed just being with you. I feel as though we are kindred spirits," said Micco.

"As do I. Goodbye!"

He and Meg walked outside to the carriage and Jim helped her up. He turned and waved at the two men who were standing on the porch. Then he got into the buggy and Chotskee drove off.

The ride was still bumpy, but not nearly as bad as when Meg had first ridden from the lighthouse in the cart. This time, Chotskee took them directly to the keeper's house. Captain Armour and his wife were in the yard. Chotskee jumped down and pulled Jim's suitcase from the seat while Jim was helping Meg out of the carriage. Then Jim started to pick up his bag, but Chotskee wouldn't allow it.

"Me carry."

"That isn't necessary," said Jim.

"Me carry 'um. You talk 'um," answered Chotskee as he began walking with the suitcase towards the dock.

"It's good to see you again, but I am sorry it has to be under these circumstances," said Captain Armour.

"I am, too. We have been so busy at the house, setting up the clinic, and getting Meg's schoolhouse built that even I haven't had a chance to come over for a visit," Jim said regretfully.

"Good day to you, Miss Riley," greeted Captain Armour.

"How have you both been?' asked Meg.

"Good morning. We keep busy," answered Mrs. Armour. "I hear the clinic is busy and that your school has plenty of students. Do you think you would have room for two more? It would be a lot easier for my two grandchildren to go there than to take the boat to Lake Worth like they do now."

"Of course I do. Send them tomorrow. We start classes at seven thirty and I dismiss them at noon. I don't want to keep them all day, at first. It might be too much. Later on, I will probably extend the school day."

The Armours were walking along with them as they talked. They crossed over the little bridge and then walked down the shore to the dock.

Meg felt nostalgia and sadness when she saw the valiant Annie Marie tied up at the pier.

"Oh, Uncle. I can't believe you're leaving me."

"I'll be back, dear. Now don't cry or you'll make me sadder than I already am," said Jim, taking out his handkerchief and dabbing her cheeks.

"All right," sniffed Meg.

Davy came out to greet them. "Hello everyone. How are you, Meg?" Davy asked, his eyes lighting up at the sight of her.

"I'm fine, I guess," she replied.

Davy was hoping she would offer her hand so he could hold it, but she didn't. She was too emotional to think about it.

Disappointed, he turned to Jim, "Your luggage is already on board, Sir. We're ready to sail."

"Oh no!" cried Meg, her eyes starting to fill again.

"Remember what you said. Now give me a hug and a kiss. I promise I will return next year with Leland and Stephanie and probably Lucy, Bob, the children and Alexandria, too. You'll be so busy this year that you will be surprised when we come knocking at your door."

Meg hugged Jim as hard as she could. "That will be wonderful. Now write me just as soon as you get there."

"I will write you a letter on my trip back and post it along the way, and then I'll send you a telegram when I arrive in New York." He paused. ""Meg, I want you to look after your father. He doesn't appear strong and I am afraid he will overdo. He'll listen to you."

"I promise, Uncle Jim."

"Goodbye dearest niece, until next year," said Jim, trying to hold back the tears himself, as he kissed her.

He climbed up the rope gangplank and then Joey and Tim cast off the lines and jumped on board. The ship drifted out into the outgoing tide and the sails were hoisted. Jim was in the stern, waving, and then the wind caught the sails and the Annie Marie seemed to take wings.

Meg waved until the ship had disappeared from view. She finally turned, and with a heavy heart, walked back to the carriage.

"Please come to visit us. We can have a nice long chat," invited Mrs. Armour.

"I will. My father is getting me a horse to ride. Then I'll be able to come over often." Meg bid them goodbye and Captain Armour helped her up into the buggy.

"Remember. You are welcome anytime," he said.

Meg rode off, felling more desolate than she had ever felt in her life.

Chapter Twenty

Andre and Jamie set sail in the gig, headed for Jupiter Inlet. Andre had left information with Anderson about when certain merchant ships would be passing by Juno and Lake Worth. He instructed Anderson to go ahead with the raids. He had great confidence in the man and believed he would follow orders. They had ventured on two other raids, plundering ships carrying cargoes worth thousands of dollars. He had explained that he had important business in Jupiter and would not return for a fortnight.

Jamie was happy to be sailing alone with Andre, but he felt a little uneasy. He always had the fear that somehow he would displease Andre and then once again be left alone and friendless.

"Andre, why are we sailing to Jupiter without the rest of the crew?" he asked timidly.

"Why? Aren't you glad to get away from that scurvy crew?"

"Yes, but I just wondered why you would leave your ship and crew. We should be buying cargo to sell in other ports."

"Certainement, but first I have unfinished business to take care of," responded Andre, aware of Jamie's uneasiness, "and you are going to help me."

"I am? How?"

"You see there is a young lady, tres belle, that I must see. I met her in Beaufort and promised to meet her again in Jupiter, but there is a problem."

"Oh? What is the problem?" asked Jamie, completely surprised by what Andre was telling him.

'The problem is this. Another man is vying for her affection, but he is not right for her. He is so jealous that he would harm me, even try to kill me, should I appear on the scene."

"Then you shouldn't go there if he wants to kill you," Jamie said anxiously.

"Ah, but that adds spice to the chase, n'est pas? This is where you come in, Jamie. The young lady, whose name is Megan Riley, has just opened up a school and I want you to attend classes there."

"I knew it!" cried Jamie. "You want to get rid of me. What did I do wrong? I'll try harder!" he pleaded.

"No, no, no! I do not want to get rid of you, as you put it. You are to be my messenger and my lookout."

"But I won't be your cabin boy anymore," said Jamie, almost in tears.

"Oui, you will. This is just a temporary plan. I am depending on you. Won't you help me?" asked Andre in his most persuasive manner.

"Well, if you really need me and you're not doing this so you can leave me, I'll do it," said Jamie.

"Bon!" exclaimed Andre, clapping Jamie on the shoulder. "Now let's enjoy our sail to Jupiter Inlet. The sun is shining and the breeze is brisk. What more can a man ask?"

"Okay," mumbled Jamie, still not convinced.

In two hours, they had sailed into the Loxahatchee River and the current was stronger. Sea grapes and driftwood floated past with minnows playing leapfrog over the sticks.

"Look, there are porpoises ahead," cried Jamie excitedly.

"Ah, that's a good omen. Maybe they'll guide us to the Inlet," said Andre as the little sailboat picked up speed and seemed to be on the trail of the dolphins.

In another hour, they had reached the mouth of Jupiter Inlet and the playful porpoises were far ahead of them.

"Keep a lookout for shoals," warned Andre. "Anderson said they appear as if by magic."

Within another hour, the lighthouse appeared quite close.

"I can see the light when the sun hits it," said Jamie, now eager to reach their destination. "You did say I could go inside, didn't you?"

"Mais oui."

In another half-hour, they were tying up at the lighthouse dock. Jamie was eager to climb to the top of the lighthouse.

"Come along and we'll talk to the keeper," said Andre.

They walked across the little bridge as Meg had done just a few weeks before and went to the coquina house. Andre knocked on the door and Mrs. Armour opened it.

Andre bowed slightly and took off his hat. "My name is Marcel Dupois and this is my son, Jamie."

"I am Mrs. Armour. Come in," she invited, thinking what a handsome and charming man he was. "Won't you sit down?"

"Thank you. I won't take up much of your time, Madam Armour. I have heard that a young woman has recently opened a school."

"Yes, that's true."

"I wish to enroll my son. Jamie's mother died two months ago. Unhappily, I had no one with whom to leave him. I had to take him on my sailing vessel, but he needs to go to school, not be a cabin boy."

"I am sure Miss Riley could take your son."

"That's a relief, but there is another problem. Where will he live? I would be only too happy to pay for his room and board, whatever the price. He must have an education."

Mrs. Armour was looking at Andre thoughtfully. "Let me contact Miss Riley. She may have a suggestion."

"I would be most grateful. My ship is anchored outside the inlet. If you could have the information for me at this time tomorrow, I will return. Would your husband object if I took Jamie up in the tower? He so wants to go to the top."

437

"No. That will be perfectly all right. My husband has gone to Lake Worth for supplies, but the assistant keepers are over there. Just tell them I sent you. I'll send one of my boys with a message to Miss Riley right away."

Andre then took Jamie to the lighthouse where they both climbed to the top. Lafitte was able to see the lay of the land and noticed a house in the northeast near the shore. It was the only house anywhere, other than a small building behind it. All else was forest, shore, and ocean. That had to the Riley home. Jamie was thrilled with the lighthouse and one of the keepers patiently explained everything to him.

"Thank you, Sir, for giving us your valuable time," said Andre. "I know you are busy, but my son is absolutely ecstatic over what you have told him. Come Jamie, we must leave now."

"Yes, Sir," said Jamie regretfully. "Mr. Tyler, I sure do appreciate you telling me about everything."

"Not at all, Jamie. I was glad to give you a short history. Come back. Maybe you can help me light the lamps next time," said Mr. Tyler.

"Oh boy! Could I? I'll be back!" Jamie said joyfully.

He ran down the spiral stairs, whooping all the way. Lafitte and Tyler exchanged indulgent looks.

Jamie and Andre went back to the gig. As they cast off the lines, Andre told Jamie his plan.

"We'll spend the night on shore. I saw a cove on the way in where we can shelter out of sight. I also brought along food and water just in case we needed it. Then we'll sail back in at the appointed time tomorrow. How does that sound?"

"All right, I guess," replied Jamie.

It was strange, but Andre felt a companionship with Jamie, something he had never felt before. It almost was as if the boy were his son. 'The sun must be affecting my brain,' he thought.

They spent the night and returned the next day. Mrs. Armour was waiting to greet them.

"I have good news for you. Miss Riley and her father will be happy to let Jamie live at their house, for the time being, until you can make other arrangements. She says they have plenty of room."

"That is wonderful news! Thank you so much for all your trouble."

Andre smiled at Mrs. Armour and she just wished she could have done more. He was such a charming man.

"Not at all. I was happy to do it," she replied.

"May I leave Jamie with you now? It is imperative that I return to my ship at this time; however, I would like to buy a horse, perhaps from some local Indians, and keep him stabled with them nearby. That way, when I come into port, I can visit Jamie."

"That can be arranged. As a matter of fact, Chotskee will be in shortly to pick up Jamie and you can talk to him. Would you like some lemonade while you wait?"

"That would be wonderful. What do you say, Jamie?"

"Yeah, I'd sure like some."

When Mrs. Armour left to get the lemonade, Andre handed Jamie a letter. "You are to give this to Miss Riley. Don't let anyone else see you do it. Is that understood?"

"Yes," said Jamie, putting the letter in his pocket.

Chotskee arrived fifteen minutes later, and Andre handed him Jamie's suitcase with the few clothes he possessed.

"Now remember, Jamie, you are to have Miss Riley send me a note about your behavior by the end of two weeks. I will return on Friday, two weeks from today."

"Yes Sir."

Jamie got up into the buggy with Chotskee and Andre arranged to buy a horse.

"Me bring. Twenty-five dollars."

"That's a deal. You can keep it stabled for me and I will pay for its feed, of course."

"Me do."

439

Jamie was fighting to keep from crying when he bid Andre goodbye.

"I will be back in two weeks, Jamie. This isn't forever, you know. Study hard and do not give Miss Riley any trouble. I will bring back money for your room and board. Also, if there is any way you can help around the house, do it. Au revoir."

He left and sailed back to Lake Worth. When he arrived, the Osprey was tied up at the dock. He quickly moored his boat and ran over to the Osprey. Anderson was on deck talking to McGuire.

"What news, Anderson? Did you have a successful trip?"

"That we did, Sir. The hold is full of cargo that you'll be able to sell easily."

"Any casualties?" asked Andre, looking around for Dory.

"No. I cracked that devil over the head with my billy club before he was able to stab a sailor in the back. He's lying in his bunk, moaning like he was dying."

It wasn't necessary to mention names. Both men knew exactly who Anderson was talking about.

"I wanted to toss him to the sharks, but I thought you might not approve," said Anderson sarcastically.

"You're right. I wouldn't have," replied Andre with an expression on his face that made Anderson glad he hadn't gotten rid of Dory.

"I'll go find the buyer and have him arrange to pick up the merchandise. I won't be back until morning."

Andre walked off in the direction of Sally's house and Anderson and McGuire smiled knowingly at each other.

As Andre strode along, he was thinking of Meg. How he burned to make love to her, and he wanted to be sure that he had her first. He could just envision caressing that warm virginal flesh. By the time he reached Sally's house, he wanted a woman, any woman. He didn't bother to knock, but barged in unannounced. Sally was in the kitchen. Startled, she turned around to see who was there.

440

"Oh, Andre, you're back," she said happily as she moved towards him, arms outstretched.

"Go in the bedroom and take off your clothes," he ordered harshly.

She backed up, and then seeing the look on his face, went in to the bedroom. Andre followed her in, closing the door behind him.

Later, as she was dressing, Sally felt hurt and used. He had barely spoken to her, but had just taken her like a rutting deer.

Watching her expression, Andre knew he had to placate her if he still wanted to use her services as middleman for his stolen cargo.

"Amour de ma vie, can you forgive me for being so impetuous in my lovemaking? I have thought of you constantly," he lied," night and day, but in my passion, I did not mean to crush so delicate a flower."

He gently tilted up her chin, so that she was looking into his pleading blue eyes. "Am I forgiven, ma cherie?"

Sally couldn't resist him. "You acted as though I was nothing, just an animal in mating season, but I guess sometimes men are like that." She didn't really have any basis for comparison. Her husband certainly had not been like that. He had always made her feel she was special, though he was no Don Juan.

"That is sad, but so true. We are no better than animals. Today I was a swine." He pulled her gently towards him, holding her and touching her hair softly. "Please say you forgive me or I will be devastated."

"I do," she said tremulously.

"Bon. Then, let's go into the parlor. We have business to discuss and then I have a present for you," said Andre. He took her hand and led her into the parlor.

Sally smiled, her unhappiness banished by small attentions and flattering words. "May I see the present first?" she asked timidly.

441

"Oui, so you shall," he said, taking out an object wrapped in paper.

Sally tore off the paper and her eyes widened as she looked at the shining gold bracelet that was part of the booty taken last night.

"Ooh! It is beautiful!" she cried. She slipped it on her wrist and then hugged Andre. "Thank you!"

"De rien. It is fitting for a beautiful woman. Now, to business. Would you contact my buyer right away? If he can come to the ship and arrange for buying and removing my cargo, my first mate will be there to handle it."

"I'll go right now."

"Bien, and I shall stretch out on your bed. I am a little tired," he said with a satisfied smile on his face.

"You should be," she said as she went out the door, her good nature restored.

"Oh, what a bauble will do," murmured Andre as he plumped the pillow and fell asleep.

Chapter Twenty-One

In the week that followed, Meg plunged into her work and gradually the pain of separation from her uncle eased. Every day was a challenge. She had never had such a willing captive audience. Rows of children stared at her with shining black eyes that never wavered in attention. She was determined that every child learn to read and write English as if it were their native tongue. After class, she spent hours preparing her lessons. The schoolroom was light and airy and was pleasantly cooled by the breezes that wafted through the open doors. Meg was grateful to Micco's friends every time she entered the schoolhouse.

This morning, as she entered the classroom, a small nervous, freckle-faced boy accompanied her. "Come Jamie. It will be okay. The Seminole boys and girls are very friendly. After a while, you will feel right at home."

He had spent the night at her father's home last night and Meg felt sorry for him. He seemed lost and he missed his father so much.

"Uh, Miss Riley," said Jamie with his head bowed slightly.

"Yes, Jamie. What is it?"

"I have a letter for you," Jamie murmured, pulling an envelope from his pocket.

"A letter?" Meg asked in a surprised voice.

"Uh huh."

She took it and opened it. Color flooded her face as she read the letter.

"Ma Ange,

You see, I have never forgotten you! At last we can be together again. Jamie is my cabin boy. No, he is more than that. He is like my adopted son and he is very loyal to me. I have told Jamie that you will send a report of his progress in two weeks, on Friday. I will be there at Jupiter to receive your note, telling me where to meet you. I have purchased a horse and can ride to rendezvous with 'La plus belle fille du monde'.

Toujours,
Andre"

Meg gasped, holding the note to her breast. She went inside and sat down at her desk, dipping Lazy Bear's quill pen in the ink well. She thought and then wrote:

March 6, 1887

"Andre,

I cannot believe you are here. I am so happy! Every morning at daybreak, I ride along the beach in the direction of Juno. There is a hammock of cypress about two miles from my house. I will wait there for you at daybreak on Saturday morning in two weeks.

Meg"

She enclosed the letter in an envelope, sealing it with sealing wax. Then she handed it to Jamie.

"Today after school, walk to the lighthouse. Andre will be there, waiting for you to give him this letter. Do not let anyone see it except Andre."

"Yes, ma'am," said Jamie as he put the letter in his pocket. Then he went over and sat down in a desk at the back of the room.

For once, the morning seemed to drag. Finally, the class was dismissed and Meg watched as Jamie struck out for the lighthouse.

She walked slowly back to the house. She couldn't realize she was actually going to see Andre again. She had been so involved in her job that she had actually pushed him out of her mind. Everyone was busy. The only chance she had to talk to Micco and her father was at the dinner table. Their schedule was less hectic than it had been at the beginning, but they were still busy every minute of the day. After dinner each night, Micco reviewed patient files and her father went to bed early. Micco even had office hours on Saturday and Sunday. Meg felt that he had completely forgotten about her. She wouldn't even mind if he teased her. At least he would be paying her a little attention. She went up to her room and re-read Andre's letter, savoring each word. He said she was the most beautiful girl in the world. She sighed, remembering how complimentary he always was. Micco could take lessons. Finally, it was time for dinner. It was almost four o'clock. She was having to adjust to eating so early. In New York, they never ate before six o'clock and usually seven. She brushed her hair, pinched her cheeks and walked downstairs. Jamie was just coming in the door.

"Did you give him my letter," she asked, first looking around to see if they were alone.

"Yes, he said to tell you he would be there." Jamie went into the kitchen and sat in a chair, looking up at Sheyokee.

"You no eat cookie. Me cook big dinner."

Meg smiled. Sheyokee had taken Jamie under her wing just like she had the homesick Meg. She had even measured him and was sewing pants and shirts. Sean came into the dining room, followed by Micco.

"Did you have a good day?" asked Micco.

"Yes, I did. Jamie is going to fit in just fine. Little Tiger has promised to show him how to make a pipe."

Micco smiled at Jamie. "Excellent! He'll probably take you hunting and fishing, too. His father is a great hunter."

Micco, too, felt sorry for Jamie. He seemed so lost. Hopefully, he would become more cheerful as he became accustomed to his surroundings.

"How are you feeling, Father?" asked Meg solicitously.

"Fine, Meg. Micco insists that I quit work at one o'clock and lie down. I have to keep my top assistant happy, so I do what he says."

"Good. You need to do that. What's the news in the paper?" The mailman had brought them a week-old paper from Jacksonville.

"There are two articles about piracy. I cannot believe that pirates are attacking our ships. Blackbeard ravaged the eastern seaboard 125 years ago. How is this possible in this day and age? And why can't the Coast Guard catch them? Not only have they pillaged ships, but they have murdered two men." Jamie gasped when Dr. Riley said this.

Dr. Riley continued. "They have no clues as to their identity because they have blackened their faces. They wear caps or bandanas to hide the color of their hair. In most cases, the boarded ship's crew simply surrenders and the marauders take the cargo, but in some cases, there had been resistance. On the last ship plundered, a single gold earring was discovered on deck."

This struck a cord of remembrance in Micco. There was something Jim had said about an earring concerning a murder in Beaufort. Micco dismissed this as irrelevant.

After eating a filling dinner followed by Sheyokee's pie- a delicious confection of baked sour oranges topped with fresh coconut, they rose from the table.

"I am going to take a walk along the shore after that dinner," said Meg.

"Good idea, Daughter. I'm going over the books and there is an article on infection I want to read."

He didn't need to walk off his meal because he hadn't eaten enough to sustain a grasshopper, much to Sheyokee's annoyance.

Micco merely said, "Have a nice stroll," and went back to his office.

Meg had been hoping that Micco would offer to go with her. Well, obviously, she no longer held any charms for him. Fine. She'd go alone! She stomped outside in poor grace, but no one noticed.

Two weeks later, Andre was mooring his boat at the Jupiter Lighthouse pier. 'Now I shall see what "ma belle" Meg has to say,' he thought. He whistled as he walked down the dock, supremely confident that she would arrange to meet him. He occupied himself by sitting under the banyan tree reading a book on navy battles. Mrs. Armour saw him when she came out to hang up the wash in her back yard. She insisted on bringing him a glass of cool water, and then went back to her duties. An hour later, Andre saw Jamie trudging over the sand, headed towards the lighthouse.

"Jamie, over here," called Andre. The boy came over and handed him the letter. Then he sat down, wiping his brow. Andre handed him his cup of water. He opened the letter and skimmed it, smiling with satisfaction.

"Ah, soon I shall see my delectable Meg." He spoke to Jamie. "How is everything going at school?"

"It's okay, but I never did like writing much. They always want you to practice them circles, over and over."

"Soon that will become easy for you. And what of your living quarters? Are they satisfactory?"

"Oh, yes. It's a real nice house and I have my own room. You don't even have to go outdoors to relieve yourself."

"The doctor has indoor plumbing. Who would have thought it in this remote area? And what do you think of Miss Riley? She is pretty, n'est pas?"

"She sure is, and smart, too." Jamie looked down at his feet, "But Andre, I want to be with you. I don't want to stay here."

"Remember, you won't be here forever. You are here to help me right now. You do want to do that, don't you?"

"Yes. Sir."

"Well then, make the best of it and enjoy your stay here. I expect you to take advantage of the schooling offered you. It can be very important in life. I read every book I could get my hands on when I was your age. Now go on back to the house, and tell Miss Riley that I will meet her."

Jamie surprised Andre by putting his arms around the Frenchman's neck and hugging him. Then Jamie jumped up. "Goodbye," he said and ran across the grass.

"Adieu," responded the startled Andre. That was a first for him. He got up and walked down the dock to his gig. He cast off and sailed down the inlet a little ways to a piece of land that jutted out from the bank. He lowered and furled the sails and then lifted out the mast, laying it across the thwarts. Before sunrise, he would slide the boat beneath a tangle of vines so that it would be hidden from curious eyes. He pulled out his sandwich, wrapped in oilcloth, from the bow of the boat and settled down for the dawn to break. He had arranged with Chotskee to take his horse from the stable at anytime. This would be satisfactory because Chotskee would know that Andre had taken the horse since no Indian would ever steal.

Meg's heart was pounding as she dressed for her early morning ride. Today she would see Andre. She went to the small barn behind the house, taking a carrot with her. The dappled gray pony whinnied a greeting. Meg loved her horse already.

"Here, Dumpling. This is for you," she said, giving the mare her carrot. When the pony finished, Meg put a saddle blanket across the horse's back to prevent galling her and then she saddled Dumpling with a lightweight English saddle. Meg absolutely refused to ride sidesaddle, and so she dressed in riding breeches. No one saw her since she rode so early in the morning. She took hold of the bridle and led the frisky Dumpling out of the barn. The horse was ready for a run and so was Meg. She galloped off down the beach to the copse of cypress trees, as arranged. It was still dark as Meg flew along the beach, but by the time she reached her destination, dawn was breaking. She tied Dumpling to a tree near some grass and walked down to the shore. She had only been there a few minutes when she heard the sound of hoof beats. She looked to the south and saw a rider galloping towards her. The rising sun gleaming on his blonde hair made it look like a halo. 'I should have known he would ride a black stallion,' thought Meg. Man and beast moved as one. Andre was as graceful on a horse as he was striding across the deck of a ship. Meg's pulse quickened as she waited to meet this sun god, Apollo's twin. He rode in the edge of the surf, the water splashing with every hoof beat. When he was a few feet from Meg, he reined the horse and stopped, leaping from the saddle.

"Stay, Thor," he commanded, and the horse obediently stood still, tossing his head as if to say 'I understand'.

"Meg, ma ange," cried Andre. He pulled her roughly to him and captured her lips like a sultan bussing his slave girl. Meg could smell leather, horse, and that elusive, woodsy fragrance that she associated with Andre. She was excited, but a little frightened by his violence. Using a woman's wiles, she collapsed against him, and he loosened his hold. When he did, she was able to push him away a few inches.

"Andre," she said panting. "You promised to control your impulsiveness."

"So I did," he said, breathing hard. His eyes were consuming her as if she were a mouth-watering confection he would gobble up, bite by bite. Gradually his breathing slowed, and he released her. "I apologize. It seems I am always doing that with you, Cherie."

"You frighten me a little. You kiss me as though I were a tasty morsel you are devouring," said Meg, still a little breathless.

"I have never been so attracted to anyone as I am to you. You are so beautiful and so sexy. Meg, you are unlike any other woman I have ever known, and I have known myriad women. Your sweet lips are like nectar and I could sip it day and night.

Ah, Meg, let me make love to you and send you soaring to the stars."

He was so appealing, so earnest. He looked like a lover completely enamored by her charms. Meg could not know that he had said these very same words over and over to countless women. He made Lothario look like a callow youth.

"No, Andre. I don't want to make love like this. It is wrong outside marriage."

Andre almost laughed. "Ma petite, you are so innocent, so unused to the ways of the world. Most men and women do not suffer under this yoke of Victorian conduct."

"Be that as it may, I cannot engage in an illicit affair."

"Then you need not fear me. I shall not impose my will upon you until the day you decide it is your wish, also." Andre was almost grinding his teeth as he said this. It would be so hard to keep his hands off her tantalizing body. But he could wait. He knew he could eventually seduce her. It would just take longer.

Meg relaxed as he began to talk, entertaining her with tales of his travels to faraway places. Andre took Thor over by the mare and tied him close by. Then he and Meg strolled along the shore talking and laughing. They held hands like any couple falling in love and Meg was happy. She really didn't like that violent side of him, but he was so contrite afterwards, it was as though it had never happened.

"I must go, Andre. It's almost time for my classes and I have to change clothes. Father and all the students would be shocked to see me in britches."

"They don't know what they are missing," said Andre as his eyes roamed her slender hips and legs. "What about your Indian friend? Would he be shocked, or has he seen you dressed his way before?" asked Andre with suppressed anger in his voice.

"Well, he hasn't seen me, but I am sure he wouldn't be shocked. Nothing shocks Micco."

"Are you seeing him? I mean, as a sweetheart?" he asked jealously.

450

"No. I told you before. He means nothing to me, except as a friend."

"And does he reciprocate that feeling?"

"Of course. He thinks of me as a sister." Meg felt a little pang as she said that. She did not want him to think of her as a sister. 'How fickle can I be?' she thought.

They had walked back to their horses and Andre helped her mount, enjoying the feel of her rounded bottom as he lifted her up. After she was seated, he mounted his horse and they trotted down the beach, the rising sun warming their left shoulders. All too soon, they were in sight of the house. They stopped and Andre grabbed Meg's hand, kissing it passionately.

"Until we meet again, mon rouge fleur," he said.

"Goodbye. When shall we meet again?" she asked.

"In three weeks. I will be at our rendezvous on Saturday. Adieu."

Meg turned off to take Dumpling to the barn and Andre continued down the beach at a gallop. She watched as he flew along, almost expecting him to take flight on his black-winged Pegasus, drifting up into the sky. Meg smiled at her fantasy, but Andre was a man who invoked fantasies. She stabled Dumpling, promising her a treat later on for being such a good horse.

Meg again became immersed in her teaching and was encouraged to see amazing results in just a few short months. She saw Andre from time to time and each meeting was more passionate than the last. Could he be right? Was she the only mature woman in the world who had not experienced sexual fulfillment, as he implied. 'No, I know I am right, but it is getting harder and harder to resist him,' she thought, troubled by her ambiguous feelings. That night at dinner, Micco gave her a surprise.

"You know the time of the Green Corn Dance is approaching. You said you wanted to attend the festival. Do you still want to go?" he asked.

"Yes, of course. I have been so curious about it. The children have been talking about it. Gray Wolf and his friends, and Sheyokee speak of nothing else. I want to go, too. Are you going to take me?" she asked, amazed that he would consider leaving the office for even one day.

"Yes, I promised you I would. It is the biggest celebration of the year for the Seminoles. I am going to close the office that day. No one would come into the clinic, even if they were dying."

Meg was filled with anticipation waiting for the Green Corn Dance day to arrive. She was very curious about it, plus she would be with Micco all day, even though he was sure to tease her. Actually, she missed their verbal sparring. When Sheyokee heard that Meg would be attending, she insisted that Meg wear the Seminole dress. She measured Meg, tut-tutting at her narrow waist, small hips and slim legs, but felt there was some hope because Meg was very full bosomed.

"Brave no like. You eat," she advised.

"I know. Lazy Bear told me I would be an old maid if I didn't fatten up."

Meg smiled, thinking about Miss Molly and how both she and Sheyokee tried to arrange her love life. Apparently, according to them, if she weighed in at two hundred pounds, men would be dropping at the sight of her like Mayflies in their death throes. She didn't think Sheyokee had Micco picked out, however, as did Miss Molly. Perhaps she had in mind a sea captain or merchant that happened to come by. 'Someone like Andre,' Meg thought dreamily.

Shontee dropped by later the next day. She had visited only a few times and had come by the schoolhouse once, but Meg knew that Micco went to see her often later at night, after office hours. Meg felt a little resentment because Micco did not neglect his grandmother, but he couldn't spare five minutes for her. She could not know that this was part of Micco's campaign. He was playing a waiting game, hoping that Meg would come to him.

"Good afternoon," said Shontee. "Micco told me you would be attending the Green Corn Festival with him, so I brought you something to wear that day."

"Good afternoon,' replied Meg in surprise. She and Shontee did not have a warm relationship, though Shontee showed no animosity. So Meg wondered why she would be bringing her a gift.

Shontee handed her a pouch.

"Thank you," said Meg, looking inside. "Oh, they are lovely." She pulled out ten strings of multi-colored beads, some of glass, some of shells, and some of semi-precious stones.

"It is appropriate that you wear these to the Green Corn Dance. Sheyokee told me she is making you a dress to wear. This will complete the outfit."

As usual, the Seminole wild grapevine was working with the speed of a telegraph wire. Meg didn't know what to say. She always felt a little uncomfortable in Shontee's presence. She didn't think Micco's grandmother disliked her, but she knew instinctively that Shontee would not approve of her as a prospective bride to Micco. The Seminole code of conduct was far more rigid than the white man's. What a paradox that Micco seemed more a part of Boston or New York society then he did Seminole society. He loved his friends, of course, and enjoyed being with them, but Meg realized for the first time how difficult it must be for him. She had never thought about his feelings on the subject before.

"I really appreciate your thoughtfulness and will enjoy wearing these beads. Did you make them yourself?" asked Meg.

"Not all of them. As a chief's wife, I received many beads in my lifetime."

"I remember when your son, Tall Chief, Micco's father died, though I was just a little girl, but I don't remember your husband."

"He died many moons before his son."

"Oh, I am sorry, " said Meg, not knowing what else to say.

453

"Both had funerals for great chiefs. I myself painted my husband's face and dressed him in new clothes and placed his rifle beside him. I prepared the safki for his journey to the Happy Hunting Ground."

"You painted his face?" Meg asked in a puzzled voice.

"Yes, it is the custom to paint one cheek red and the other black. This honor is accorded only to chiefs. No other brave's face is painted. My people even allowed me, a squaw, because I was the daughter of a chief, to light his funeral pyre. I did not dress my hair for a year, so that all would know I was in mourning. When my son, the mighty Tall Chief, went to the land of his fathers, his squaw had to leave while the braves lit the logs that would consume his body. The mighty Osceola, with the death struggle already upon him in his dank prison cell, rose in his bed and painted one half of his face, his neck, throat, wrists, and the back of his hands with vermilion paint. He also painted the handle of his knife red, for these were the symbols of a great war chief."

"How tragic and cruel his death was," said Meg hotly. "That such a man should die in that shameful cell was unforgivable. It was horribly ironic that his own honesty and belief in the white man's honor brought him to that state."

"It was. He died of a broken heart and spirit, mourning for his people and his lost land, unable to fathom the deception of the white man."

Shontee's eyes were bleak, filled with an age-old sadness. Then her mood changed. "But now his soul is with the Great Spirit. He is hunting with Tall Chief, and Micanopy, and all the great chiefs, where they always bring down game and have cool water to drink. After the big sleep, the bad Indians hunt and hunt, but they never find any animals, and they have only hot water to drink."

"There are many parallels in your beliefs and the white man's," said Meg. "We too, dress the deceased in their best clothes, bury them with their jewelry and wedding rings. We believe the soul lives on as you do, with the heavenly father in a

454

place of eternal peace, called Heaven, and we believe the wicked people go to a separate place called Hell where they suffer eternal damnation. This is comparable to the bad Indian who cannot find game and drinks hot water." Meg thought for a minute. "Does this apply to women, too?"

"Yes, though their primary job is not hunting, they do know how, and some are as skilled as the braves. I was brought up by missionaries and was taught your religion. You are right that there are many parallels. In your society, the widow wears black for a year after her husband's death. The squaw must live with disheveled hair, and take off her beads. At the end of a year of mourning, she may arrange her hair, don her beads and marry again, if she chooses."

"And the brave, is he in mourning, too?" asked Meg, always on the alert for inconsistencies between male and female culture.

"When his squaw dies, the husband may not hunt for four days, and for four moons, he must not wear his neck handkerchiefs or his turban."

"I see," said Meg. "Whenever a brave is without his head covering, he is in mourning."

"That is true. There are other parallels in our societies, one of which is very interesting. The Seminoles believe that a Christ-like figure came down to earth, where he was met by three Indians. They carried him around on their shoulders while he sowed the seeds of the coonti root, which was God's gift to the red man. At that time, all the Indians were starving; the ground was parched, no corn grew, and all the animals were gone. During this period, while the Seminoles were waiting for the coonti to grow, God rained down bread that the Indians gathered and ate."

"That is unbelievable," gasped Meg. "It is exactly like the Mosaic account of Manna from heaven."

"Yes, it is. As well as believing in a supreme being and the immortality of the soul, the Seminole also believes in the resurrection of the dead."

Meg was fascinated by Shontee's account. There were links to the Aztecs, the Jews, the Christians, and even the ancient Egyptians. Meg had seen pictures of the pharaohs and sultans of Arabia wearing a headdress that was similar to the turbans worn by the Seminoles.

"Our beliefs are connected in many ways, aren't they?" asked Meg.

"They are. The big difference between the Seminole and others is that he believes in the purity of body and soul. He maintains a strong body, and he does not lie, cheat, or steal." Shontee had a cynical expression on her face. "Chief Tallahassee once took a white man on a hunting expedition. When they were leaving, the hunter asked if it would be safe to leave some of his belongings in the chief's wigwam. 'It will be perfectly safe,' responded Chief Tallahassee, 'there is not another white man within fifty miles.'"

Meg could see the way Shontee had been pulled in two directions by her upbringing. She was raised with the white man's religion and philosophy, but had married an Indian. It must have been difficult to reconcile the two. Changing the subject, Meg talked about the Green Corn Dance.

"I feel honored that I am to be allowed to attend the festival. I understand that white people are not welcomed with open arms. Micco had instructed me to remain a part of the background."

"We are not so unbending as that. The Seminole is always polite. He opens his home to a guest, no matter who it is," said Shontee..

"Oh, I know," replied Meg, eager not to offend. "Everyone had been so helpful to me. I couldn't have asked for a more gracious welcome. Micco explained that it is a religious ceremony, as well as a time for celebrating. I recognize that and intend to show a reverent attitude."

Shontee appeared to be mollified, for the expression softened. "It is time for me to leave. I will stop in to say a quick hello to my grandson. My people are happy with your school. I think you will have more and more attending. It is a good thing that you have done." She paused. "Micco is proud of you." Shontee arose and walked towards the clinic.

"Thank you. I hope you come back to visit soon," said Meg, hoping for a smile of friendliness. But it was not forthcoming.

Meg was surprised that Shontee had complimented her, but then she realized that even though Shontee might not like her very much, she was fair. She felt it her duty to tell Meg what the others were saying.

Sheyokee came into the room, having waited for Shontee to finish her conversation.

"You put on dress. Me see," ordered the meticulous seamstress.

A month later, the Green Corn Dance was just one day away, and Micco had arranged for Jamie to go with them. He had become very fond of the shy, lonely, little boy. He had even forgone dinner several times to take the child fishing, persuading Sheyokee to fix a picnic for them to take along. They had borrowed Gray Wolf's canoe and paddled in the quiet lake, catching enough fish for dinner. Micco showed him how to spear the mud cat. It was harder to spear a trout that darted more quickly than the sluggish cat, but Micco caught five of them. He also showed Jamie how to capture crayfish that were hiding beneath the rocks.

Jamie was thrilled with these outings. He had fished a few times with a baited line in Beaufort, but this was really exciting, especially with Micco, who knew the names of all the fish and animals. Jamie even saw an alligator sunning on the bank, but Micco told him not to worry, that the alligator was too sleepy to move. He kept comparing Andre to Micco, but felt disloyal doing it. He loved Andre and treasured the time they spent together, but he was horrified by the crimes he had committed. He also was worried about Andre, Micco, and Meg. He knew Andre was seeing Meg regularly, and Andre had told him that Micco hated him and wanted to kill him because Meg had chosen Andre over Micco. He just couldn't believe that Micco, who spent his days curing people and saving lives, could be capable of taking a life. Jamie was worried and he didn't know what to do. He even suspected that the reverse was true, that Andre wanted to kill Micco.

Micco knew that something was bothering Jamie, but he thought it had to do with homesickness and missing his father. He hoped that with time, the boy would adjust. He seemed to be happy when he was fishing with Micco, but as yet, Micco had not been able to persuade Jamie to call him by his first name.

"Dr. Ravenwing, do you like Miss Riley?"

"But of course I do. Why do you ask?" asked Micco, wondering at the question.

"Well, I was just wondering. Are you going to marry her?" Jamie asked anxiously.

Micco laughed. "That is the kind of question you never ask a gentleman, Jamie. It puts him on the spot, so to speak. It's in the same category as asking a lady how old she is."

"Huh?"

"Never mind. I doubt if Miss Riley thinks of me in that way, but we are close friends," said Micco.

He wondered how Jamie could have gotten the impression that he was seriously interested in Meg. He certainly hadn't been paying attention to her lately.

"It's getting late and we need to get home. You should have been in bed by now."

"Do we have to?"

"Yes, we do." Micco had brought a sorrel that he kept stabled with Meg's pony. If he ever had the time, he intended to ride with her some morning. He had brought Jamie on his horse to the lake for it was too far to walk.

He put the fish and crayfish in pouches and attached them to his saddlebag, and then slid the spears into deerskin cases. He swung up into the saddle and then reached down for Jamie.

"Up you go," he said, swinging Jamie up behind him. If Micco had been riding just for pleasure, he would have ridden bareback, Indian style, but since he had Jamie and equipment, he was using a saddle. They reached the house about 8:30.

"Time for bed, Jamie. Scoot on upstairs, but do not get in bed until you have bathed and brushed your teeth."

"Do I have to? I'm tired."

"No excuses. I'm going to come up and check on you," said Micco, giving him a swat on the rear. "If you have bathed and are in bed by the time I come up, I'll tell you a story about how an Indian Chief tricked his pursuers."

"Oh boy! I'll be ready." Jamie liked Micco's Indian tales, especially if they had a happy ending.

Micco gave the fish and crayfish to Sheyokee who would then put them in a stew, and then he ran upstairs, bathed quickly, and changed into fresh clothes. Meg was still sitting in the parlor reading a book when he entered the room.

"Are you all ready for the festival tomorrow, Red?"

"Do not call me 'Red". Yes, I'm ready. Sheyokee has outfitted me as an Indian maiden, and your grandmother completed my ensemble with ten strings of beads. I don't think they can do anything about my hair, though. Sheyokee is bemoaning the fact that I don't weigh eighty pounds more. Of course, YOU think I am fat already," said Meg, set for battle, just waiting for him to agree.

Micco sat down and stretched out his long legs, watching her lazily. "As always, you are so perceptive, my Chick--, I mean, Meg. Most of the men in my tribe prefer plump, robust women. I, too, once felt that way as an untutored youth, but my ten years among the svelte ladies of Boston convinced me otherwise. Now while you are well-endowed above the waist, below it you definitely need some padding!"

459

"How dare you!" shouted Meg. "How dare you speak to me in this manner!"

"Now, now, Meg. You are the one who said I was not 'polite society'. Remember when Jim scolded you for mentioning bustles and corsets in my presence?"

Meg was simmering. "Of all the unmitigated audacity! You, you…" Words failed her at this point.

"Cad? Scoundrel? Worm?" offered Micco helpfully. His eyes traveled up and down her figure. "I'd say you need to lose five, no, possibly ten pounds. Then you could compete with the best of them."

"I'm not going with you tomorrow," stated Med emphatically.

"Yes, you are. You are too curious to miss it. You'd go if I compared you to a baby hippopotamus. Just be ready on time, and make sure Jamie's ready, too. Well, it's past my bedtime," he said, yawning mightily as he arose and headed for his room.

Meg heard him laughing as he ran up the stairs. She was so angry she slammed her book down on the table. It was a conspiracy- Micco, Shontee, Sheyokee. Only her father was on her side, but he wasn't much of a champion. She knew Micco thoroughly enjoyed it when she rose to the bait, but she couldn't help it. He was so infuriating. She wished she could have thought of a satisfactory name to call him. She'd work on it, and the next time she would be ready for him. She couldn't handle Micco verbally, and she was having increasing trouble handling Andre's physical advances. How she wished her uncle were here. The last time she met Andre, after a passionate kiss, he had put his hand on her breast. It was all she could do to stop him, but the frightening thing was, she was excited as well as shocked. No man had ever touched her there. No man had ever kissed her the way he did, either. Micco's kiss had been gentle, but exciting too, in a different way. At times like this, Meg really missed her mother. Her aunt was wonderful, but Meg could never have discussed anything really personal with her. She felt that she could have with her mother. She could with her uncle, but only to a certain extent. He was a man of the world, but he regarded Meg as his baby, almost. She would have to figure these things out on her own, but it was difficult. She was just too naïve. She was starting to get a headache, mulling over her situation. Were Andre's intentions honorable as far as she was concerned? Did he plan to ask her to marry him? She would go to bed and sleep on it, and perhaps tomorrow she would see more clearly. She did not intend to speak to the insufferable Micco all day, if she could help it. At least the blouse and skirt that Sheyohee had made were pretty.

Meg was awakened early in the morning by the aromatic fragrance of night-blooming jasmine wafting through her window. She arose and walked onto the veranda. The birds were lifting their heads from beneath their wings, twittering a welcome to the coming dawn. She could hear the litany of crashing ocean waves upon the far shore. She was in her nightgown and the breeze caressed her body like a lover. Then she felt someone else's presence.

"You're up early, Love." Micco was in the shadows, staring at her.

Meg crossed her arms across her bosom, aware of her scanty gown. "I was just going back inside," she muttered. "You said to be ready on time, and I did not want to run the risk of arousing your ire."

"Don't go," he pleaded. "Dawn is the most beautiful time of the day. Let's enjoy it together." He started to walk over to her.

"I prefer twilight. If you'll excuse me, I have to get dressed," she said coolly.

She went inside her bedroom and closed the window as hard as she could. This was the absolute limit! Last night he compared her to a hippopotamus almost, and this morning he called her 'Love'. Did he think she would swoon and fall into his arms and forget what he had said last night? When coconuts grew in Brooklyn!

Micco had forgotten his plan to appear detached to Meg. She was so beautiful standing there, the wind blowing her glorious hair around her shoulders, and her thin gown molded to her perfect body. How he longed to kiss her and hold her! But he couldn't. He knew she would reject his advances as surely as the dawn was breaking. He sighed, regretfully. The battle to break down her defenses was frustrating. How could he do it? He had thought a dozen times, that with Andre out of the way, she would be more receptive to him. He shook his head. 'It's time for me to get dressed, too."

By seven-thirty, Micco, Meg, and Jamie were on their way. Micco was riding his horse, Chips, with Jamie holding on to his waist, riding behind him. Meg rode her beloved Dumpling. She was really annoyed that she could not wear britches instead of this skirt that must have had ten yards of material. Every time there was a slight breeze, her skirt blew up, exposing her legs and bloomers. Thankfully, she was following behind Micco. Then, just as the wind caught her skirt, he turned around to see how she was doing and grinned like a small boy in a candy store. The look on Meg's face warned him not to say a single word.

He turned back around and said over his shoulder, "Are you doing okay?"

"Fine," Meg gritted between her teeth. "Just keep looking straight ahead for ruts."

"I'll do that, Red."

They finally arrived just before nine o'clock with Meg worrying all the way about how she was going to get down without showing her legs and drawers.

She needn't have. Micco slid off his horse. He plucked her off hers, and then placed her on the ground in one swift motion. Her skirt hardly had time to fly.

He murmured, "sotto voce, must not shock my kinfolks."

"If you dare say one word…" sputtered Meg furiously.

"I will be as mute as the Sphinx about your lovely, uh, green and purple skirt."

As they approached the camp, Jamie was looking all around with great curiousity. There were at least twenty thatched-roofed huts under moss-hung trees in the encampment. A few chickees were without walls, and were made of palmetto leaves and the skins of wild animals, but most of the huts were made of pond cypress logs and poles with thatched roofs of palmetto. They had floors of split cabbage palm logs very similar to Meg's schoolhouse, except her building was rectangular. Nearly every hut had a hammock close by, strung between two trees.

The village was near a lake and many dugouts, carved from bald cypress, dotted the shoreline. Some of the canoes contained bamboo fishing poles, and quite a few were fitted with mast and sail.

"What kind of a house is that?" asked Jamie.

"That's a cooking hut and inside is a coonti strainer." Unlike the other huts, this structure was floorless and had a fireplace in the center. Two squaws were working over a very elaborate construction of poles and deer skins.

"They use that to strain the poisonous juices from the coonti plant. After this process, the roots are quite edible," explained Micco. "And of course, they make coonti flour using large wooden mortars and pestles. They also make rubber from the milky latex of the strangler-fig."

"This is fascinating," said Meg, forgetting her vow not to speak to Micco.

The camp was stirring with life. Delicious aromas were arising from other cooking huts as the squaws prepared the food for the very special day. Several braves were bringing fresh fish from their canoes. There would be smoked trout and charcoaled mullet at the feast, along with safki, roasted bear meat, oysters, scallops, blue crabs, and stone crabs. The Seminoles got their seafood from the shore as well as close-by lakes. Micco, Meg, and Jamie strolled by numerous garden plots filled with tasselling corn, peas, and beans climbing over trestles, and squash vines bursting with plump squash ready for the picking. Further away from the huts were fields of sugar cane, alongside patches of pineapple. Most huts had banana trees growing in their yards, and cattle were grazing in a field nearby.

"Oh, look over there!" Meg cried in delight.

They looked where she was pointing. In one yard, two tame white-plumed egrets with alert, piercing eyes stood with their long slender necks craning at the doorway, waiting for their beef to be thrown to them.

"The Seminoles actually domesticate those beautiful birds. I can't believe it."

"Why not?" asked Micco. "Sailors have pet parrots."

"You're right. I guess most animals could be tamed."

They passed by an Indian carving a model of a Seminole dugout. He smiled amiably at them and continued his absorption in his work.

"As you can see," said Micco, "the Seminoles are an industrious people. They are proud and will not accept a handout. They make canoes that they sell to hunters and trappers. They also find a market for moccasins, baskets, coonti starch, plumes, smoked skins, and venison, as well as bamboo pipes and boxes."

Meg was intrigued by all the sights and sounds. "I really admire them."

They watched as little girls came running in from the fields with containers of blackberries and huckleberries. One intrepid girl had managed to get honey from a hive. Another child had climbed a tree and picked a basket of wild sour oranges.

"You know the rule is that those who would dance at the Green Corn Festival must work or hunt. Every member of the camp, to the smallest child, must hunt until twelve noon. These children left camp at daybreak and they have been working ever since. The men left to hunt large game, and the boys will get rabbits, birds, and squirrels. The women hunt hogs and dig potatoes. Even the smallest children 'hunt' water and bring in sticks of wood," Micco told them. He was smiling.

"Why are you smiling?" asked Meg.

"Seeing that girl with the oranges reminded me of a story about sour oranges. They have to be cooked to make them palatable, of course. Well, the Indians know this from experience, and think that everyone else does, too. Billy Cypress traveled great distances to sell his wares. He had gone all the way to Titusville to meet the train carrying visitors from the North. They were delighted to see sweet, fresh, juicy oranges for sale as they stepped down from the train. Billy was happy, too, and soon sold all of his oranges for a penny a piece. The visitors could not believe their good fortune in getting the fruit at such a bargain. Billy drove off counting his profit, and the buyers got back on the train and sat down, ready for a feast of sweet, juicy oranges. Their faces puckered as they bit into the sour fruit. They called Billy every kind of name, and talked about double-dealing Indians. Later on, when word of this got back to Billy, he was genuinely surprised. He thought they knew if you sold an orange for a penny, it had to be a sour orange. A sweet orange was worth three cents."

Meg and Jamie laughed, picturing the looks of the visitors' faces when they bit into the oranges.

"We probably won't see Gray Wolf and the others until noon when they come back in with their game," said Micco.

They continued to wander around the camp watching all the activity.

"That dance must be really special, if even the tiny children are willing to work in order to dance," Meg remarked.

"Oh, it is. It is the high point of the whole celebration. The Seminoles like to play as well as work, so they are willing to do it. There are several activities that they enjoy. One is dancing around the Festal pole. Tonight, which is the night of the Full Moon, they will dance from sunset until sunrise. The women throw a ball at the center pole, and the men catch it in their bags. When the dancing is over, the circle around the pole is perfectly symmetrical and about ten inches deep, made by running and dancing. There is another ball game that is played by a code of rules more than 150 years old. The object is to strike the pole with the ball that is knocked with a stick made of hickory. It has a netted pocket made of deer thongs. The ball is tossed up and caught in this pocket, and then hurled at the pole. The opposing side endeavors to prevent the ball from touching the post. If the ball should happen to strike the ground away from the line of play, everyone goes after it; men, women, and children. The one who captures the ball has the next play. A scorekeeper stands by the pole, keeping a record of the play."

"The women sound as if they compete with the men," said Meg.

"They do. Both men and women are strong and healthy. Some women are even more fleet of foot than the men. There will be much feasting after the games when twilight falls. And then the 'piece de resistance' will begin. You will enjoy seeing the Medicine Man who leads the dances."

"I can't wait," said Meg.

Jamie had slipped his hand into Meg's, somewhat cowed by all the people and activity.

"Jamie, I know you'll like the Medicine Man and all the dancers," Meg stated assuringly, giving his hand a squeeze.

"I'll even put you up on my shoulder if we don't have a good spot," offered Micco.

Jamie didn't say anything but he moved closer to Meg when two men dragged in a bear, carrying it to their hut.

They walked everywhere watching men carry huge deer on their shoulders, apparently without fatigue.

"How can they do that?" questioned Meg admiringly.

"The men have wonderful physical endurance and they are fearless. To test their endurance, some of the old chiefs have been known to take a live coal from the camp fire and place it on their wrist, allowing it to burn until the heat is exhausted without showing the slightest sign of emotion. Then they would remove the cool ember and replace it with a hot one from the embers."

"That must hurt!" exclaimed Jamie. "Their arm would be burned."

"Amazingly, it isn't, at least not badly burned. The Indian boy is taught that no merit is so great as bearing pain without complaint. They also develop their strength by walking or running many miles, jumping, wrestling, or poling a canoe. With the Seminole male, the Spartan spirit is expected."

When the sun was straight overhead, someone hailed them.

"Micco, we're glad you are here. Hello, Meg. And who is this?" Gray Wolf greeted them.

He was accompanied by his close inseparable friends, Spotted Deer, Lazy Bear, and Little Fox.

"Hello," Meg greeted them warmly. "This is Jamie. He is staying at Dr. Riley's house and attending school. His father arranged it because he didn't want to keep his son at sea with him. He wants him to get an education."

"Hello," said Micco, so happy to see his friends. He hardly ever saw them because he was so busy.

"Little brave, we are happy to have you visit us," said Spotted Deer to Jamie.

Jamie timidly shook his hand. "Is that a real bow and arrow?" And can you shoot with it?"

The bow was so long that Jamie didn't see how anyone could bend it.

"Yes, it is. See what I shot this morning?" offered Spotted Deer, as he opened his pouch.

Jamie peered inside the pouch and saw two rabbits and a squirrel.

"Oh, are you gonna' eat those?"

"Of course, I only kill something if I am going to eat it, not like white hunters who kill for sport," replied Spotted Deer.

He had already brought two deer to his chickee for his squaw to prepare. Little Fox and Lazy Bear were looking at Meg admiringly.

"You pretty," said Lazy Bear.

467

"Ojus pretty," agreed Little Fox.

"Thank you," said Meg, looking down at her colorful skirt.

"Shontee is waiting to see you," said Gray Wolf. "She wants to make sure you know where you'll be sitting for the dancing tonight."

They all made their way through chickens and pigs that were running around randomly.

Meg hoped she met with Shontee's approval. Along with friendly smiles, she noticed the squaws staring curiously at her hair. It floated around her head and spilled down her back like a river of fire. In New York, she would have caught it up in a chignon, but here in Florida, she felt less structured and unfettered. Micco looked at her with a burning desire to run his fingers through those silken tresses, though he hid it well.

"Meg, you are going to enjoy our great feast day of the Shotcaytaw, the Green Corn Dance," said Gray Wolf, who was walking beside her. "It is kind of like your Christmas celebration. Our feast is for sorrowing and purifying, as well as rejoicing."

"I am so honored to be allowed to attend. I know it is just for your clans."

"We are happy to have you because we know you would not show disrespect for our traditions." He said, smiling at her.

Lazy bear and Little Fox had managed to push their way up beside her. Lazy Bear actually bumped Gray Wolf aside, which was like being hit by a tree trunk.

"Me dance tonight. You watch?" asked Lazy Bear.

"Oh yes. I can't wait to see it."

Micco had to smile. Lazy Bear and his sister Sheyokee dancing was indeed something to see. He was walking behind, talking to Spotted Deer. Gray Wolf fell in with them.

"Lazy Bear bumped me out of the way like a pebble," muttered Gray Wolf, rubbing his shoulder. "He is smitten with Meg. You better watch out, Micco, you've got competition," he said, grinning.

"I know. It's all around me. Little Fox wants to kill a deer and leave it at her doorstep."

Both Gray Wolf and Spotted Deer howled with laughter.

"A marriage proposal?" asked Spotted Deer.

"No less," replied Micco.

"Well, you better claim her at the dance tonight before she's whisked off into the forest," said Gray Wolf.

Both men were thoroughly enjoying kidding Micco.

"Right. I'll enter her in the race, then catch her before she realizes she's been selected as my future wife."

"Somehow I don't think Meg will go along with that. Better still, she might beat you in the race and what can be more humiliating than that," said Gray Wolf.

It was perfectly obvious that Meg, or any other at the camp, would have no chance of outdistancing Micco, but they were all going along with the joke. All of Micco's friends had no qualms about a Seminole marrying a white woman, unlike Shontee, who would be horrified.

They had reached a hut at the far end of the camp. It was a little bigger than the others.

"Is this Shontee's home?" asked Meg.

"Yo. She not here now," answered Little Fox.

Meg was relieved, in a way. She'd just as soon put off meeting as long as possible. Meg didn't know why she always felt that she was being judged or criticized. What had she done to cause this reaction? She didn't realize that Micco's grandmother viewed her as a prospective bride for him, and that this was unthinkable. Shontee saw how Micco looked at Meg. She was able to read her grandson well. So she was subtly trying to ward off that possibility. To Shontee, Micco might as well disappear into the bowels of the earth if he married this white woman.

The afternoon gradually wore on. It would soon be time for the games to begin and then the feasting.

Micco finally caught up with Meg.

"Remember how I told you that the Indian cannot hold his liquor?"

"Yes, I remember it well. It was the night of the eggnog episode."

"They are well aware that firewater can adversely affect them. So on a night like tonight when there will be feasting and celebrating, they practice caution. One of the men is selected to stay sober. It is his duty to watch his brothers carefully. He will stand guard over all the weapons and see that no one gets hurt."

"What a wise precaution," said Meg. Too bad members of other societies do not practice that."

"Come," said Spotted Deer. "I want you to meet my wife. She is in the Cooking Hut."

He and Meg walked into the hut. A very pretty woman was chopping up meat into a kettle with boiling water.

"This is my wife, Hotiyee," said Spotted Deer, "and this is Meg Riley."

"Hilippithashaw," said Hotiyee.

"How do you do," responded Meg.

Hotiyee's eyes were smiling, but uncomprehending. She obviously understood little English.

Spotted Deer spoke rapidly to his wife and then kissed her on the cheek. "We'll go now. My wife thinks you are very beautiful."

"Tell her I think she is, too," said Meg, smiling at Spotted Deer's wife.

Hotiyee giggled and Meg wondered what else she had said.

They went outside and by this time, the men, women, and children were gathered for the ball games.

Micco, Meg and Jamie sat on the grass under a shady tree to watch. Micco felt a little nostalgic, remembering the times he had thrown the ball at the pole. Meg was amazed at the enthusiasm and agility of the players. While they were sitting there, three men walked by surrounded by four or five others. None wore friendly expressions.

470

Meg whispered to Micco, " Who are they?"

"They are men who have committed some minor crime. Although we have very few who do commit crimes, still there are always some who are transgressors. They will be placed in a closed skin tent where a large stone has been heated on the fire. Then they will be given Osceola's drink, 'the Black Drink'."

"What is that?"

"It is a really nauseating emetic made from herbs."

"What happens after they drink it?" asked Jamie nervously.

"More water is poured on the stone, and the culprits are shut up in the tent in suffocating heat. If they survive the ordeal, they'll be forgiven and be allowed to join in the feasting and dancing."

"Does anybody ever die?" asked Meg.

"It has happened, but not very often, for the Seminoles can endure great physical torture."

Meg shuddered.

Noticing this, Micco told her, "It is tribal justice. Everyone understands this. None think it unfair. Of course, in the case of a serious crime, the chief can decree death."

"I see."

"This same 'Black Drink' is taken by everyone on the first day of the Dance, which is today, incidentally. It cleanses the system and enables them to eat, drink, and be merry to the fullest extent."

"Well, it is certainly different," said Meg, for lack of anything else to say about what she considered a barbaric custom.

Micco knew very well what Meg was thinking and he could empathize with her, but he understood and had been a part of those customs himself.

"There are other interesting medicines in which they have a superstitious faith. Some of these medicines are derived from roots and herbs. Some have healing powers; others, absolutely none. Certain knowledge has been handed down through the generations. One root in which they have complete faith is called 'hilliswaw'.

It was obtained by some members of my tribe when they were encamped in Tampa sixty years ago. It has been carefully treasured ever since, being handed down from father to son."

"Does it work?" asked Meg.

"Their absolute faith in its healing is incredible! Can you imagine it? They think the smallest amount made into tea can practically raise the dead. Those who are fortunate enough to own one small piece the size of a pea are considered to own a great treasure."

"But do you believe in its efficacy?" asked Meg curiously.

"Absolutely not. It has no physical healing properties; mental perhaps. It is hard to change their beliefs. In many cases, a person might be on the point of death before he would be brought to a medical doctor. Then it is often too late. During Osceola's time, some Indians went into a camp where the soldiers had died of yellow fever. They took their clothes and blankets back to their wigwams and shortly thereafter contracted the disease. They believed that bathing in cold water would cure the fever. When they did this, they all died."

"How tragic!"

"On the other hand, they do have some healing herbs. Paishaw is the Indian name for a plant that the Indians regard as a cure for snakebite. Most of the time it works."

"Do the Medicine men act as doctors?"

"Oh yes. That's what they are. They are the most respected members of the tribe, next to the chief."

"I thought they just danced around, waving rattles."

"No. Well, not exactly. They do dance around in full regalia, waving magic sticks. Today their powers of healing are not thought to be as great as they were in olden times. At one time, the Medicine man healed with brews of herbs by chanting or sucking the evil from a patient's forehead."

"Are you serious? You have traveled along way from the Everglades to the halls of academe, Dr. Ravenwing."

"I have indeed," said Micco, thoughtfully.

"The Medicine man cured such diseases as rat sickness, mosquito sickness, and fever caused by dreams of fire, or of the bear. There was another disease of distracted wandering called the 'giant disease'. The magic of the Medicine man had to be powerful in order to protect warriors and fell enemies."

"But surely they don't believe this in this enlightened age."

"Not as strongly, but they still trust the Medicine man more than the physician." Micco paused. "It looks like the ball games are over and it is the time for feasting. I'm starved. How about you, Meg and Jamie?"

"I am. I haven't eaten anything since yesterday and that wasn't much," said Meg.

"Trying to take my advice about losing ten pounds?"

"I suppose you prefer someone like Alexandria?"

Micco looked as if he were seriously trying to decode. "Now that you mention it, Alexandria is quite slender."

Meg glared at him jealously.

"I'm really hungry, too. I'm ready for dinner," chimed in Jamie.

"Jamie, you and I will eat with the men. Meg will have to join the women. Perhaps she can sit with Sheyokee, a dainty eater if I ever saw one."

"What? I don't want to eat with them. I don't even know them, and they can't speak English," protested Meg, now doubly annoyed with Micco.

"Unfortunately, this is part of an ancient tradition."

"Hang tradition!"

"Meg, such unladylike language. Remember you promised to revere our customs."

"I didn't think that would be one of them."

Just when Meg thought Micco was being an agreeable companion, he started teasing her again. But did he really think she was too fat?

"We had better go while there is still food." Micco helped her up, with Meg giving him her hand grudgingly.

Twilight was beginning to fall and Meg could hear the hoot of the Great Horned Owl and the soothing cadence of crickets. They walked to the tent and edibles were distributed in parts to the men and to the women and children, who went to separate locations to eat.

Micco did feel sorry for Meg as she went off to the women's area. Fortunately, Sheyokee saw her and took her along. It wasn't too bad. The fresh fruits and vegetable were delicious. She avoided the meat, then sampled the seafood offered. The smoked mullet was quite good, as was the grilled trout. She simply ate and tuned out conversation around her. It was like the Tower of Babel. She didn't understand one word. She saw Shontee in the crowd of women, but Shontee merely nodded and did not come over.

Finally the meal was over and Sheyokee said, "Come. Me show."

Meg got up and went with her. She was being taken to the Council Lodge where the women and children were gathering. They wore yards and yards of brightly colored ribbons floating everywhere- from their head, necks, and shoulders. A plethora of colored beads encircled their necks. Meg wondered why they didn't fall to the ground from the weight of them. They wore beaten silver ornaments fastened at their waists. Sheyokee was a splendid sight. Her six foot two frame was bedecked with what looked to Meg to be a hundred ribbons, and her multitudinous beads clinked and jingled as she walked. 'Now I really can't wait to see her and Lazy Bear dance," she thought.

They all walked outside and the men were standing there, resplendent in brilliant coats and enormous turbans. They wore leggings with fringes of doe skin, and fresh new moccasins. She noticed Gray Wolf and Spotted Deer with brightly beaded sashes and waist-high red-beaded leggings. They wore high-topped moccasins of buckskin.

Micco and Jamie found Meg and led her over to be seated in a place of honor. This was because she was Micco's guest.

'Thank goodness they had provided some chairs,' she thought. She was thoroughly tired of sitting on the ground.

It was dark now and campfires were burning all around the dancing square. The flames flickered as a breeze fanned the fire and shone on the dancer's fantastic attire.

"This is the beginning of the new year when old fires are allowed to go out. The new fire, the Sacred Fire, must be made with the flint rock of our ancestors," explained Micco. "This ancient flint-and-steel set is kept by the Medicine man with his other religious materials. He is the only one who may light the fire."

"Fascinating," said Meg, almost mesmerized by the flames. "Oh, look!"

The Medicine Man had appeared, his coat adorned with ruffled epaulettes. He wore a high-plumed turban on his head, and high-topped moccasins.

"He will lead the dance," said Micco.

Jamie was staring at the Medicine Man as if he were Beelzebub's agent come straight from Hades.

"Don't be afraid," said Micco. "He is just going to dance."

"I'm not," Jamie said softly, but he took Micco's hand too. He was already holding Meg's.

Meg looked down at Jamie. He was a bright boy. Already he was ahead in his studies, but something was really bothering him. She knew he missed Andre; but it was more than that. Micco had noticed it too, and had mentioned it to her, but neither could figure out a reason for it. Meg decided that the first chance she had, she was going to have a serious talk with him.

They all looked up as the dancers were poised on the sidelines, ready to begin. In the center of the square, the Sacred Fire flashed, and at each corner of the square stood a pole. All was quiet and there was an excited air of expectancy. The Medicine Man began a weird melody and the band of chanters and dancers locked hands, marking time as they took up the strange chant.

475

Then the Medicine Man led the entire fantastic procession, the performers' faces lit by the flickering flames.

Meg felt a chill as she watched the weaving bodies, moving to the rhythmical cadence of the owl song, then the wild turkey, and then another. Their songs and their dances showed how close they lived to nature. Finally, never missing a beat, the Medicine Man led the men from the circle. Now the women entered, their ankles strapped with clusters of the highland terrapin shell, partly filled with pebbles or seeds of the wild canna. These shells were concealed by their long dresses, and as they danced barefooted, they sang the song of their fathers, making ancient melodies. Meg was caught up in the beauty of their graceful movements. Even Sheyokee moved as one with the others, graceful and light-footed. Then, like foxes in the night, they glided off, and not a sound could be heard. The clusters of shells were as silent as the bated breath of the viewers. How could they steal away without making a sound. Not one rattle of the shells could be heard.

"A Broadway production could not have topped that," said Meg, sorry that it was over.

"They will return, both men and women, and will dance around the festal pole until sunrise. But first, there is a most interesting feature of the Green Corn Dance- the racing for a wife."

"What is that? How do you race for a wife?" asked Jamie. "I thought you had to take a girl to church and marry her."

"That is true in your society, but here, the conventions are different. Look over there. They are laying out a course."

Jamie watched intently as young men and women lined up.

"The young brave has already had his eye on a girl that he would like to marry," said Micco, "But he can't just ask her, Jamie. He has to go through a certain procedure. He also cannot choose a girl from his own clan. That is forbidden."

"This is beginning to sound like a typical male idea to me, with no input from the female," said Meg, still annoyed with Micco.

"That is where you are wrong, Meg. The young brave selects the girl he wants to court, but he has to catch her first before he courts her. The Indian girl is often his equal, and even superior in fitness and swiftness."

"Do you mean to tell me that they are actually going to race with the idea that if he catches her, she will have to marry him? I never heard of anything so ridiculous."

"Well, the girl doesn't have to lose unless she wants to."

"What girl could outrun a man? It's a fixed race," said Meg.

"I agree that she'll allow herself to be beaten and captured, fainting in his arms, in most cases, but if she doesn't like her would-be suitor, you'd be surprised at how fast she can run," said Micco laughing. "And if she does win the race, the poor guy has to give up. He won't risk further humiliation by trying to court her."

"Humph!" muttered Meg.

"What happens if he catches her?" asked Jamie.

"He has already secretly conveyed his intention to the girl's parents. Having been given permission to woo, the lover shows some token of affection. He might kill a deer and leave it at the door of the wigwam. If the gift is received, he is happy. If it remains untouched, even if he has already captured her at the race, he will seek a more willing bride. But if she does accept the present, she will show some token of her appreciation, such as making him a shirt and presenting it to him."

"Now what do they do? It seems like it's a lot harder than just saying 'Will you marry me'?" said Jamie.

"Now the marriage day is set and the groom-to-be goes to the intended bride's house at sundown. He is now her husband and he lives at her home for a period of time. When the young couple finally build their own home, they may build it at the camp of the wife's mother, but not among the husband's relatives. There had been no pressure from the parents, forcing her to marry him. That is left entirely up to the girl."

""That seems like a funny way to get married to me," said Jamie.

"From the mouths of babes," quoted Meg .

"Jamie, you will discover when you are older that the relationship of men and women is an up and down situation in any society.. You see, women are, how shall I put it? Fickle? Yes, that's it. One minute, they are sure they want one thing, and the very next day, they want the opposite. This confuses men, who are quite logical. They cannot figure out what women want. Right now you haven't reached that state of perplexity, but you will, believe me, probably as soon as you reach puberty."

"What's puberty?"

"That's when you reach that point where annoying girls becomes your sole purpose in life," answered Meg.

"Meg, don't confuse Jamie. It is that stage in life when you begin to change physically, from a boy to a man."

"Without a doubt, Micco Ravenwing, you are the most irritating man I ever met!"

"I don't think Miss Riley is whatever that word was you called her. She always explains things so everybody can understand. And she's nice, too," said Jamie loyally.

"Jamie, bless your heart. I agree with you. She is very nice. I was only teasing her."

"Oh."

"Do you want to stay and watch more of the dancing?"

"I enjoyed it, but I am sleepy." said Meg. "Aren't you, Jamie?"

"Yes, ma'am." He had been desperately trying not to fall asleep for the last hour.

"Let's go home, then," said Micco.

They found their way back through myriad people, still eating and drinking, to where they had tied the horses. Micco helped Meg mount. Then he mounted and pulled the sleepy Jamie up behind him. Seeing how tired Meg looked, Micco said, "I wish

I could take you on my horse, too, Meg. Then you could just fall asleep in my arms and not have to worry about riding Dumpling."

Meg wished she could do that, also. How pleasant it would be to relax in his arms and go to sleep, in spite of how annoying he was.

"I appreciate your thought. I can manage, though."

As before, she followed behind Micco. At this point, she didn't care if her skirt blew over her head; she was so tired. It was dark, anyway.

An hour later they were home. Meg wearily climbed the stairs, following Micco. He was carrying Jamie, who had fallen sound asleep. Meg undressed and fell into bed, wondering how she would get up in time for school. She certainly didn't plan to take her early morning ride. It would be hard enough just to face her students.

Micco undressed Jamie and put him to bed. He was growing fonder of the boy every day. Tomorrow he would have a talk with him to find out what was troubling him. Then Micco found his own room, pulled off his clothes, and fell into bed. He was asleep in five minutes.

Chapter Twenty-Two

Andre was growing impatient. He wanted Meg, but she wouldn't surrender completely to his advances. He was wasting his time coming into Jupiter when he could be doing more profitable things. Then he had a plan. Why hadn't he thought of it before? 'Sacre bleu; I am an idiot!' he thought. He would simply take her on his ship, away from any possible encounter with the Indian. He would have mumbling, even mutiny from his crew for they were superstitious about having a female aboard ship. It brought bad luck. But Andre could handle them, especially if he promised to let them have her after he finished with her..

Meg wouldn't go willingly, of course, unless he married her, which he was not going to do. After they were seduced, women became an annoyance. Sally wanted to get married, too. They all did. He grew tired of them when he no longer desired their bodies, and that didn't take long. They were just like his mother—sluts, all of them. Each desirable woman that he encountered was like a mouth-watering sweet that he had to consume, the next piece of candy beckoning him when he finished that one. He was madly enamored of Meg and he was tired of being frustrated. He would get her on his ship, rip off her clothes, and take that luscious body as often as he pleased, slaking this lust that was consuming him. At the moment, he thought her physical charms might hold his interest a little longer than the rest, but he knew that she would finally love him, as they always did, and that would end his interest. Why couldn't they be satisfied with a physical relationship? The more he thought about it, the more eager he became. He smiled as something else occurred to him. Dory had been a help in spite of his bloodlust. He would reward Dory for his loyalty by letting him rape Meg first.

He was to meet with Jamie in two days with a message from Meg. He hadn't been able to meet her at the appointed time last week because he was involved in a raid. He knew she was disappointed and this would make her even more eager to see him. When they did arrange to meet again, he would bind her legs and arms and gag her. Then he would wrap her in a blanket and throw her over the horse, carrying her to his gig. He could take a roundabout way to reach the boat, put her in it, and sail out to the Osprey, which he planned to have waiting in the channel. They could sail away and she would be all his to do with as he pleased. He went over his strategy again and could find no flaws in it. No one would ever know where she was. If, by some freak happenstance, the Indian did discover where she was, he would have the pleasure of killing him when he boarded the ship. That would be almost as enjoyable as raping Meg. In just two days, he would be reading Meg's note, and the next day he would have her. She would plead with him to stop, but he knew she wouldn't really mean it. Not many women had ever been able to resist him. Only one before Meg. Helen, the one exception, was a pretty sixteen year-old virgin. He had made the acquaintance of her father, a blacksmith. Then one night when the man went to work, Andre visited the girl. She invited him in, and when he threw her down and tore her dress, she scratched him. Andre was so enraged that he pulled out his knife and cut both her cheeks. He smiled remembering her screams. He had left town that night. Helen would never attract a man again.

Micco managed to get through the next day after the Green Corn Dance festival. He had really enjoyed himself, and he

482

thought that Meg had, too. He must find time to see her more, even if she became annoyed. Then he thought about Jamie, wondering why he was so troubled. When he could get a moment of free time, sometime this week, he was going to find out what it was. He was completely surprised when Jamie came to him after dinner two days later and said he wanted to talk to him privately. They went into Micco's office and he closed the door.

"Well, Jamie, what did you want to talk about?"

Jamie hesitated.

"Is it something I can help you with? You know I will, and it will be just between us if you are afraid of someone else finding out about it. Nothing is so bad that we can't fix it," said Micco kindly. He thought it was probably some schoolboy problem, perhaps a trick he had played on someone.

"It's about Miss Riley."

"What?" said Micco in amazement. "Do you feel she is unfair to you in class?"

"No. It's worse," said Jamie miserably.

"What could be worse?" Micco was completely thrown off track. He couldn't imagine how Jamie could be so upset with Meg. The boy had always appeared to be fond of her.

Jamie was twisting his hands in his lap. "You know when I first came here and I said my father had brought me to get an education?"

"Yes, I remember."

"Well, that's not true. He is not my real father, though I think of him as one."

"I see," said Micco, trying to figure out where this was leading.

"What he really wanted was to see Miss Riley," Jamie blurted out.

Micco was so taken aback that he just looked at Jamie in amazement.

"He already knew her," said Jamie, still struggling with what he was trying to say.

"Where did he know her from?"

"He met her in Beaufort, but I didn't know that until we came to Juno."

"You came from Beaufort to Juno with this man whom you regard as a father?" asked Micco.

"Yes. My parents had died and I was living with this old woman who didn't want me. He came to the house and asked me if I wanted to be a cabin boy on his ship, and I said 'yes'. I was so glad because I had been so unhappy before. He said it would be an adventure."

"So you embarked on an adventure and it hasn't turned out to be one? Is that it?"

"It's turned out to be much worse," said Jamie, almost on the verge of tears.

"Did he mistreat you?" asked Micco angrily.

"No, that's just it. He's the only person, up until now, who's ever really been nice to me. That's why it's so hard to tell."

"I understand, Jamie. Let's start with when you arrived in Juno, all right?"

"Okay. He told me that he was going to be a merchant and buy and sell stuff. He had just bought his ship in Beaufort and that's why he needed a cabin boy. But when we got here, he didn't do that." Jamie paused, not wanting to say the words that would condemn Andre.

"What did he do?" asked Micco gently.

"He, he robbed people and somebody was killed," said Jamie, now in tears.

Micco was really concerned now, but he could see Jamie's distress and didn't want to worry him more. "You realize, Jamie, that this must be reported to the authorities. I know you love this man who treated you so well, but you can see that he is not really a good man, can't you?"

"Yes. I probably wouldn't even have told you about that, except I am worried about Miss Riley."

"How does this involve her?"

"He's been meeting her secretly on the beach. I've been taking messages back and forth. I've been worrying and worrying because he said that you wanted to kill him because Miss Riley chose him over you. But I know you couldn't kill anybody. I'm afraid he wants to kill you."

Micco sat there, the blood draining from his face. He had a horrible suspicion that somehow it was Andre the boy was talking about.

"You said your father's name was Marcel Dupois?"

"That's what he told Mrs. Armour, but it's not. His name is Andre Lafitte."

Micco jumped up and his chair crashed to the floor. He was so enraged that Jamie was afraid. Seeing this, Micco tried to calm down. He spoke in a quiet tone.

"Jamie, this is even more serious than you realize. What is the name of his ship? I need to notify the Coast Guard. I am assuming that these robberies took place at sea. Is that correct?"

"Yes. Andre found out when ships would be passing by and then they sent up a distress signal, and when the ship came to help, they boarded it and stole the cargo. This real scary man called Dory shot the captain of the ship for no reason. I heard them talking about it in the general store and later on, when they thought I wasn't listening, I heard the crew talking about it. That's how I know it was Dory who did it. Even that crew didn't like him. I told Andre that it was wrong, but he said it was just that one time. But it wasn't. They've done it four times! I'm glad I'm not on that ship. The name of it is the Osprey. I'm worried about Miss Riley because he told me that he's going to have his ship just outside the harbor, and he's going to take me back with him in two days. I'm afraid he's going to take Miss Riley, too."

"Great Spirit, no!" moaned Micco. "When and where will he meet her?"

"Tomorrow morning when she goes for her ride. I think she has a place where she stops down the beach. He told me to wait at the gig and be there at seven o'clock in the morning."

"Jamie, don't you say anything to anyone. Do you understand?"

"Yes. I won't."

"You will not be going with Lafitte and neither will Meg. Now go to your room and go to sleep. Everything is going to be all right."

"You're not going to hurt Andre, are you?" asked Jamie anxiously.

Micco stooped down in front of Jamie and took his hand. "Jamie, this man has committed terrible crimes, and he may hurt Meg. I will have to do what is necessary to stop it and hand him over to the authorities. Do you understand that?"

"Yes."

"Go on to bed. I'll take care of it."

Micco watched as Jamie walked up the steps, and then he ran out of the house and got Chips out of the barn. He leapfrogged over the horse's rump and urged him into a gallop. Within minutes, he had reached the telegraph office. The operator was still there, just getting ready to leave.

Micco bounded into the office. "This is an emergency! Send this telegram immediately to the Coast Guard Station in Lake Worth."

The operator, alarmed by Micco's urgency, sat down at his table. "Go ahead. I'm ready."

Ship named Osprey responsible for piracy and murder. Stop. Will be anchored off Jupiter inlet 7:00 A.M. tomorrow. Stop. Apprehend.

Micco Ravenwing,
Jupiter Inlet

"Oh, my God! Is this true?" asked the shocked operator.

"Yes, send it now before it's too late."

"I've known you all your life. I'll send it." He tapped the keys quickly. "I've sent it."

486

Micco ran out the door. Now he needed to contact his friends. Not that he needed them to handle Lafitte. Heaven and hell combined couldn't keep him from hurting the slimy devil, but he wanted them to take him to the authorities. He rode into the village and found Gray Wolf, telling him what to do. Then he went back to the house, waiting for six o'clock to arrive. He seethed and burned with a fury. He didn't know if he could control it. He put his knife in his belt and waited. Everyone else was in bed. His thoughts of Meg weren't very pleasant, either. How could she possibly have done this? The grandfather clock in the hall ticked away in half-time. Finally, at 5:00 A.M., he took Chips out of the barn and rode down the beach. A few miles away, he found what he knew must be their meeting place. It was the only likely spot. He hid his horse far back in the woods and waited. An hour later, he heard a horse galloping. It was Meg. She tied Dumpling to a tree and waited for Andre. A few minutes later, another rider approached. Meg ran down to the beach to meet him. Micco was so furious; he was almost blinded. Andre slid from the horse and captured Meg in his arms, kissing her passionately, and then he lowered her to the ground.

"What are you doing?" he heard her yell.

"I can't wait until I get you back to my ship. I'm going to take you now, " he panted as he began to tear her clothes.

That was the last move he made. Micco jerked him backwards and hit him so hard that Andre's head snapped. He was lying on the ground, blood running from his mouth, and Micco hit him again. He was about to smash his nose when Gray Wolf caught his arm. His friends had just driven up in the wagon.

"No more, Micco. You'll kill him!"

A red haze had enveloped Micco and he didn't even hear Gray Wolf. If Spotted Deer hadn't grabbed his other arm, Gray Wolf couldn't have stopped Micco. It took both of them to pull him off the semi-conscious man. They continued holding him and then Micco relaxed.

"I won't hit him again. Take the bastard away. God damn him to Hell!" If they were shocked to hear Micco curse, they did not show it.

Lazy Bear walked over to Andre, and Little Fox went along to help him, but Lazy Bear picked up the moaning Andre like a bag of feathers, tied his hands with the rope he found looped to Andre's saddle, and dropped him in the back of the wagon the four had driven to the beach. Then he hitched Thor to the back. They drove off with their prisoner and would hold him until the authorities arrived to take him away.

Meg was still sitting on the ground, too stunned to move. Micco was furious. He pulled Meg up, none too gently.

"Let's go back to the house. You'll need to change that torn blouse before anyone sees you."

He got Meg's horse, picked her up, and set her on it. Then he untied Chips and leaped onto his back.

As they rode back home, Meg was so shocked at the violence in both men that she couldn't speak. She glanced at Micco, and his expression was forbidding. She had never seen such a look on his face. They rode in silence to the house. To Meg's dismay, Shonte was waiting on the porch.

"Graywolf told me what happened. She looked at Micco. "Was this man truly the one who has been robbing ships?"

"Yes. He is the one."

Meg thought she was beyond being shocked.

"It can't be. Andre may be impulsive, but he is not a pirate and murderer."

"Impulsive? What a quaint, Victorian word," Micco said. He fought to control himself. He did not want to upset his grandmother by saying what he really thought to Meg.

"Jamie told me Lafitte's plan to kidnap you and take you on his ship. He also told me that Lafitte was responsible for the piracy. Do you think that innocent child made this up? He was so upset when he told me because he actually loved that bast... man."

"I can't believe it."

"Well, believe it."

Micco turned to Shonte. "Did the authorities arrive and take him away? Was the ship captured?"

"Yes, my grandson. You did well. He and the others will be punished," said Shonte.

"I hope they don't kill him. That's too quick. I hope he rots slowly in a dank, rat-infested cell for the rest of his life."

"It will be as God wills."

Meg looked at both of them and then ran to her room.

"I'd better talk to Jamie. I know he's worried. Wait here and I'll take you home." Taking his grandmother's hand he led her to a chair. "I'll be back in a few minutes."

He went to Jamie's room and knocked on the door.

"Come in."

Micco entered the room and he felt so sorry for Jamie when he saw the boy huddled in a chair, crying.

"Jamie, son. Don't cry. I know how you loved Andre and felt disloyal for telling me what he had done. I also know that it took a great deal of courage to do what you did. Sometimes in this life we have to do things that are painful. We have to make a choice, and you made the right one. Never feel guilty for doing what is right. I am so proud of you for making that choice. Jamie, you are like my own son. We can go through life together. Don't look back in regret, but look forward to the good things."

Jamie looked up, and he had stopped crying.

"You don't think I was a bad person for telling?"

Micco bent down beside Jamie and hugged him. "Dear child, there is nothing bad inside you."

"And you want me to be your son?"

"I do with all my heart," said Micco as he held the boy against him.

Jamie was comforted by Micco's words. Now, for the first time in his unhappy, young life he was truly loved by a man who could be his father. He would listen and try his hardest to learn from Micco.

489

"You know, Jamie, you can help me in the clinic after school. I need someone to run errands and do odd jobs. That's what I did for Dr. Riley when I wasn't much older than you. As I worked with him and watched him heal the sick, I discovered that I wanted to be a doctor, too. I was just a poor, uneducated boy, but he saw something else in me and gave me a chance to do more with my life. I see something else in you, too. We shall work side by side. Who knows? Maybe you'll want to become a doctor. If not a doctor, you have the potential to be whatever you want to be. But whatever you do, you'll know that I will be there, always. Okay?

"Yes. If you're there, I can do it."

Micco stood up. "We will still have plenty of time to go fishing and canoeing, though. I'll expect you to study hard. It is important to learn everything you can. Never slack in your studies."

"I will study. You know how good my teacher is, too." Jamie's face glowed when he talked about Meg. "She is never mean to anybody. I had a teacher in Beaufort who would slap your hands with a ruler if you gave the wrong answer."

Micco's face tightened when Jamie mentioned Meg's name.

"You are lucky to have her. She is a good teacher. My grandmother said the children in the village are already learning to read. Their parents are all pleased with her."

"I wish..."

"What do you wish?"

"I wish Miss Riley could be my mother. You're going to be my father. You could chase her in that Indian race. And then when you caught her, she would have to be your wife. Are you mad at her?"

"Why do you ask that?" asked Micco, hiding a smile.

"Because, oh, I don't know. We had such a good time at the Green Corn Festival and you don't seem like you want to talk

490

to her after what happened. I heard her run by my door, and she was crying, too."

"Sometimes ladies become emotional in a stressful situation. But they are as changeable as the spring tide. She will get over it. I need to take Shontee home now. Get in bed and sleep well, but brush your teeth first."   He leaned over and kissed Jamie on the forehead.

As Micco passed Meg's door, he almost stopped, especially when he heard her crying, but he steeled his heart against her. When he came downstairs, Shontee was nodding as she sat in the chair, her head slumped on her shoulder. Micco walked over to awaken her.

"My Shontee, it's time to go."

Then he saw her deathly, white face.

"Oh, no. Please God, no."

He lifted her wrist and felt a faint pulse. Then he picked her up and carried her into the clinic and put her in bed. Frantically, he fought to save her life, and this was the most important battle he had ever fought.   After twenty minutes, Shontee began to breathe normally and her face regained color. Micco looked at her beautiful, bronze skin, and he gently held her hand against his cheek. When he felt it was safe to leave her, he went to awaken Dr. Riley.

"Doctor, hurry. Shontee has had a heart attack. I have stabilized her. Please stay with her while I go to the village and get someone who will remain with Shontee day and night, if necessary.

Dr. Riley arose and threw on his clothes.

"How long ago did it happen?" he asked, buttoning his shirt while they walked.

"An hour ago. I thought she was dead." said Micco, so emotional he could hardly speak.

Sean put his arm around Micco. "My dear boy. She didn't die. You saved her life."

When they reached her room Dr. Riley pulled up a chair and sat down beside her. "Her color is good. Don't worry. Go to the village. I won't leave your grandmother for a second."

Micco ran out and got Chips from the barn. Horse and man were one as they galloped down the path on that fog-shrouded morning.

A half an hour later, Micco returned with Gray Wolf and an Indian girl.

"Go to Shonte," said Gray Wolf to the girl. "I'll stable the horses, Micco."

The two went inside and the girl sat down beside Shonte.

"No change," said Dr. Riley. Both Micco and Dr. Riley were watching Shonte when she opened her eyes.

"My grandson, why do you look at me as if I am about to meet Tall Chief?" She asked in a surprisingly strong voice.

"Grandmother, you gave me such a scare I am still shaking." Micco knelt down beside her and put his arms around her.

"You weren't shaking so much that it prevented you from saving her life," said Sean..

"I am not yet ready to go to the Happy Hunting Ground. Now everyone leave me except Kiki. I feel sleepy."

Even as weak as she was, Shonte still ordered them around. "You have really sick patients to take care of.." And having the last word, she went to sleep.

A much relieved Micco stood up. "I guess we'll have to do what she says. No one has won an argument with her yet." The two men walked out, amazed at her resiliency.

"Dr. Riley, go back to bed. It's still early. I'll awaken you in two hours."

"I will if you promise me one thing."

"Anything. What is it?"

"Please call me Sean when we're not with patients. I am not your father though I feel like I am. But I know you would not

492

want to call me 'Father' because you have wonderful memories of your natural father."

"Dr. .. .I mean Sean, you honor me. I cherish both of my fathers—Tall Chief who loved and sired me and Dr. Riley who loved me and made it possible for me to become the man that I am."

Sean coughed to cover his embarrassment. "Well, I will go back to bed. Don't fail to call me in two hours."

"I won't, my second father."

Micco watched as Sean walked slowly to his room. He intended to go straight to the clinic, but his conscience was bothering him. He knew Meg would want to know about Shonte. Though he still didn't want to talk to her, he went upstairs and knocked on her door.

"Yes. Who is it?" she asked.

"It's Micco. Shonte has had a heart attack."

"What?" said Meg, opening the door.

"She survived it and is downstairs."

Meg was still dressed and her tear-streaked face made Micco feel terrible.

"Let me wash my face and I'll be right down."

"That isn't necessary. I have someone staying with her. If there is any change, she will get me immediately."

"I will be down in ten minutes," Meg said, turning away from him, her eyes downcast.

Without another word, Micco turned and went downstairs. Already patients were waiting. Meg heard him close the door and felt her heart was breaking. He was so cool to her, so detached. Then, she thought 'Forget about your small troubles. Shonte needs you.'

Meg went into Shonte's room and sat, quietly, on the other side of the bed. The Indian girl did not speak English but gave Meg a friendly smile. Shonte opened her eyes some time later and did seem pleased to see Meg. Meg stayed a long time, but finally she left because she had to prepare for school.

Days passed into weeks as Shontee slowly recovered. Meg was by her side every day, early in the morning and after school. She read to her and brought her special treats. And gradually Meg and Shontee bonded. The coolness between them vanished and Meg felt that Shontee loved her as a daughter. Meg poured her heart out to Shontee, tears running down her cheeks, and Shontee comforted her. "I just can't bear it because Micco is so cold to me. It's as if I don't exist."

"Don't grieve, Meg. I will talk to him."

Micco and Sean were as busy as ever. One day when Micco came into the clinic, Stemolakee, the little girl Shonte had taken in, stood by a neighbor who had brought her to see the doctor. The child had a wire-covered basket in one hand and a burlap sack in the other.

"Don't you feel well, little one?" asked Micco in Hitchiti.

The neighbor answered him. "Her stomach has been hurting her ever since Shontee had a heart attack."

"I will fix that. You miss Shontee, don't you?"

The child nodded.

"I am going to give you some medicine to stop the pain and then we will go see her."

Stemolakee's black, olive eyes were as round as polished pebbles tossed by the sea, and relief flooded her little face at the thought of seeing Shontee.

She held out her basket and sack.

"What is this?" asked Micco.

"It is her pet frogs, and those are live crickets that she feeds to them. She wants to give them to you for making her well."

"What lovely green frogs and they're red bellies, too. I'd like to have them, but I really don't have room and no one to feed them. Why don't you take them back with you and I'll come over to visit them from time to time. It is a wonderful gift. Thank you."

He patted her arm. They left and Micco worked non-stop until four o'clock.

494

Meg saw Micco only when he visited his grandmother and they exchanged polite greetings. He asked how Jamie was doing in school and Meg reported that he had become a straight 'A' student. He never asked Meg how she was getting along.

One day Micco walked in to examine Shontee. Meg had not yet arrived from school. "Sit down, Micco. I want to talk to you."

Micco wondered at her tone, but sat down obediently.

"What is it, grandmother? Is the hospital food unappetizing?"

He liked to tease Shontee, especially because she never knew when he was kidding her.

"Of course not. Why would you think I didn't like it? I have something very serious to discuss with you. It is about Meg," she said, watching his startled look. I know that you are in love with her."

Micco started to interrupt.

"No. Do not talk until I have finished. During these weeks when I have been convalescing, I have grown to be quite fond of her. She is kind and thoughtful and we have had many interesting conversations. I have noticed, however, that when you are around, you two barely speak to each other. I realize that something unpleasant must have happened to have caused this rift. When I first met Meg, I saw how you looked at her and I disapproved because I wanted you to marry one of your own kind. Our customs are strict and have been handed down through the ages. It is hard for me to change, but I see how others in our village are changing. You would have my approval to marry Meg."

"We can never be reconciled. I, I can't forgive her."

"Micco, I cannot believe that Meg could do anything that was unforgivable. I can see that she is very unhappy."

"We cause our own unhappiness. Grandmother, I need to examine you. Other patients are waiting."

Shontee sighed. She knew that Micco could be unrelenting if he believed he was right.

495

After examining her, Micco said, "If you keep improving, I'll have to send you home in a few days."

"Good. I need to get busy."

"Not too busy or you will be right back here."

He bent down and kissed her cheek. "I'll see you tonight."

Micco went to his office thinking of what she had said. 'Could he forgive Meg?' Every time he thought of Andre and how Meg had deceived him he became angry again. He didn't know that his grandmother had changed her attitude about marriage until today. Maybe he should try to reconcile with Meg. Maybe she didn't even want to be friends with him anymore.

'Tomorrow I'll talk to her,' he thought.

The day was so busy he became completely immersed in his work, forgetting his problem with Meg. Then, like every other night, he fell into bed, exhausted.

The next morning he saw Meg walking towards Shonte's room.

"Meg, wait a minute," he said.

She turned at the sound of his voice.

"What is it?"

"I wondered if you would like to take a ride early tomorrow morning. I'm sure Dumpling needs the exercise, and I know Chips does. You've been working so hard at school, and then taking care of my grandmother. She told me how much she enjoys talking to you."

"I didn't think you would ever want to ride with me again."

"Meg, I want us to be friends again. I know I've been distant, but can't we try to be friends?"

"I have missed our rides and conversations, too. Yes, I will ride with you tomorrow. What time?"

"Is six o'clock too early?"

"No. I'll be ready."

"Good. Until six, then," said Micco. He felt a lessening of the band that had been around his heart.

Meg watched as he walked away and she felt happy for the first time in weeks. She was going to be with Micco. She could hardly wait until the next morning.

It was foggy when Meg walked outside, but she could see the outline of Micco holding the bridles of Dumpling and Chips. She walked quickly to him.

"Right on time. That's my Meg," said Micco as he lifted her up on the horse.

He took a little run and leaped up on Chip's back.

Meg caught her breath. He had said 'My Meg'.

"Let's ride through the woods near your school and then go along the shore," said Micco.

"All right. I'd like that."

As they rode, Meg was thinking how she had missed him so much. She missed his teasing, his flirting, his conversation, his kiss. Would he ever kiss her again?

Micco was remembering how Andre had held Meg and kissed her. And he remembered how madly jealous he was when he saw them. He had wanted to kill Lafitte.

They passed through the woods and onto the beach. Micco reached for Dumpling's reins and brought both horses to a halt."

"Why are we stopping?"

"I want to walk on the beach," said Micco as he leaped to the ground and lifted Meg from her horse.

"Oh."

Suddenly, he pulled Meg against him, holding her so tightly with one arm that she could not even wiggle.

"Is Lafitte the kind of man who attracts you? One who takes you by force? Kissing you until your weak protests die? Pinning you down against your will?"

She looked up at him and her startled green eyes met smoldering black ones.

"I can be that kind of man, too."

"No," she said.

"Yes." Micco held her head with his left hand and leaned down to meet her parted lips. He began kissing her with such ardor that Meg's head was spinning. She was seeing stars on a starless night. She felt boneless.

When he finally stopped kissing her, Meg opened her eyes in a daze. She felt completely bereft without his lips. She looked at him, unaware that her own eyes were filled with passion. Was this the considerate, protective Micco she knew, this fierce, erotic man?

"Dear, sweet Meg," said Micco in a ragged voice, as he began to slowly unbutton her blouse. "Is this what you want, Sweetheart?"

"I, I..Yes."

Micco looked at her, his eyes blazing with desire, and then he buttoned up her blouse.

"No, you don't. Not this way. When we're married, Meg, I'll make love to you all night long, but you'll still beg for more in the morning."

"Married!"

"Yes, married, my dearest red-haired chickadee. I love you Meg. I have always loved you ever since we were children."

He looked at her with such a tender, amorous expression that Meg almost melted. He waited expectantly, but Meg said nothing. Then he walked over to the woods and brought the horses back.

"Well, up you go," he said, picking Meg up easily and sitting her on her pony, disappointment etched on his face.

"I love you too, Micco Ravenwing, but you'll have to catch me to prove it," she said, pressing her knees gently in Dumpling's sides. The horse obeyed her command and galloped down the beach.

Micco leaped onto his horse and shouted, "Yohoeehee" joyfully, at the top of his lungs as he raced after Meg. He caught her and pulled her from her horse, putting her astride his horse in front of him. And then he kissed her.

As soon as she could catch her breath, she asked, "Am I too fat, Micco?"

"My dearest, darling Meg, you are perfect."

She smiled contentedly. They cantered along, Meg leaning back into his arms with Dumpling following docilely behind.

A mist veiled the rising sun and a double rainbow arched across the horizon as they journeyed home.

LaVergne, TN USA
06 November 2009

163306LV00003B/11/P